Enigma Books

Also published by Enigma Books

Hitler's Table Talk: 1941–1944
In Stalin's Secret Service
Hitler and Mussolini: The Secret Meetings
The Jews in Fascist Italy: A History
The Man Behind the Rosenbergs
Roosevelt and Hopkins: An Intimate History
Diary 1937-1943 (Galeazzo Ciano)
Secret Affairs: FDR, Cordell Hull, and Sumner Welles
Hitler and His Generals: Military Conferences 1942–1945
Stalin and the Jews: The Red Book
The Secret Front: Nazi Political Espionage
Fighting the Nazis: French Intelligence and Counterintelligence
A Death in Washington: Walter G. Krivitsky and the Stalin Terror
The Battle of the Casbah: Terrorism and Counterterrorism in Algeria 1955–1957
Hitler's Second Book: The Unpublished Sequel to *Mein Kampf*
At Napoleon's Side in Russia: The Classic Eyewitness Account
The Atlantic Wall: Hitler's Defenses for D-Day
Double Lives: Stalin, Willi Münzenberg and the Seduction of the Intellectuals
France and the Nazi Threat: The Collapse of French Diplomacy 1932–1939
Mussolini: The Secrets of His Death
Mortal Crimes: Soviet Penetration of the Manhattan Project
Top Nazi: Karl Wolff—The Man Between Hitler and Himmler
Empire on the Adriatic: Mussolini's Conquest of Yugoslavia
The Origins of the War of 1914 (3-volume set)
Hitler's Foreign Policy: 1933–1939—The Road to World War II
The Origins of Fascist Ideology 1918–1925
Max Corvo: OSS Italy 1942–1945
Hitler's Contract: The Secret History of the Italian Edition of *Mein Kampf*
Secret Intelligence and the Holocaust
Israel at High Noon
Balkan Inferno: Betrayal, War, and Intervention, 1990–2005
Calculated Risk: World War II Memoirs of General Mark Clark
The Murder of Maxim Gorky
The Kravchenko Case: One Man's War On Stalin
Shattered Sky
Hitler's Gift to France
The Mafia and the Allies
The Nazi Party, 1919-1945: A Complete History
Encyclopedia of Cold War Espionage, Spies, and Secret Operations
The Cicero Spy Affair
A Crate of Vodka
The First Iraq War: Britain's Mesopotamian Campaign, 1914-1918
Hitler's Intelligence Chief: Walter Schellenberg

Salazar: A Political Biography
The Italian Brothers
Nazi Palestine
Lenin and His Comrades
The Decision to Drop the Atomic Bomb
Target Hitler
Truman, MacArthur and the Korean War
The Eichmann Trial Diary
Working with Napoleon
Stalin's Man in Canada
Hunting Down the Jews

Mysteries

Operation Neptune
Paris Weekend
NOC
Code Name: Kalistrat
Pax Romana

Other Winston Churchill thrillers by Michael McMenamin and Patrick McMenamin

The De Valera Deception
The Parsifal Pursuit

Also by Michael McMenamin

Becoming Winston Churchill, The Untold Story of Young Winston and His
American Mentor (with Curt Zoller)
Milking the Public, Political Scandals of the Dairy Lobby from LBJ to Jimmy
Carter (with Walter McNamara)

The Gemini Agenda

A Winston Churchill Thriller

by

Michael McMenamin
and
Patrick McMenamin

Enigma Books

Published in the United States by
Enigma Books
New York
www.enigmabooks.com

ISBN: 978-1-936274-37-6
eISBN: 978-1-936274-38-3

Library of Congress Cataloguing in Publication Available

To Carol and Becca, the loves of our lives.

And to the next generation, Dorothy, Meredith, Teddy, and Arthur, "the big A"

Publisher's Note

Some may question casting Winston Churchill as a key character in a series of historical thrillers set during 1929-1939, his "Wilderness Years" when he was out of power, out of favor and a lone voice warning against the rising danger posed by Adolf Hitler and Nazi Germany. They shouldn't. Saving Western Civilization in 1940 when England stood alone as a beacon of liberty in a sea of tyranny tends to overshadow Churchill's earlier accomplishments.

Churchill is, in many ways, a perfect historical figure around which to craft a period thriller. Winston was an adventure-seeking young man, a fencing champion in prep school, a championship polo player in the Army and a seaplane pilot in the early, peril-filled days of flight in 1910. In between, he was a much-decorated war hero in bloody battles on the Afghan-Indian border, in the Sudan, and in South Africa where his commanding officer nominated him for the Victoria Cross, Britain's highest military honor, and where he escaped from a prisoner of war camp and made his way to freedom over hundreds of miles of enemy territory. In World War I, while other politicians, safely abed, sent millions of young men to their death, Winston was with his troops in the trenches of the bloody Ypres salient daily risking death himself.

More importantly for this new series, Churchill maintained a private intelligence network in Britain and Europe during the 1930s which often left him better informed than his own government. The writing team of the critically acclaimed Churchill biographer Michael McMenamin and his journalist son Patrick McMenamin use this fact as a catalyst for their stories. With Churchill at the center spinning his own web, he lures into many adventures his fictional Scottish goddaughter, the beautiful Hearst photojournalist Mattie McGary and the American law professor Bourke

Cockran, Jr., a former U.S. Army counter-intelligence agent. Winston, a romantic at heart, brings the two young people together. Romance blooms but it is not a match made in heaven. Both characters are strong-willed individuals and their Celtic tempers frequently clash. Cockran is the fictional son of Churchill's real life mentor Bourke Cockran, a prominent turn-of-the–century New York lawyer, statesman, orator and presidential adviser whose life is chronicled in *Becoming Winston Churchill, the Untold Story of Young Winston and His American Mentor* by Michael McMenamin and Curt Zoller (Enigma Books, 2009).

The first three novels take place during 1929-1932 before Hitler's ill-fated, but entirely legal, appointment as the German Chancellor. In *The DeValera Deception,* Winston, Mattie and Bourke tangle with the IRA and a real-life, pre-Hitler, Russo-German conspiracy to dismember Poland. In doing so, they discover a plot in the US to assemble arms for an IRA *coup d'etat* in the new Irish Free State and Cockran seeks revenge for his wife's murder by the IRA in the 1922 Irish civil war. In *The Parsifal Pursuit,* Winston sends Mattie on a grail quest in the company of a handsome villain intent on her seduction, a journey shadowed by the Nazis who want the ancient Christian artifact for Hitler. Also at Winston's behest, Cockran travels to Germany to represent a beautiful blonde heiress who is the victim of a Nazi fund-raising tactic—extortion of her business by a protection racket worthy of Al Capone. In *The Gemini Agenda*, Winston and his private intelligence network put Mattie and Bourke on the trail of a plot by Nazi scientists to kidnap and conduct lethal eugenic experiments on American twins. Shockingly, they learn the conspiracy is funded by Wall Street financiers and elements of US Army Intelligence who hope to unlock the secret to creating a master race.

I hope you have as much fun reading these stories as I did. A new Winston-Mattie-Bourke trilogy set in 1933–1934 is in the making so stay tuned…

Robert Miller
Publisher
Enigma Books

The Gemini Agenda

The march of Science unfolding ever more appalling possibilities... the fires of hatred burning deep in the hearts of some of the greatest peoples of the world & fed by the deepest sense of national wrong. . .

Winston Churchill, 1924

PART I

England, America, and Germany

9 May — 20 May 1932

Eugenics is the science which deals with all influences that improve the inborn qualities of a race. The aim of eugenics is to bring as many influences as can reasonably be employed to cause the useful classes in the community to contribute more than their proportion to the next generation.

Sir Francis Galton, 1904

[T]here is now no reasonable excuse for refusing to face the fact that nothing but a eugenic religion can save our civilisation from the fate that has overtaken all previous civilisations.

George Bernard Shaw
1904

1.

There Are Worse Things Than War

Chartwell
Kent, England
Sunday, 8 May 1932

WHY did you have me make those inquiries in Germany?"
Winston Churchill stopped walking but otherwise ignored the question as he looked out over the weald of Kent, the most beautiful view in the world. And it all belonged to him. The view, that is, not the weald. He may have been out of power—and certainly out of favor with his own Conservative Party—but he still had the view.

It was a glorious spring day in the south of England. Churchill stood on the back lawn of his country estate, Chartwell, with two people very close to him. One was Professor Frederick Lindemann whose question he had not answered. Known fondly to Winston as "the Prof," he was an accomplished mathematician and scientist. The Prof, whose father had emigrated to England from Germany, still had many contacts there among the scientific community and that was why he was here today.

The other man was Churchill's son Randolph, a budding young journalist attempting to follow in his father's footsteps, both as a writer and, if he were fortunate, a politician. He had recently returned from Germany after covering Adolf Hitler's campaign for president where the Nazi leader had received over 13 million votes, second only to President Hindenburg himself.

The trio walked slowly along the lawn, toward the artificial lake whose digging Churchill had personally supervised. They were walking slowly because Churchill had not yet fully recovered from the injuries he had suffered the previous December in America. While crossing Fifth Avenue en route to the home of his friend, the financier Bernard Baruch, Churchill looked in the wrong direction and had been struck by an automobile traveling forty miles an hour. He had been thrown up over the hood, sustaining broken ribs, facial lacerations and a concussion.

Churchill had been home for several months now and Chartwell was just the tonic his bruised and battered body needed. He had to conserve his strength while his body healed if he were to carry through with his plans to visit Germany later that spring. The public reason he gave for his upcoming visit was the biography he was writing about his famed ancestor John Churchill, the first Duke of Marlborough. Churchill wanted to tour the battlefields where the first Duke had made his name and secured his fortune. But there was another reason for his forthcoming visit that he chose to keep to himself. Whispers out of Germany on certain matters had reached his ear and troubled him greatly. Matters of life and death.

Churchill turned to the Prof. "So, your sources turned up nothing new?"

The Prof withdrew his pipe from between his clenched teeth and shook his head from side to side. The Prof was taller than Churchill and his hair was short and dark, matching his mustache—below which was found his ever present pipe. In contrast, Churchill was a cherubic man with thinning red-hair, no more than five foot nine inches tall when his shoulders weren't slumped forward—which hardly ever happened. His face was pink and clean shaven and between his lips—a twin to the Prof's pipe—was a long unlit Havana cigar.

"That is a shame," Churchill replied, his voice a low growl. He turned to his son. "What are your plans for later this spring, my dear boy?"

Randolph was an exceptionally handsome young man, slightly taller than his father, with long blond hair combed back from his forehead. Having turned twenty-one earlier in the year, he had dropped out of Oxford—much to his father's dismay—to pursue a career in journalism. Lord Rothermere had hired him for the *Sunday Graphic* and sent him to Germany to cover the presidential election.

"It depends on what happens in Germany."

"Pray elaborate," Churchill replied.

"Chancellor Brüning is on his last legs. He could be forced out at any moment and new elections held. As the number of unemployed grows, so does Hitler's popularity—and all the street violence that goes with it. It's positively bad for your health, Papa, to be a Socialist, a Communist, or a Jew in Germany today. And the Brown Shirts don't spare women either,"

Randolph paused and then chuckled. "Given Hitler's views on the Jews, you would think Jewesses at least would be safe from rape. Racial pollution, mongrelization and all that nonsense, eh? But my sources tell me their women aren't any more safe from the SA thugs than blonde-haired German maidens." Randolph laughed again. "Actually, I suppose they are all safe from the SA types who are queer. Plenty of those, starting at the top with Rohm."

Churchill frowned. "I see nothing humorous in rape."

That was about as close to a rebuke as Churchill was capable of giving to his only son. Churchill knew that he spoiled Randolph but he couldn't help it. He so wanted his son to have a different relationship with him than Churchill had with his own father, Lord Randolph, who had been distant and, at times, cruel. He wanted it to be more be more like the one he had with his mentor, Bourke Cockran, the late Irish American statesman and orator who was a close friend to his mother and his Aunt Leonie. Churchill smiled. Indeed, as Leonie told it, Cockran once had been much more to his mother than just a friend after his father had died. He had never asked his mother but secretly he hoped it had been true. He liked Americans. His mother was American.

Churchill and Cockran had treated one another as equals with due deference given by the younger man to the older man's wisdom and experience. For if Churchill had striven throughout his life to accomplish great things in order to prove his father wrong in his low opinion of him, the opposite had been true with his mentor Cockran. With him, Churchill was always conscious that he had to prove Cockran right about the glittering future the American had predicted he would have. He liked Americans but he had loved Bourke Cockran.

Churchill briefly explained to the Prof and Randolph the plans for his holiday in Bavaria—touring Marlborough's battlefields—with Munich as their base of operations. The Prof promptly accepted Winston's invitation, but Randolph demurred.

"I'll come with you as far as Munich, Papa, but if there's another election, I must cover it. Hitler may well win. You don't have to understand German to see the mesmerizing effect he has on crowds. He exhorts them to rise above their petty individual interests and do what is right for their country. His appeal is extraordinary. During the last campaign, Hitler once arrived late for an address in a small rural town. His airplane landed at three in the morning and 40,000 people were still there, in the rain, waiting to hear him speak. Can you imagine that?"

Churchill chewed on his Havana cigar but said nothing.

"That's where the action will be, Papa. I don't have wars to cover like you did when you were young, but this is as close as it gets. For if Hitler takes power in Germany, war will certainly follow."

Again, Churchill did not reply and the three men resumed their walk.

"I am pleased you will be able to join us," Churchill said to the Prof before responding to his son, "and I don't blame you, Randolph, in the slightest for wanting to cover an election in Germany. Were I your age, I would do the same thing."

"Why did you have me make those inquiries in Germany, Winston?" the Prof asked for the second time after Randolph had returned to the house to take a telephone call from his editor.

Churchill kept walking. If the rumors were true—and right now that was all he had—it was all too monstrous to contemplate. They reached the edge of the lake and Churchill turned to his friend. "Randolph is right. There will be war if Hitler comes to power. But there are worse things than war, Prof. Far worse things."

"You're not going to tell me, are you?" Lindemann said but it wasn't a question.

Churchill did not answer. After a long silence, they turned and walked back towards the house. "I'll tell you this much," Churchill finally said. "People are being kidnapped and killed in America in an alarming fashion. But I don't know why. And no one in America appears to be paying any attention. A person who has my trust believes there may be a German connection. But that's all I know. I've passed what information I have to my friend, W.R. Hearst, a powerful American publisher. Needless to say, he has vast resources at his disposal. I stayed at his estate in California when I was on holiday there in 1929. I haven't given him much but someone risked his life to bring the information to me. I hope it will help. I pray to God it will."

LATER, alone in his upstairs book-lined study after dinner, a roaring fire at the far end of the room, Churchill stood before a rough-hewn stand-up writing desk and made corrections on page proofs with bold strokes from a red pencil. A weak Johnnie Walker Red and soda was on the shelf above the proofs next to a half-smoked Havana. Was Hearst the right man to have been given the information? For now, yes. Hearst had more than enough money but he also had an incomparable resource in his employ, someone with the tenacity of a terrier in pursuit of prey and the courage of a lioness protecting her cubs. His god-child Mattie McGary, the daughter of his great friend James McGary , who had been the first member of the Liberal Party to befriend the twenty-nine year old Churchill after he crossed the floor of the House of Commons in '04 and left his father's Tory party over their new-found opposition to free trade. He shook his head and took a sip of scotch as his thoughts took him back. To the fight for free trade. And to Bourke Cockran, the man who taught him that voluntary exchange was the very cornerstone of liberty. It was in many ways a more simple and happy time. Before all the horrors the 20th century had brought so far and, he greatly feared, was still to bring.

Certainly a happier time than now. Nevertheless, he was optimistic. If, as he hoped but was not so bold as to suggest, Hearst did assign Mattie to investigate the alarming information he had supplied, that meant the son of his old mentor Cockran would not be far behind. He smiled. It had not been his intent to act as a matchmaker but he had more or less brought the children of his two old friends together several years ago and they seemed to have quite a romance going. It had brought him great pleasure for he was a romantic at heart. Churchill was mildly surprised they were still not engaged. Once he decided it was to be Clemmie—and that hadn't taken very long—Churchill certainly had wasted no time in proposing and then marrying that stunning young woman a few short months later. Before she changed her mind. Faint hearts never won fair ladies. His god-child was equally attractive and no less a catch. Why hadn't young Cockran proposed to that girl?

2.

Improving the Race

Fifth Avenue
New York City
Monday, 9 May 1932

BOURKE Cockran, Jr. knew from long experience that accepting a written invitation to meet another man's stunningly beautiful wife, sent without her husband's knowledge, would rarely be innocent. Enjoyable? Possibly. Perilous? Almost certainly. Innocent? No. Especially not when it came from the wife of a powerful and dangerous adversary. But that only made it more of a challenge and Cockran had never thought for a moment of declining. A certain protocol had to be followed, however, before accepting.

The morning sun was streaming in the Florida room of his Fifth Avenue town house and, wordlessly, Cockran handed the scented note across the breakfast table to a tall and ravishing red-haired beauty from Scotland, Mattie McGary. Mattie was William Randolph Hearst's favorite photojournalist and she was just back from a month-long assignment covering the war between Bolivia and Paraguay. Clad only in a green silk dressing gown, carelessly knotted so that it revealed more than it concealed of her freckled breasts, she looked gorgeous, her tousled locks a crimson version of Amelia Earhart. They had been lovers for nearly three years.

Mattie took the pale blue sheet of paper, raised it to her nose and lifted her eyebrows.

"It arrived late yesterday afternoon at my law school office," Cockran said.

"Strange you didn't think to show this to me last night."

"My mind was occupied with other things."

"Your mind?" Mattie said, arching her eyebrows again. "I distinctly recall something else being occupied last night," she said and began to read aloud:

Dear Mr. Cockran:

Please do me the favor of meeting me tomorrow evening at Carnegie Hall for the reception following Dr. Lothrop Stoddard's lecture. I was not able to make an appointment with your law firm as they advised me you do not keep regular hours there. I wish to consult you professionally.

> *Sincerely,*
> *Ingrid Waterman*

P.S. Please do not make reference to this note in front of my husband. He would not approve.

"Ingrid Waterman. Isn't she the wife of . . . .?"

"Wesley Waterman, the chairman and president of International Calculating Equipment, I.C.E.," Cockran replied, enunciating each letter of the acronym forming the company's name.

Mattie raised her eyebrows once more. God, he loved her eyes but he knew what she meant. He and Wesley Waterman III had an unpleasant history. "His wife is a blonde knockout with a wicked sense of humor. I told you about her. We met after oral argument in Judy Dill's appeal."

Mattie nodded. "I remember. That poor girl who was sterilized, wasn't it?"

"The third sterilization case I lost, yes. I notched number four while you were in Bolivia. Anyway, not only was Ingrid easy on the eyes, but she poked fun at her husband right in front of me. He's the head of the American Eugenics Society as well as I.C.E., and she joked with me about her husband entering her in the annual American Breeders Association contest for Nordic Females. I forget exactly how she phrased it but the gist was that ABA conventions would be ever so much more interesting if they had public matings between the "best in show" winners in the male and female classifications.

Mattie laughed, almost choking on a sip of tea. "She said *that*! In front of her husband? I like her already."

"It sounds like she needs a lawyer. Should I go? What do you think? You'd have to fly yourself to Long Island tonight for your meeting with Hearst."

Mattie spooned some marmalade onto a piece of toast and held it up in the air. "I've seen photographs of her on the society pages. She *is* very blonde and very beautiful but I suppose it's okay. I'm a big girl. I can fly myself. On one condition."

"What's that?"

"That you don't show her your birthmark."

Cockran laughed. "I promise. I've learned my lesson."

Mattie smiled. "Good. Me too."

COCKRAN stepped out of the taxi in front of Carnegie Hall and looked up at the darkening clouds. What had started out as a beautiful spring day was turning into something else entirely. He tipped the cabbie and saw a flash of lightning. To the east, he saw the high, dark clouds which foreshadowed the storm to follow. He was worried. He had read the weather reports and had been concerned about his flying Mattie out to Long Island himself but now, with the storm definitely approaching, he hoped Mattie wouldn't attempt to fly on her own.

Mattie was a good pilot but "risk-taking", not "cautious", more aptly described her approach to life. He put the thought out of his mind. It was something he couldn't control and he no longer criticized her for it. It previously had been the subject of many arguments between them because he once believed his criticism could curb her recklessness. But the unintended consequences of doing that had persuaded him otherwise. He had learned his lesson the hard way. She was who she was and risk was part of the package.

The humor-tinged exchange between them at the breakfast table was a healthy sign that the hurt each had caused the other a year ago over this very subject was continuing to heal. While apart from him after one of their arguments over her risk-taking, Mattie had come to believe that Cockran had thrown her over and was having an affair with a new and beautiful blonde client. He hadn't but it had been a damn close run thing. In the process, his client had gotten a really good glimpse of the birthmark on Cockran's ass while she had been tending a bullet wound he had incurred in defending her from a ruthless business competitor—Wesley Waterman to be precise. All very innocent—really—but enough to make a saint suspicious.

Mattie was no saint and, for reasons he never understood, his client had told her about seeing his birthmark and used that to imply she and Cockran were lovers. A heartbroken Mattie thought their argument over risk-taking was responsible and that he had found someone else. Shortly thereafter, a vulnerable Mattie had an affair with a man accompanying her on what became a dangerous assignment. Cockran didn't know that last part exactly. Her affair, that is.

Once she learned Cockran hadn't been sleeping with his client, Mattie tried to confess what she had done but he put her off. He had met the guy who was tall, fair-haired and one tough bastard. He and Cockran had even joined forces later to rescue Mattie from several tight situations. Under other circumstances, he might even have liked the guy. But if it were true about him and Mattie, he didn't want to hear it. He loved her and simply wanted it all to stay in the past while they moved forward. That was when he had decided her taking risks was one of those things he couldn't control. But his previous plans to propose marriage were temporarily on hold for a variety of reason.

For one thing, she didn't really know him that well if she thought he was the kind of guy who would have an affair with another woman without first telling Mattie that it was over between them. For another, he thought she still had tender feelings for the man who had so swiftly swept her off her feet and into his bed. He needed to come to grips with both because he didn't want her accepting a marriage proposal out of guilt over the affair or her misreading of his character. And he sure as hell didn't want to talk about it. Guys didn't do that even if girls did.

Cockran looked again at the ominous sky. He had taught Mattie to fly himself last summer in Italy and she would be flying the safest aircraft known to man, a Pitcairn autogiro, Cockran's personal plane, the *Celtic Princess*. Mattie *was* a good pilot and good pilots knew better than to fly in bad weather like this.

"Please, Mister? A penny, if you can spare it?" The voice of a boy reached Cockran through the depths of his thoughts. He turned and saw a small boy in threadbare clothes, clearly unwashed, standing outside the entrance to Carnegie Hall and begging passersby. Ever since the Depression deepened, he had been disturbed at how many beggars were children these days — their parents off looking in vain for work that did not exist. Cockran often wondered how his father would have responded to the Depression, wishing his great oratorical presence were still alive to protest the Republicans' high tariffs, higher taxes and greater government spending which they promised would return prosperity. It hadn't and things were getting worse. "Governments create nothing" his father once had said and his father's protégé Winston Churchill had said it even better: "A government can no more tax itself into prosperity than a man standing in a bucket can lift himself by the handles."

He opened his wallet for a ten dollar bill to place in the boy's outstretched palm. "Oh, thank you, Mister! Thank you, God bless you!" the boy shouted. Cockran gave him a smile. It would only help for so long, Cockran thought, as he walked up the steps to the entrance to Carnegie Hall, but his father had taught him to be generous with those less fortunate.

Cockran opened the brass door, walked inside and examined the glass-enclosed placard announcing the evening's entertainment:

LECTURE TONIGHT
"Our Moral Obligation to Future Generations"

By Dr. Lothrop Stoddard
Author of: *The Passing Of The Great Race;*
The Rising Tide Of Color Against White World-Supremacy; and
The Revolt Against Civilization: The Menace of the Under-Man

Cockran shook his head. How could you shove so much crap inside one Harvard Ph.D.?

Cockran was late, a not uncommon occurrence, but it was usually unplanned. Tonight was different. He knew what Stoddard would be saying. He didn't need to hear it again. He had heard it all before at the Army War College where Stoddard had been a regular lecturer to the Officer Corps of the U.S. Army and MID agents like Cockran. All three of Stoddard's books listed on the lobby poster were required reading at the war college. What kind of government would employ Stoddard as an educator for its young military officers? Democrat or Republican, it apparently didn't matter. Predictably, Stoddard had started during the reign of that Southern racist Woodrow Wilson but he was still there today with Herbert Hoover in the White House.

Stoddard was one of the leading advocates of "eugenics," the science of human heredity which contained both positive and negative components. Cockran's father had said to him on more than one occasion that, in a society where there was democratic tolerance and freedom under the law, many kinds of evil would crop up. But give them a little time and they would usually breed their own cure. It wasn't that the science of eugenics was evil *per se*. Science, properly understood, was neutral. It could be used for good or ill. But when science—or some scientists—began to serve politics, bad things could happen. Eugenics was a case in point.

Cockran, like his father, fiercely believed in individual liberty. Hence, he was more tolerant of "positive" eugenics whose core consisted of encouraging upper class Protestants to breed more of their own kind so as to keep Irish, Italians, Jews and other undesirables out of their superior gene pool. Having grown up as an Irish Catholic on Long Island's Gold Coast, Cockran came to appreciate that most Protestants didn't want their offspring sleeping with Catholics, let alone marrying them. Cockran thought it had more to do with bigotry than science but small-minded bigots only marrying their own kind might well breed its own cure.

The problem was that its twin—"negative" eugenics—was definitely not breeding its own cure. States were passing laws left and right mandating sterilization of mental defectives — already over 40,000 women in twenty six states had been permanently deprived of their ability to reproduce by wise and well-meaning governments. He couldn't help recalling the phrase "three generations of imbeciles are enough" from the judicial pen of the octogenarian Mr. Justice Oliver Wendell Holmes which had opened the constitutional floodgates for forced sterilization based on a cooked-up record which the senile bastard had not bothered to analyze.

After that unfortunate Supreme Court decision, Cockran had taken on the lost cause of four women condemned to forced sterilization because they were "mentally defective." Cockran had done this because he could see where it would all end. Weeding out the weak was only the first step. State-sanctioned euthanasia would be next. Scientific treatises were already advocating just that. Could the courts be far behind? With judges like Holmes, who knew?

People talked about the impatience of the populace but sound historians knew that most tyrannies had been possible because men moved too late. It was essential, his father had told him, to resist tyranny before it gained a foothold. A blow from a hatchet, Cockran knew, could only be parried while it was in the air. Cockran's seemingly Quixotic defense of women facing forced sterilization was his effort to parry the hatchet while it was still in the air. Was it working? He didn't know. All he knew was that people like Lothrop Stoddard were still wielding the hatchet of "science" to further their political agenda.

As Cockran entered Carnegie Hall's main auditorium, he was encouraged to see that it was only three-quarters full. Maybe civilization still had a chance. Stoddard's slicked-down dark hair and mustache beneath his hawk-like nose were a distinct contrast to the other man on the stage. Harry Laughlin was the bald, clean-shaven chief of the Eugenics Record Office research facility and clinic at Cold Spring Harbor, Long Island, fifteen miles up the road from Cockran's own country home in Sands Point. Neither Stoddard nor Laughlin fit the fair-haired Nordic stereotype. Laughlin had a round, moon-shaped face while Stoddard's nose had a Semitic cast to it. In contrast, the Irish Cockran, six feet two inches tall with sandy hair and green eyes, towered over them. No one would have called him handsome but there was a rugged angularity to his Celtic features, a long face and aquiline nose, which more approximated the Nordic ideal than either Stoddard or Laughlin, an irony which neither would appreciate.

Stoddard slapped the podium with his left hand for emphasis: "Our particular job is stopping the prodigious spread of inferiority which is now going on. We may be losing our best-stocks, but we are losing them much more slowly than we are multiplying our worst. Our study of differential birth-rates showed us that if these remain unchanged, our most intelligent stocks will diminish by one-third to two-thirds in the next hundred years; it also showed that our least intelligent stocks will increase from six- to ten-fold in the same time."

Cockran smiled. Obviously, Stoddard considered himself to be among the most intelligent stocks and positive eugenics encouraged them to breed more than their less intelligent brothers. He wondered if Stoddard used this line to pick up women in bars—blondes, naturally.

Stoddard had more in mind, however, than the most intelligent stocks simply outbreeding their inferiors. He paused for effect: "Obviously, it is this prodigious spawning of inferiors which must at all costs be prevented if society is to be saved from disruption and dissolution. Race cleansing is apparently the only thing that can stop it. Therefore, race cleansing must be our first concern." The crowd burst into applause.

Who *were* these people? Unfortunately, Cockran knew all too well. Did the science of heredity support what they were doing? To Cockran, it didn't matter. One didn't need to deny the science of heredity in order to resist legislation mandating sterilization any more than one needed to deny the spiritual world in order to resist an epidemic of witch-burning.

With the cheers of the audience now fading, Cockran wanted nothing more than to go home and take a long, hot shower to cleanse himself from having spent so much time among people who could applaud what he just heard. And, as soon as he had found the bar; had a stiff drink; and talked with Ingrid Waterman – in that order – he intended to do precisely that. Halfway to the bar, Cockran felt a big hand suddenly clamp down hard on his right shoulder.

"Cockran! We need to talk." A deep, masculine voice cut through the noise of the crowd.

Cockran turned and looked up at the face of the Chairman of I.C.E., Wesley Waterman, III. Waterman was a big man. Six feet, four inches tall and easily two hundred and forty pounds. He did have those Nordic blue eyes but his light brown hair was thinning at the crown. Cockran wondered if this were a genetic defect from which future generations should be spared. A moral obligation perhaps? Right now, however, he needed a drink. Maybe two.

."You cost me a lot of money in Germany last year. I've not forgotten," Waterman said as he tightened his grip on Cockran's shoulder.

Cockran tensed. He did not like Wesley Waterman. "Take your hand away. Now. Or I'll return it with a broken wrist." Coming from a former MID agent, it was not an idle threat.

Waterman smiled broadly as if they were old fraternity brothers and released his grip. "Don't make the same mistake twice."

"Buzz off, Waterman. I have no idea what you're talking about," Cockran replied, disappointed at being deprived of an opportunity to break the man's wrist.

"My wife," he hissed. "*Who*. Not what. Don't even *think* about becoming her lawyer. You'd live to regret it." Waterman paused and smiled. "Or maybe not. The choice is yours."

"To become her lawyer?"

Waterman shook his head and smiled. "To live."

Cockran didn't reply and resumed his journey to the bar, shouldering Waterman aside with perhaps more force than was really necessary. In addition to manners, Waterman needed to learn not to stand in the way of an Irishman and his drink. As he ordered a martini at the bar, Cockran noticed lightning flash outside, the sound of thunder immediately following, rain pelting the window. He turned to watch. The threatening thunderstorm had entered with a vengeance. He was relieved. Mattie would have had his chauffeur Jimmy take her in the Packard to Long Island. Even experienced pilots knew better than to fly in weather like this.

3.

Thanks For Leaving The Lights On

MATTIE McGary was thoroughly frightened. She used the sleeve of her leather flying jacket in a vain effort to wipe her goggles. She had flown at night before and she had flown in rain. But never both at the same time, let alone in the middle of a thunderstorm and into the teeth of gale-force winds which slowed her forward progress to twenty-five miles per hour, fifty miles per hour less than the cruising speed of the Pitcairn autogiro. Its four giant blades rotated above her head, providing lift as the propeller of the Wright Whirlwind engine pulled her forward and she ruefully reflected that Cockran once had told her it was the world's safest aircraft.

Normally, the flight from Manhattan to Sands Point in Long Island would have taken less than thirty minutes and five more minutes after that to reach Hearst's mansion. She had been aloft for nearly sixty. She took a deep breath. No aircraft was safe from pilot error.

Mattie could not recall the last time she had been so scared. Well, actually, she could. It had been the previous summer on the *Graf Zeppelin*. Three hundred feet above the Atlantic Ocean. From the safety of a hatch on top of the immense airship, she had been taking spectacular photographs of four riggers as one of them stitched up a tear in the silvery fabric of the dirigible's outer shell. The other three riggers were braced on top, holding the ropes from which the fourth dangled halfway down the side of the ship. But Mattie's field of vision had been blocked by one of the riggers and she had climbed onto the top of the dirigible, away from the safety of the hatch in order to take better photographs, clutching onto what she mistakenly believed to be a safety line. It wasn't. Mattie nearly died but had been saved by the strong hands of the man she was to take as a lover a few short weeks later in a moment of vulnerability following an unfortunate misunderstanding on her part.

The guilt she felt for that brief affair was with her still. Cockran was the best thing that had ever happened to her and she had almost screwed it up. Fortunately, that big, beautiful Irish bastard still loved her and things were back on track. Or at least she hoped so. To bring them both closure, she had tried to tell Cockran how it had happened but he had put her off. Did that mean he loved her but hadn't forgiven her? She didn't know. Thank God the man with whom she had the affair was an ocean away and out of their lives forever if she had anything to do with it.

Mattie had taken off at 7 p.m. from the skyport on the lower tip of Manhattan and she had seen the storm clouds building in the east over Long Island. But, to the west over New Jersey, the sky had been gloriously clear, and she could tell the sunset would be stunning. And the meteorologist's report said that landfall for the storm was a good hour away, more than enough time to make it safely to Sands Point. What the report hadn't said was how soon and how strong the winds would be.

Mattie was literally flying blind now, using only the compass to keep her headed due east. She nosed the stick forward in an attempt to break below the cloud cover and hopefully pick out some local landmarks. She was grateful for the autogiro's inability to stall, even at the slowest speeds, but right now she would have given anything to be safely on the lawn at Hearst's beachfront mansion, followed by her sipping a very large single-malt scotch in front of a roaring fireplace, listening to the details of the newest adventure Hearst had in store for her.

Lightning flashed again very close, quickly followed by the crack of thunder just as she broke free from the cloud cover, barely 100 feet from the ground. She could smell the ozone, so close had the lightning passed. Then, blessedly, less than a mile ahead, a blazing circle of storm lamps nearly 50 yards in diameter appeared in front of a castle-like structure that looked as if it had leaped from the pages of *Ivanhoe*.

Mattie wiped her goggles once more and pushed the stick forward as she headed for the safety of Hearst's estate. She banked gently to her left until the huge circle was barely 100 yards away. Lightning flashed again and Mattie saw she had been coming in too low, heading straight for the electric wires on the road in front of the mansion. Quickly, she pulled back on the stick to regain altitude, the aircraft's wheels barely clearing the wires. She cut power to the engine and the autogiro floated safely towards the ground.

Mattie breathed a sigh of relief, unbuckled her seatbelt and climbed out of the cockpit onto the wing. She hopped down to the ground and saw the tall figure of William Randolph Hearst dressed in oilskins and a nor'easter hat, followed by six similarly clad servants moving toward her. She took off her white leather flight helmet and shook out her hair. Hearst was carrying another set of oilskins which he wrapped around Mattie's shoulders as she embraced him and kissed him on the cheek as the others tethered the autogiro.

"You're a sight for sore eyes, Chief," she said. "Thanks for leaving the lights on."

Hearst embraced her in return. "Let's get you inside, my dear, and out of those wet clothes. You'll catch your death of cold."

MATTIE, bundled into one of Hearst's old flannel robes, held the crystal tumbler in both hands as she sat in a leather armchair on one side of the fireplace, savoring the heat from the fire and the warm glow the single-malt scotch produced. Hearst stood beside the fireplace, sipping from a cup of hot apple cider. He was a big, shambling bear of a man and, even in his late sixties, several inches taller than the six foot two inch Cockran. His face was long and when it spread into a smile, Mattie could still see more than a trace of the handsome young man he once had been, his blue eyes as clear and sparkling now as they must have been then.

The fire provided the only illumination in the room as Mattie sat there, naked beneath Hearst's flannel robe, her feet tucked under her. Hearst's wife Millicent rarely ventured out to the castle, he had explained, so none of her clothes were kept there that Mattie could have borrowed. Mattie had smiled at this because Hearst's wife Millicent rarely ventured out to his other castle as well. San Simeon, California, Hearst's pride and joy, was presided over by Hearst's mistress, the smart and beautiful young actress Marion Davies, with whom Mattie had become good friends.

"So, I'll make you a deal, Chief" Mattie said.

"What's that, my dear?" Hearst asked as he sat down across from her.

"I won't tell Marion that we had drinks together in front of a roaring fireplace with me wearing only your robe, so long as you don't tell Cockran that I got caught up in the thunder storm and barely made it here in one piece. You know how he feels about my taking risks."

Hearst chuckled. "Of course, my dear. You have my word. It's bad enough that Marion is jealous of Millicent. We certainly can't have her suspicious of you as well. Besides, you always get your way with me, my dear. The only other person who does that is Marion."

Mattie smiled back. "She'd better, Chief. She's the best thing that ever happened to you. So, fill me in. What's so important?"

Hearst's smile faded as he placed down his cup of cider. "I have a new assignment for you," he said in a voice oddly high-pitched for such a large man as he reached for a large sheaf of newspaper clippings on the side table and handed them to Mattie.

Mattie took them and began to read. They were from Hearst papers all over the country. Pittsburgh, Cleveland, Detroit, Chicago, St. Louis, Milwaukee, Portland and San Francisco. The stories varied in size and location within the paper. Some were small, three or four paragraph matter-of-fact stories buried on page eight or nine. More than half were given this treatment. A few more were on page three, with bigger headlines and a few more paragraphs. Two were actually front page stories, but below the fold.

Mattie was horrified. What the stories had in common was that they involved murder victims whose naked bodies all had been discovered in a similar condition in remote locations near major metropolitan areas. Their throats cut from ear to ear. Their collapsed bodies virtually drained of all blood. Their eyeballs missing.

"There's no detail in any of these stories about the eyeballs" Mattie said. "Don't you think it's strange? I can understand how some of the bodies were missing eyes. Rats or other small animals could do that. But *all* of them with no eyeballs?"

Hearst nodded. "Good girl. I thought of that myself. So I had my editors send their reporters back to read all the coroners' autopsy reports on the victims."

"And?" Mattie asked.

"Animals weren't to blame. All the victims had their eyes surgically removed. Clean incisions."

"Oh my God!" Mattie gasped. She took a healthy sip of scotch and picked up the last article she had read, the front page story in *The Chicago American* with what was clearly the most lurid headline:

VAMPIRES? POLICE BAFFLED BY EYELESS CORPSE ON THE SOUTH SIDE

"Vampires? What's going on here?"

"Ignore that. That particular editor has always had an overly active imagination." Hearst said in an annoyed tone, "but, taken together, those articles show that most Hearst editors only read their own paper and not the other Hearst papers. I read them all, of course. Cover to cover."

"So you picked up this pattern, Chief?"

Hearst looked away and then back at Mattie. "Not exactly. In all fairness to my editors, I didn't spot the similarities at once. These eight murders occurred over a six month period."

"So how'd you figure it all out? Did you have a source?"

Hearst waved her off. "Yes, but that's not important now. What's important is to get to the bottom of this. Alert the authorities to common threads among these crimes," Hearst paused and smiled. "And, of course, supply us with an exclusive story. The usual priorities apply."

"Come on, Chief," Mattie said. "Don't keep me in the dark. If you trust me with the story, you've got to trust me with your source."

Hearst frowned. "This is most sensitive. He swore me to secrecy but I believe he would not object if you knew," he said as he paused and took another sip of cider. Then, he looked directly at her and spoke one word. "Winston."

"My godfather? Really? And who were his sources?"

Hearst shook his head. "He wouldn't tell me except to say that they were reliable. And German."

Mattie grinned. "Okay, that sounds like Winston. But let's make sure I have your priorities straight. The exclusive story is paramount. You want me to go vampire hunting and investigate these crimes but I only let the police in cities who cooperate with us know that there were similar crimes committed elsewhere."

"That's my girl," Hearst said. "How soon can you start?"

"Give a girl a break, Chief. I just got back from Bolivia a week ago. I haven't seen Cockran in over a month. Can't it wait a few weeks? What you're talking about could take me months, and I still might come up with nothing."

"Our competitors aren't stupid, Mattie, and Winston may well decide to tip off Pulitzer or Scripps-Howard. We can't have that happen."

"That won't happen, Chief. If Winston knows it's my story, he'd never do that."

"Perhaps but I'm not willing to take that risk. I'm putting my two best reporters on this and I want you and Ted Hudson to start at once."

Mattie was startled and nearly spilled her drink. Ted Hudson? Or, more precisely, Theodore Stanhope Hudson IV? This was a big problem. An extended assignment in the field with Ted Hudson was *not* a good idea. She and Ted had dated a few times in the 20s. OK, well… more than a few times and they were more than just dates. Tall, blond, handsome and rich, he was a good guy, if a trifle self-centered. But he also had a dark side that sometimes flashed across those all-American good looks. Before she got him an interview with Hearst in '29, he had been in the U.S. Army's Military Intelligence Division just like Cockran once had been. In fact, she later learned, the two MID agents had worked on several assignments together before she had met either man. But Hudson wasn't the problem. The problem was Bourke Cockran and it long predated her relationship with both of them. Cockran couldn't *stand* Ted Hudson.

4.

The Assassin

KURT von Sturm looked good in black. He knew this in a matter of fact way like a man knows how tall he is or how fast he can run. His blond hair, combed neatly back from his forehead, was in sharp contrast to his black dinner jacket, crisp white wing-collar shirt, and formal black bow tie. Only a two-inch scar on his left temple marred what was otherwise a classically handsome face which most woman found attractive and some even irresistible.

Sturm looked out across the crowded ballroom, filled with the elite of Europe — bankers, industrialists, diplomats, and politicians, each dressed much like Sturm, but none of them pulling it off with quite the same perfection. The occasion was a fund-raising ball for Berlin's Kaiser Wilhelm Institute. To Sturm, the mistresses and young second wives here tonight provided a more splendid impression, sparkling like diamonds in their color-splashed evening gowns, standing out against the sea of black coats—all ripe for seduction. For Sturm was a predator and, on any other night, they would be his prey. But not tonight.

A tall raven haired beauty named Juliette stood at the far end of the ballroom, her sleek backless red dress stretching across her small taut breasts. She had been his prey the evening before and was the mistress of his prey tonight—Pierre Reynaud, the silver-haired arms dealer with the long Gallic nose to whose arm she clung, a clear look of boredom the only sign of her independence.

From the other end of the ballroom, Sturm made eye-contact with Juliette and her eyes lit up with excitement. He could see that she was making excuses to her consort and began to glide her way through the crowd, sliding her thin body between guests, moving with haste to reach Sturm at the other end of the ballroom. Before she could reach him, Sturm turned and made his way to the back of the ballroom. Once in the corridor, he made his way to an unused kitchen where they had agreed to meet.

Inside the empty kitchen, he turned to greet her, but she was already pressing her long lithe body against his and he allowed her to push him back against the stainless steel countertop of the kitchen. She kissed him fiercely and he kissed her back, spreading his hands across her bare back as her breasts stiffened in anticipation. She reached her hand down to his groin, and he felt himself begin to stir, causing Juliette to smile.

"There he is," she said in French, with a lazy grin. "I've been missing him all day."

Sturm pushed her away gently. "There's no time, *mon amie*," he answered back in his slightly accented French. "You must get back to him before he suspects anything."

"To hell with him," she said, reaching to unbutton his pants. "He is not my husband. Fuck me again, right here."

Sturm seized her hand and quickly spun it around behind her back, causing the length of her body to rest firmly against his. She purred in delight at his suddenly rough turn. "But you are his mistress and he will notice your absence."

"I'll make it quick," she whispered.

Sturm smiled, "'Quick' is not what I have planned for you."

"You won't have any choice in the matter," she said.

"You've said that before," he said. She leaned to kiss him, but Sturm pushed her away firmly. "No. I have much more in store for you and nothing about it could be described as 'quick.' When can you free yourself from him?"

She sighed and sagged back into his arms. "He expects me to fuck him after these events. Once he's finished, he sends me away and orders room service for himself. That's how you found me in the hotel bar last night."

Reynaud's voracious appetite was well known and Sturm had discovered his habit of ordering a post-coital meal during his early reconnaissance of the Frenchman. Vintage Bordeaux and a wedge of Roquefort were his room service order of preference. "Then my staff will alert me when Monsieur Reynaud makes his order and I will find you in the hotel bar, just as the night before," he said. Juliette had been given the false impression that Sturm was heir to the aging owner of the hotel she was staying in, the *Bayerische Hof.* Good looks and a tailored tuxedo can go a long way.

"You don't understand," she said. "The room won't be under his name. Pierre never uses his real name when he travels outside of France—especially in Germany. He says there are people here who want him dead. He even brings a pair of bodyguards with him. They stand outside his room every night."

"Then tell me your room number."

"He'd kill me if he knew I told you," she said.

"He'd have you killed if he knew what you have been doing with me," Sturm said, pulling her closer to him, his strong hands pressed firmly against the small of her back. "He'd have us both killed."

She turned her face up to his and sighed, her lips nearly touching. "Suite 803," she whispered and Kurt von Sturm kissed her deeply before pushing her away.

Juliette left him alone in the kitchen and he remained, gathering his thoughts, slowing his heart-rate, regaining his self-control. Then he left the kitchen and was soon walking down the night streets of Munich towards the *Bayerische Hof.* Sturm knew that his self-control was not complete. Last summer, a woman had nearly cost him his life. She too had been prey but, during the chase, she had stolen the hunter's heart.

Sturm knocked carefully in a pre-specified pattern on the back door to the staff quarters of the *Bayerische Hof.* The door opened to reveal a tall man with close-cropped light brown hair. Sturm's protégé, Bruno Kordt.

"It's about time you showed up," Bruno said, smiling. "I was beginning to think all the dancing and fucking had gone to your head."

"Juliette wanted me to take her right there in the kitchen," Sturm said. "I can see why you keep asking to take my role in these operations."

"And I can see why you keep saying, 'No.'"

Sturm shrugged. "Women find me irresistible. God has blessed you with other gifts."

Bruno laughed and stepped aside to let him into the staff quarters of the *Bayerische Hof.* His entire team, or "staff" as he had described them to Juliette, were there, dressed as waiters.

REYNAUD'S order came in two hours later, settling for an assortment of cheeses in lieu of his favored Roquefort. The room service cart rolled down the corridor to Suite 803, under Sturm's gentle pressure. He was dressed in the red-trimmed white tunic of the *Bayerische Hof* staff which had replaced his black dinner jacket. He didn't need to look at room numbers to see Suite 803. Only one room had two large men in gray suits standing outside it and they both had stared at him from his first step out of the elevator.

As expected, they searched every inch of the room service cart before moving on to a search of Sturm's own body, hands brushing over the spot by his right ankle where he normally kept a knife hidden. But not tonight. They were thorough, forcing him to open the bottle of wine outside the room before taking the corkscrew from him. Finally, they nodded their approval and knocked on the door. From within, they heard the permission to enter and opened the door. Sturm was about to push his cart and his weapon into the Frenchman's room, but one of the guards suddenly seized his arm. Sturm's muscles tensed automatically to make the counterstrike that would break the man's arm, but he was able to control his instincts and remain outwardly calm instead.

"Hold it," the guard said in French. "Did you think I would let you in with this?" He held up a razor sharp, perforated cheese knife.

"But that is for the hard cheeses," Sturm protested.

"He can use this while you are here," he said, gesturing to a small butter knife. "I will bring the other to him after you leave. Now go. Be quick about it."

Sturm nodded his assent, watching the guard pocket the sharp knife. He pushed the cart into the expansive corner suite, his back to the guards, and began pouring a glass of wine. He could hear one of the guards follow him into the room, while the other one presumably stood watch outside, the door remaining open. At this very moment, Sturm knew the guard outside would be tense and occupied watching the tall man with close-cropped light brown hair—Bruno —walking down the hallway towards their door. But Sturm waited patiently, moving the plate of cheeses, laying out the bread and the small plate of butter alongside it.

The Frenchman entered from the bedroom wearing a loose silk robe and slippers, a cigarette in one hand, a strand of his sleek silver hair hanging loosely over his forehead. "It's about time you arrived," he said. "I ordered this twenty minutes ago." He walked closer to the cart, pointing at the bread. "I don't recall ordering a baguette."

"No Sir," Sturm said. "Compliments of the house with all orders of our special cheese selection."

Finally, Sturm heard the bell of the elevator ring as its doors opened onto the eighth floor and he knew exactly what would happen outside in the hallway as though he were there watching it like a spectator. A man on Sturm's team would walk onto the floor, his silenced Mauser pistol in plain sight of the guard still in the hallway, whose head would spin instinctively towards the sound. The sight of the gun would grab his attention long enough for Bruno to take an uncontested shot, eliminating the first threat with a bullet in the back of his head.

Just as Sturm saw the action playing out in his mind, he heard the muffled retort from Bruno's pistol. He reached for the butter knife resting harmlessly next to the bread, swiftly jabbed upwards with the knife at the Frenchman's throat and punctured his neck. Reynaud gave a choking cry as Sturm jerked free with his right hand, tearing through the carotid artery. He brought a thick napkin up with his left hand to absorb the blood pouring out of the Frenchman's body as he let him drop to the floor.

There wasn't time to waste. He turned, butter knife in hand, and saw that the guard was completely focused on him, his gun almost out of his holster. Sturm lunged forward with the knife, aiming for the same spot on his neck, but the guard's head exploded in a shower of blood and bone before he could reach him. His body crumpled lifelessly to the ground and Sturm found himself staring at Bruno Kordt, his silenced Mauser pistol held in both hands.

Sturm had not expected Bruno would be able to reach him so quickly, certainly not with enough time to take out the second guard. That was why they had planned for Sturm to take out the second guard. But Bruno had timed it flawlessly and was much faster than Sturm had anticipated.

He took note of Bruno's progress. He would be aware of it the next time they worked together.

Outwardly, Sturm conveyed an appearance of mild irritation. "A Mauser at point-blank range is not a clean affair, Bruno." Sturm gestured to the mess left against the wall and tiled floor of the entrance — not to mention the specks on his white coat. "That is why I had you take out the guard outside, because the distance would be enough to keep the bullet inside the skull, killing cleanly and efficiently."

"I understand," Bruno said. "But the second guard had his weapon drawn and I had to make certain the result was not in doubt."

"The result was never in doubt, Bruno. You know that. You must trust your team to carry out their function," Sturm said. "Still, it was good, quick work. An acceptable improvisation. Nevertheless, you must clean up this mess and dispose of the bodies."

"And what will *you* be doing?" Bruno asked, displaying curiosity rather than resentment.

"Me?" Sturm took off his waiter's jacket as one of his men approached, holding out his black evening jacket from earlier. Sturm put his arms through the sleeves and adjusted the cuffs to display a hint of his onyx cufflinks. He smiled. "I'm late for my date with Juliette."

5.

A Fine Nordic Specimen

Hollywood, California
Monday, 9 May 1932

NANCY Anne Neumann was naked; she had been born naked; she had been naked last night on his hotel room bed; and—the man checked his watch—in precisely twenty-four minutes and fifteen seconds, she would die naked.

The man ran a hand through his prematurely silver hair as he raised the ophthalmoscope to a dark blue eye that seemed almost violet. He brought his eye in close to examine each of hers, a lighter blue. Like an unclouded summer sky. Yes, he thought, they would do nicely. They both were fine specimens. The rest of her presented a fine Nordic specimen as well from the top of her pretty blonde head past plump, pink-tipped breasts down to long, well-formed legs, all of which had been placed in service the previous night for "sperm migration studies". The speculum-aided examination he had performed moments ago, the results recorded in his precise handwriting, was the first but by no means the last of the scientific contributions the lovely Nancy would make to the next generation.

The man stared impassively at the woman lying flat on the metal surgical table. She attempted to move her head but a soft leather band pulled tightly over her forehead kept her from doing so. A cotton cloth tied around her mouth meant that any sound, including the inevitable screams, would be muffled through several layers. She struggled in vain to move her arms and legs but her wrists and ankles were firmly bound in soft leather restraints as well.

Nancy wanted to be an actress. *Didn't they all?* When he told her his name was "Victor Volbrecht" and that he produced films for UFA, he could tell from the look on her face that was all the aphrodisiac she needed. A trip to his penthouse suite at the Hollywood Roosevelt Hotel was a foregone conclusion. Besides, he consoled himself as he placed a large syringe and scalpel on the tray beside the metal table, she wouldn't have been a particularly good actress, not if her feigned orgasms the night before were any indication.

No, not much of a loss to humanity, especially when she had so much more to contribute this morning. After aligning the syringe and scalpel, he walked to the telephone in the corner of the room and placed a long distance call to Denver. Once the call came through, he waited until he recognized the voice on the other end. "Are you ready to begin?" he asked. "Yes, Josef, everything is ready here as well." He chuckled. "Of course. The migration study results have been recorded. Let's synchronize our watches. On my mark," he said and paused. "Seven-ten a.m. I'll telephone you when it's over. You keep careful notes as well."

The silver-haired man picked up the large syringe. He swabbed the inside of Nancy's right arm and then injected the needle into a vein, her blue eyes growing wide, as he began to draw her blood into the syringe. Once full, he replaced it with an empty syringe. He repeated the process ten times more until, at last, she lost consciousness. He smiled. She had already contributed more than her proportion to the next generation and now she was ready to make her final contribution. He opened her left eyelid and reached for the stainless steel scalpel, its silver surface flashing once in the overhead light before it moved down to Nancy's eye.

6.

I Prefer Vodka With My Caviar

Carnegie Hall
New York City
Monday, 9 May 1932

IF Cockran had been surprised by Waterman's clumsy threat, he was not surprised to find two full bars set up in the reception area. Prohibition was on its last legs and, in New York at least, the police no longer bothered. Now that good gin was again being imported from Canada as opposed to the bathtub variety, Cockran had ordered a dry Gordon's martini with two olives and looked out over the crowd, hoping to spot Ingrid Waterman.

Cockran began to circulate, carefully avoiding the small knots of conversation as he walked through the room, taking an occasional sip from his martini. He disliked cocktail parties and polite conversation. Five minutes later, he felt a warm presence behind him and a soft, seductive voice was whispering in his ear. He liked this a lot better.

"Thank you for coming. I wasn't sure you would, but I want you to know I appreciate it."

Cockran turned and there before him, in a form-fitting strapless royal blue silk dress, was the blonde Nordic vision that was Ingrid Waterman, every bit as beautiful as the woman he remembered meeting nearly a year ago in the rotunda of the state appellate court on East 26th Street.

Cockran put out his hand and she extended hers. "Mrs. Waterman, how nice to see you once more."

"Please, Mr. Cockran. Call me Ingrid," she said and smiled.

Cockran smiled back. "And I'm Bourke."

"So that's how you pronounce your name? "Burke"? The "o" is silent?"

"That's what my father told me. It's the same as that *Fortune* photographer, Margaret Bourke-White. I think we're distantly related."

"I feel silly asking you to meet me like this, but I was afraid if we talked on the telephone you might not remember me."

Cockran smiled. "I don't think there was ever any danger of that. I have an excellent memory when it comes to beautiful women."

Ingrid returned the smile. "Some of my girlfriends told me the same thing about you."

Cockran took a sip of his martini rather than reply. He knew she and her husband had a place on Long Island's north shore and they undoubtedly moved in the same circles as some of Cockran's former married lovers. He didn't believe that comparing mutual female acquaintances with Ingrid Waterman would be a wise exercise.

Before he met Mattie in the summer of 1929, his love life had consisted of dating a number of attractive married women, mostly from the north shore of Long Island where he had grown up. The Gold Coast. Why he had done so was complicated but logical. After the tragic death of his young wife Nora in the Irish Civil War in 1922, he determined not to remarry and to raise their two year old son Patrick by himself. Nora's widowed mother had come back with him to America to help. After breaking the hearts of a few single women, he decided that romancing married women out for revenge on their husbands posed less of a danger to his continued bachelorhood. He had started with an old high school sweetheart whose Episcopal parents hadn't wanted their daughter dating a Catholic. Once she moved on to the local tennis pro, Cockran's reputation had quietly spread among other dissatisfied North Shore wives who were in no short supply. No strings for Cockran. None for them. Life was good. Then along came Mattie who changed his world forever.

"As I said in my note, I wish to consult you professionally."

Ingrid appeared more nervous to Cockran than the self-assured young woman who a year ago had gently mocked her husband to his face about being "Best in Show" at the American Breeders Association annual convention. Also she was wearing more make-up now than before.

"I need a lawyer."

"I plead guilty to being a lawyer," Cockran said, "but mostly I teach at Columbia's law school and I take on an occasional case in international law. That, plus my writing, keeps me pretty busy."

"A writer? What do you write?" Ingrid asked.

"Books and articles on politics. But now mostly books," Cockran replied. "Biographies."

"Really?" Ingrid began and then her eyes lit up. "Wait. You mean you're W.B. Cockran, the one who wrote *A Life In The Saddle* about Teddy Roosevelt? I love that book. It made him seem both human and heroic at the same time."

Cockran smiled and modestly dipped his head. "Guilty. And you're right. Colonel Roosevelt was very human and he would be the first to admit his flaws. But, deep down, he was proud of his heroism as well. I knew him when I was a boy. His place was just up the coast from ours. His sons were my playmates. I called him 'Uncle Teddy'."

Ingrid shook her head and smiled. It was a beautiful smile. "W.B. Cockran. Bourke Cockran. I should have connected them but somehow I didn't. You were so fierce last summer in defending that poor woman, Judy Dill. It never occurred to me that someone like that could write something as sensitive as your biography of Roosevelt."

Cockran shrugged and gave her a crooked grin. "Well, what can I say? I guess I'm a fierce, sensitive kind of guy. And I'll need to be for the book I'm writing now. It's a biography of my father and the great men whose lives he touched. Grover Cleveland. Theodore Roosevelt. Winston Churchill. The last two will be a real challenge. They only met once but for reasons I've yet to discover, TR could not stand Winston. Too much alike, I guess."

Ingrid laughed and her face lit up. She really was beautiful.

"But I need someone tough for a lawyer. Someone who's not afraid of my husband and his wealth."

"I don't know about tough. But I'm not afraid of your husband."

"Good. I know he doesn't like you and I sense that there's more to it than your defending those poor women facing sterilization. But Wesley won't talk about it."

Cockran didn't reply. Well, he thought, she was right. There *was* more to it. Wesley Waterman didn't like him and had reminded him of that only moments ago. Cockran knew why. He really *had* made the takeover of his client's company last year in Germany far more expensive than Waterman had intended. Apparently he didn't appreciate that if Cockran's opponent wasn't playing by the rules, he didn't either.

"So, may I have an appointment?"

"Give me some idea what your problem is, Ingrid. My practice is fairly specialized," Cockran replied. "International trade and finance."

"But when I met you last year, you were arguing a sterilization appeal. I also saw you in trial last month. Another sterilization case."

Cockran nodded. "My fourth. And I lost them all. I don't know why you need a lawyer, but you might be better off with someone who actually wins a case now and then."

Ingrid placed her hand on Cockran's elbow and guided him over to a window.

"I am going to divorce my husband and he is not going to be pleased. I was carefully selected to be Mrs. Waterman Number Two after he committed his first wife to an asylum and then divorced her. He really believes all that breeding theory nonsense and he expects us to have perfect children. He plans to raise them as 'international citizens.' Earlier this year, he bought a large *schloss* in Bavaria where he expects me to spend six months of the year. That was the final straw. I am *not* leaving this country," she said, "and I will *never* bear him children."

Cockran turned from the window to Ingrid. Apparently she was unaware her husband already knew of her plans. "I've never handled a divorce in my life, and I don't know a thing about it," Cockran said and then noticed a slight frown cross her face. "But I'm sure there are lawyers in my firm who do. Tomorrow morning. 9:00 a.m. sharp. The Chrysler Building. OK?"

The frown was still there. "But I want you personally, Bourke, not someone else."

"Don't worry. I may need help but if I take your case, I'll handle it myself."

"Thank you," she said and squeezed his arm.

"Where the hell have you been?" Wesley Waterman boomed, startling Cockran and Ingrid as he laid a heavy hand on his wife's shoulder. Cockran could see her wince. "I've been looking all over for you. I'm leaving now. The Whartons' dinner party starts at nine o'clock and you know how Millicent absolutely hates it when people are late. Let's go," he said with a peremptory nod of his head toward the door.

Ingrid coolly looked down at her husband's hand as if an unwanted insect had lighted there until, at last, he withdrew it. "I'll meet you there,

Wesley. Mr. Cockran and I have several friends in common and much to catch up on. I may be late. Give my apologies to Millie if I am."

Waterman started to object but Cockran looked him straight in the eye and extended his arm to Ingrid who hooked her arm through his. He looked down at Ingrid and then gave Waterman a big smile as he walked off with the businessman's beautiful wife, leaving behind one unhappy and humiliated husband. It felt great. Just like old times on the Gold Coast.

Ingrid turned her head to him and said, in a loud voice for the benefit of those nearby, "The Russian Tea Room? Of course, Bourke, I would absolutely love that. I prefer vodka with my caviar rather than champagne, don't you?" she said, squeezing his arm with her free hand and snuggling close.

Cockran looked at her and tried to conceal the surprise in his eyes. He had said *nothing* about the Russian Tea Room. Or caviar. Outside, Cockran turned to her. "What was *that* all about?"

"You have not yet outlived your reputation, Bourke. When I confided in two of my best girlfriends that I was contemplating retaining you in divorce proceedings, simply the mention of your name caused them to think we were having an affair. So I thought . . . what if we were seen together publicly in front of Wesley's friends, arm in arm, having a cocktail, chatting like old friends and then going off to a rendezvous at the Russian Tea Room? Isn't that wicked? Wouldn't that rub my husband's face in it?"

"Well . . . ." Cockran began, "is that entirely wise?"

Ingrid laughed. "It's just payback for my husband's bimbos, Bourke. As I'll show you tomorrow, I have ample grounds for divorce apart from that. Now, let's leave. I really do love vodka with my caviar and I intend to spend the rest of the evening with you celebrating the beginning of the end of my unfortunate marriage."

7.

Some Dinner Dates, Nothing Serious

Long Island, New York
Monday, 9 May 1932

MATTIE pulled the robe tighter and took another sip of scotch. There were only three people whom both Cockran and Mattie had known prior to their being introduced in the summer of 1929. One, of course, was Winston, Mattie's godfather and someone Cockran had known since he was five years old. Another was Cockran's childhood friend, Anne Darrow, at whose cocktail party they first met.

Unfortunately and, to Mattie's chagrin, the third person whom both she and Cockran knew was Ted Hudson. They had served together in military intelligence in various capacities during and after the war and, for whatever reason, Cockran thoroughly despised Ted.

Cockran had never volunteered why but when he learned that Mattie had once dated Ted, he was *not* happy. In fact, that was when Mattie first learned her new lover could be a jealous man. She made a mental note at the time never to raise Ted's name in Cockran's presence and she hadn't.

"I met him in 1924," she had told Cockran. "We would occasionally run across each other in our travels. The last time was in Paris, the spring of '29, a few months before we met. He was back in military intelligence then and he told me he was leaving the army and asked me to get him an interview with Hearst. We had dinner a few times and went dancing. That was it. It's not as though we were seriously seeing each other." Or, Mattie had thought at the time but had left unspoken, that Hudson once proposed to her and she had turned him down.

What she selectively had told Cockran, however, was all literally true. As for "seriously" seeing each other, that depended on how you defined seriously. When she was younger, Mattie had been to bed with a few men she met by happenstance during the course of an assignment, relationships which ended with the assignment. She thought of them as "*aventures*". Some were intense. None were serious. At least to her. Had Ted been one of her little *aventures*? That was a different question, one Cockran hadn't asked and she had no intention of ever answering. Cockran had his own past—with married women, no less, if you believed Anne Darrow—and Mattie had never asked about them. Well, girls were entitled to their secrets too.

Still she knew there was no way Cockran was going to be happy about her traveling on an assignment alone with Theodore Stanhope Hudson IV. "Chief, it really looks like a great story but I think I'm going to have to pass on this one."

Mattie winced internally when she saw the disappointment on Hearst's long face.

"Why is that, my dear? You've never turned me down before."

"It's not the story, Chief. True, I've only been back a week from Bolivia and I could use some more time off. It's just… well, it's Ted Hudson."

"You have a problem with him?" Hearst asked. "I thought you two once had been … "

"Romantically involved?" Mattie said, completing his sentence. "Yes, you might say that, in a casual sort of way. Some dinner dates, nothing serious. And, as you know, I stopped seeing him after you hired him."

"That wasn't necessary, not for me." Hearst said. "Ted wasn't happy about that?"

"No, Ted wasn't happy, but that's not my problem. Cockran is my problem. He and Ted were MID agents together. The fact Ted and I once dated really rubs him the wrong way."

"I'm sorry if this poses a problem but this is an unusual story and it requires two reporters. My best reporters. You're one. Ted is the other…"

"Maybe, but he's not as good as me."

"No one is. But there may be a European connection. I asked him about it because he's our European bureau chief and he volunteered to return to the States to cover the story. I had already decided it was your story. It still is but Ted may be a big help. Please say you'll do it."

Mattie sighed. Disappoint her boyfriend? Or her boss? A helluva choice. She paused but she knew what she was going to do. She had always known. Saying no to Hearst would be like saying no to her father. She just couldn't do it. No matter how much she loved Cockran, she couldn't disappoint the Chief. Besides, this was one of Winston's ideas. That made it twice as difficult to turn down.

"Okay, chief. I'm your girl. But you owe me one for this. Big time."

Hearst beamed. "Certainly, my dear. If you want, I'll speak to your Mr. Cockran."

Mattie smiled. "Thanks, Chief but that won't be necessary. I'll do it myself."

Mattie phoned Cockran's Fifth Avenue townhouse but, after ten rings, Mattie placed the receiver down and looked at her wrist watch. 12:15 a.m. The lecture had been over at 8:30 p.m. Where was Cockran? She looked out the window. The thunderstorm had passed and the night sky was clear, a full moon illuminating the autogiro tied down fifty yards away. Mattie was tempted to fly back to Manhattan but she decided not to. No need to press her luck.

"Chief, could I persuade you to have your chauffeur give me a lift back to Manhattan? I'll send someone for the autogiro in the morning." She'd soften Cockran up tonight and then she would find just the right time tomorrow to tell him about Ted. Men were so predictable. Bourke was no different.

8.

Stay Away From Other Men's Wives

Fifth Avenue
New York City
Tuesday, 10 May 1932

COCKRAN sent Ingrid home in a taxi after midnight when she made clear to him that she had no intention of joining her husband at the Wharton's dinner party. He then walked east on 57th toward Fifth Avenue and his townhouse in the sixties. Cockran had literally never handled a divorce case in his life. Notwithstanding his having lost four sterilization cases in the last three years—all bench trials—Cockran thought he was a fairly decent trial lawyer when the occasion arose. For some reason, juries liked him and trusted him which was, in his experience, half the battle. That much he knew he owed to his father, either to his genes or the example he set for his son. Maybe a little of both.

Still, much as Cockran enjoyed a good courtroom fight, he wouldn't have taken Ingrid's case were she not the wife of Wesley Waterman. Waterman wasn't the one directly responsible for the tragic death of Cockran's young blonde client the summer before, but Cockran still had a score to settle with Waterman and this was the first opportunity he had been given to do so. He hoped that Donovan & Raichle, the law firm where he was "Of Counsel", had a divorce expert.

Later, Cockran reflected that he had been too focused on the thought of settling the score with Waterman and not enough on the fact that his public humiliation by his wife in rejecting a dinner party with him in favor of a cozy evening at the Russian Tea Room with Cockran had given Waterman ample grounds for a pre-emptive strike.

They had been waiting for Cockran in the shadows beside his Fifth Avenue townhouse. Both of them were big, with thick necks and blond, closely cropped bullet-shaped heads. Each man outweighed him by a good forty pounds. One grabbed him from behind and pinned his arms. The other, the one with a mustache, was set to use Cockran's stomach as a punching bag.

"We've come to give you a message, Cockran," he said with an odd, difficult to place accent as he drove his fist deep into Cockran's midsection.

Great, Cockran thought, trying to recover his wind. Just what he needed. These guys looked like overweight Katzenjammer Kids. They were probably named Hans and Fritz. Still something about them seemed familiar but Cockran had a terrible memory for names.

"Stay away from other men's wives," the man holding him said as Fritz the mustache once more hit Cockran a heavy blow in the stomach, again driving the breath from him.

Their advice was wise but not well-intentioned and Cockran swung his right foot in a wide arc as Fritz began to deliver another punch. His shoe hit the side of Fritz's left knee and the man cried out in pain as the knee buckled under the impact and he crumpled to the ground.

Hans momentarily loosened his grip on Cockran's arms, unsure of how to help his fallen comrade. Cockran rammed his right elbow into Hans' gut, causing him to drop his arms. That was all Cockran needed. He spun around, grabbed Hans by his lapels and smashed his forehead down squarely on the bridge of the thug's nose. He heard the satisfying crunch of cartilage as he did so. Hans howled in pain, bringing his hands to his nose. Cockran came even with the man on his right side and leg-whipped him, knocking his legs out from under him. As he fell heavily to the ground, Cockran knelt down, grabbed the man's right elbow with his left hand and his wrist with his right. Using the elbow as a fulcrum, he bent the man's wrist back in an unnatural position until he finally heard it snap and the man howled with the pain of a broken right wrist.

Fritz had regained his feet by now and limped only a little as he threw a roundhouse right at Cockran's head. Cockran dodged the punch and hit him with a left jab. Fritz raised his hands to defend his face and Cockran hit him in his ample belly, knocking the wind out of him. An upper cut drove him back until he stumbled over a still prostrate Hans and fell to the ground. Cockran was on top of him in an instant and a moment later Fritz had suffered the same fate as Hans, Cockran using the man's own left elbow as a fulcrum to break his left wrist, the audible snap of bone nearly drowned out by the other man's cries.

How to incapacitate an enemy within ten seconds had been one of the more useful skills Cockran had acquired in the exacting training course given to Army MID agents assigned to the Inquiry, the secret agency created during the war by Woodrow Wilson. His old MID hand-to –hand combat instructor would have been proud of the head butt especially.

And then it hit him. MID! It had been well over ten years ago but these guys had been in several classes with him at the Army War College for a few weeks in the summer of 1920. They hadn't gone through MID training together but their size and mid-western accents made them stand out in class. Wisconsin? No. Minnesota? Yes, that was it. At times, their accents almost sounded Canadian. Minnesota and MID agents both. But now, he amended, probably ex-MID agents. He still couldn't remember their names but he had friends in MID who might. As he recalled, they weren't bad guys and, on occasion, they had beers together after class. Strange to think they were now just hired muscle for Wesley Waterman.

Cockran looked around. Where the hell was a cop when you really needed one? He watched the two men rise unsteadily to their feet and, clutching their ruined wrists, walk down the street. He watched from inside the door until they turned the corner and were out of sight. Inside, the phone was ringing, but by the time he picked up the receiver, the caller had hung up.

BOURKE Cockran was woken from a sound sleep by the familiar pressure provided by the erect nipples of two very naked breasts pushed firmly against his back, followed by the rest of her body up against his backside. God, he loved the fact that Mattie always slept in the nude.

"No more, Ingrid. Please. You're insatiable. You've worn me out. Ow! That hurt," Cockran cried out as he felt the force of Mattie's punch to his kidneys.

"It was supposed to hurt. Where have you been? I called at 12:15."

Cockran rolled over and faced Mattie. "It's a long story, but Ingrid is now my client. I can't tell you what we discussed. But it's serious. Her husband warned me not to represent her and sent two thugs over later to reinforce the message. I was probably busy with them when you called. What time is it, anyway? I thought you were going to spend the night at The Cedars."

"Two-thirty in the morning. Once I couldn't reach you, I decided to drive back here."

"Why?"

"To spend the rest of the night with the man I love. What else?"

"What else indeed," Cockran replied as he reached out for her. "But I'll bet that also means you have a new assignment from Hearst, one on which you'll be leaving soon."

"I do. So, come on sailor, you're wasting time here."

9.

My Husband Is a Very Big Man

New York City
Tuesday, 10 May 1932

IT was a beautiful spring morning and Cockran was a happy man. Mattie's new assignment—on a tip from Winston, no less—would keep her safely in the U.S. and away from war zones while he had a chance to stick it to Wesley Waterman. Life was good.

Cockran had decided to walk the twenty blocks or so from his townhouse to the Chrysler Building and the law offices of Donovan & Raichle. He met Ingrid Waterman inside the law firm's walnut paneled reception area whose dominant features were brass lamps, old oil paintings, comfortable leather club chairs and tasteful oriental rugs selected by the senior partner's wife, Ruth Donovan, herself. Ingrid was wearing dark glasses, oversized, like a film star. He was mildly surprised that she did not remove them as they walked down the corridor to his office, which faced south toward the tip of the island and the canyons of lower Manhattan. He noticed that, unlike last night, she was wearing no makeup. As he had noted when they first met, she didn't really need it.

Cockran's desk faced away from the window. He and Ingrid moved toward two green leather armchairs placed against the far wall, near a small table on which was a yellow and green Tiffany lamp. They placed their coffee cups on the table and sat down, the morning sun glowing over the skyscrapers. Ingrid did not remove her glasses.

Cockran briefly contemplated telling her about the assault last night, but decided not to. Cockran didn't believe in coincidence. He couldn't prove Waterman had hired the goons but the chances were remote that some other jealous husband from Cockran's romantic past was responsible. More importantly, he found the men's MID background was troubling.

"Thank you again, Bourke, for agreeing to see me this morning," Ingrid said as she took a sip of coffee and removed her dark glasses.

Cockran gasped. One eye had been blackened and there was an ugly red bruise on her right cheek which the glasses had hidden.

"Would you be so kind as to close the door?" Ingrid asked.

Cockran walked over to the door and closed it. He turned back toward Ingrid and did a double-take. She had been dressed in a dove grey suit and cream colored blouse. Ingrid was standing, now wearing only her skirt and a lacy, low cut brassiere, her blouse draped over the arm of the chair. But it was not her breasts which grabbed Cockran's attention. Rather, it was the ugly bruises on her shoulders and abdomen.

Wordlessly, she turned and offered a view of her back, which was criss-crossed with vivid red welts as if she had been beaten with a leather strap. Before Cockran could speak, she lifted the back of her skirt above the top of her silk stockings to the edge of her garter belt and the silk panties beneath, revealing more red welts on her thighs.

It took a second for a startled Cockran to find his voice. "Stop, Ingrid. That's not necessary. I get the picture."

Ingrid lowered her skirt, turned around and without a trace of embarrassment put her long-sleeve blouse back on, tucked it into her skirt and sat down.

"He did this?"

Ingrid nodded. "The black eye is a week old. That's when I decided to contact you. Last night when I returned, he ripped my favorite gown right off and beat me with a belt again."

"We can have him arrested for assault and battery."

"I don't want arrested, I want a divorce. I don't want this all over the papers. I want out."

"But why does he beat you?" Cockran said.

"I want children someday, but not by him. I've always taken precautions to see that I won't conceive. We've been married three years. During that time, he's had me examined by the most expensive specialists in the world. They tell me I'm quite fertile and they don't know why I can't conceive. Wesley, of course, is too proud to be examined by specialists himself because superior stock like him are potent by definition. But since he won't be examined, I've made it clear that I consider him to be the problem, and I *always* point out that he had no children by his first wife either."

"So that's why he beats you?"

"No, he recently found my diaphragm, quite by accident when searching through my drawers for a lost pair of cuff links. Or so he said. I tried falsely confessing to an affair and told him the diaphragm was only for that. Given his assorted mistresses, I told him turnabout was fair play. He didn't think so and that's when he beat me the first time. I was so furious that I finally told him the truth. The diaphragm was to prevent my conceiving *his* child."

"You mentioned that you 'falsely' confessed to having an affair. I take it you haven't had any affairs?"

"Affairs?" Ingrid asked and then turned her head and looked out the window at the Manhattan skyline. "No, none. I'm certainly ready for an affair but things just never seem to work out for me. Timing is everything and my luck has been lousy."

Cockran walked over to his desk, picked up the phone and dialed an interoffice number. "Sarah, I'm with the client I spoke to you about. It seems her husband has been beating her. Do you have a female photographer we could send her to this morning to document her bruises? You do? Fine, give me her name and address and make an appointment for her."

Cockran wrote down the name and address and gave it to Ingrid. "Go right over. I want full body photos, long view and close-ups of all your bruises. The lawyer in the firm who will be helping me is a woman and the two of us are the only ones, for now, who will see the photos." Cockran paused. "Actually, I may have to show them to one other person. Our managing partner. Our firm doesn't specialize in divorce, although we do it to accommodate good clients. The managing partner needs to approve the case."

Ingrid frowned. "Is that really necessary?

"Maybe the photographs might not be necessary, but . . . ."

"I don't care about that. I want to know if he has your courage. Or will he be intimidated by my husband or his wealth?"

Cockran laughed. "He won the Congressional Medal of Honor. Trust me. His nickname is 'Wild Bill.' He fears no one. I'll call you after I've talked with him."

COCKRAN hung up the phone after his conversation with Major Timothy O'Hanlon in Washington. Tim was an old friend who had been in the same MID training class with him and had stayed on in the peacetime army. He had been in the War College classes with Cockran in 1920. He gave Tim a description of the two MID thugs and O'Hanlon had quickly identified them as the Schmidt brothers, Peter and Wilhem.

"Check them out," Cockran said. "See if you can find what they're doing now."

"I seem to recall hearing some scuttlebutt that they had left MID and gone private. I'll have their files pulled and then I'll ask around and get back to you," O'Hanlon said.

10.

Wild Bill Donovan

The Chrysler Building
New York City
Tuesday, 10 May 1932

COCKRAN shook hands with William B. Donovan, the managing partner of Donovan & Raichle. They had known each other since Cockran's tenth birthday party when Donovan, Columbia University's quarterback and a friend of his father, had been the guest of honor. Donovan was a big man, a few inches shy of Cockran, with a broad frame, expensively barbered brown hair, and a perpetual smile on an Irish face marked by sparklingly clear blue eyes.

During the war, Donovan had been a colonel and commanded New York's 69th Regiment, the "Fighting 69th." Cockran, then a captain, had been Donovan's chief intelligence officer but a leg injury from a shell fragment during the Battle of the Ourcq River after only five months in the trenches had sent Cockran back to the states for a long rehabilitation and an eventual assignment from MID to the Inquiry.

After the war, Donovan rose to be head of the Antitrust Division of the Justice Department in the Coolidge administration. In the waning months of Silent Cal's second term of office, Donovan had become acting Attorney General. Donovan declined Herbert Hoover's offer to be his running mate in 1928 and served instead as his campaign manager with a promise to be Hoover's Attorney General. Elected in a landslide, Hoover promptly reneged on his promise to Donovan. Anti-Catholic feelings against the Democratic candidate Al Smith were so strong among Hoover supporters that the multimillionaire engineer didn't think it politic to appoint even a Republican Irish Catholic to his otherwise all-white, male and Protestant cabinet.

Donovan then had formed what he termed an international law firm for American business with offices both in New York and Washington. He had invited Cockran, a tenured professor at Columbia's law school, to join the firm as "of counsel," which meant that Cockran took on his own cases or assignments from Donovan on an *ad hoc* basis. Joining Donovan's firm also was one of the two events which brought him out of the introspective shell he had created for himself after his wife's tragic murder where he had focused only on writing, teaching, and raising their son. The second was meeting Mattie McGary which felicitously had occurred at the same Anne Darrow cocktail party where Donovan extended the invitation to join his firm.

"I haven't seen you in a month. Bourke. How is Mattie? Have you proposed to that girl yet? You know she's far better than your…."

Cockran laughed. "Than my sorry Irish arse deserves? You're beginning to sound like Bobby Sullivan."

Donovan frowned. "Ah yes. Your Irish gangster friend."

"He's not a gangster, Bill. He's a private detective licensed by the state of New York."

"That he is but the two terms are not mutually exclusive. So, what can I do for you?"

"I need you to sign off on that new divorce client. I left a message about her with your secretary this morning."

Donovan nodded. "Right. Mrs. Wesley Waterman. You talked with Sarah Steinberg as I suggested?" Donovan asked.

"I did. She's young, but she really appears to know her stuff."

"That she does. Our only lawyer of the fairer sex. So tell me about Mrs. Waterman. What are the grounds for divorce?"

Cockran didn't reply. Instead, he reached into the file folder and pulled out a manila envelope containing the photographs of Ingrid Waterman which were delivered to Sarah Steinberg thirty minutes earlier. He silently slid the envelope across Donovan's broad desk.

Donovan undid the metal clasp on the envelope and pulled out 8" by 10" glossy photographs and slowly went through them, one at a time, his frown deepening as he viewed each photograph, turned it face down and went on to the next. When he finished, he put the photographs back in the envelope, refastened the metal clasp and slid the envelope back across his desk to Cockran.

"Her husband did this?" Donovan asked.

"He did."

"We'll take the case. Tell Sarah to start working up papers for a temporary restraining order and have them ready for our client to review and sign tomorrow morning. If she approves, haul your ass into court tomorrow afternoon and get a TRO keeping Waterman away from their primary joint residence. Hire a PI right now and start tracking down all of his assets and his girlfriends. I want him tied up so tight he can't take a piss without permission from the Court. You got all that?"

"Got it."

"Good. Who's your private investigator going to be?"

Cockran didn't reply. Donovan didn't like Bobby Sullivan, the instinctive reaction of a man steeped in the law toward someone who wrote his own laws. Still, Donovan had grudgingly conceded that Cockran had made the right choice in hiring Sullivan the year before for a client assignment in Germany where he had crossed swords, literally, with Wesley Waterman. When the German authorities had done nothing to protect the people and property of Cockran's client from Nazi extortion, he let Sullivan off the leash. Donovan hadn't asked and Cockran hadn't said if Sullivan had been responsible for the car bombing and other mayhem visited upon the SS goons hired by Waterman to terrorize Cockran's client. But Bill Donovan was nobody's fool.

Finally, Donovan broke the silence and acknowledged the inevitable. "All right," he said, a resigned look on his face. "Given what happened to you in Germany and that it's Waterman as an adversary again, I suppose it's okay to hire Sullivan. He's probably as good a choice as any to get the dirt on Waterman and his showgirls. But is he up to doing the kind of financial investigation you're going to need in this case?" Donovan asked.

"He is," Cockran replied. "We're going to need inside information, probably from his accountants, and Bobby can be . . . ." Cockran paused and searched for the right words. He smiled. "Peculiarly persuasive, is how I would phrase it."

Donovan smiled, laughed softly and shook his big head from side to side. "I'll bet he can."

11.

Keep Your Damn Autogiro!

The Cedars
Sands Point, Long Island
Tuesday, 10 May 1932

COCKRAN'S Packard pulled up in back of the large shingled, multi-gabled house his father had purchased back in the 1880s after marrying Cockran's mother, the mercantile heiress Rhoda Mack. As he stepped out of the Packard's front passenger seat, he told his chauffeur Jimmy to take the motorcar back to Manhattan. He would drive himself tomorrow in the Auburn boat-tailed speedster which Mattie had driven out earlier in the day. Walking to the front porch, he noticed the early evening sun shining off the kelly green fuselage of his autogiro, *The Celtic Princess*, Hearst's Metrotone News logo a pale yellow against the bright green. Cockran smiled. Once Hearst heard he and Mattie were planning a cross-country flight in July intending to break Amelia Earhart's record, he offered to pay all their expenses if they would give him exclusive rights to "*The Great Autogiro Race: Hearst Papers' Own Mattie McGary vs. Amelia Earhart*" and let his autogiro be used as a flying billboard for Hearst's Metrotone News.

Cockran crossed the long covered porch at the back of the house and let himself in. He turned toward the dining room and kitchen beyond, calling out for Mattie as he did so. Mattie had said she would cook a going-away dinner for the two of them. She wouldn't tell him what it was but promised that it would include his favorites. Cockran was counting on steak. He pushed through the swinging door into the large airy kitchen to find Mattie McGary facing away from him, stirring a pitcher of martinis on the countertop next to a plate containing two fourteen-ounce New York strip steaks and wearing nothing but an apron. He stopped short, his face breaking into a broad grin as he gazed at Mattie's gorgeous ass.

Something a lot better than steak was also on the menu tonight. A good thing Patrick and his grandmother were back in Manhattan.

"Leave the groceries over there, Wally," Mattie said, with her back to Cockran. "You're just in time for cocktails," as she poured two martinis into stemmed glasses on a silver tray.

"Oh, Bourke! It's you. You're early," she said as she turned to face him, her grin as broad as his. "I wasn't expecting you for another hour."

Cockran laughed. "I'll bet. So what's on the menu besides steak?"

"I've got two desserts for you tonight," she said. "Over there is the crème brulée. Would you like to risk spoiling your supper having the other dessert before I grill the steaks?"

"And the other dessert would be?" Cockran asked.

"Me."

"Where?"

"The pantry. Isn't that where you country squires typically take your kitchen help, bend them over a serving table, then ravish them to your heart's content?"

"Usually, but it depends."

"On what?"

"The only reason to go all the way to the pantry is if you would otherwise have an audience in the kitchen while you subdued the wench," Cockran said.

"Well, there's no one else here," Mattie said, "and the wench is defenseless and completely at your mercy."

"That she is," Cockran said, as he put aside his martini glass and reached out for her.

MATTIE took the last bite of her Caesar salad and then a sip of the 1923 Medoc she had opened for dinner. They had showered together after their kitchen floor adventures and they were each wearing thick, white terrycloth robes.

"Bourke, have you given any more thought to my borrowing the *Celtic Princess*? Two more victims were discovered yesterday. In Denver and Los Angeles. Everyone agreed it would be ever so convenient if we weren't bound by train schedules. If we could just take off for the next city whenever we wanted. The sooner we get to all these cities, the sooner I'll be back. Plus it will give me good cross-country experience for our publicity flight in July."

"We?" Cockran asked, raising his eyebrows as he sliced a piece of steak. "Hearst has given you an assistant on this story?"

"Sort of. He thinks it's a big story, big enough for two reporters, especially now with ten victims. I tried to talk him out of it. You know how I hate to share a by-line. But no luck."

"Anyone I know?" Cockran asked, slicing off another piece of steak.

Mattie sighed. "I'm not happy about this. But, well… it's Ted Hudson."

Cockran didn't reply. He kept his courtroom face on, betraying no emotion—or so he hoped—as he took in what was *not* good news. The woman he loved was going on an extended assignment with a charming, handsome and thoroughly unprincipled snake. A man whom she once had dated, if not more. And Cockran instinctively knew it had been more

But that's not what bothered Cockran about Hudson or why he thought a trip with Ted might prove dangerous. By unspoken agreement, he and Mattie had never talked about previous romantic liaisons, including Hudson and Cockran's Gold Coast matrons. The only exceptions were Cockran's late wife Nora and Mattie's late fiancé Eric. What bothered Cockran about Hudson was both professional and personal. Cockran and Hudson had been together in military intelligence in the same training class where they had been fierce competitors. Each topped the other in some areas but not others. They finally ended up together in the same unit, the Inquiry, Woodrow Wilson's ultra-secret intelligence outfit where Hudson served as the liaison from MID. Their true antipathy had started with a woman even if it hadn't ended there.

Unbeknownst to each other, they both had dated Harriet Vine, a history professor at Stanford who, like Cockran, was on the staff of the Inquiry. She had ended the competition between them by abruptly returning to her tenured position in Palo Alto. Cockran later learned from a mutual friend that the reason for her abrupt departure was that she had become pregnant and the reputed father wouldn't do the right thing. Cockran had been astonished. So who had it been? It didn't take Cockran long to learn that the other man Harriet was dating was none other than Ted Hudson. When Cockran confronted Hudson in a bar near the offices of the American Geographical Society on upper Broadway, the headquarters for the Inquiry, he laughed and admitted that he had been seeing Harriet. Then he claimed that she had tried to "blackmail" him after she had been "knocked up" by someone else. "I gave the Jewish slut her walking papers."

The words had been barely out of Hudson's mouth before Cockran sucker-punched him, commencing a monumental brawl between the two. Hudson got in a few good shots but Cockran had paid no attention to his own bruises. He only cared for the damage he had inflicted on Hudson, leaving his handsome face far less handsome than before and requiring extensive surgery on the arrogant nose which had been the target of Cockran's first punch.

Their relationship had gone downhill after that when the Army, in its infinite wisdom, had teamed them up on several assignments. And it didn't improve when Cockran filed formal charges against Hudson for torturing and mutilating a suspect—a Russian émigré baker in Brooklyn with a young family—who turned out to be innocent of being a Bolshevik spy. The Army had covered it up. Shortly thereafter, a disillusioned Cockran had left the Army late in 1920 and rarely thought of Hudson again until that fateful Hearst Christmas party in 1929. He would never forget the mixture of envy and hatred on Hudson's face directed at him when he learned Mattie and Cockran had been seeing each other for the past six months. Hudson had put his arm securely around Mattie's shoulders, occasionally staring down at Mattie's breasts as if he were re-staking his claim and then looking over at Cockran. He had been about to deck the bastard when Mattie's withering glare put Hudson in his place. And Cockran too.

Cockran's concern over Hudson, however, went beyond any competitive rivalry between them about women or anything else. It was why Cockran had tried—and failed—to end Hudson's military career. He knew Hudson was a patriot who loved his country but once Ted decided that certain ends were justified—his opposition to "godless Bolshevism" being one example—then he was coldly prepared to use any means necessary to accomplish those ends. Did that include bedding women? He knew from their MID days that Ted had quite a reputation as a ladies' man, the sort who never took "no" for an answer until, as their fellow agents crudely phrased it, a woman had "spread for Ted". He had never heard Ted use the phrase himself but he was never part of Ted's circle. All he ever heard Ted profess was that a gentleman never tells. But he had no doubt the phrase originated with Hudson. It sounded just like him. So, despite her denials, he believed Mattie had been a Hudson conquest and he knew from friends in the Hearst organization that Hudson claimed Cockran had "stolen" Mattie from him. Would Hudson make a pass or two at Mattie during the course of their assignment? Of that he had no doubt. Would Mattie shoot him down? He had no doubt of that either.

Cockran's concern was what Ted would do when Mattie rejected his advances. Would Ted take "no" for an answer? He didn't know and it worried him. With Hudson based in Europe as a Hearst correspondent, it hadn't seemed important. Now it did, Still, how best to respond to this unpleasant development? He had to be careful. Ted Hudson brought out the worst in him. "Look. Is Hudson qualified to fly an autogiro?"

"I don't know. Probably not. Why?"

"Short flights to Long Island without a co-pilot are one thing. A cross-country autogiro flight on a holiday with your old boyfriend who isn't a trained pilot isn't the safest thing in the world. In fact, it's pretty damn risky."

"That's not fair," Mattie protested. "It's *not* a holiday, it's a story. It's my *job*. And Ted Hudson is *not* my old boyfriend." Mattie paused. "We've been over this before, Bourke. I don't know why you have it in for Ted Hudson. Maybe he hates you as much as you hate him. I don't know but he never let on to me that he did even when he knew you and I were having difficulties."

"How did he know *that*?" Cockran demanded, unable to keep the anger from his voice.

"What do you mean? He's Hearst's bureau chief in Europe. You know I had lunch with him last year in London before my interview with Hitler. Ted asked me out to dinner like he always does and I said no like I always do. I told him that even though we were having arguments over my career, we were in love and we were going to work it out."

Cockran was furious. The fact that she and Hudson once may have been lovers was no big deal. He could live with that. He could even live with her going on this assignment with him. He didn't like it but it wasn't her fault. The fact she had discussed with Ted Hudson the problems they had been having a year ago, however, was almost a betrayal. He knew he might regret it later, but he couldn't help himself. Ted Hudson brought out the worst in him.

"You discussed *what* with Ted Hudson?" he asked, his voice cold.

"That silly argument we had last year about my job and the risks I was taking. Why?"

"First, it wasn't a *silly* argument. It was deadly serious. It was your possible *death* I was concerned about," he said, enunciating each word precisely. "Second, I don't appreciate your talking over our personal disagreements with *any* of your old boyfriends, let alone that asshole Ted Hudson."

Mattie stood up and threw her napkin down. Anger flashed in her green eyes. "Damn it, Cockran! I don't know what your problem with Ted is, but he's *not* an asshole, at least not to me. And for the last time, he is *not* an old boyfriend and I wish you'd stop saying it. It's starting to piss me off."

"Well, I'm already pissed off about your discussing *any* of our problems with Ted Hudson."

"Well, then, I'm sorry. I apologize. But I didn't discuss anything with him in detail. I merely mentioned it to him in passing while I was telling him how much I loved you." She paused and Cockran could see tears in her eyes. "So, sue me! I'm going to bed. Keep your damn autogiro! I'll take the train!" Mattie said as she shoved open the swinging door to the pantry and swung it back with such force that it banged against the wall.

12.

You're Not in His League

WESLEY Waterman was not a happy man. He kicked himself for using Van Deman's boys last night to settle what was a purely personal matter—sending a message to his faithless wife's lawyer. He had thought no one would be the wiser. It wasn't his fault that two experienced ex-MID agents had botched a simple mugging and ended up with broken wrists on a mission that had nothing to do with Project Gemini. Besides, how could he have known that those two ex-agents would recognize Cockran and likely had been recognized themselves? He would have to find some other way to deal with Ingrid. Gemini was too important to jeopardize. He was already using some of the Irish mobster Owney Madden's thugs to supplement the MID agents. Owney would charge him an arm and a leg for more of his thugs but you got what you paid for. As those two MID agents had proved.

Waterman walked to the sideboard and splashed three fingers of Canadian whisky into a short crystal glass. He added a few cubes of ice and surveyed the room with its leather sofa and club chairs, hunting prints on its green lacquered walls, and a golden glow cast by brass lamps. *His room.* A fire burned in the corner fireplace beneath the head and impressive antlers of a stag Waterman had killed on a large estate near the Bavarian National Forest. *His stag.*

The stag reminded him of Ingrid who refused to allow the trophy in their Central Park West penthouse. *His wife.* The one who made a fool of him last night by openly going off for a *tete à tete* with another man and standing him up at the Wharton's dinner party. Her new found desire to divorce him was one more problem he didn't need especially since the new threat to the Gemini Project was far more real and immediate.

Waterman was looking forward to later in the evening when he would be joined by Pamela Powell, a dancer at the Latin Quarter and a woman who knew her place; who did what she was told; and who presently, albeit temporarily, resided in this elegant apartment. *His mistress.* He most assuredly was not looking forward to his two 10:00 p.m. visitors. But 1787 protocol demanded it. The future of Project Gemini demanded it.

The telephone rang. He looked at his watch. It was 9:30 p.m. He had been expecting the call from Chester Bowles. *His lawyer.*

"Waterman here. What do you have for me?"

"A lot, Boss," the familiar voice of Chet Bowles replied. "It's just what you expected. She went to the Donovan law firm this morning. Spent several hours there."

"Whom did she see?"

"Can't be sure. But that guy you mentioned to me?"

"Cockran. Bourke Cockran."

"Yeah, him. Well, his name is listed in the lobby as 'of counsel' to Donovan & Raichle.

I already knew that, you cretin, he thought but he said nothing "Where did she go next?"

"To a fancy society photographer's studio on Madison. After that she went back to Central Park West. She's been there ever since."

"Has she called anyone?"

"Yeah. Some dame named Anne Darrow. We got it on the wiretap. Your wife thanked her for recommending Cockran. She's going to file for divorce and Cockran's now her lawyer."

"That ungrateful bitch!"

"She sure is, Boss. But at least we'll be ready for her," Bowles said.

Waterman smiled. Oh yes, they were ready for her. In ways she couldn't possibly imagine. "Prepare the counter-suit. I've got an important project in Germany early next month. I want this business with Ingrid well in hand before I leave. Make it happen."

GENERAL Ralph Van Deman wore an angry scowl on his face as Waterman handed him a crystal tumbler of Jack Daniels over ice. His companion beside him on the leather sofa—Lothrop Stoddard—looked uncomfortable. A retired Army intelligence chief, Van Deman was a member of the secretive 1787 Society where Waterman had become an adjunct member for the limited purpose of managing Project Gemini. Other than its chairman—Waterman's childhood friend and I.C.E.'s investment banker, R. A. Lowe, Jr. — Van Deman was the only 1787 member whom he knew. The Society valued its privacy.

Stoddard was uncomfortable because he was the Gemini project's godfather and had come to Waterman for help once the ubiquititious "Dr. V" had persuaded him of the scientific breakthroughs the project promised. Waterman had more than sufficient contacts in Washington and Wall Street to ensure adequate funding. And, he also had sufficient contacts and manpower in Europe to handle that end of the project. What he didn't have was enough manpower in place in America to get the project off the ground.

Enter the 1787 Society. Lowe and Waterman had been in prep school together at Choate from their pre-teen years on, followed by undergraduate degrees at the Wharton School of Finance and Economy at the University of Pennsylvania in Philadelphia. Their business paths had diverged after that but their personal lives had not. Like many rich men, they supported each other's pet charities. Lowe, for example, was a major contributor to the Waterman-led American Breeders Association and the American Eugenics Society. Waterman had been equally generous to the 1787 Society which was solely dedicated—or so he once thought—to anonymously promoting and preserving the ideals of the Constitution by supporting the research of historical scholars. He had been disabused of that notion by his friend five years ago over brandy and cigars following an evening of wine, women and song without their respective wives.

Lowe had confided that the sudden death of the beloved President Harding in the early 1920s had been "arranged" by the 1787 Society as had been his successor Coolidge's decision not to run for re-election in 1928, thus paving the way for Herbert Hoover. How had this been accomplished? In addition to awarding scholarships and research grants to deserving history scholars, the Society also had at its disposal a private intelligence network of ex-MID agents to enforce its own peculiar ideas of how best to promote and preserve constitutional ideals. Lowe suggested that Harding was not the first nor the last politician to have been removed from the public arena for the good of the country. All it had taken to persuade Coolidge was the sudden death of several close friends of the now ex-President.

Once Waterman had explained the scientific significance of the Gemini project, Lowe agreed to lend 1787's support. That led to a meeting with the #2 man in the Society, the unhappy General Van Deman who controlled the Society's ex-MID agents network.

"Damn it, Waterman, my men are too valuable to be used in some petty domestic squabble," Van Deman said, after taking a generous swallow of Jack Daniels. "You know I agree completely with the goals of Project Gemini. We've got no choice unless we want to leave the future to the Bolsheviks and the Jews. You and your friend Stoddard, here," the general said, referring to the man on his left who seemed to flinch at the sound of his name, "are in operational charge of the project but my men are to be used *only* on the project and nothing else from here on out. Is that clear?"

"Yes, General, perfectly," Waterman replied. He was not used to being dressed down like some junior officer and he damn well didn't like it. But Van Deman was right. "It won't happen again. I apologize for using them. It was a spur-of-the-moment thing. It never occurred to me or them that they knew the target from their days together in MID."

Van Deman laughed, stood up and walked over to the bar to refresh his drink, talking over his shoulder as he did so. He was a tall, gaunt man over six feet tall with closely barbered graying brown hair. "Yes, if they had known, I suspect they would have turned you down. The Schmidt brothers know that on their best day they couldn't take Bourke Cockran on his worst. I've read the commendation for his Silver Star at the Ourcq River, the one where Donovan got his Medal of Honor? Cockran is as ruthless and crazy an Irishman as Wild Bill himself. I daresay he sent a lot of the Schmidts' German cousins to Valhalla that day. Give him a wide berth, Wesley. You're not in his league."

We'll see about that, Waterman thought, but otherwise said nothing. He hadn't been aware of Cockran's war record and he'd be more careful next time.

Drink in hand, Van Deman turned to face the other two men. "Professor Stoddard says he's concerned about the investigation this woman reporter for Hearst is undertaking into our affairs. What's being done about that?"

Waterman smiled in reply. He was not about to let Van Deman know just how serious a danger he believed the Hearst organization posed to the project. "We've learned that Winston Churchill—he's an out-of-office British politician—was Hearst's source. We walked that back to Germany and our people there were able to figure out who tipped off Churchill. Now, he's dead. Churchill and Hearst will learn no more through him. As for the woman, I don't think she'll be able to discover anything about the project. As a precaution, however, I have her under close surveillance. One of the usual teams of a Madden operative and an MID agent will be around in the event she learns more than she should. I take your point on Cockran but the Hearst reporter is nothing to worry about."

Van Deman nodded. "Good. Keep me informed," he said as he donned his trenchcoat and headed for the door.

"That's all for now, Lothrop," Waterman said to Stoddard after the general had departed. "I'm expecting guests and I have no further need of you tonight. See Dr. V and make all the necessary arrangements for the remainder of the project."

But Waterman did not leave things to chance. He hadn't conceived the project but his money and influence had given it life. It was *his*, he thought as he placed a phone call.

"When does the Hearst bitch leave? Tomorrow morning? Fine. Give her enough rope but only enough to hang herself. Just make sure she's scared off the story." He laughed. "No, I don't care how you do it. But tell them it's business before pleasure."

As he replaced the receiver in its cradle, he heard the apartment's door open and Pamela Powell appeared, still wearing heavy make-up from her appearance at the Latin Quarter.

"Sorry I'm late, sweetie. I won't be but a minute," she said and headed for the bedroom.

Waterman smiled. Five minutes later, Pamela Powell reappeared, her face scrubbed, her hair in pigtails, an oversized white shirt her only clothing. *His shirt.* She looked all of fifteen years old. "Has my Pam been a bad girl?"

She lowered her eyes and stared at the floor, biting her lower lip. "Yes, she has.

13.

He Made Me Like Him

The Cedars
Sand Point, Long Island
Tuesday, 10 May 1932

COCKRAN heard two more doors slam as Mattie made her way upstairs. That certainly went well, he thought. Pick another fight with Mattie the night before she leaves on what could well be a long assignment with a man who obsessively believed Cockran had "stolen" her from him. A man who would love to turn the tables on Cockran and to whom the ends justified almost any means.

You idiot, Cockran. Apparently he hadn't learned his lesson from last year as well as he thought. What was that phrase? Ah, yes. His late wife Nora's oft-repeated favorite: "Thick-headed Irishman". Cockran carefully pondered his next move. He had to apologize. That was obvious. But it had to be just right. Then it came to him. Mattie knew he didn't much like bourbon and, hopefully, the symbolism would not be lost on her.

Cockran walked into the library, picked up two snifters and poured bourbon into one and brandy into the other. Then he walked up the stairs to the master bedroom where he hoped he would find Mattie. If she were in a guest bedroom, that would *not* be a good sign. He was in luck. She was sitting up in bed, still in her terrycloth robe, making notes on a legal pad, a pile of newspaper clippings on the bed beside her. Her eyes were filled with tears.

"Cognac for you, my love, Old Crow for me." Cockran handed her a snifter. "I'm sorry, Mattie. I apologize. I was an idiot. You can use my autogiro whenever you want. Ted Hudson just brings out the worst in me. Please forgive me."

"Apology accepted, you big Irish bastard," Mattie said with a laugh as she took the brandy snifter from Cockran. "But we need to talk. Not about Ted. He's nothing to me. He never was. You know that. There's an elephant in the room which you're trying to ignore. What happened to us—to me—last year in the Alps. I know you don't want to hear it, but you've got to let me talk about it. How I made a fool of myself by letting that woman convince me the two of you were having an affair. I blamed myself. I thought I had driven you away by our arguments. And, yes, you're right. They weren't silly. You weren't trying to control my life. You just wanted to keep me safe. I can see that now. He helped me see that even before . . . ." Mattie paused.

Cockran said nothing. Before what? He damn well knew. She was right. He didn't want to hear it. What was it with women, anyway? Why did they have to talk about the past? Men didn't do that. They left the past where it belonged and focused on the future.

"He took your side, you know. He told me not to draw too many conclusions from such limited evidence. But it didn't matter. I really thought I had lost you and then I went and made an even bigger fool of myself. I'm ashamed to admit it. But there it is. He seduced me. I let him make love to me. I wish I hadn't but I was feeling so low right then. I don't think I've ever told you how much you mean to me. I had been alone for so long. Eric and my brothers taken in the war. Mum and Dad soon after. I lost everyone I loved in less than two years. I spent the next ten years looking for love in all the wrong places with all the wrong men. Then I found you. And Paddy. You've both made me so happy that the thought I had lost you and was all alone again was too much to take."

She paused, wiped away her tears and took a deep breath. "I know it doesn't make it better but it wasn't like with us where it was me who had to seduce you."

She had tears in her eyes again and, ill at ease as he was, Cockran knew he needed to break the tension. "True. But I *am* irresistible. Besides, I let my guard down. You lied and promised my virtue was safe with you. I really thought we only were wrestling for the bottom bunk in that Pullman compartment."

Mattie laughed through her tears. "You? Irresistible? I just wanted the goddamned lower bunk. And once I got on top, what happened next would hardly count as resistance on your part. After that, the lower bunk was mine. You're lucky I let you stay."

Cockran was relieved at her levity even if he found this entire line of conversation uncomfortable. Her sleeping with other men before they met was one thing but just thinking about Mattie with someone else after they had been together hurt. Hearing it from her was worse. He hoped it would stop right here but, somehow, he knew she wasn't finished.

"I told you he saved my life. First on the zeppelin and then several times after that. When we were in Egypt together and then in the Alps. He's just like you in that respect," Mattie said, then blushed and looked away. "My safety, I mean. He didn't lecture me the first time he saved me after that stupid incident on top of the zeppelin. Like you would have done. Or the second time in Egypt. But the next two times he saved my life—in the Alps—he lectured me just like you. And he sounded just like you."

Mattie paused and bit her lip, tears in her eyes. "That's where it happened. In the Alps. He saved my life two days in a row and made love to me each night." she said and dropped her head, still avoiding Cockran's eyes.

Cockran let the silence build. Only twice? She had been with him for nearly two weeks. That was some solace but he still didn't want to think about it. He wanted the memory to fade as it had been doing. Until now. This was *exactly* why he had never wanted to have this conversation. Mattie might feel better afterwards, but he damn well knew he wouldn't. And but for that damn Ted Hudson, this talk might never have occurred. Still it was his own fault. Both tonight and for what happened in the Alps. He had come a lot closer to sleeping with his lovely blonde client last summer than he would ever admit to Mattie.

" I've never been so scared in my life. And I felt safe with him. Like I do with you. He was concerned for my safety just like you were. Men are like that, I guess, about the women they love. I know that now too."

" He loves you?" Cockran asked. He already knew the answer from seeing the way the man had looked at her last year. Mattie couldn't help but know as well, but he wanted her to admit it. And to admit her feelings for him, whatever they were. Now that she had come this far, he might as well know the worst.

Mattie paused and bit her lip again. "Maybe. I'm not sure. . ." she sighed, closed her eyes and then opened them, making eye contact with Cockran where earlier she had not. "Yes. I think he does. Or did. I certainly knew at the time that he had feelings for me that were more than physical."

"Do you love him?"

"No. I only love you," Mattie said quickly and emphatically. Too quickly? "Even though I thought you had left me, I never stopped loving you. Because of you, I'm not alone any more. You're the only man I want. Or need. I never made love with him again because I decided to find you and win you back. I felt so small when I learned I had never needed to win you back. That there had been nothing between you and your new blonde client."

"But you had feelings for him?" Cockran asked, his heart aching because he knew the answer to this question as well. Damn but he hated this conversation.

"I did. I can't deny it. I thought I had lost you and he was interesting. A complex man. Ruthless and, at the strangest times, kind and caring." She paused. "I guess . . . I'm not sure how to describe him. But he made me like him."

Cockran nodded. She liked him and felt safe with him. Who wouldn't after he saved her life? He was interesting. Complex. Kind. She liked him. Could he live with that? Hell, he had no choice. Not if he wanted Mattie to be with him. Which he did.

"Okay, I can understand that. But I don't like his politics and I don't like him."

"No, my darling, you don't. I don't like his politics either, but he's not like the others. He's an honorable man. And, in his own way, a good man. I'm convinced of that. Anyway, he's out of our lives now, an ocean away and he's not coming back."

Cockran pulled her close and kissed her. He undid the sash to her robe. It was long past time to end this conversation. Besides, what more could he ask? The bastard who seduced her in the Alps was in her past and she was in his arms.

14.

Bobby Sullivan

THE morning sun was on his left as Cockran steered his Auburn speedster onto Lexington Avenue. Mattie had promised to call him every day, something she couldn't do on her overseas assignments. He had left the Cedars at dawn because he was meeting Bobby Sullivan at 8:00 a.m. and he didn't want to keep him waiting in the reception area on the off chance Bill Donovan might see him there and change his mind about Cockran using Bobby on the Waterman case. Also, Cockran had planned an early morning breakfast at his Fifth Avenue townhouse with Paddy and his grandmother before they set off by train for a flying visit to her cousins in Philadelphia.

Cockran parked the Auburn in a nearby garage and entered the glorious art deco lobby of the Chrysler building. Bobby Sullivan was already there waiting for him. After shaking hands, they rode in silence to the 53d floor. He took Sullivan down the hall to his office. Once there, he sat behind his desk and contemplated his friend. Unless he looked at you, most people would not notice Bobby Sullivan if he passed them on the street. A shade under six feet tall, his only prominent feature was a broken nose which, at first glance, might lead you to think he had once been a prize fighter. But if he looked at you with those cold blue eyes beneath his black hair, you would wish he hadn't and you would not forget him. For Sullivan was an assassin by trade, trained by Michael Collins himself in the Anglo-Irish war of 1919 to 1921, a bloody war which had ultimately led to Ireland's freedom with the creation of the Irish Free State. Its aftermath led to the death of Cockran's young wife Nora by the IRA in the Irish Civil War of 1922.

Bobby Sullivan would always reflect that dark and hidden side of Bourke Cockran. He had first met Sullivan on the evening of his wife's funeral. He could see it still in his mind's eye. McDade's Pub in Dublin. The paper bag which Sullivan handed him containing a British Army Webley revolver. The list of three names given him by his friend Collins—the IRA paymasters in America who controlled funds that could have extended the savage civil war that claimed Nora's life.

Cockran was a lawyer and a writer, two peaceful professions. But the Great War and its aftermath had made him a trained killer as well. He became quite skilled at what the Brits called "bloody mayhem" or "dirty work at the crossroads", both planning and fieldwork. He enjoyed the former, the latter not so much. Killing was not pleasant. But if the war made him a trained killer as a soldier, Michael Collins had turned him into an assassin. For one bloody summer. Fueled by revenge, he had enjoyed planning the executions of the three IRA paymasters and had taken equally grim satisfaction in the fieldwork which followed. He only wished he could have taken out his wife's killers as well during that same killing season. He knew his father would not have approved. But Cockran hoped he would have understood.

A few years ago, Sullivan had emigrated to America and sought out Cockran to discuss his future. Cockran had vouched for Sullivan's good character when he applied for a New York state private investigator's license and Sullivan had made a fairly decent living out of it. So what if he occasionally worked a little too closely with gangsters like Owney Madden? Contacts like that were useful tools of the trade, as far as Cockran was concerned. Bobby's status as a former assassin for Michael Collins made him a minor legend among the Irish thugs in Madden's mob. Cockran strongly suspected that Sullivan occasionally did favors for Madden that resulted in somebody being killed but the two friends never talked about that.

Sullivan sat in the same green chair where Ingrid Waterman had sat the day before. It was 8:00 a.m. and his long legs were stretched out in front of him.

"Marital infidelity, you say? And we're representing the wife?"

Cockran nodded.

"That's getting to be one of me specialties. Ever since your Mattie gave me those lessons in photography. Speaking of Mattie, how is she? You know she's . . . "

"More than my sorry Irish arse deserves. And no, I've not proposed yet. Christ, you're as bad as Bill Donovan."

Sullivan just smiled. Cockran knew it was a smile but people who didn't know Bobby wouldn't have thought so and a shiver of fear would have gone through them had that smile had been directed their way.

"That's good about your photography," Cockran continued, "because I've got the name and address of the bimbo his wife calls his showgirl of the month. She's in the chorus at the Latin Quarter. But I also need all his financial holdings tracked down as well."

"Would you by any chance be having the name and address of his personal accountant?" Sullivan asked, an innocent Irish lilt to his voice.

Cockran grinned and shoved a sheet of paper across his desk. Sullivan pushed himself to his feet and in two long strides reached Cockran's desk. He picked up the sheet of paper and began to read. "Would I be correct in assuming Ms. Pamela Powell is the showgirl?"

Cockran nodded.

"Which means the other one must be the accountant."

Cockran smiled. "You don't miss a thing. I can't imagine why Bill Donovan thinks you're more of a thug than a detective."

Sullivan nodded. "He may be right. One doesn't preclude the other. But I like to think I'm a selective thug. I do what needs to be done but no more. So who's the mark?"

"Our old friend Wesley Waterman. He's a customer of Madden who's been known to hire his thugs from time to time. Will that pose a problem for you?"

Sullivan ignored the question. "Tell me. Is Pamela a good looker?"

"I wouldn't know," Cockran replied. "But here's a photograph of his wife. Judge his taste in women for yourself," Cockran said as he pushed across his desk the society photograph of Ingrid at a charity function, her dark gown cut low in front.

Sullivan looked at the photo and whistled. "Sod Owney," Sullivan said. "He should worry more about staying on my good side than me on his. I'm your man."

Ingrid Waterman arrived at 9:30 a.m., wearing a severely cut navy blue suit and white blouse. The suit was obviously made from the same pattern as her dove gray suit of yesterday. Cockran introduced Ingrid to Sullivan and to Sarah Steinberg. "Ingrid, I know it will be painful but, as my co-

counsel in this case, Miss Steinberg needs to hear your story directly in case she has questions that did not occur to me. She's an expert in divorce law where I'm not."

Sarah Steinberg was a short, dark-haired woman with a full figure and a youthful face. Cockran didn't think she looked a day over twenty-one.

"If you say so, Bourke, you're my lawyer. But I must say, Miss Steinberg," Ingrid said, turning to Sarah, "that you look fairly young to be much of an expert in anything."

Sarah smiled and if she took offense, she didn't show it. "I know. I get that all the time. Even my mom says that when I lose my baby fat, I'll be gorgeous and finally able to find a husband. In her book, I'm almost an old maid because, after all, I will be twenty-eight on my next birthday. But I assure you that I know what I'm doing. . . ."

Cockran cut her off. "She was first in her class at NYU and editor in chief of the law review. She's our only woman lawyer and she's stuck for now in domestic law. I promised to teach her all about international finance and arbitration if she helps me on this case. Trust me."

"I do," Ingrid said with a smile and told her story a second time. Sarah took extensive notes as Ingrid talked. Cockran watched Sullivan's eyes narrow as Ingrid's story continued, his hard face growing harder as he listened.

Cockran was surprised when Ingrid recounted for them what she did not tell him yesterday. Why she married Waterman. The simple answer was security. She already had an advanced degree in psychology. Her parents died in a plane crash in the late 1920s but her brother and sister were about to start college and what she could earn as a psychologist was not enough to pay their tuition, room and board. A friend had invited her to a charity affair where she met Wesley Waterman who had recently committed his first wife to an asylum and had commenced divorce proceedings. He made a determined effort to woo her and what sealed the deal was his promise to pay her siblings' tuition to Princeton and Smith, where they were now in their junior years, taking the spring semester off to travel together in Europe. She hadn't discovered his fanatical interest in eugenics until after their wedding.

Ingrid paused and looked at Cockran. "May I have my photographs, please, Bourke?"

"There's no need. . . ." Cockran began.

But Ingrid cut him off in a firm voice that brooked no opposition. "Give me my photographs."

Cockran did and watched as Ingrid handed the brown envelope to Sullivan who opened it and quickly skimmed through the photographs, taking barely fifteen seconds to look at them all.

When he finished, Sullivan stood up. "There's no need for you to be hiring these high-priced lawyers to solve your problem, Mrs. Waterman." Bobby smiled and Cockran could tell by the facial expressions from both Sarah and Ingrid that they didn't recognize it as a smile.

"By this time tomorrow, Mrs. Waterman, I can guarantee you won't have any more problems with your husband. T'is a well-known Irish solution I have in mind. "

Ingrid looked confused. "Irish? I don't understand . . . "

"You'll be a grieving widow by then with all your friends sending flowers."

Sarah Steinberg gasped and clasped her hand to her mouth. Almost simultaneously, Ingrid Waterman did the same and they both turned to Cockran.

"Mr. Sullivan misspoke," Cockran said, giving Sullivan a stern and familiar look. "He's new to America. He grew up in County Donegal where, if a husband did to his wife what Mrs. Waterman has endured, her brothers would have taken care of the bastard in a permanent fashion which I'm sure Mr. Sullivan did not mean to suggest for your husband. He's still adjusting to the fact that America is a nation of laws and that we do things differently here."

Cockran nodded to Sarah who handed him a manila folder. He took the folder and walked over to where Ingrid was seated and handed her the papers inside it.

"This is a verified complaint. Please read it carefully. Make sure everything in it is factually accurate and then I will have you sign it after you swear to me, under oath, that it is all true. After that, we'll file it in court and arrange a hearing before a judge this afternoon."

They all sat silently while Ingrid read the verified complaint. After she had done so, she looked up at Cockran and smiled. "Do you have a pen?"

15.

Ted Hudson

The Cedars
Sands Point, Long Island
Wednesday, 11 May 1932

IT was a glorious morning in Long Island, a perfect day for flying. Mattie couldn't wait to be airborne. The sun had been up for only an hour when Theodore Stanhope Hudson, IV, made his typical grand entrance in a chauffeur-driven maroon Cadillac Phaeton, its glossy surface sparkling in the sunshine as it pulled up the long driveway to the Cedars.

"Mattie, darling," Ted's voice boomed out. "Aren't you a sight for sore eyes? It's been too long," he said as he embraced her and kissed her on the cheek.

Hudson was dressed in what was obviously a brand new leather flying jacket, holding an equally new leather helmet and flying goggles in his right hand. His khaki trousers held a crease so sharp you could cut your finger on it. Almost as tall as Cockran and somewhat stockier, his thick blond hair was slicked back from his forehead.

"It's good to see you, too, Ted," Mattie replied. "How've you been?"

"Never been better. Especially now that we're going to be working on the same story. Just like old times."

Just like old times. Right. Hudson was a military attaché at the U.S. Embassy in Prague when they first met in 1924 and when she ran across him in Munich in 1925, he was working for the investment bank Goldman Sachs. Two years after that in London, he said he was with the State Department working on the Dawes Plan, negotiating with the Allies to ease the burden of reparations on Germany. And then, of course, there was Paris.

"Not exactly old times, Ted. We've never worked together. Just keep in mind I'm the senior correspondent on the team and the Chief made it clear that you'll be assisting me."

Hudson bowed at the waist. "And I'm yours to command. Still seeing that shanty Irish law professor of yours?"

"This is his estate, Ted. We're flying to Pittsburgh in his aircraft. You were in military intelligence. See if you can figure it out."

Hudson flashed his million dollar smile. "Well . . . you can't blame a fella for trying. They say the Irish have the luck of the devil and that sure was true for Cockran when he found you. Just let me know if his luck ever runs out."

"Things are fine with us Ted." Mattie said, as she motioned for him to follow her around to the back of the house.

"But things weren't so hot a year ago as I recall. Until there's an engagement ring on your pretty little finger, a fella can dream, can't he?"

Mattie sighed. And wouldn't Cockran just love this conversation? "Get in the plane, Ted. The front cockpit. You can dream all you want up there. I'll be doing the driving. It's a good six-hour flight to Pittsburgh with two refueling stops in between."

Hudson did a double take. "We're going to fly in that? What in hell is it?"

Mattie chuckled. People usually had that impression once they saw a Pitcairn-Cierva autogiro up close on the ground. Aloft, it didn't look quite as strange, like any other two-cockpit monoplane with a large rotary engine-powered propeller. What made it different was the shaft rising up from the fuselage above the passenger compartment in front. The shaft was a pyramid formed by three steel struts, each a yard long, on top of which was a large, four-bladed rotor, poised as if it were sitting atop a child's beanie, each of the drooping four blades longer than the aircraft's wings. In fact, they acted as the plane's "third wing," a rotary wing.

"It's an autogiro, a PCA-2" Mattie said, "but most people call it a flying windmill. Cockran bought it last year to fly to his auto races. The Pitcairn Company in Pittsburgh manufactures it in America, but it was designed by a Spaniard, Juan De La Cierva."

"So you know how to fly this thing?"

"I do," Mattie said. "Hop in and I'll show you."

Hudson settled wordlessly into the two-passenger cockpit in the front of the plane, while Mattie climbed into the pilot seat in back and fired up the Wright Whirlwind 420 HP radial engine. Slowly, the nose propeller spun into life and the rotor blades above her head started rotating, as a small amount of power from the engine gave the rotary wing a boost to get it going. Unlike the propeller attached to the engine, however, the large rotor blades on top were not powered by the engine once in the air. They auto-rotated — hence the name autogiro — as the aircraft moved forward, providing lift just as wings did. Unlike its propeller, the rotor blades on top of the autogiro were clearly visible to the naked eye once they were moving at speed.

Mattie opened the throttle and the propeller began to pull them forward in a modest acceleration. After ten yards, Mattie pulled the stick back as the autogiro topped fifteen miles per hour and began to rise in the air. The autogiro continued to accelerate and to gain altitude nearly as fast, climbing to about five hundred feet and on toward their western destination.

At cruising altitude, Mattie began to reflect on her "history" with Ted Hudson. It wasn't something she was proud of and reflected a side of her that, until last spring in the Alps, she thought she had outgrown. She had to admit Ted was still one good looking guy which is what attracted her to him in the first place. But, she thought things would be fine between them on this assignment so long as he followed the two rules she had carefully explained prior to take-off. Rule #1: She was the boss on this story. He was her assistant. Rule #2: There was no chance he was ever again going to be back inside her knickers. Well, she hadn't phrased it in just those terms but her meaning was clear. Paris had been the end of things between them.

Mattie had told Cockran she only had some dinner dates with Ted, which was true as far as it went. But those dinner dates happened *each* time she ran across Ted and, after their first three dates, had been followed by visits to his bedroom, Prague in '24 and Munich in '25. They saw each other maybe twice a year. It wasn't a serious relationship, at least not to Matttie, but that all changed two years later in London. Ted's comments on that occasion made it clear he was planning a future for them and talked of taking her home to Stanhope Hall, his family's estate on Long Island, to meet her parents. He hadn't proposed but Mattie could see where it was leading and she didn't want to go there. She liked Ted well enough but he definitely wasn't "the one". He just didn't make her heart flutter as her fiancé Eric had done. She wanted that again.

Mattie had been struggling over how best to let him down gently when, during a seafood dinner at Wilton's on Jermyn Street, Ted provided the answer. Despite their common interest in world affairs and related problems, Mattie was careful never to use Hudson as a source for any of her stories, even on background. She had a professional reason for doing so—she never slept with sources. Well, almost never. She had done so once, and only once, back in '23 which led to a ring-side seat at Hitler's failed Beer Hall *putsch* and the launch of her career. She vowed never to do it again. And she hadn't.

At Wilton's, Ted had proudly given her a copy of a classified State Department paper from its Division of Russian Affairs titled "Judaism and the Present World Movement" by DeWitt Poole to which Ted had authored Appendix "C" on Bolshevism in Russia. Mattie had glanced at it over cocktails and wasn't impressed. The rationale for the study was to understand the involvement of Jews in so many world events and its thematic breadth encompassed Bolshevism, European affairs and Zionism. Ted's Appendix "C" contained the unstartling revelation that many Bolshevik commissars were Jews, starting with Trotsky! Not exactly the *Protocols of the Elders of Zion* but it wasn't news.

Mattie had been about to hand it back when she had a thought. "Is this for me? Can I use it as background for a story and share it with my colleagues?" Hudson assured her she could. "Are you entirely certain?" she had asked. He was, Ted replied. Later, when she declined an offer to join him in his hotel suite for a "night cap", a distraught Ted had been told of her strict policy not to sleep with a source of which Ted was now definitely one.

As a consequence, after London, Ted had ceased being one of her *aventures*. Mattie still continued to have dinner with him whenever their paths crossed over the next few years. But, Ted's passes notwithstanding, only dinner and nothing more. Until Paris in early 1929.

Mattie had become seriously involved in 1928 with André, a painter she met in France who had formerly been in the French Foreign Legion. She really thought he might be the one. He made her heart flutter. Mattie had run into Ted in Istanbul late in the year and they had dinner, Mattie rebuffing Ted's usual pass. But, while Mattie was being faithful to André in Istanbul by only having dinner with Ted and nothing more, André in Paris had broken her heart with a dancer at the *Follies Bergère*. When Mattie found out, she promptly dumped André and then Ted helped her even the score. He met her in Paris in early 1929 and it was for more than a few dinner dates. Mattie had taken him and his blond American good looks to every haunt she and André had enjoyed together. The payback had been delicious. They ran across André and his new girlfriend on five different occasions, André looking progressively less happy each time. Mattie's smile at André's discomfort could not have been sweeter.

Of course, nothing is free and there had been a price for her payback. In bed. With Ted. All week long. Ted made her admit it had been over two years since he had been a source and he made her admit that the statute of limitations had expired on her "no sleeping with a source" policy insofar as it applied to him. She agreed but, with her payback to her faithless French lover complete, Ted had served his purpose. The sex had been nice but that was all, nothing more.

You could have knocked Mattie over with a feather when, at the end of the week, Ted told her he was in love with her and proposed. Except for her late fiancé Eric, it was the only marriage proposal Mattie had ever received. She hadn't declined immediately. Her friends would have considered him a great catch. He was third generation wealthy with a family estate on Long Island's North Coast—Stanhope Hall—whose size literally made Cockran's estate, the Cedars, look like a modest guest house by comparison.

Mattie had declined the next night over dinner. She told him she felt guilty if she had given him the wrong impression but she hadn't healed from her break-up with André. More to the point, she didn't love Ted. He just wasn't the one. So she told him what she should have said in the first place—they could still be friends and occasional dinner partners but not lovers. Ted did not take it well. It may have been a line but he made a guilt-ridden Mattie believe that he had been in love with her all along. At the time, Ted had been back in MID as military attaché at the U.S. Embassy in Paris but was looking for a new civilian cover. To console what he claimed was a broken heart, she had done two things for the crestfallen Ted.

First, she had arranged an interview for him with William Randolph Hearst himself. Then, out of guilt, she agreed to one last night. In bed. With Ted. The last night bothered her still. She had way too much liquor and couldn't tell you all they had done. But her headache the next morning was monumental, her memory a virtual blank. It must have been a helluva night.

The next thing she knew, Ted was a European correspondent for Hearst and soon his London bureau chief. But no good deed goes unpunished, as Mattie learned at the Hearst Christmas party in 1929 where she and her new boyfriend Cockran had run into Hudson. If she hadn't obtained that job for Ted with Hearst, Cockran would never have known about the two of them and Mattie would have had one less complication in her life.

THE flight to Pittsburgh was uneventful. They stopped only once for refueling in Harrisburg, rather than twice as Mattie had anticipated. An unexpected head wind helped. They landed in Pittsburgh at12:45 p.m. Mattie placed a phone call to the offices of the Pittsburgh *Examiner*, the Hearst paper in town. Within fifteen minutes, a Hearst reporter arrived in a rented motorcar, a long blue Reo Royale. They drove into downtown Pittsburgh and checked into the William Penn Hotel. After settling in their rooms, they met in the lobby to plan their next move.

"Let's visit the police station first," Mattie said. "If we have time, I'll go see the coroner after that and you can interview some of the victim's neighbors before dinner."

Hudson nodded as he topped his head with a gray fedora, running his finger along the brim. "That would be great. I've missed our dinners together these past few years, our nightcaps even more."

Mattie shot him a disapproving look but Hudson only flashed his million dollar smile. "I know the rules, boss lady. You're Hearst's golden girl. Trust me, I'll behave."

Mattie sighed. Hearst really owed her for this one.

16.

Blood and Steel

Lake Constance, Germany
Wednesday, 11 May 1932

KURT von Sturm stepped out of a long closed Mercedes motorcar and smelled the fresh late afternoon air drifting from the shores of Lake Constance, hidden from view by the mansion that lay before him. He walked over the carefully combed stones of the driveway toward the entrance, feeling the oblong shape of a stamped and sealed envelope within his breast pocket. The letter weighed more on his mind than it did within his crisp, Saville Row tailored suit.

The butler led him into a large octagonal foyer and directed him towards the expansive Great Hall, a room with a massive, barrel-vaulted ceiling and an inner balcony lining all four sides of the room. Paintings and tapestries hung from the wood-paneled walls and a fire blazed within an enormous hearth at the end of the room, where four of the most powerful men in Europe stood talking over cigars and cognac. They greeted Sturm warmly.

These men were four of the five members who comprised the Executive Committee of the Geneva Institute for Scientific and Industrial Progress. The Geneva Group, as it was known informally among its members, was comprised of major players in the international arms trade. Raw materials, manufacturers, middlemen, financiers. They used their influence to promote violence throughout the world, then supplying the deadly tools to prolong it. Small conflicts. Little wars—controllable, profitable. Their business was blood and steel and business was good.

Each member of the Geneva Group had a code name representing the cities from whence they came: Amsterdam, Berlin, Brussels, Lisbon, Milan, Madrid, Munich, Manhattan, Stockholm and Zurich. It was an anachronism dating to the Group's initial formation at the turn of the century. The cities and the men representing them changed over the years, as power and influence waxed and waned. Now, power was in full force for the four men in front of him, 4/5th's of the Geneva Group's Executive Committee: Amsterdam, Milan, Zurich and Berlin.

Zurich finished his snifter of cognac and placed it on a silver tray held by a hovering servant. "Well, gentlemen? Shall we proceed to business?"

Sturm raised an eyebrow. The fifth member of the Executive Committee was not yet present. "Aren't we waiting for Manhattan?" he said.

"No," Zurich said. "I spoke with him by trans-Atlantic telephone today. Manhattan has been experiencing some difficulties in America. He will not arrive in Europe until next week."

The four men sat down at one end of the large mahogany table which dominated the center of the room. Sturm took his customary seat off to the side, sitting upright in a comfortable straight-backed chair and tuned out the opening moments of the meeting.

Zurich asked for a report from the Geneva Group's Executive Director on his recent journey to Munich and Sturm was grateful for the early request. There were no smiles as Sturm methodically detailed the operation he undertook with Bruno Kordt to assassinate the rival arms dealer Pierre Reynaud in Munich. Zurich thanked him and Sturm moved back to his seat at the side of the room to listen. Their discussion typically did not include soliciting his opinion.

That suited Sturm. He did not share a major political goal of the Geneva Group — the replacement of the German Chancellor Brüning with Franz von Papen — which was the next item on the agenda. He listened with half an ear. He had heard it all before. The key appointment was not von Papen but rather making General Kurt von Schleicher the Defense Minister. That was but a prelude to lever the good general himself into the chancellorship. The unsuspecting von Papen would merely be warming the seat for him.

Sturm understood this and, at one time, he shared Geneva's vision of Germany as a great nation led by a strong leader like von Schleicher whose appointment to the defense post would increase his public visibility. But all that was long ago, before Sturm met and was instantly captivated by the confident voice and piercing blue eyes of the man he knew was destined to become Germany's true savior. Adolf Hitler.

There were others in the Geneva Group who agreed with him, Berlin prominent among them, but they were in a minority. That would change. It was only a matter of time. Brüning had ruled by presidential decree, his power coming from the 80 year old German President Paul von Hindenburg. Von Papen's power and von Schleicher's would come from the same source. Adolf Hitler's power came from the people, the ones who had made his National Socialists the second largest party in Germany. He could not be kept much longer from the leadership role for which he was destined. His day was soon coming, the dawn of a new era for Germany.

Sturm tuned back into the meeting as the men of Geneva convinced themselves anew that democracy was not a good thing if it produced a dangerous man like Hitler. Geneva knew what was best for them and the German people would just have to accept it. They always had.

"The final item on the agenda," Zurich said with a smile to Sturm "is a six-week holiday for our Executive Director." Sturm was mildly surprised. He'd forgotten his request.

Zurich continued, "It has been nearly three years since his last holiday and, considering the future profits we all stand to enjoy thanks to his latest success, I fully endorse the request and cast my vote. All in favor?" The other three men around the table quickly added their consent.

THE meeting over, Sturm left the men of Geneva to talk amongst themselves and walked onto the terrace of von Thyssen's mansion. He rested his arms on the marble balustrade and looked out onto the sunset dappled water of Lake Constance.

Sturm let his weight sag on the railing. He was tired. He had been working for the Geneva Group for ten years. He did not feel the satisfied exhaustion one feels at the end of a long day's work, the way one should feel on the eve of a well deserved holiday. He felt the fatigue that plagues a man when he's spent too many years fighting someone else's battles. Sturm was tired, tired of the lies, tired of the intrigue and, yes, tired of the killing. The last time he had felt the satisfied exhaustion that let him sleep the sleep of the just, secure in the knowledge that he had fought his own battles and fought them well, was when he commanded an airship during the Great War, flying side-by-side with his father—the legendary head of the German Naval Airship Service, Peter von Strasser.

Something in the sky above Lake Constance caught Sturm's eye and he turned to see the familiar shape of an airship, the LZ-127, the *Graf Zeppelin* as it was popularly known, on a tourist excursion. He marveled at the timing of the zeppelin's appearance in the sky, as though his thoughts had willed the silver ship into existence. But he was not surprised. Friedrichschafen was the home of *Deutsche Zeppelin Reederei* where more passenger zeppelins were being built.

His father's old friend and airship architect Hugo Eckener was president of the famed Zeppelin company and it was his name scrawled in careful gothic letters on the envelope that still rested in Sturm's pocket. The letter inside asked Hugo Eckener to allow him to once more command an airship. A part of him had always wanted to return to the sky, but he had resisted the impulse. Even now, he had not yet decided to send the message to Eckener. Germany had to be restored to greatness first. Yet Sturm knew Geneva's current scheme was fatally flawed. He knew von Schleicher was not the answer just as he knew there were a few key men in Geneva who agreed with him. Sturm could help determine Germany's future. He knew what had to be done. Could he turn away in order to indulge his desire to once more fly? He didn't know.

"Kurt? I've been looking all over for you." Sturm turned to see Zurich walking onto the terrace, a cigarette in hand.

"I'm sorry, *Herr* Dressler. I needed some time alone. I was thinking of my father," he said. "And my mother and sister, in turn. It will be good to spend time with them."

Zurich smiled sympathetically. "It is a long-overdue holiday, Kurt."

Sturm nodded and Zurich took a long drag on his cigarette. He could see that Zurich was hesitating, stalling for time. He recalled Zurich's strained voice during the meeting.

"I told you before the meeting that Manhattan has problems in America. Apparently, they are severe enough that he has made a request for your particular…services. It is unrelated to Geneva business but he offers to pay you well."

Sturm raised a hand to cut Zurich off. "I don't need to hear details. Manhattan is not a person I care to work for on a personal basis," he said.

"In truth, I do not know the details. Manhattan did not volunteer them. I know only that Manhattan is a valuable member and worth keeping happy. I told him that your request for a holiday would be on the agenda. He said he understood, but asked that I appeal to you directly."

"I'm sorry, *Herr* Dressler. My holiday on the North Sea is not negotiable," Sturm said. "But I understand your position. I do not want to let a member of the Geneva Group down. Suppose I send my number two, Bruno Kordt? He is a protégé of mine and quite capable."

"I trust your judgment, Kurt. If you vouch for him, I will send word to Manhattan."

"It will be good for the men of Geneva to see Bruno in action, without my direct guidance. There may come a day when you'll need to rely on him even more."

"*Ach*, Kurt, don't talk like that. There will always be a need for you here."

"Perhaps," Sturm said. "but I am 38 and I am not getting younger. There is only one man whom I expect, one day, will surpass me and that man is Bruno Kordt. It is time you gave consideration to my successor for you will always have a need for an Executive Director with my specific skill set, even after Geneva succeeds in placing von Schleicher in power."

"Time," Zurich said, placing a fatherly hand on Sturm's shoulder. "There is never enough of it, is there?"

"No sir, there is not."

"Enjoy your holiday," Zurich said. Sturm watched as the older man walked across the terrace and back into the mansion.

Sturm turned toward the lake again. A stiff breeze was blowing up white caps on the water and, in the distance, he saw the silver speck of the *Graf Zeppelin* grow larger, almost glowing in the fading rays of the setting sun. If Bruno Kordt proved himself to the men of Geneva, Sturm would be free to take a more fulfilling role while Germany returned to greatness. In the air. With his father's spirit by his side.

17.

She's Fair and Even-handed

The Chrysler Building
New York City
Wednesday, 11 May 1932

I'VE got good news and bad news."

Cockran looked up from his legal pad and saw Sarah Steinberg standing in the doorway. He stopped working on an outline of Ingrid's testimony. "Good news first. What's the scoop?"

"We got the best judge down there," she replied.

"Who's that?"

"Miriam Perkins." Sarah said. "But her maiden name was Friedman. She doesn't come often, but we go to the same synagogue. She went to law school at NYU, just like me. About fifteen years ago. She's my role model. There aren't many woman lawyers, let alone Jewish ones. Unlike my family, she's rich, but she's not stuck up at all."

"So what's the bad news?"

"She's fair and evenhanded," Sarah replied.

"That's bad?" Cockran asked.

"Mr. Donovan always tells me we want a judge or jury biased in favor of our client."

Cockran laughed. Donovan was right and Cockran's father had taught him the same thing. "I agree, but what's the practical effect of that going to be today?"

"She scheduled a hearing late this afternoon on our motion for a temporary restraining order, but she insists that we give notice of the hearing and a copy of the motion to Waterman's attorney. I tried to tell her that we didn't know who his attorney was, but she told me that was my problem to solve before 4:30 this afternoon. If I can't certify to her under oath that we've notified Waterman's attorney of the hearing, there will be no hearing. So what can we do?"

Cockran didn't reply. He swiveled his desk chair around and looked out the window.

"Chet Bowles," said a voice from behind him.

Cockran turned around and looked at Ingrid, who had been sitting quietly in the corner, leafing through the current issue of *Vogue* magazine, heretofore showing no sign of interest in the conversation between Cockran and Sarah.

"Who?"

"My husband's personal lawyer. Chester Bowles. He has an office on Park Avenue in the sixties. He handled the commitment of Wesley's first wife as well as the divorce. I'm sure Wesley will use him again. I've met him a few times at cocktail parties. He thinks he's smooth, but he looks oily. Wears a pencil-thin moustache. He resembles the groom on a wedding cake, only a lot fatter."

"Fine," Cockran said, looking over at Sarah who was still standing in the doorway. "Have the motion, the TRO and the notice of hearing delivered to Mr. Bowles office by messenger immediately. Prepare an affidavit; sign it yourself; and have it notarized."

COCKRAN, Ingrid and Sarah sat in the chambers of Judge Miriam Perkins. Judge Perkins was a petite woman in her early forties, her dark hair drawn back from her face in a severe bun. She had angular, attractive features and flashing green eyes. Except for lipstick, she did not appear to be wearing make-up. Her demeanor so far had been firm but friendly.

Judge Perkins looked at her small gold wristwatch. "It's 4:40, Mr. Cockran. Ten minutes after the hearing was scheduled to start. I believe we need wait for Mr. Bowles no longer." The judge looked to her left where, beside her desk, a court stenographer stood, fingers poised over the keyboard of her Stenotype machine. "We'll begin now, Agnes. Mr. Cockran, tell me why you're here. Then, call your first witness."

Seating in the Judge's chambers was informal. The Judge sat behind her desk with the stenographer slightly behind her. There were five chairs arranged in a row in front of the Judge's desk, Cockran in the middle chair, Ingrid to his left, and Sarah on the outside. The two chairs to his right were empty.

Cockran explained in a conversational tone what their purpose was in seeking a temporary restraining order. He did not employ the resonant voice he usually did when appearing in court, the one he had inherited from his father. He could have. He knew lawyers who used their courtroom voice every time they appeared before a judge. But Cockran thought that a bit much especially since the Judge was sitting only five feet away.

"My client seeks two things, Your Honor. First, we ask that you freeze Mr. Waterman's assets prohibiting him from transferring or otherwise encumbering them absent a court order permitting him to do so. We don't seek to prohibit him from conducting normal day-to-day business, customary and usual expenses and the like. Our complaint seeks half of Mr. Waterman's assets as is Mrs. Waterman's right under New York law. We would settle, however, for only half the assets Mr. Waterman has acquired since his marriage to my client four years ago." Cockran paused and grinned. "Plus, of course, half of any appreciation in the value of assets he held at the time of his marriage to my client."

Cockran thought he saw a small smile on Judge Perkins face as she nodded, a signal Cockran took to mean that she understood what he was asking. "Our first witness is Ingrid Waterman."

Cockran then reached into the briefcase, pulled out a manila folder and handed it to the Judge. "Your Honor, we would like these photographs identified as Plaintiff's Exhibits 1 to 5." The court reporter did so and gave them back to the Judge. She gave them to Cockran.

Cockran then turned to Ingrid. "Mrs. Waterman, I give you what have been marked as Plaintiff's Exhibits 1 through 5. Please identify each of these exhibits for the Court."

Ingrid did so, testifying as to each bruise, welt and black eye. As Ingrid finished identifying each photograph, Cockran thanked her, handed the photograph to the Judge and asked that it be admitted into evidence. The Judge kept a good courtroom face, displaying no emotion. But by the time the fourth photograph was handed to her, a frown began to form on her face, her green eyes growing narrow. By the fifth photograph — which showed deep red welts on Ingrid's naked back, buttocks and thighs — the Judge lost her courtroom face completely and he heard an audible gasp.

"Please describe for the Judge the circumstances under which you received these injuries and identify the individual responsible."

Ingrid told her story in a calm and clear voice, looking directly at the Judge as Cockran had advised her. By this time, the Judge had her courtroom face back on and was taking notes in small neat handwriting on a legal pad. She looked up at Cockran when Ingrid had finished describing the circumstances under which her husband had beat her with his fists and a belt.

"Is that all, Mr. Cockran?" the Judge asked.

"That's all we have, Your Honor. We would ask that you enter the temporary restraining order we've submitted with our motion and set a trial on the merits as soon as the Court's calendar permits."

Before the Judge could reply, Cockran heard the door to the Judge's chambers open behind him and a loud courtroom voice boom out. "I object!"

Cockran turned around and was surprised to hear such a deep voice coming from such a short creature.

"I apologize for being late, Your Honor. I'm Chet Bowles. We met last fall at the opening exhibit of the Metropolitan Museum of Art."

Bemused, Cockran watched as a short, fat, balding man with a pencil-thin mustache circled around the five chairs in front of the Judge's desk and extended a sweaty palm towards the equally bemused jurist, who hesitated before she extended her own hand.

Chester Bowles looked to be in his late fifties. He wore a double-breasted brown plaid suit which simultaneously emphasized his short stature and his wide girth. Cockran knew it was all an act. Chet Bowles was no buffoon. When it came to divorce court, Sarah Steinberg had assured Cockran that Bowles was a shark amidst minnows. His reputation may have been sleazy but, Sarah told him, Bowles had a first-class legal mind. Bending rules and cutting corners were second nature to him. Cockran could only hope that Judge Miriam Perkins was as equally aware of Bowles' reputation as was Sarah Steinberg.

"Your Honor," Bowles began, "we oppose any TRO being granted to the plaintiff, let alone the shameless motion she has filed in this court. We have filed our own counterclaim for divorce," Bowles said as he handed a blue-backed set of pleadings to both the Judge and to Cockran, "in which we ask the court to permanently bar this faithless adulteress from all of

Mr. Waterman's residences and to cut her off without a penny. Starting today."

Cockran handed his copy of Waterman's pleading to Sarah and watched while Judge Perkins picked up her copy and slowly leafed through it, her eyes occasionally narrowing. Cockran took this as a good sign. Bowles' appearance had been theatrical but he wasn't aware that Judge Perkins had already seen dramatic evidence of Waterman's cruelty toward his wife.

Judge Perkins looked up. "Mr. Bowles. I note that your client accuses his wife of adultery. Having read her complaint, I note that she has made the same accusation against your client. You will have ample time to file an answer, but I want your reply right now. Did your client commit adultery as alleged in the complaint."

By now, Bowles had settled into the far right hand chair, leaving the chair between him and Cockran vacant.

"Absolutely not, Your Honor. It is this . . . this . . . ," Bowles began, theatrically stammering, "faithless slut. I apologize, Your Honor, but there is no other word for it — who is the only person in this room guilty of adultery. And I can prove it."

Judge Perkins looked at Bowles and lowered her reading glasses down to the tip of her long nose. "Really, Mr. Bowles? Would you be so kind as to enlighten us?"

Bowles shoved his meaty hand into a cracked and battered brown leather briefcase and extracted a crisp brown envelope. "I have the photographer waiting outside in the courtroom, Your Honor, to validate these photographs. But I believe it will be apparent once you look at them," Bowles said, casting a sidelong glance at Ingrid, "that the photographs will be self-authenticating once I'm allowed to question the plaintiff as if on cross-examination."

"It's late, Mr. Bowles. We'll take this up in the morning. Meanwhile, tell your client to stay away from the penthouse on Central Park West until I've heard all the evidence.

"No problem, Your Honor. He's out of town until Saturday."

"Good," the Judge said as she rose from her desk. "I'll see you gentlemen in my chambers tomorrow at 9:00 a.m."

Ingrid placed her hand on Cockran's arm as they left the Judge's chambers and placed her lips close to his ear. Cockran angrily shook her arm off and walked away. "Tell it to Sarah" he snapped. Clients. Cockran hated it when they lied to him.

BACK in his office, Cockran's messages included one from Tim O'Hanlon. Once Ingrid left, he had his secretary return the call and moments later O'Hanlon was on the line.

"It's not good news, Bourke. I can't even tell if the Schmidt boys are still in MID. Both their personnel files are classified 'Black Drape'. They're available only on a need-to-know basis and—here's the kicker— the only person who approves access is General Ralph Van Deman."

"The former head of MID?" Cockran said. "Hell, he retired 10 years ago. What gives?"

"Van Deman runs a private intelligence network and has a lot of corporate clients. He only hires ex-MID agents. He told me so himself a few years ago when he tried to recruit me. The pay is good, twice what I'm making in the Army. I also know he does contract work from time to time for MID. So my best guess is the two Schmidts left MID to work for Van Deman who still has the clout to have a Black Drape placed over all the MID agents he's recruited."

"Thanks, Tim. I appreciate it."

"A word to the wise, Bourke. Watch your back. Van Deman has important friends all over Washington and that includes the current resident at 1600 Pennsylvania Avenue. You don't want to make an enemy of him. He plays for keeps."

Cockran replaced the receiver and walked over to the window and looked out over the New York skyline. Waterman was hiring a better class of thugs nowadays. Last year, he had two of Owney Madden's men try to persuade Cockran not to take on a certain client. Now it was two ex-MID guys doing the same thing. This was beginning to be a bad habit.

18.

Get the Hell Out of My Office

Pittsburgh
Wednesday, 12 May 1932

HUDSON surprised Mattie during dinner in the hotel's dining room when, after she made a cutting comment on Stalin, he bitterly criticized the 1918 Allied intervention in Russia, ostensibly to keep supplies there from falling into Bolshevik hands after they made peace with the Germans. After all, that had soon turned into Allied support for the White Army against the Red Army, something she thought Ted and his anti-Bolshevism would have supported.

"That's not the point," Ted said. "We didn't adequately support our forces there once we started to back the Whites. Plus the officers in charge were a couple of incompetent limeys with double-barreled names. Then, once we decided to pull out, our goddamn Navy took their sweet time in getting there and a lot of good men—and women too—were butchered by the godless Communists at Archangel."

Mattie tried to draw Ted out on why he felt so strongly about this but he coldly cut her off. "Look, I don't know why I brought it up and I'm sorry I did. Someone I knew died there. Let's just leave it at that."

Changing the subject, they each recapped their day and Ted even agreed with her that Albert Stewart, the short, bald-headed Chief of Detectives in the Pittsburgh Police Department was a patronizing bastard. He hadn't given them a thing, even off-the-record, except a smug lecture about the police not needing out of town reporters telling them how to do their job. Well, he had given them the address of the victim — Elizabeth Adams — in Mount Lebanon. But nothing more.

The check arrived and, as Mattie reached for it, Hudson snatched it first. "Ted, this is my assignment. I'm the chief correspondent," she said "and the expense account goes through me. Give me the check."

"Allow me my male pride, Mattie." Hudson replied, flashing a smile. "If I don't pay the check for dinner with a beautiful woman, I'll look like a kept man. A gigolo even."

Mattie laughed as Ted slipped their waiter two twenty dollar bills. "You can pay me back later in my hotel room over a nightcap."

"Only in your dreams, Ted, only in your dreams." she replied. "Just keep a running tab of your expenses each day and give them to me the next morning at breakfast."

Hudson grinned. "You're the boss but you can't blame a fella for trying."

Thursday, 13 May 1932

MATTIE nibbled on a piece of bacon as she gave Ted his marching orders for the day. "Go down to Mount Lebanon. Question all her neighbors. Find out as much as you can about her background. The victims may have been randomly chosen but we need to find all we can about each one if we're going to piece it all together. It's a giant jigsaw puzzle but, unlike the police, we know there has to be a common thread. We just have to find what it is."

Hudson nodded. "Okay. I'm on it. May I have the automobile?"

"Yes. I'm going to see the coroner first. Then I'm going to check some public records. Elizabeth Adams was a widow. But the article said her late husband George was a Pittsburgh native. His birth certificate may give us some leads. If they were married in Pittsburgh, their marriage certificate may give us even more. This is not going to be an easy story. Unless we get lucky, it may take weeks, if not months of work."

Hudson flashed her a dazzling smile. The man knew just how handsome he was. "The longer, the better, so far as I'm concerned. A day outside your presence is a like a day without sunshine."

Mattie sighed and shook her head. "You're irrepressible."

"Most women say it's one of my more redeeming qualities."

Mattie laughed. "I'll bet they do. I'll see you back here this afternoon."

Mattie's morning did not prove fruitful. She had read the coroner's report but her interview with the physician who performed the autopsy was no more illuminating than her conversation with Detective Stewart the day before. She had next reviewed birth certificates which had provided her, at least, with the identity and former address of the parents of the victim's late husband. It was a lead she would have Hudson follow up tomorrow.

After a quick cup of coffee at a diner, Mattie headed back into the bowels of the Pittsburgh bureaucracy to wade through marriage certificates. What had she been thinking when she agreed to take on this assignment? The story was superficially exciting. Eyeless bodies drained of blood. But she wasn't a detective. Unless she got lucky, this assignment could take the rest of the spring and the summer too. She sighed. She wished Cockran were here.

Mattie sat down at a table in the basement of the Allegheny County Archive Center and, within minutes, a clerk had brought her the file drawer containing the marriage certificates cataloged under "A." Who would have guessed so many men with the surname of Adams had been married in Pittsburgh in the past thirty years?

By lunchtime Mattie had not come across the marriage certificate for George and Elizabeth Adams. She wasn't hungry, but she needed a break. She walked back to the William Penn; went up to her room and ordered a pot of tea. While she waited for the tea to arrive, she decided to call Cockran and get her daily phone call out of the way. She placed a call to the Donovan law offices but was told he was in court. Disappointed, she finished her tea and headed off to work. She left a message for Cockran to call her.

Back at the archives, Mattie went through the records for over an hour and at 2 p.m., she finally found the marriage certificate for George Clark Adams and Elizabeth Ann Miller. Miller? That name rang a bell. Wasn't one of the male victims named Miller, Mattie wondered? She picked up the canvas mail pouch at her feet which served as her briefcase and pulled out the file of clippings she had received from Hearst. She'd organized them by city and she quickly leafed through them. San Francisco, Chicago, Los Angeles, Denver, Cleveland.

Yes, Mattie thought, Cleveland. James Roger Miller of Cleveland. According to the news clipping, James Miller's body, eyeless and drained of blood, was discovered three days before the body of Elizabeth Miller Adams. Coincidence? Mattie didn't believe much in coincidence. Could the victims somehow be related? Cleveland was next on their itinerary and she sure as hell would fly there the next morning and check it out. But, in the meantime, there was a certain Chief of Detectives of the Pittsburgh police force she intended to revisit.

" I must see Chief of Detectives Stewart immediately," Mattie said.

"I'm sorry, Miss. Your name please? Do you have an appointment?" a very young brown-haired girl with a heart-shaped face asked as Mattie stood at her desk, towering over her.

"McGary," Mattie snapped. "The Hearst papers. I don't have an appointment but he damn well better see me. Now." Mattie gestured imperiously with her finger. "Move."

Seconds later, Mattie was standing in front of Detective Stewart's desk. She thrust a photostat of the Adams-Miller marriage license at him. "Look at that. Your victim's maiden name is Miller. Someone named Miller turned up dead in Cleveland that same week in the same condition. Eyeless and drained of blood. Were you aware of that?"

Detective Stewart hesitated and didn't meet Mattie's eyes as he looked off into the distance. "Well, no, I wasn't aware of that. But I hardly see the relevance. . . ."

"Two people named Miller turn up dead in the same unusual condition only two hundred miles apart and you can't see the connection? Are you daft?"

Stewart stood up to his full five foot seven inches, placed his knuckles on his desk and looked up at Mattie, who was staring down at him. "You want to be a detective? Take a Goddamn civil service exam. Otherwise, lady, get the hell out of my office."

"You don't think this is significant?" Mattie asked.

Stewart narrowed his eyes. "Get the hell out of my office."

At dinner that night with Ted Hudson, Mattie was still furious at Detective Stewart's reaction. "How the hell can he call himself a detective?" Mattie asked.

Hudson was soothing, the voice of reason. "You've embarrassed him. That's all. Don't read any more into it. In his mind, you're an amateur and you found something which may be of significance. Or it may be a coincidence. But you found it and he didn't. Don't judge him too harshly."

"Well, the hell with Detective Stewart," Mattie said, as she sliced a piece of her veal chop, impaled it on her fork and looked at Hudson. "We're flying to Cleveland first thing tomorrow morning and we're damn well going to get to the bottom of this."

19.

That Is Certainly Not My Husband

New York City
Thursday, 12 May 1932

I T'S not that a client had never lied to Cockran before, he reflected as he rode in the back of the big green Packard on his way to court. They had. They always did. Never trust a client, his father had told him, and he didn't. Still, he was surprised and he shouldn't have been.

Cochran replayed the conversation he had with Ingrid yesterday afternoon after he had cooled down and they were back in the office.

"You told me that you hadn't had any affairs." Cockran had said in an accusing tone.

"It wasn't really an affair. It was more like a one-night stand a year ago with a man I met at a reception given by the Swedish Consul General."

"So that was the only time?"

"Well, I've had no other lovers, if that's what you mean, and it was a one-night stand because the gentleman in question was returning to Europe the next day. I saw him again six weeks ago. He was staying for a day in America on business on his way to somewhere else. Wesley was in Germany that week, so I figured, why not?" She shook her head. "He was really good looking and even better in bed. Much better than Wesley. So when he telephoned me out of the blue last month, I accepted. I knew it was shameless of me but he had been such a good lover before that I couldn't resist. I could tell you a lot more but I'm afraid I'm embarrassing you."

Well, yes, she was. This was much more than Cockran needed to know.

"And you didn't think your husband knew? Or suspected?"

"Before now? No, he was out of the country both times."

"So, it was twice with one lover? Two one-night stands?"

"Well, mornings too. It seemed a shame to waste them."

Cockran shook his head. Clients. "This is not good, Ingrid. I hope he was worth it."

Ingrid had given him a beautiful smile. "He was. Believe me, he was."

The only good thing that had happened after court was when he learned from Ingrid that her husband was *not* out of town as his lawyer had claimed.

"He spent last night with that bimbo and I bet he'll be there the rest of the week."

"How did you find this out?"

"As I told you before, her name's Pamela Powell. She has a one bedroom apartment at Park Avenue and 77th Street which she clearly can't afford. One of my best friends from college lives in the building and she saw Wesley come in with her one night. The doorman told my friend everything else, including the regular nights that Wesley visits."

"How do you know he'll be there tonight?" Cockran had asked.

"That's what Wesley's chauffeur told the doorman yesterday and my girlfriend told me."

Cockran smiled. Courtesy of Bobby Sullivan and a photo lab open 24 hours a day, they now had some photographs of their own. It was going to be an interesting day.

COCKRAN watched the Judge closely. Occasionally she raised her eyebrows as she leafed through the photographs Chester Bowles had given her, taking no more than a few seconds with each one. Twice, she looked over at Ingrid and then back to the photo before moving on. That was not a good sign. On the other hand, her face was relatively impassive. It did not register shock or disgust. In fact — but he could not be sure — he even thought he detected a barely perceptible smile at one of the photographs. Interesting. He wondered if he would be able to pick out which one had caused that sly little smile.

Notwithstanding, Cockran was tense when Judge Perkins finished reviewing the photos, put them back in the brown envelope, and handed them to Cockran.

"You and your client may examine these exhibits, Mr. Cockran. And then I will permit Mr. Bowles to question Mrs. Waterman as if on cross-examination."

"Yes, Your Honor," Cockran said as he pulled out the photographs.

Oh, my God, Cockran thought as he looked at the first one. Bobby Sullivan's snapshots of Wesley Waterman cavorting the night before with his nubile young showgirl were good, but this glossy halftone was spectacular. Broad daylight and everything in focus as if she had been posing for a society magazine photo spread. A frontal shot of a naked Ingrid reaching out to her lover, her blonde hair around her shoulders, her firm high breasts, a narrow waist, voluptuous hips. Why would Waterman ever pass that up for a teenage showgirl?

In the foreground of the photo and off to the right was a partial view of a toned male backside that displayed none of the sagging Cockran had seen in the naked photos of Waterman.

Wordlessly, he handed the first photo to Ingrid and looked at the second. If Cockran had been embarrassed during Ingrid's prior discussion of her sex life, that was nothing compared to now as he realized the truth of the Chinese saying that a picture was worth a thousand words. Ingrid was astride her lover, hands pressing down on his chest, her mouth parted, her head thrown back. He caught himself thinking of Mattie and how beautiful she was when he looked up into her face while they were making love. Ingrid's face had that same incandescent quality.

Cockran quickly passed the second exposure over to Ingrid. He didn't want the Judge to think he was lingering over any one of the revealing exhibits and, notwithstanding his embarrassment, he hoped the Judge couldn't tell. He skimmed the remaining images, noticing only the contrast between these and the ones Bobby Sullivan had taken of her husband. It was clear that the photographer had been instructed to keep Ingrid's face visible in every shot because you never got a good look at who her lover was. Big, blond and well-muscled, but that was all you could see. Never his face. Only her face and her breathtaking body.

Cockran passed the last exhibit over and Ingrid's face remained impassive as it had through every photograph. She was acting as if these were nothing more than unremarkable family portraits. She had followed his instructions. To the letter. Appearing in court was like being on stage. You had to assume every movement you made, every small gesture, would be noticed and interpreted by a jury or a judge. He had to admire her self-control.

But then Ingrid surprised him. She casually leaned over. "These photographs? They're really quite good. Can I have copies made?"

Cockran almost swallowed his tongue. Had he kept his placid demeanor intact in front of the Judge? He hoped so. But inside he was grinning. Ingrid was one hell of a woman.

Sarah Steinberg put the last exhibit back into the envelope and handed it to Judge Perkins who nodded to Bowles. "You may cross-examine the plaintiff, Mr. Bowles."

Bowles handed all the exhibits to Ingrid. "Mrs. Waterman. These have been marked for identification as Defendant's Exhibits A through J. Are they photographs of you?"

"They are," Ingrid replied, her head erect and looking directly at the Judge.

"And who is the man in these pictures?"

Ingrid paused as Cockran had instructed her, and a thoughtful expression came across her face, her brow ever so slightly narrowed. "It's not important who he is."

"Listen, lady," Bowles snarled. "I decide what's important, not you. Tell us who he is."

"No," Ingrid calmly replied, once more making eye contact with the Judge.

"But it's not your husband, is it?" Bowles asked.

Ingrid gave a slightly repressed smile, implying that, were she not in court, she would grin broadly. "No, Mr. Bowles, that is certainly not my husband."

Bowles sat down. "No further questions, Your Honor. But based on her testimony we ask that you deny her motion and grant my client's instead."

"Thank you, Mr. Bowles," Judge Perkins said. "Do wish to question the witness and will you have any more evidence or testimony, Mr. Cockran?"

Before last night, Cockran hadn't intended to introduce any snapshots they obtained of Waterman and his show girl at this early stage. He had thought it unnecessary overkill with this judge, based upon what Sarah had told him about her reputation. Bowles' unexpected exposure—literally—of Ingrid's love life altered the landscape dramatically. Mere allegations of adultery in the complaint would not be sufficient to counter those explicit photographs. For Cockran knew if he didn't get his temporary restraining order today, Waterman would have more than ample opportunity to place the bulk of his assets outside the jurisdiction of the Court and Ingrid's reach. That was not going to happen if Cockran had anything to say about it. It was payback time for Waterman having sent his MID thugs to mug him the other night.

"No more questions for this witness, your Honor, but Plaintiff calls Robert Michael Sullivan." Cockran walked into the courtroom where Bobby Sullivan had been patiently waiting for the past hour and a half and motioned for him to join them. Once in the Judge's chambers, Cockran directed him to the empty chair beside Chet Bowles. Sullivan stared down at Bowles before he took his seat, and Bowles quickly averted his eyes. Cockran smiled. Sullivan did have that effect on people he met for the first time.

Sullivan was sworn in as a witness and Cockran took him through the story of how he came to be in Pamela Powell's apartment on Wednesday evening. In his retelling, however, Sullivan did not volunteer how he had secured Pamela's cooperation; or that she was no longer a member of the chorus line at the Latin Quarter; or that she would be appearing for the first time tonight on Broadway in the Gershwin brothers' latest musical hit, *Of Thee I Sing*, in which Bobby's patron Owney Madden had an undisclosed interest.

After that, Cockran handed Sullivan the photographs he had taken last night. As with the images of Ingrid, the Judge viewed them first and passed each one on to Bowles who, in turn, handed them back to Cockran. Cockran focused on Judge Perkins' facial expressions as she viewed each new exhibit. The fifth one produced the exact reaction from the Judge he was hoping for. She frowned. All six feet four inches of Wesley Waterman and his sagging backside was wedged between the widespread thighs of an eighteen year old Pamela Powell who, without her make-up, didn't look a day over sixteen. The pigtails Pamela was wearing certainly helped convey that impression and Cockran had to hand it to Bobby Sullivan for coming up with that suggestion.

After Bobby had identified the last photograph, Cockran looked at the Judge. "No further questions for this witness, Your Honor."

"Do you wish to cross-examine this witness, Mr. Bowles?" the Judge asked.

"You bet, Judge. I sure do," Bowles said as he bounced to his feet and took several steps to the side so as to put a good five feet between him and Bobby Sullivan.

"How'd you gain access to the apartment?"

"Miss Powell unlocked the door to her apartment and invited me in."

"How much did you pay her for letting you in?"

"I paid her nothing," Sullivan said.

"Not even a gift?"

"Not even a gift," Sullivan said, and then smiled.

It wasn't a pretty smile but it was directed only at Bowles. Unlike Ingrid, Cockran had given different stage directions to Sullivan, should he have to appear as a witness. Bobby had followed the script as perfectly as Ingrid and delivered all of his answers directly to Bowles and not the Judge.

"Why were you in her bedroom closet?" Bowles demanded.

"Miss Powell told me the bedroom was where they usually had sex," Sullivan replied.

"But why did she let you take these . . . . these . . . "

"Filthy pictures?" Sullivan added helpfully.

"These *photographs*!" Bowles snapped.

Sullivan paused as if weighing his answer and then turned his face to the Judge. Cockran was surprised. He had told Sullivan to look directly at the Judge only if his testimony was going to be critical. Based upon what Sullivan had told him, he couldn't imagine what that could be.

"Miss Powell told me she was afraid of Mr. Waterman. That sometimes he would beat her before having sex with her; and that she thought allowing me to take these photographs would get him out of her life forever." Sullivan said this all in an even and quite sincere tone of voice, but it was all news to Cockran.

"Objection! Judge! That's hearsay! I move to strike."

"Motion denied," Judge Perkins said. "I know what hearsay is, Mr. Bowles, but I am not admitting the testimony based on truth but simply on the basis of what Mr. Sullivan heard Miss Powell say, whether it be true or not. Be assured I will give it the weight it deserves. The motions are heard and submitted." She looked at her wristwatch. "Be back here in one hour. I'll deliver my decision from the bench at that time."

THE four of them stood outside the courtroom, talking quietly. 55 minutes later, they were back in the courtroom. Sullivan took a seat at the rear while Cockran, Ingrid and Sarah sat at the plaintiff's table in front of the bench on the right-hand side of the aisle. Four minutes later, Chester Bowles showed up and took his seat on the left-hand side of the aisle.

One minute later, the bailiff rapped his gavel and said in a loud voice, "All rise!" Everyone did and Judge Miriam Perkins entered the courtroom. She took her seat on the bench, motioning with her hand for them all to be seated.

"I am granting plaintiff's motion for a temporary restraining order, both as to finances and Mr. Waterman's staying away from their Central Park West penthouse. Mr. Bowles, I do not mean to unduly restrict Mr. Waterman's ability to conduct both his personal and business affairs. But he is not to move any assets outside the jurisdiction of this court without my written permission. Is that clear?"

Bowles stood. "Yes, Your Honor."

"Good. Temporary alimony is granted in the amount of $10,000 per month; $5,000 on the first of the month, and $5,000 on the fifteenth, delivered to whatever bank is designated by the plaintiff. Is that clear, Mr. Bowles?"

Bowles scrunched his face. "But Judge, that's awfully steep, considering she comes into court with unclean hands. Couldn't you . . . "

Judge Perkins cut him off. "Is that clear, Mr. Bowles?"

Bowles' chin slumped onto his chest. "Yes, Judge," he said in a resigned voice.

"Good. One more thing. I am placing today's testimony and all the exhibits under seal. I don't want to see any photographs in the tabloids. If any photographs of Mrs. Waterman's injuries or the ones of Mr. Waterman appear in the papers, I will issue an order to show cause why plaintiff and her counsel should not be held in contempt. Is that clear, Mr. Cockran?"

"Yes, Your Honor," Cockran replied.

The Judge then turned her attention to Bowles. "And if the photos you introduced today of Mrs. Waterman show up in the papers, Counselor, the same will happen to you."

Bowles nodded but otherwise said nothing.

"Don't try the court's patience, gentlemen. If you do, believe me you will not like the consequences." With that, she rose from the bench and walked off.

Cockran walked up to the bailiff who gave him a copy of the signed restraining order. Cockran turned and gave it to Sarah Steinberg. "Sarah, get five certified photocopies made of this order. Deliver one to Central Park West. Have a second sent to I.C.E.'s chief financial officer. Deliver the others to the banks where either I.C.E. or Waterman have accounts.

Cockran then walked to the back of the courtroom where Ingrid and Sullivan were talking quietly. "Bobby, I believe Ingrid needs a body guard. Are you free?"

"I am," Sullivan replied.

"No, Bourke," Ingrid said, laying a hand on Cockran's forearm. "I'll be perfectly fine. It's Central Park West and Wesley may be many things but he'd never violate a court order."

20.

You Need To Be Taught a Lesson

MATTIE and Hudson left Pittsburgh early in the morning and landed at the Cleveland Municipal Airport shortly before noon. Home of the National Air Races since 1929, the airport was located southwest of the city and, at 1000 acres, was the country's largest air field. Hearst had placed a bright red LaSalle sedan at their disposal and Mattie laughed when she saw it. "The Chief sure doesn't want us to be inconspicuous, does he?"

"On the contrary, Hearst knows that the natives in towns like Cleveland are impressed by appearances," Hudson said as he slid an appreciative hand over the gleaming front fender. "Besides, Ted Hudson in a lesser motorcar would raise too many eyebrows."

Mattie laughed again. "Just get in the bloody car, Ted."

The drive into downtown Cleveland took nearly forty-five minutes and Mattie dropped Hudson off at the police station at 22nd and Payne Avenue. "Grab a taxi to the Hotel Cleveland when you're finished here," she said. It's in the Terminal Tower complex. I'll be at General Electric at Nela Park to interview Miller's employer. First one to finish can check us in."

Hudson gave her a mock salute as he stepped out of the LaSalle. "Aye, aye, Cap'n."

At Nela Park, Mattie was treated well. The plant manager was an older man in his late fifties with a full head of grey hair and a florid nose which offered evidence of repeated violations of the Volstead Act by his local liquor purveyors. "I am Matthew Parnell, Miss McGary. It's an honor to meet you. How can I help you?"

Mattie flashed him a smile in return and thanked him. "I'm working on a story about an employee of yours who was killed recently. James Miller."

Parnell's face darkened and he shook his head. "A tragedy. A terrible tragedy. Jimmy was one of my finest engineers."

"Do you know whether he had any relatives?" Mattie asked.

"I don't know. Jimmy was an excellent employee but he pretty much kept to himself. Engineers can be like that, you know. Why do you ask?"

"There may be a connection to a recent murder in Pittsburgh. The woman's maiden name was Miller and her body was found in a similar condition as Mr. Miller's."

"You mean she was . . . " Parnell began and then hesitated, as if embarrassed to continue.

"Yes, she was found naked," Mattie said matter-of-factly, "drained of blood and her eyeballs were missing."

Parnell grimaced at Mattie's description. "Gruesome. Who would do something like that?" He paused. "I had to identify Jimmy's body, you know. It wasn't pretty."

"I'm sorry," Mattie said.

Parnell shrugged it off. "So there may be a connection, you think?"

"There may be a connection," Mattie said. "Do you still have his personnel file?"

"It's not in the active files any more, but I'm certain we do."

"May I see it, please?"

Moments later, Mattie was seated in a conference room off the plant manager's spacious office, a steaming mug of coffee to her right, and James Miller's personnel file open in front of her. Miller had been a bright and accomplished man. Electrical engineering degree from Case Tech and then a job with General Electric right after graduation. He had authored several articles for industry publications which she also found in the file, along with his evaluations. They were uniformly excellent. At the bottom of the file, she found what she was looking for. She quickly skimmed it, noting he was unmarried. She turned to the second page and there it was. His date and place of birth. November 3, 1895 in Findlay, Ohio. She made a note of it, closed the folder, and knocked lightly on Parnell's door. He opened the door.

Mattie handed the file to him. "You've been a great help, Mr. Parnell. Thank you."

"Did you find anything?"

"Yes, perhaps," Mattie replied. "Can you tell me where Findlay, Ohio is located?

"Sure." Parnell said. Northwest Ohio, about fifty miles due south of Toledo. Why?"

"Jimmy Miller was born there. I'm flying cross-country and I just may drop in."

MATTIE McGary was furious. "Scotch!" she demanded from the waiter. "On the rocks. Make it a double." The fact that the waiter had been staring down the front of her little black halter top dress, the backless number, didn't improve her mood.

She settled herself across from Ted Hudson in a cozy booth illuminated by a small brass lamp and gave him a look that would freeze any other Hearst reporter working on a story with her. But Hudson only gave her a bemused expression and placed his martini back on the table. They were in Marie Schreiber's Tavern Chop House which the concierge at the Hotel Cleveland had assured them was the best restaurant in town.

"Whatever possessed you to register us in the hotel as Mr. and Mrs. Theodore Stanhope Hudson, IV?" Mattie demanded.

"I'm no more to blame for there being a Shriners' convention in town than I am for all those funny hats they're wearing."

"Don't dodge the question."

"Look, every place is booked solid. All they had left was a single suite. I'll sleep on the sofa but I thought it would raise fewer questions to register us as man and wife. I didn't want it to look like we were shacking up."

Mattie took a deep breath and exhaled it slowly. The Hearst publisher in Cleveland had bloody well better find her separate accommodations tonight or heads were going to roll. Right now, however, she needed to refocus.

Mattie was certain that she had been followed from Nela Park by a dark grey Chevrolet. Worse, when they had walked six blocks up Euclid

Avenue to East Sixth Street and then over to Short Vincent, she was positive they were being tailed. While waiting for their drinks to arrive, Mattie excused herself to visit the ladies' room and spotted the tail nursing a drink in the bar of the Tavern Chop House, the map of Ireland written all over his face. A bruiser, six foot tall, curly black hair, blue eyes and a cauliflower ear, suggesting time spent in the ring.

Their drinks came and Mattie drained half of hers in one long swallow, savoring its fire as it coursed down her throat and left a warm glow in her stomach. Another round of drinks arrived with their appetizers, foie gras for Hudson, and Oysters Rockefeller for her. Mattie had just finished her oysters when the waiter brought her a phone and plugged it into the jack.

Mattie picked up the phone. "McGary here." She listened for a moment to the voice on the other end. "Okay. Excellent. Thank you so much. The twelfth floor. I understand. Thanks again," Mattie said as she hung up the phone.

Mattie smiled. "You're officially out of the dog house, Ted. Hearst still has influence. They've moved my bags to something called the Van Sweringen Suite, downtown apartments of the Van Sweringen brothers, the two guys who built and own the Union Terminal complex. There's an unmarked door to the left of room 1236. The concierge will have the key."

Hudson grinned and flashed her a smile, displaying his even white teeth. "Well, I'm glad that's settled. I only did what I thought best. I wasn't trying to embarrass you. Really."

Mattie was mollified. Maybe it was her second drink. Maybe it was not having to spend the night with Ted. She had overreacted. Ted was trying to make the best of a bad situation

"We need to find out who he is," Mattie said. "The guy who followed us."

Hudson placed his big hand on her arm, grasping it warmly. "You're being paranoid. We weren't followed. Trust me, I'm a professional. I know these things."

"Don't patronize me, Ted. I know when I'm being followed, and I'm going to find out why. You can either help me or go back to your cozy little hotel suite and have a nightcap by yourself," Mattie said just as their steaks arrived.

"A nightcap with you? Sure, why not? I hate to drink alone."

"So, are you carrying?" Mattie asked, changing the subject. She hadn't exactly offered him a nightcap but she didn't want to be rude about it. Besides, this was more important.

"No, I'm not," Ted replied. "I didn't see the need. Given the fit you threw over our accommodations, you forgot to mention that you thought you were followed from Nela Park."

Great. What help was he going to be without a weapon? Mattie always carried one, even tonight, in her purse. She sighed. "Did they teach you hand-to-hand combat in MID?"

"Of course. Number one in my class. Tied for second in hand guns. First with a sniper rifle as well. Ask your boyfriend. He finished well back in the pack. I was never second to him in anything."

Mattie sighed. Well Ted, she thought—but didn't say—you weren't even close to him in the Mattie sweepstakes. Instead, she said "OK, here's the plan." She then laid out the scenario of the argument they would have within earshot of the man in the bar. Hudson agreed to play along

Mattie promptly rose. "We're finished, you bastard!" she said and threw the remains of her water glass into a surprised Hudson's face. That hadn't been part of the plan but she liked to improvise. Moments later, she took her long navy wool coat from the coat check girl and had started to put it on when Hudson caught up with her.

"Please, dear, forgive me. If you take me back, I promise I'll change."

"We're through!" Mattie said. "Leave me alone or I'll call a cop!" As she buttoned her coat and walked out the door, she could tell from the corner of her eye that the man in the bar had heard it all. While the stained glass in the restaurant's window made it difficult to see clearly, she could see a figure stand and pay the bartender.

Mattie turned left on Short Vincent, away from Public Square. A soft mist was falling, and she pulled a beret from her pocket and put it on. The street itself was a garish display of color and people out for a Friday evening. Nightclubs, strip joints, restaurants, hookers and bars vied for the attention of passers-by with nary a cop in sight. What Cockran had told her about Cleveland was true. The most corrupt police force east of Chicago. Pittsburgh had been positively sedate compared to this. Mattie was propositioned by drunken sailors twice before she reached Ninth Street. She hesitated, unsure whether to head south to the main thoroughfare, Euclid Avenue, which would take her back to Public Square and their hotel, or north toward the lake. She looked north and it seemed darker, more foreboding. And better, she thought, for what she had in mind. She surreptitiously removed her Walther automatic from her purse, slipped it into the right-hand pocket of her coat and turned left towards the darkness of Lake Erie.

The lights faded in the distance as Mattie crossed Superior Avenue. She looked both ways before crossing and spotted her tail. She was hoping to find an alley but none presented itself. Halfway down the block she found what she needed. She turned left onto Rockwell and sprinted twenty yards more until she found the recess of a loading bay. She stepped into the shadows, her navy coat and beret making her nearly invisible. When the tail turned onto Rockwell, he would see an empty street.

The man passed her place of concealment and Mattie, automatic drawn, jammed it into his back. "Don't move," she said. "Raise your hands and turn around slowly."

The man did and Mattie instantly recognized him from his tan overcoat and fedora as the bruiser in the bar, the one who had followed her from Public Square.

The man laughed. "A woman! The boys are never going to believe this. A frail got the drop on Eddie Monahan." The face was Irish, but the voice was pure New York, straight out of Hell's Kitchen. "Listen, sister, you better give Eddie that little pop gun of yours before it goes off and someone gets hurt."

"Move it, buster, or you're the one who's going to be hurt. We're going to have a little talk," Mattie said. Just then, Mattie felt a big arm circle her waist and felt a gun barrel pressed firmly into her back.

"Hey, Eddie," a voice behind her said, "need some help taming this skirt?"

Bloody hell! Mattie thought. There were two of them! How had she missed it? And they were armed and Hudson wasn't. Damn!

"Nah, Frank, I can handle it," Eddie said as he relieved Mattie of her weapon and tucked it into his belt. Then Eddie sent his fist deep into her belly. She gasped and folded over.

"Hold the bitch up," Eddie said. Mattie felt herself pulled upright and then another fist buried itself in her belly and she thought she was going to be sick.

"Take her back to that loading bay," Eddie said. "That bitch pulled a gun on me."

Mattie, weak from the blows, felt herself almost lifted off her feet as she was dragged further back into the dark alcove where she had been hiding. Where the hell was Hudson?

Eddie followed them into the loading bay. "You need to be taught a lesson, Missy, to keep your nose out of places it don't belong. Drop the story you've been working on. Or else. Now, in case you're hard of hearing," Eddie said, taking off his coat and grinning at her, "I'm gonna give you that lesson. I guarantee you won't forget it. "

Frank laughed and bent her over the front edge of the loading dock, her face flat on the rough wooden surface. Drop the story? Who were these guys working for? She had caught her breath by now and shouted in a loud voice "Let me go, you bastards! Help! Someone help!"

Frank, one big hand in the small of her back holding her down, clamped the other over her mouth, stifling her shouts. When Eddie lifted the back of her coat, she felt the chill night air on her legs followed by Eddie's big hands on her hips sliding her dress up and realized the lesson he had in mind posed a more immediate problem than the identity of whoever had hired these thugs. Damn it! Where was Hudson?!?

21.

Make Yourself At Home

New York City
Friday, 13 May 1932

COCKRAN tipped the garage attendant and stepped into his Auburn Speedster. He'd spent most of the day and a good portion of the evening in the *Wall Street Journal* morgue and was pleasantly surprised to find out how much information there was publicly available about Wesley Waterman and a lot of other wealthy individuals as well. The Journal's morgue was well indexed and many famous names had equally fat files. The family Rockefeller alone had an entire file cabinet. Cockran had filled two legal pads with notes on Waterman holdings which would find its way into the trial record. He had checked in with his secretary at the law firm and Sarah had left a message for him indicating that she was having comparable success at the *New York Times* morgue. Who would have guessed that Waterman owned a major gun powder company in Cleveland and small arms manufacturers in Connecticut and California?

Cockran turned left and headed uptown on Broadway away from the financial district and lower Manhattan. He wondered how Mattie was doing. She had called him, as promised, the last two nights. She had sounded in better spirits last night when she told him she had a good lead in Cleveland. Caught up in thoughts of Mattie, he did not spot the black Lincoln sedan. It was after 10 p.m. and, while there were no other motorcars on the street, he did not pay particular attention when the Lincoln pulled up abreast of him at a red light. Casually glancing to his right, he saw that the rear window of the car was rolled down. The temperature was in the high thirties and a lowered window was curious.

He was turning his head back to focus on the traffic light when he saw movement in his peripheral vision.

It happened in an instant. His head stopped. He looked back and chilled. The ugly but unmistakable snout of a Thompson .45 caliber submachine gun was poking out of the open window. Without hesitation, Cockran slammed the accelerator pedal to the floor and the Auburn shot forward as Cockran heard the chatter of automatic weapons fire and several metallic pings on the rear of his car. Cockran had run a red light but, with no other traffic, he shifted the Auburn smoothly to second, then to third and within a block was at sixty miles per hour, the Lincoln giving chase behind. Ignoring red lights, Cockran began to put distance between himself and the Lincoln. The big black motorcar had a powerful engine also, but the Auburn's engine at 240 horsepower was equally powerful; the chassis was lighter; and the suspension was more finely tuned. The machine gun kept firing as Cockran accelerated, but he was now a much smaller target than when they were alongside of him. He could still hear the rattle of the machine gun and he instinctively flinched when a lucky shot tore through the rear window and out the windshield. Seconds after that, a shot hit the right rear view mirror, tearing it loose.

Cockran downshifted and turned right onto 23rd, tires screeching as he took the turn at forty miles per hour. The Lincoln had been a block and a half behind. He turned left at Madison Square, sped past the Court of Appeals and hung a right on 27th. He slowed at Park Avenue, looked for traffic on the left and right, and ran another red light. He turned left on Third Avenue and barreled uptown, hoping no police car was patrolling nearby, as he kept the Auburn close to sixty miles per hour. At 57th he turned right, headed over to First Avenue, took another left, pulled into the first available side street, stopped the car and took stock. He had lost the Lincoln.

Cockran figured that if the bastards had followed him from his midtown parking garage down to the *Wall Street Journal* building, they also probably knew the regular garage he used near his Fifth Avenue townhouse. So prudence dictated that he not park there for the night. He selected one on Second Avenue in the sixties, a good fifteen blocks from his residence.

Cockran tipped the garage attendant and inspected the damage on the Auburn with dismay. Damn it! He might well have to replace the sheet metal on the rear half of the car, not to mention the windshield and the right-hand rear view mirror. This was serious. He needed to find Bobby Sullivan. Someone was going to pay. He made a mental note to increase his final bill to cover the Speedster's repairs if the court ordered Waterman to pay Ingrid's legal fees.

COCKRAN cautiously approached his townhouse from the alley behind it, running between East 79th and 80th Street. He pulled his keys from his pocket and unlatched the rear gate, walked through the patio and up a flight of three steps to the rear entrance and froze. The left pane of glass above the door handle had been broken. Someone had gained access to the house and might be waiting for him inside. Cockran tried the doorknob but it was still locked. Rather than shove his hand through the jagged opening, he used his key to unlock the door and silently opened it. He stepped into the kitchen and stopped, alert for noise or movement. He drew his .45 automatic from his shoulder holster and held it beside his thigh, its barrel pointed down. In his stocking feet, he walked from the kitchen into the hallway, moving along the wall. The hallway was dark, the only illumination coming from the clerestory window above the front door. Once he reached the entrance to the dining room, he carefully put his left foot around the corner of the entrance. There were no windows in the darkened dining room. Cockran's eyes had adjusted to the low light by now, but as he turned to face the interior, he was alert for any movement but saw none. The dining room was empty. He retreated to the hallway and continued along its right-hand side until he reached the sitting room which had windows facing onto Fifth Avenue. He repeated the procedure but the sitting room was also empty. That left one more room to clear — the library — before he headed upstairs.

Cockran moved back to the left-hand side of the hallway when he heard a noise, the unmistakable sound of a round being chambered. He froze.

"And wouldn't a wise man put his weapon down and step out where I can see him? T'is living and breathing you'd remain. Whereas, I can assure you, a Thompson submachine gun will rip through that wall you're standing behind like a knife through soft butter."

Cockran breathed a sigh of relief and laughed. Bobby Sullivan! Kneeling down, he placed his .45 automatic on the floor and shoved it into the entranceway to the library. Then, carefully raising his hands above his head, he stepped slowly into the doorway. "Didn't your lawyer ever tell you breaking and entering is a felony?" Cockran asked.

Sullivan smiled. "My lawyer couldn't tell his arse from his elbow," he said. "Besides, it was an accident. My elbow hit the glass inadvertently. I opened the door to come inside so I could clean up the damage."

Cockran laughed again. Sullivan was sitting in a leather armchair with the Tommy gun resting comfortably on his lap, a crystal tumbler half full of what had to be Irish whiskey on the side table beside him.

"Make yourself at home. Go ahead, have a drink," Cockran said.

Sullivan did, lifting the glass to his lips and taking a sip. "The twelve year old Jameson's is far superior to the eight year old, I would be thinking. Easily the equal of the Black Bush."

Cockran raised his eyebrows. "Bushmill's? You drink whiskey made by Protestants?"

"Even a blind squirrel finds an acorn now and then. If I were the king of Ulster, Bushmill's distillery is one of the few things I'd keep around."

Cockran moved to turn on a lamp in the library.

"I wouldn't do that, if I were you," Sullivan said.

"Why's that?"

"You have two visitors sitting in a car out front, halfway down the block. You wouldn't want them to know anyone's home," Sullivan said.

"Really?"

"Aye. I have a few friends who work for Owney who believe it's more healthy to stay on my good side than his. Imagine that."

Cockran grinned. "Yes, imagine."

"Well, they told me that one of Owney's customers had ordered a hit on you tonight and paid double to make sure it was his best men. You weren't at your office, and your secretary wouldn't tell me where I could find you. I figured they didn't know either and the only other place they knew you'd be sometime tonight is here. I thought it best if I came over to hold down the fort, so to speak."

"But what if I'd come in the front way instead of the back?"

Sullivan motioned him over to the window. He saw that Sullivan had placed his chair at such an angle that he would see Cockran approaching from his regular garage before the men waiting in the car, with their backs to Cockran, would have seen him.

"My plan was to open your front door and let the boys in the car see me holding Mr. Thompson's finest firearm."

"Do you know who is behind it?" Cockran asked, as if he didn't know.

"You pissed off one of Owney's clients the other night. Got a little too friendly with the man's wife. My friend didn't know the client's name but we both know who it is, don't we now?"

Cockran nodded.

"I think it's time we took him out," Sullivan said.

"We?" Cockran asked.

"That was a royal 'we,'" Sullivan replied. "I assumed an Anglophile like you would understand." He smiled.

"Aren't you afraid of what Owney will do?" Cockran asked.

Sullivan didn't reply for a long time. When he did, he wasn't smiling. "It's Owney who should be asking that question about me," Sullivan said. "So, are my hands untied?"

Cockran shook his head. He knew he was probably Sullivan's closest friend but they didn't share all the same values. Sullivan was an eye for an eye man, the law be damned. Cockran, on the other hand, was willing to give the law a chance to do the right thing. Once.

Cockran shook his head. "No, Bobby, not yet. This isn't Germany, like last summer, where most of the cops were corrupt or in bed with the Nazis. We had no choice but to fight fire with fire. This is New York. It's different. We give the police a chance."

A moment later, Cockran dialed the local precinct house and talked to the desk sergeant, explaining the presence of a parked motorcar, after midnight, with two men in it, staking out his townhouse. The desk sergeant promised to send a patrol car around to check it out.

Cockran refilled Sullivan's glass and then poured a Jameson's on the rocks for himself. He pulled a chair over beside Sullivan and the two men sat there in companionable silence, sipping their whiskey and waiting for the police to arrive. It took fifteen minutes, but in due course a police car arrived, two uniformed officers got out of the car, guns drawn and approached the stake-out vehicle. After forty-five seconds of the officers' conversation with the occupants of the car, the driver put it in gear and pulled away from the curb.

Cockran pulled the drapes closed and they rearranged their armchairs until they were facing each other beside the fire place. Cockran lit a fire and turned on two table lamps..

"Did you visit Waterman's accountant this afternoon."

"I did," Sullivan replied.

"And?"

Wordlessly, Sullivan stood, walked over to the dry sink where Cockran's liquor supply was on display, and picked up two envelopes. He sat back down and handed one to Cockran.

Cockran opened it and quickly leafed through its contents, noting here and there a discrepancy between what he had found in the *Wall Street Journal* morgue and what Waterman's actual holdings were. They were much more than the newspaper had imagined. He frowned when he noted a series of nonprofit corporations owned by the Waterman Foundation which were valued collectively at $11.5 million. That was a drop in the bucket of Waterman's net worth, which was well north of $400 million. If the nonprofits had been formed after Waterman's marriage to Ingrid, however, she deserved her half of that $11.5 million.

"Good work, Bobby. Find out what you can tomorrow on these non-profits."

"You got it," Sullivan said as he rose to his feet. pulled his wallet out and extracted a $20 bill, laying it on the side table."

"What's that for?" Cockran asked.

"Would you be thinking I'd be the kind of man who breaks into a house without paying for the damage he caused? That's not how my Da raised me. See you tomorrow."

22.

We're Making Some Progress

Cleveland
Friday, 13 May 1932

MATTIE was pinned, helpless and furious. She tried to struggle but Frank easily held her for that bastard Eddie who, having finished pushing her coat and dress up, was starting to pull down her knickers. Then she heard a sharp cry to her left and Frank's hands suddenly released her. As Frank's body slumped to the ground, Eddie also cried out and he fell away as well.

Mattie turned her head around to see Frank unconscious on the ground and Eddie on his knees holding his face, blood streaming from between his fingers. Above them stood Ted Hudson, looming like a golden avenging angel, blood dripping from the barrel of the revolver with which he had pistol-whipped her two tormentors. She realized she had been holding her breath and exhaled deeply as she pushed herself up.

"Are you alright?" Hudson asked. "Did they hurt you?"

"I'll be okay. This one here," she said, pointing to Eddie, "punched me in the stomach a few times but he had a lot more in mind than that had you not come along in the nick of time. Thanks." Hudson nodded and leveled a .38 revolver at Eddie while Mattie turned away and straightened her garments beneath her navy coat. That had been far too close a call. "Where in the hell were you, anyway? And what's with the gun? I thought you weren't armed."

Hudson kept the revolver pointed directly at Eddie. "I wasn't. But when I saw there were two people following you, I figured I might have need of one."

"So how'd you get it?" Mattie asked.

"From a cop on the corner of East Ninth and Euclid."

"He *gave* you his weapon?'

"Not exactly. More like *loaned*. I flashed my MID credentials and he agreed to let me borrow it for a few hours. Plan B. That's my motto. Always have a Plan B."

Mattie was impressed. Thank God Hudson knew how to take care of himself. She retrieved her Walther from Eddie's waistband and patted him down.

"You want to question him here?" Hudson asked, his eyes cold and his voice flat as he hauled the bleeding Eddie to his feet. Below, Frank remained unconscious.

"Let's take him back to my new quarters. That Van Swerigen Suite, or whatever it's called. I don't think from what I was told that we'll be disturbed there." With that, Mattie placed her Walther back in her pocket, grabbed the lapels of Eddie's coat, pulled him close and drove her knee straight up into his crotch, leaving Eddie doubled over in pain.

Mattie thought briefly of doing it again but Eddie stayed doubled over and groaning. "That should last a while," she said. "Why don't you bind Frank's hands with his belt while I pop out into the street and hail a taxi?" Hudson cracked his revolver barrel down again on the other thug's head before he began to remove the man's belt from his trousers.

MATTIE couldn't believe it. Here she was on the twelfth floor of the tallest skyscraper between New York and Chicago and she felt as if she were in an English Tudor mansion. Which, in a way, she was. A thirty-foot high, heavily beamed cathedral ceiling loomed above her from which were hung three elaborate brass chandeliers. Either side of the room was lined with English oak paneling and leaded glass windows. At one end of the Great Hall was a small balcony for musicians. At the far end, a fire was blazing in a massive stone fireplace. A grand piano sat in one corner of the room and throughout were comfortable leather armchairs. It was a room fit for a London club or a home in the English countryside. No one standing outside the fifty-two story Terminal Tower would have guessed such a baronial room was hidden inside.

Hidden was the operative word. After Mattie had found a taxi, they had taken Eddie Monahan back to the Hotel Cleveland where they had hustled him through the lobby, pretending he was a drunken friend who had tripped and fallen on his face, explaining away the bloody gash on his cheek. Once on the twelfth floor of the hotel, they had followed the directions to the unmarked door which Mattie had unlocked. As they walked inside, they saw an intercom system on the left wall, beside a small brass-gated three-person Otis elevator. They got into the elevator and Mattie closed the door. She was surprised to see that it indicated they were on the tenth floor and not the twelfth. There was no stop for the eleventh floor and so Mattie had taken them to what the elevator panel showed was the twelfth floor. Once on twelve, she stepped from the elevator, turned the corner and walked up two steps into the Great Hall, lit at that time only by the roaring fire in the fireplace at the far end of the room.

Mattie had told Hudson to tie Eddie hand and foot in front of the fireplace.

"So where in New York are you from? Mattie asked.

"Sod off, you bitch. I'm not telling you nothing."

Growing up in Great Britain, Mattie had an ear for accents. She wasn't sure why. It was just part of her. Highlands, Liverpool, the Lake Country, Cornwall, Kent. She could place them all. She'd been doing the same with Americans. She was positive Eddie Monahan was second generation Irish who had grown up in Hell's Kitchen on New York's west side.

"Hell's Kitchen, isn't it?" Mattie asked.

"What do you mean?" Eddie asked.

"I mean that you grew up in Hell's Kitchen and I'll give you two to one odds you work for Owney Madden," Mattie said.

The man's eyes widened and Mattie knew she had struck pay dirt. All she needed now was the full name of Owney's customer who had hired Eddie and Frank.

"I'll be right back," Mattie said, "after I slip into something more comfortable. Ask him who hired him and why he wanted me mugged."

MATTIE had worn her little black cocktail dress to dinner and she could tell by the expression on Hudson's face that her idea of "something more comfortable" had not met Ted's expectations. Mattie was now wearing her typical workday ensemble of tailored khaki trousers, a crisp white cotton blouse, one button open at the neck, and a pale brown pair of leather boots.

"Any luck with finding out who hired him.?" Mattie asked. She noticed Eddie's face was swollen from further blows and blood trickled from a small cut above his ear.

Hudson smiled and grasped the man's chin. Then he slapped him hard on the side of his face. Twice. "We're making some progress. Aren't we, Eddie? You said his name was "Dr. V" but what's his real name?"

"I don't know. Honest. I don't know, Eddie replied. " I just go wherever Owney sends me and do what Dr. V tells us. Just like now. Frank got a call from Dr. V yesterday. He told us to get to Cleveland and we caught the night train. Instructions were left at American Express. Wait for the red haired broad at the airport, follow her and scare her off the story."

"Let me, Ted," Mattie said as she stepped in front of Eddie. "Why scare me off?"

"Hell, lady. I don't know. I just do what Owney tells me. I don't ask no questions. Not very healthy if you know what I mean. Besides, Frank says what we're doing is patriotic."

"I assume Frank also works for Owney?"

"Frank? Nah, he's some ex-Government guy. He's pretty close-mouthed about who he works for. Told me we were a team but I didn't have a 'need to know' who he works for. He's the one Dr. V talks to and then I just do whatever Frank tells me."

"What do you do for Dr. V?"

"We mostly snatch people. Knock 'em out with chloroform and bring them to wherever we're told."

"Why?"

Eddie shrugged his shoulders. "I don't know. Frank just says we're making America stronger. We snatch the guys and take them to a warehouse."

"What about girls? Do you snatch them too?" Mattie asked.

"Sure. Both men and women. We take the women to a hotel first. We pick them up again several hours later. They look like they had a good time but they been drugged or something. Most can barely talk. Without their clothes, they weren't bad-looking broads, either. My job is to dress them and carry them out of the hotel, pretending they're drunk. Just like you two brought me in here."

"Where do you take them after that?" Mattie asked.

Eddie shrugged again. "Same kind of place where we take the men in the first place. It's different in each city. It's usually a warehouse in a rougher part of town."

Mattie smiled at Eddie and he smiled back. "Anything else you've done for this Dr. V ?"

"No, that's about it."

"Are you certain?" Mattie asked. "Did I mention that my friend Bobby Sullivan won't be happy when he learns what you and Frank tried to do tonight?"

"Bobby Sullivan is your friend?" Eddie asked, his eyes growing wide.

"A *close* friend." Mattie replied and waited.

Eddie seemed torn but finally he spoke. " Wait, there *was* something else. Not always. But sometimes, he gives us names and has us go check birth certificates. If we find them, we bring him copies."

"Birth certificates?" Mattie asked. "Why?"

"Beats me," Eddie said. "Frank told me it was none of my business. Sometimes the names are the same as people we've snatched. Sometimes they're not."

Mattie walked over to a stained glass window, turned the handle and swung it open. She looked down on Cleveland's Public Square. "Take this piece of trash out of my room. Then get some sleep. We're flying to Findlay first thing tomorrow morning."

"Sure thing," Hudson said and grinned. He cut Eddie's bonds and jerked him to his feet. "We appreciate your cooperation, Eddie."

Eddie looked down and began to rub his wrists when Hudson suddenly hit him from behind with the revolver he had borrowed from the Cleveland cop and the thug crumpled to the floor. Hudson effortlessly picked him up and slung him over his shoulder.

"We'll take the back way out. See you in a half hour for our nightcap."

Mattie looked at her watch. 12:50 a.m. She sighed. She did owe Ted a nightcap for what he'd done tonight but she just wasn't up to it. Her stomach was still sore from Eddie's two punches. She took the elevator to the tenth floor and left a note for Ted on the door with a rain check for tomorrow on the nightcap. Back in her room, she stripped and went to sleep.

23.

Going Home

KURT von Sturm arrived at the train station in Friedrichschafen and looked immediately for the post office. He walked with a light step, the stamped and sealed letter to Hugo Eckener resting in his hand. If Eckener granted his request for command of an airship, he would tender his resignation to the Geneva Group and nominate Bruno Kordt as his successor.

Sturm saw the LZ-127 soaring overhead again, surely a good omen to accompany his decision. He knew the airship's primary purpose in its regular excursions over Lake Constance was not the revenue it generated, but the training it gave the crew in between its transatlantic passenger flights. Three days to North America. Half the time it took an ocean liner.

Time, Sturm thought, recalling Zurich's words to him two days before. *There never was enough of it.* Without meaning to, he found himself thinking of the last time he crossed the Atlantic aboard an airship. With her. And wishing it had taken longer to cross.

Sturm blinked his eyes sharply, turning from the zeppelin hanging in the sky, trying to break his mind away from the memory. Why think of her now? Place her in his past and think of her no more. Falling in love had been a weakness he could not afford.

There were more important things in life. Germany. A strong Germany. One that would stand up to the insults of her enemies; one that would tear up the Versailles Treaty that crippled his country; one that would reclaim the German-speaking territories taken from the *Vaterland*, including Posen where his own family estate lay in Polish chains. Deep down, he knew that if the woman he loved had not left him for another, he would have started then the new life which the letter he carried represented. It was a weakness that would have led him to betray Germany if only she would have loved him back.

Yet now, letter in hand, he was poised to do just that. Why? Certainly not for the woman he loved. She was out of his life. Forever. No, it was the growth in his protégé Bruno Kordt that would make it possible. Thanks to Sturm, Bruno was ready. He dropped the envelope in the post box and moved on toward the platform. He checked his watch and stopped at a public telephone booth and waited. In less than a minute, the phone rang and he heard Bruno's familiar voice.

"Geneva has made a request for a mission in New York to settle some difficulties that Manhattan is having," Sturm said.

"When do we leave?"

"We don't," Sturm said. "I turned the request down. I'm heading home for a holiday with my family and I won't have it interrupted."

"As well you should, Kurt," Bruno said. "Old bones like yours need their rest."

"Just as children like you need their afternoon naps."

He could hear Bruno chuckle under his breath over the phone. Bruno was twenty-nine, almost ten years younger than Sturm. He'd been drafted when he was only sixteen years old, the Imperial German Army desperate for warm bodies to throw into the Spring Offensive in 1918. As a result, Bruno had grown up very quickly.

"Nap time must wait, I'm afraid," Sturm continued. "I think you are ready for a Geneva assignment. On your own."

"I welcome any challenge. What is the assignment?"

Sturm told him what he knew. It wasn't much other than the assignment required his travel to New York where he would be directly serving Manhattan's interests in America. He detailed Geneva protocols that he had heretofore kept from Bruno — how to communicate with Geneva, what information to send, daily updates on location and progress. Bruno took the information as Sturm named the contact in New York, Bruno's go-between for Manhattan.

"Upon learning that I turned the job down and offered you in my place, Manhattan agreed but insisted that he have no direct contact with you whatsoever, in case you fail," Sturm said. "Don't be offended. I know you; he doesn't. You won't fail."

"I take no offense," Bruno said. "A man must earn respect."

"One more thing. Manhattan needs you as soon as possible. You will return by steamship but I have booked you on this afternoon's zeppelin to New York. Catch the next train to Friedrichschafen. You will arrive early on Sunday evening in New York."

The moment he disconnected the call, Sturm felt his body lighten, as though a heavy burden had been lifted from his shoulders. He was right to have sent the letter to Eckener. Bruno would not fail. He would be a worthy successor. Sturm made one last stop at a telegraph window to wire his mother and sister to tell them he was coming home for a holiday. He needed a rest, and so did the family Alsatian "Storm." He would happily serve as his blind sister's guide dog, so Storm could spend his time chasing rabbits to ground and gulls from the beach.

Sturm suddenly felt free, free of work, free of responsibilities, free to spend time with his family, free to be nothing more than his mother's beloved, first-born child and his sister's adored older brother. The man whose *nom de guerre*—to his sister's everlasting delight—was taken from the family dog. Kurt von Strasser was going home.

24.

Twins!

Hancock County Courthouse
Findlay, Ohio
Saturday, 14 May 1932

MATTIE spied U.S. Route 224 within thirty minutes of take off and followed it straight into Findlay. They passed over the town square heading west over a large industrial complex with a tall brick chimney labeled "Cooper Tire." Beyond was the airfield where Mattie feathered the autogiro gently to earth. A hired motorcar was waiting and within minutes they were in the center of town where the county recorder's office was located in the Victorian-era courthouse. They walked down the marble halls to the recorder's office only to find a locked wooden door, its frosted glass top half announcing that this was where the county's records were kept.

Mattie was disappointed. Ted was undaunted.

"No problem," Ted said, as he began wandering until he found a janitor.

Hudson promptly flashed his MID credentials; told the janitor that this was a matter involving the security of the country; and that the president himself would be grateful for any assistance the janitor could render.

Of course, Mattie thought, the $20 bill in Hudson's hand probably played its part as well. In any event, the janitor had the necessary keys and she was soon within the county recorder's office, searching for birth certificates. Hudson left Mattie alone to do this and went to call the offices of *The New York American* to see if there were any messages from MID for him.

"Have them give you my messages as well," Mattie said, as she started to examine the labels on the many file cabinets to locate birth certificates.

WHILE Hudson placed his phone call, Mattie tried to figure out which records were kept where. She finally found the room where birth certificates were located. Mattie tugged at the door, but it didn't move. It was locked. Damn, she thought, as she went back out in search of the janitor. She walked past the telephone booth where Hudson was still talking. Then, with the janitor in tow, she walked back to the recorder's office once more. Whoever Ted was talking to clearly had upset him because, as she passed, she heard him say "Do it right the next time! Don't screw it up again! I don't care what you think, you moron! Or what someone else told you! This is not some training exercise. I don't want you exercising any discretion in the field. Just follow my instructions precisely! Or else! You got that?"

Mattie frowned as she walked. She hadn't known Ted had such a temper. Gossip travels fast in any business organization and she didn't recall having heard anything like this about Ted. Self-confident to the point of being cocky? Well, sure. Everyone knew that. But a temper? No. Not like the dressing down she just heard him give to some young reporter.

Back in the recorder's office, the janitor helpfully unlocked the door. Mattie found the file cabinet with "1895" on the label. She pulled out the drawer which had folders tabbed "M" and took it over to a nearby table. She located November and pulled it out. She opened it and began leafing through the certificates. There it was. James Roger Miller, born November 3, 1895 at 4:20 a.m. Parents John Burson Miller and Jane Brewer Miller. 311 South Main Street, Findlay. Mattie took out her reporter's pad and began copying the information into her notebook. Having done that, she began to place the certificate back into the folder. She couldn't explain why she did it but she placed the certificate face down on the left-hand side of the folder as opposed to face up on the right-hand side. She thought later that it must be how she unconsciously did things. It made all the difference. It was the key which broke the story wide open. Maybe she would have found the same key later in other cities, but maybe not.

In the event, as she placed James Miller's birth certificate face down on the left-hand side of the file, the next certificate caught her eye because it was a baby girl named Elizabeth. Curious, she picked up the certificate and examined it more closely. Oh my God, Mattie thought, as she read. Elizabeth Ann Miller. Born November 3, 1895. Time of birth 4:40 a.m. Twenty minutes later than James Miller. She quickly looked at the section where the parents were listed and found exactly what she expected. John Burson and Jane Brewer Miller.

Twins! Two of the victims were twins! Fraternal twins, to be sure, but twins. Coincidence? Nope. Her instinct yesterday about victims being related had been correct.

"Find anything interesting?" Ted Hudson asked.

"Oh!" Mattie said, startled. "How long have you been there?"

Hudson grinned and then smiled. "About five minutes. But you were scribbling in your notebook so intently that I didn't want to disturb you. Your profile is magnificent."

In truth, Mattie didn't think her profile was magnificent. She thought her nose a tad too long. Still, it was never bad to hear a handsome man tell her she looked magnificent. Mattie explained to Hudson what she had discovered but, at first, Hudson couldn't see the significance. "So they're twins. So what? It's probably just a coincidence."

"Coincidence, my ass. If two victims are twins, more of them may be as well."

Hudson remained skeptical. "But where does that get us? It doesn't solve the crimes."

"Two things, Ted. It gets us closer to finding the killer. Second, and the more important thing, is that if the other victims are twins also, we've got one hell of a story already."

"Really? I just don't see that all the victims being twins is such a big story."

Mattie laughed. "If you don't, it's probably just as well you're going back to MID."

Mattie took careful notes from Elizabeth Miller's birth certificate and then put the folder back in the file drawer. She turned to Hudson as they left the office. "You go over to the hotel and check us in. I've got to call the Chief right away and give him the news. I'm sure he'll agree with me that this is a big deal and, when he does, you find us the best restaurant in the city. This calls for a celebration. You and I are going to paint the town."

TED Hudson signed the hotel register "Mr. and Mrs. Theodore Stanhope Hudson IV" for the second day in a row. After doing so, he flashed his MID credentials at the desk clerk. "We are on a sensitive government mission and are traveling incognito. My traveling companion is Martha McGary, although she will undoubtedly refer to herself as "Mattie." Do you have that?"

The young desk clerk nodded.

"Good. She's fairly tall and a real looker. She has red hair. When she comes and asks for her key, she will tell you her name. You will give her the key to 708, which is one of the two connecting rooms I have taken. It's important. National security. Lives are at stake."

The desk clerk's eyes grew wide. "Yes, sir, I understand."

"Good lad," Hudson said, as he patted the boy on the shoulder with his left hand and slipped him a $5 bill with the other. He grinned to himself as he walked to the elevator. What was her Irish boyfriend going to think when the postman delivered copies of hotel bills from yesterday and today in the name of Mr. & Mrs Theodore Hudson along with room service chits signed by Mattie? Well, if said boyfriend were the jealous type and started making what Mattie knew were false accusations, that would make it all the easier for him to lure Cockran's girlfriend back into his bed. And he knew there would be plenty of time to do just that. Maybe he'd even get lucky tonight after they finished painting the town. She was still one hot number.

But business came first. Back in his room, he began to work the phones. Mattie's discovery was important, a critical development. Much had happened and there was much more to do. From past experience, he knew there often wasn't as much time as you first thought.

PROHIBITION was a joke in small towns as well as big cities and the dining room of the Hotel Phoenix in Findlay was reputed to have the best wine cellar in town as well as the best chef. Over martinis, Mattie filled Hudson in on her talk with Hearst. "The Chief agrees with me that this is too good a lead not to follow up immediately. He's splitting us up."

Hudson frowned. "Really? Why?" Then he smiled. "I've enjoyed dinner with you these past few evenings and I was looking forward to many more."

"Me too," Mattie said, the white lie coming easily, "but business comes first. Hearst wants to keep this story secret. Only you, me and him for now. No one else is to know about the twins angle. He's dividing up the country between us. You have Denver, Portland, Seattle, San Francisco and Los Angeles. A different Hearst reporter will meet you in each city. Track down the victims' birth certificates to see if we find more twins. I think we will. I'll drop you tomorrow in Toledo, an hour north of here. You can book passage from there to Denver."

Hudson nodded but he wasn't happy. "If I didn't have bad luck when it comes to timing, I wouldn't have any. You remember that night in Pittsburgh when I mentioned the Allied intervention in Russia and the slaughter at Archangel?"

"Yes. You were clearly upset and said you had lost someone there very close to you."

Hudson nodded. "That's what I meant about timing. My fiancée Elizabeth was a nurse in a field hospital there. Their orders to evacuate had been cut and she was supposed to be on a Navy ship a week before the Bolsheviks overran their hospital and killed everyone there, patients and medical staff alike. Except the ship never came. Beth's last letter to me said they expected the ship any day but the goddamn ship never came."

"I'm sorry. That's horrible."

"Yeah, well, I guess I mentioned it the other night because you've always reminded me a lot of Beth. She never took any crap from me either. That's probably one of the reasons why I fell in love with you and proposed in Paris. Just another example of bad timing biting me in the ass. Look, I know my timing was lousy back in '29. It was too soon for me to propose. After that French bastard's betrayal, you needed time to heal. I'm just sorry that by the time you did, Cockran and not me was lucky enough to be the right man at the right time in the right place. I once told you I never finished second to him in anything but that doesn't include you. I've gotten over my disappointment but I still feel the same way about you now that I did in Paris. Besides Beth, you're the only girl to whom I ever proposed. I hope for your sake that Cockran's the right one. Really. If he is, then I'm happy for you and I wish you both the best."

Mattie didn't reply immediately, surprised at Ted's insight as well as showing her a vulnerable side of himself he had heretofore kept hidden. It was an attractive side as was the boyish grin which accompanied it and it brought back, for a brief moment, her guilt over turning down his proposal after their torrid week in Paris. But it was neither bad luck nor timing, she told herself. It was love. She liked him well enough but she had never loved Ted. And Cockran bloody well was the right one.

"Thank you. That's very sweet. And I understand the pain of losing a fiancé in the war. I did too but we both need to focus on the future," Mattie said. "This is a big break in our story. Trust me. My instincts tell me twins are the key." She raised her glass in the air and moved it toward Ted, inviting a toast. He responded and their stemmed glasses gently clinked.

"To us," Hudson said.

"To our story," Mattie corrected.

The rare roast beef at dinner were excellent as was the wine cellar, Ted ordering a bottle of the 1921 Margaux. Mattie protested that her expense account couldn't afford it.

"My expense account can't either," he said with a wink, "but my trust fund can."

Outside Findlay, Ohio

AFTER dinner, Mattie was feeling tipsy, but she was in a light-hearted mood and full of confidence that the story was going to break exactly as she had predicted. She was surprised when Hudson suggested they go dancing to top off the evening. She readily accepted. Mattie loved to dance but Cockran didn't. As a result, she had little opportunity to indulge one of her favorite things. Had she ever told Ted that? She didn't think so but she might have.

They piled into their motorcar and headed north on Route 25. "There's a roadhouse ten miles out of town," Hudson said as he drove. "I considered taking us there for dinner because of the dancing, but I was told that the food wasn't nearly as good as at the Hotel Phoenix."

"I'm glad you didn't. The prime rib was great," Mattie said, "and so were the Oysters Rockefeller. Even better than last night. Now, we'll have the best of both worlds."

Twenty minutes later they pulled up at the roadhouse and its crowded parking lot. Hudson drove to the far end where there were fewer cars. A stand of trees was between it and the highway. Inside the roadhouse, Hudson's $20 bill secured them their own booth.

Mattie knew Hudson was an accomplished dancer from the week she spent in Paris with him. The small jazz band was hopping; Hudson knew the moves; and Mattie had a ball. They polished off a bottle of champagne and, at one point, they were the only couple on the floor as the other couples watched and cheered them on, the male voices louder than the female, Mattie suspected, because it was her silk knickers and garter belt on full display when he twirled her in the air and then brought her back between his legs. It left her breathless but she felt great.

At 2:00 a.m. the band leader announced it was the last dance. There had been few slow dances but Mattie could hardly refuse Ted's offer to dance. She felt Ted's big warm hand caressing her bare back as they glided across the room. Having shared a bottle of champagne on top of the martinis and wine at dinner, Mattie began to regret last night's promise of redeeming Ted's rain check for a nightcap tonight. Pressed together as they moved around the floor, she could feel what one part of Ted had in mind beyond a nightcap.

The dance over, Mattie and Hudson returned to their booth where, against her better judgment, she let Ted order two brandies. She barely touched hers and a half hour later, he checked his watch. "Time to call it a night." Hudson got their coats, tipped the hat check girl and then tossed the keys to Mattie. "Go ahead and warm the car up. I've got to visit the little boys' room and I wouldn't want you waiting in the cold."

Mattie's reflexes were quick and she grabbed the keys in midair. Maybe the alcohol hadn't affected her that much. "All right. I'll drive the car around to the front."

25.

The Bitch Deserved It

Woolworth Building
New York City
Saturday, 14 May 1932

WESLEY Waterman had been in Washington on Thursday and Friday and taken the night train back to New York to which his private railcar had been attached. He had been outraged upon arriving at I.C.E. headquarters that Saturday morning to find the court order freezing his assets, and keeping him away from his penthouse on Central Park West. But he put off summoning his lawyer because he had real work to do during the day. That bitch of a Hearst reporter was in the home town of one of their clinical subjects and that was *not* a good development. Hopefully, the peril she posed to the project would soon be a thing of the past. He wished he could say the same for his gold-digging wife. After making a few phone calls to ensure the Hearst reporter would not present a further problem, he had summoned the incompetent fool who allowed this travesty of justice to happen.

The ugly little toad was now sitting in an arm chair, cowering in front of him.

"You idiot!" Wesley Waterman shouted. "My assets frozen! Ordered out of my own home! What do you think I'm paying you for?"

Chester Bowles nervously wiped the perspiration from his brow. "I'm sorry, Mr. Waterman, but they had photographs."

"Photographs!" Waterman roared. "I gave you photographs of my two-bit whore of a wife being thoroughly fucked by her lover. That should have been enough to sink her forever. Even an idiot could have done that. Why couldn't you? Just how incompetent can one lawyer be? Explain that!"

"They had other naked photographs of your wife showing how she had been beaten up."

"So what?" Waterman said. "The bitch deserved it. She was screwing around on me."

"Unfortunately, Mr. Waterman," Bowles continued, "There also were photographs of you and a blonde-haired young woman taken Wednesday evening in her apartment on Park Avenue."

"Pamela!" Waterman said and pounded the table. "Those bastards broke into Pamela's apartment and took photographs of us?"

"No. According to their private investigator, she let him into the apartment and set him up in her bedroom closet."

Waterman frowned. Pamela was going to learn that Wesley Waterman was not a man whom you could double-cross with impunity. But for now, that could wait.

"What moron did you draw for a judge?"

"We didn't have good luck there. The judge is Miriam Perkins and I doubt if she approves of wives being beaten. Frankly, the photographs of you and your wife in bed with other people was a wash. The photographs of her beating is what tipped the scales."

Waterman frowned. He had met her at society balls. Friedman was her maiden name. A Jew *and* a woman, he thought. What was the American judiciary coming to? Tomorrow was going to be a busy day.

"Look, Bowles. I want you to call Foster Dulles. Here's his unlisted telephone number. See him tomorrow. I want you acting on my behalf and Sullivan & Cromwell lawyers acting on behalf of I.C.E. to be in court first thing Monday morning and get those assets unfrozen. OK?"

"Yes, sir," Bowles said, "but I don't think Judge Perkins is going to be willing . . . "

"I don't care what you think. That's why I'm sending you to Dulles. I want to know what someone with brains thinks about this. As for that Jewish judge, let me worry about her."

Alone again, Waterman pondered his next steps. Ingrid? Right now, death was too good for her. That would come soon enough. Meanwhile, screw General Van Deman. What he didn't know wouldn't hurt him.

Tomorrow night, he would pay a conjugal visit to his Central Park West penthouse accompanied by the two ex-MID agents. They couldn't take Cockran down but he assumed they at least could strip and hold a wife down while her husband exercised his marital rights. An eye for an eye. He smiled. And an eyeful for them plus a small cash bonus would keep them from telling Van Deman that they had again been used for something other than Project Gemini.

Waterman paused. Project Gemini. Of course! Why hadn't he thought of it before? Perhaps there was an additional way to get even with his faithless wife and advance the interests of national security at the same time. There were those close to her who were vulnerable and he wondered if there were a way, before she died, for her to be told the real price he had made her pay for her infidelity. Time to telephone Dr. V.

26.

A Sitting Duck

Outside Findlay, Ohio
Sunday, 15 May 1932

MATTIE was surprised to see how quickly the parking lot had emptied, no more than three or four cars remaining. She swung her small purse by its metal chain as she walked, heavier than usual because it contained her Walther PPK . She quickly thought back to those thugs in Cleveland. Who the hell had put Owney Madden on to her story and her itinerary? And why was some ex-government guy his partner? Eddie's confession proved it hadn't been her imagination that someone had followed her car from Nela Park to Public Square in Cleveland. Hudson had been wrong about that. But she couldn't worry about it now. Checking out additional birth certificates was more important.

Mattie approached their motorcar and rested her right foot lightly on the running board as she unlocked the driver's side door. She had just opened the door when the first shot rang out. It came from the dark woods behind her while she was bathed in the bright glare of the overhead lights in the parking lot. "Ted!" she screamed as she dropped to the ground and a second shot shattered the glass of the rear door on the left-hand side of the car. She crouched behind the motorcar's long hood, pulled the Walther from her purse and cautiously peeked up. She ducked again as two more shots were fired. She was safe here for now and, even if there was more than one shooter, they wouldn't be able to outflank her, not in this light.

Mattie saw a shadow move in the woods to her right, and she fired a shot. Then she saw in her peripheral vision a shadow in the woods to her left and fired another shot just as all the lights in the parking lot suddenly shut off. Damn! she thought. There were two of them, for sure. And, from the direction they were moving in, they were trying to outflank her and take her from either side. "Ted!" she shouted again. Where the hell was Hudson when you needed him?

"Mattie!" a voice hissed from behind a blue Chevrolet twenty feet away. "Are you OK?"

"Yes, but there are two of them," Mattie replied.

"Stay where you are," Hudson said. "Watch out to your left. Cover me. It's Plan B time."

"You're covered," Mattie said and snapped off two quick shots as Ted made a dash to the woods. There was no return fire. Thirty seconds passed and still no shots were fired. Finally, she heard the crack of two shots coming from a .45 caliber automatic and saw a man emerge from the trees to her left, a good thirty yards from her, moving fast. It wasn't Ted. Mattie brought the Walther to bear and hesitated. It was a waste of ammunition trying to hit a fleeing man at what was now forty yards.

Mattie saw Hudson also bolt from the woods to her left. He knelt on one knee, held his .45 Colt automatic in his right hand, steadying it with his left under the pistol grip, arms fully extended. The fleeing man was a good fifty yards from Hudson when he squeezed the trigger. The Colt jerked upwards and the front of the man's head exploded in a shower of blood.

Mattie gasped, startled at the carnage, only dimly aware of how impressive Ted's shot had been. She stepped from behind the car, put the Walther in her pocket and began to shake uncontrollably as the reality of almost being killed hit her. When Hudson tucked his Colt in the small of his back and came over to check on her, her heart was still racing as she instinctively embraced him. She needed to be held. Ted put his arms around her and pulled her in close.

"Thank God you came when you did," Mattie said at last, finally pulling back from the warmth of his body while he continued to softly stroke her hair. "Did you get the other man?"

Ted pulled back also, his hands on her arms and nodded. "You were right. These are the same guys from last night." He shook his head and snorted. "Incompetent bunglers, both of them. They're better off dead. If they had been decent shots, you wouldn't have stood a chance. I was just coming out of the nightclub when I heard the first shots. You were clearly illuminated, a sitting duck. That's why I killed the lights after you weren't hit. You should have been dead twice over. I don't know how they missed you. You are one lucky woman."

"You got that right. Who's the one you just shot?" Mattie asked.

"Eddie, our guest in your suite last night," Hudson replied.

Mattie handed the car keys to Hudson. She wanted to find out more about the other shooter. "We need to get out of here before the police arrive. I've got to get you to Toledo tomorrow and myself to Detroit so we can't hang around Findlay giving statements to the sheriff or police, or whoever has jurisdiction here. Take the motorcar out to the road and wait with your lights off on the side of the road a hundred yards south of the nightclub. I'll meet you there."

"I agree we need to leave quickly," Hudson said, "but why aren't you coming with me?"

"I'm going into the woods to check out the ID on the first guy you shot. I should have done it last night. Who those guys were and why this Dr. V hired them is critical to finding out who's responsible for these murders," Mattie said.

"I can do that for you," Hudson said. "No need for you to get your slippers dirty."

"No," Mattie said, "get moving, Ted. We're wasting time. I'm already dirty and I can buy new shoes. You need to be out there with your lights out before the police arrive."

Hudson reluctantly got into the motorcar and Mattie headed toward the woods between the nightclub and the highway. By the time she reached the edge of the woods, some thirty yards away, she could hear the wail of sirens in the distance.

MATTIE sat soaking in the tub back at the hotel and took a healthy sip of scotch from a crystal tumbler on the floor beside her, her second drink since returning. Being held by Ted had been comforting but a hot bath and a drink were better. She went over once more what she had found. Or rather, had not found. Unlike Eddie last night who had both a billfold with a driver's license, the ex-Government guy called "Frank" had neither. The only thing in his pockets was a Chinese laundry ticket from Washington, D.C. Also, Frank's weapon was a Colt New Service 1917 revolver which Mattie knew was standard U.S. Army issue in 1918. The death of Frank was bothering her. Hudson had shot him execution style in his forehead. Up close, because the powder burns were evident around the wound. How had the man allowed Ted to get that close?

She had asked Ted about that, but his only reply had been, "He never heard me coming. By the time he did, it was too late. I haven't been in the field for nearly three years but some things you never forget. Quietly coming up behind an adversary is one of them." He had turned his face toward Mattie. A cold face that carried no trace of his trademark smile nor the comforting warmth of his embrace. "I'm very good at what I do." She supposed he was.

Mattie heard a knock at the interior door between her room and Ted's. "Yes?"

"We need to talk. And I'm carrying that rain check." Ted's muffled voice said through the door, which Mattie had securely locked from her side. Mattie sighed, once more regretting the rain check. A nightcap with Ted Hudson at 3 a.m. was the last thing she needed. It was bad enough she hadn't called Cockran now for two nights running.

"Just a second," Mattie called out, as she stepped out of the tub and began toweling off. She wrapped the green silk robe over her still damp body, well aware it would be obvious to Ted that she was naked beneath its clinging, filmy fabric. But she sure as hell wasn't going to bother getting fully dressed at three in the morning when all she wanted to do was crawl into bed.

Would Cockran approve of her being alone with Ted so late at night and so barely dressed? Not bloody likely! But that was more than Cockran needed to know, she thought and opened the connecting door. Her adrenalin and alcohol levels were high but she knew how to handle Ted. She always had. Except that hazy last night in Paris. What in hell *had* happened?

Ted Hudson was standing there in his own blue silk dressing gown sporting a TSH monogram. It was loosely knotted, giving Mattie a full view of a broad chest covered with tight golden curls. He was holding a bottle of Martel in one hand, two brandy snifters in the other. His blond hair was boyishly tousled and he was flashing that million-dollar smile, all too aware of just how good looking he really was. Mattie sighed. This was not going to be easy.

"Hello, beautiful," he said, his eyes undressing her as they slowly roved up and down her body, his unspoken intentions unmistakable.

"Hello yourself," she replied and self-consciously pulled the sheer silk of her robe more tightly around her but this only made her naked breasts beneath more obvious. Impeccable timing, she thought. Ted *was* intent on making his way back inside her knickers and an accommodating Mattie wasn't even wearing any. The fact that Hudson was also naked under his robe wasn't lost on her either. Still, what else could she do? After all, when a man twice saves your life, a girl shouldn't seem ungrateful.

"Make yourself comfortable" she said, as she waved him in with a sweep of her right hand, a movement which briefly opened the top of her robe more than she expected. Belatedly, she pulled the robe closed with her left hand. Damn! Had she done so in time to deprive Ted of his own private peep show? She sadly concluded she had not. Ted's face was impassive but his eyes had never left her body. No, this nightcap was not going to be easy. She really hoped she wasn't going to regret in the morning her display of gratitude tonight.

MATTIE woke up and was pleasantly surprised she had no hangover from having overindulged the night before. Her luck was still holding. She slipped from beneath the sheets where she had slept alone, walked naked to the window, threw back the curtains and looked across Main Street to the courthouse where sunshine reflected off windows and its golden dome. She called room service and ordered breakfast for two, with plenty of coffee for Ted.

As Mattie turned from the window, she realized she had no regrets. She felt refreshed and energized from all her adventures yesterday—the twins discovery, dancing, a gunfight and even that nightcap. Still, she *was* a tad sore but that was only to be expected after a semi-naked wrestling match with a determined man who mistook an accidental opening of her robe for an invitation. It had required no small effort to persuade him otherwise. But she had given as good as she got and the end result was a satisfying climax to an eventful day. Well, satisfying for her. Ted, quite drunk by then, would have to speak for himself. But her godfather Winston had got it right. Last night proved there was nothing as exhilarating as being shot at without result. True, having a handsome blond Adonis lust after her 32 year old body came in a close second even though, to her regret, it had been only Ted, two sheets to the wind, and not Cockran, doing the lusting. But unlike Paris, she thought with a smile, this time it would be a hungover Ted left wondering what in hell had happened between them last night. It served him right.

Mattie signed the chit for breakfast and knocked on Ted's door. Hearing no reply, she opened it and laughed. A completely starkers Ted was sprawled face down on his bed clutching an empty brandy bottle. She hadn't gotten a good look when he staggered back to his room in that same state last night but now, framed in the sunlight, she saw Ted still had the same attractive and well-muscled body he did in Paris. Who cared? Cockran had a much cuter ass.

27.

We Weren't Painting the Town

The Cedars
Sands Point, Long Island
Sunday, 15 May 1932

COCKRAN, dressed in khakis and a navy blue cotton sweater, was standing on the porch and about to head down to the stable for an early morning ride on the beach with his son Paddy when he heard the telephone ring. He hoped it was Mattie. He had been worried when she hadn't called the last two nights. He had phoned her hotel in Cleveland but was told she was never registered there. He waited expectantly and was relieved a few seconds later when an eager eleven year old boy with tousled red hair opened the screen door.

"Dad! Telephone! It's for you. It's Mattie," he said in an excited voice.

Cockran smiled at his son's enthusiasm. Mattie had made an instant impression on Paddy and he looked forward to her frequent visits and the adventure stories she would tell him. He avidly followed her articles when they appeared in *The New York American*. He was her biggest fan and Cockran knew he loved her. When he grew up, Paddy had once told Cockran, he was going to be a journalist, just like Mattie and his Mom, whom he knew only from photographs and the stories Cockran and his grandmother told him. Cockran was pleased and had teared up. He didn't deserve two women like Nora and Mattie. But Patrick did.

Cockran picked up the receiver from the telephone table in his study. "Mattie. I was worried when you didn't call. Are things OK? You weren't registered at the hotel in Cleveland."

"That's because we left there yesterday. We're in northwest Ohio now. Findlay."

"Findlay? What's in Findlay?"

"Not much," Mattie said and laughed softly. "Except it's where I found the answer to the connection among all the murder victims."

"Really? So soon? What is it?"

Cockran listened as Maddie recounted all that had happened since she found her first lead in Pittsburgh through her mugging in Cleveland to being shot at in a nightclub parking lot.

"Shots? At a nightclub with Ted?"

"Relax. We were meeting a source. We weren't painting the town. Anyway, Ted went into the woods after them. Killed one of them at point blank range in the woods and got the other in the parking lot as he was running away. You should have seen it! A fifty yard head shot in the dark with only a pistol! I've never seen anything like it. I didn't know Ted was that good."

Cockran didn't reply. He knew all too well how good Hudson was. They had been in MID training together and Ted had received high scores in marksmanship in both pistols and rifles. In fact, if Ted hadn't been in MID, he could have been a sniper. He was that good with a long-range rifle. But Cockran still didn't trust him. Or like him.

Finally, he broke the silence, choosing his words judiciously. He couldn't let Mattie's favorable report card on Hudson weaken his resolve to refrain from criticizing her conduct in the field. "You need to be careful, Mattie. This is obviously more dangerous than you anticipated."

"I know. In more ways than one. But trust me, after all that happened last night, I'll be a lot more careful in the future." Mattie replied, "Now, could I ask a favor?

"Sure. Name it."

"One of the guys was named Eddie Monahan. He admitted he was one of Owney Madden's men. The other was Frank or possibly Franklin. No last name. I'm not sure who he's with. Eddie said he wasn't with Owney and claimed he was an ex-Government guy. Said he was the one in charge. But he may have been lying. Can you have Bobby check them out for me? See if he can find who this Dr. V character is who hired them?"

"You got it," Cockran said, making a note of their names and Frank's Chinese laundry ticket. "I'll call him this morning. So what's next? When do you think you'll be home?"

Mattie laughed again, her voice excited. "There's good news and there's better news."

"What's the good news?"

"I'll be back in New York by Friday after I check out some of the other victims to see if they were twins also. I'll be in Detroit tonight and tomorrow, Chicago on Tuesday and St. Louis on Wednesday. If I'm right about the twins angle, then it's straight home to write the story. After that, it will be in the Sunday Hearst papers all over the country."

"That *is* good news. But what's better than that?" Cockran asked.

"How about Ted Hudson will no longer be traveling with me?" Mattie asked.

"Dumping your golden boy? That *is* good news."

"Watch it, Cockran. I told you he's not. . . ."

Cockran cut her off with a laugh. "I know. Seriously, this is great news." Cockran paused. It was great news and yet it wasn't. Mattie without Hudson was good but Mattie alone in Detroit was not. Owney Madden wasn't going to be happy to learn one or possibly two of his thugs had been taken out. Would he want to get even? With Madden, you could never tell.

Cockran listened with half an ear as Mattie began to give him the details of where she would be staying. He was analyzing the import of Hudson's absence on an assignment that had suddenly turned very dangerous. His philosophy was not to worry about things he couldn't contol and, reluctantly, he had put Mattie's safety into that category as most of her work was abroad and out of his reach. Not now. This was different. She was only an overnight train away. If Hudson wasn't there to look out for her, he would be. "Mattie, wait." Cockran said, interrupting. "I don't like your being alone. Whoever sent those two thugs after you may send more. I don't have to be in court this week. I can catch a train to Detroit today."

"No, Bourke," Mattie replied firmly. "I'm not going to let you ruin the rest of Patrick's weekend with his father. That boy looks forward to it all week."

"But Mattie. . . ."

"Don't start, Cockran. No. That's final. Saddle up and go for a ride with your son."

Cockran didn't reply. He let the silence grow until Mattie got the message. Finally, he spoke. "OK, I'll come tomorrow. I'll wire the details to your hotel. You have your Walther?'

"You bet."

"Locked and loaded?"

"It is. I love you."

"I love you, too. Be safe."

"I'll try my best."

"You'd better."

SULLIVAN'S call late that afternoon disturbed Cockran. Eddie was one of Owney's thugs but no one knew where he was, let alone that he was dead. But Frank? The only Frank in Owney's outfit was a 56 year old accountant. Remembering that Mattie had said he might be an ex-Government guy, Cockran called O'Hanlon in D.C. and gave him the name of the Chinese laundry and the ticket number. The MID man agreed to track the lead down and run any name he found through MID personnel records.

28.

This Is a Travesty

Fifth Avenue
New York City
Monday, 16 May 1932

COCKRAN was in the library, revising the proofs of his father's biography. Lifting the tea cozy from the teapot on the side table, he poured himself another cup, added milk and half a teaspoon of sugar. He had returned to the page proofs when the doorbell rang. Cockran was puzzled. It was only 8:45. He had bundled Paddy into a taxi for school fifteen minutes ago and his mother-in-law was on her daily trip to shop for groceries, a Galway habit which could not be broken. Even with Cockran's new Frigidaire, food must be shopped for every day.

Cockran walked to the front door, opened it, and was astonished to see Ingrid Waterman standing in front of him with a bruised and battered face. She now had a second black eye to accompany her first, and her upper lip was swollen.

"I'm sorry to disturb you so early, but I got away as soon as I could," Ingrid said.

"Come in, come in. Don't worry about it. What happened? Who did this to you?"

"My husband. He raped me last night," she said. "The two men with him, bodyguards I suppose, stripped me and held me down while he did it. After that, he beat me with a belt."

Cockran was furious. He had always had a temper from a very young age. Unlike his father who joked — gently, of course, as was his father's way — that Cockran's temper must have come from his mother, the Mack side of the family. Cockran believed this if only because he had never seen his father lose his temper. The same could not be said of Cockran. Growing up as an Irish Catholic on Long Island's Gold Coast as a son of privilege when most other Irish were servants had involved Cockran in more than one fist fight over his ethnic and religious heritage.

Right now, his temper was at the boiling point. Ingrid still didn't want to file criminal charges so if he dwelled on what Waterman had done, he would call Bobby Sullivan right away and let nature take its course. Waterman would be dead by nightfall and not a pleasant or painless death either.

Instead, Cockran took a deep breath to control his anger; called Sarah Steinberg; and had her arrange for a court stenographer to be sent to his townhouse to take Ingrid's new sworn statement. More photographs to follow. Meanwhile, he asked Sarah to try and schedule a hearing before Judge Perkins as early in the afternoon as possible. Then he called his secretary and had her switch his early afternoon Pullman reservation to the night train to Detroit..

Sarah called back an hour later. Judge Perkins would see them at 3:00 p.m. Ingrid signed a new sworn statement later in the morning. At 2:00 p.m., they took a taxi down to the courthouse where they met Sarah Steinberg and Bobby Sullivan. Upon entering Judge Perkins' chambers, Cockran found the Judge's secretary in tears and her bailiff close to it.

"George," Cockran said, "what's the problem? What happened?"

George Kahn, Judge Perkins' bailiff, looked up at Cockran for the first time.

"She's dead, Mr. Cockran. We just heard from the police. A bar association luncheon. The Judge was struck by a hit and run driver afterwards. She was dead on arrival," George Kahn said, and then he burst into tears along with the Judge's secretary.

"Oh, my God, Bourke," Ingrid said, "how horrible. That poor woman."

Cockran's eyes narrowed. This *wasn't* an accident. This was Wesley Waterman. Cockran looked over at Sullivan who moved his head almost imperceptibly. But Cockran knew that Bobby agreed. It was almost a sign language between them. Bobby raised his eyebrows, a question asked:

Should I go and kill the bastard now? Cockran shook his head slowly from side to side. No, not now.

The resulting glare from Bobby Sullivan would have chilled the blood of anyone who didn't know him as well as Cockran did. But Cockran made eye contact and held it until Sullivan looked away, conceding the point to Cockran. For the moment. Bobby Sullivan was an untamed tiger over whom Cockran had some control. Not a lot. And it wouldn't last long.

Cockran whispered in Sarah Steinberg's ear. "Go down to the assignment commissioner. Have him appoint a new judge. After he does, get a hearing scheduled this afternoon."

"Right away, Mr. Cockran," Sarah said and headed for the door.

COCKRAN, Sarah, Sullivan and Ingrid were ushered into the chambers of Judge John Donnelly at 4:00 p.m. Sarah was surprised, she had told Cockran, to find that the assignment commissioner had already appointed a new judge to the case.

"I've never known them to be that efficient," she had told Cockran.

If Sarah had been surprised to find that the assignment commissioner had already assigned the case to Judge Donnelly, Cockran was even more surprised upon arriving at the Judge's chambers to see a smiling Chet Bowles emerge from the Judge's private office.

"What's Judge Donnelly's reputation?" Cockran asked Sarah in a stage whisper.

"Scuttlebutt in the court is that he's a dirty old man. None of the female clerks like to be assigned to work even for a week in his court because their bottoms end up black and blue from being pinched and squeezed so often."

Cockran walked over to the bailiff, a brunette in her late twenties. She was quite attractive but dressed for business in a crisp white blouse, black skirt and dark stockings.

"The Judge will hear this in the courtroom in a few minutes," the bailiff told Cockran.

Moments later, they were in the courtroom. "All rise," the bailiff said as she rapped a gavel on the desk in front of her and stood while the black-robed Judge Donnelly ascended to the bench. He looked to be in his mid-seventies, compact, maybe five feet eight inches tall. There was a ruddy glow to his sagging face but the nose was even brighter. A hard-drinking man.

"Be seated," the Judge said as he sat down himself. "I've read the file, all the pleadings and looked at all the exhibits as well," he added. "So why are we here today, Mr. Cockran?"

Why the hell was he asking that if he had read the pleadings? Cockran's motion made clear he wanted Waterman held in contempt of court and fined for disobeying Judge Perkins' order to stay away from the Central Park West penthouse.

Cockran stood and began to explain this to the Judge in the courtroom voice he had not used in Judge Perkins' chambers. It was a mellow baritone and the words seemed to flow from him effortlessly. Cockran paused. The Judge was actually smiling. He stopped speaking and looked quizzically at the Judge. "Does Your Honor find any of this amusing?"

The Judge started and shook his head, as if coming out of a trance. "Uh, no, I don't, Mr. Cockran. I apologize, but your voice reminds me so much of your father's. I was a delegate at the 1920 convention, you know, when your father nominated Al Smith. It was the grandest speech I've ever heard. Hearing you now took me back in time. I apologize. Please proceed."

Cockran was annoyed and distracted. Probably it was what Donnelly intended. Eventually he concluded and the Judge asked if he had testimony to offer the court.

"I do, Your Honor. We call Ingrid Waterman."

Ingrid and her testimony were as impressive as she had been before Judge Perkins. If anything, it was even more painful for her than before because it had transpired so recently. The late night arrival of her husband and two other men, each one with a plaster of Paris cast on a forearm. They ripped off her robe and nightgown and held her arms tightly while her husband raped her. After he finished, the two men rolled her over onto her stomach and held her arms and the other her legs while her husband beat her with a belt until she lost consciousness.

Cockran introduced a single photograph that had been taken that morning. A full view, clearly showing the marks of her earlier beatings overlaid with fresh, new welts.

"No further questions, Your Honor," Cockran said.

Chester Bowles sprang to his feet, but the Judge held up his hand. "Sit down, Chet. I'll handle this. I realize you have filed for divorce, Mrs. Waterman," the Judge said in an even voice. "But as of last night, you were still legally married to Wesley Waterman. Correct?"

Ingrid nodded her head.

"You'll have to speak up," the Judge said, admonishing her. "The court reporter can't record a nod of the head."

"Yes, correct," Ingrid said in a tight voice.

With that, the Judge smiled triumphantly and turned to Cockran: "Your contempt motion is denied and your temporary restraining order keeping Mr. Waterman away from his Central Park West apartment is dissolved. I am also dissolving the TRO as it pertains to Mr. Waterman's holdings in I.C.E. I will leave the TRO in effect as to all his other holdings."

Cockran was instantly on his feet. "Your Honor. . ."

But Judge Donnelly cut him off. "Mr. Cockran, the common law is clear that a husband is legally incapable of raping his wife. If he managed to have marital relations with her last night, I say more power to him. Until they're no longer man and wife, your client would be well advised to try and enjoy what the law will not allow her to avoid. I've looked at the photographic evidence and she's a good looking woman," he said, holding up two graphic photos of Ingrid and her blond lover. He had a sly smile on his face as he looked at one, then the other.

"It seems to me she was thoroughly enjoying herself there. Her husband certainly deserves his piece of her even more than her lover. "

"Your Honor! This is a travesty!" Cockran shouted. "He beat her unconscious!"

The Judge looked down at him and this time he did make eye contact. "Mr. Cockran, any red-blooded American husband who discovered his wife with another man doing the lewd and disgusting things this. . . this *woman* is shown doing in these photographs, would have done the same thing. No jury would convict him. In short, Mr. Cockran, she *deserved* it and I have good reason to believe she didn't object in any event. I understand that she's something of a masochist and often asks her husband to punish her." He shook his head. "I don't understand it myself but I suppose married couples can do what they want in the privacy of their own.bedroom."

The Judge rose from the bench, his voice more high-pitched. "So don't use the word 'travesty' to me again, Mr. Cockran, unless it's you who wants to be held in contempt and spend a night in jail. You want to see a travesty?" the Judge asked. "I'll show you a travesty. *These* are a travesty." With that, the Judge took all the glossy photographs of Ingrid with her lover and threw them from his bench. Cockran watched them flutter to the floor at his feet.

"Court's adjourned," Judge Donnelly said, and rapped his wooden gavel on the bench.

29.

How About Europe?

New York City
The Chrysler Building
Monday, 16 May 1932

THEY held a post-mortem in Cockran's office, Sarah and Ingrid sitting in the green club chairs in front of him, Bobby Sullivan in the corner to his side and slightly behind him.

Cockran had been silent and furious the entire ride back from the courthouse. He knew there were bent judges, just like there were bent coppers. He learned that from his father. Tammany Hall politics as usual. But this was so much worse. Waterman had bought a judge, that much was clear. Chet Bowles emerging from Judge Donnelly's private office and the judge saying Ingrid was a masochist was proof of that. But, a hit and run accident killing Judge Perkins? Coincidence? Cockran didn't believe in coincidence when it came to Waterman.

Cockran turned to Sullivan. "Bobby, is there any way you can find out from your contacts if Waterman was behind Judge Perkins' hit and run murder?"

"No, I don't think so. I know Eddie Monahan, and he has his own enemies. Those are the ones who gave me the lowdown on him. I'll ask around. But a hit on a judge is too hot. Odds are it was out of town talent."

Cockran didn't reply and swiveled his chair around and stared out towards the towers of lower Manhattan. What the hell could he do to keep Ingrid safe?

Finally, Sullivan broke the silence. "And would you be finished communing with St. Thomas?" Sullivan asked. "Will you look the other way while I do what needs to be done?"

Cockran knew what Sullivan wanted. The two men lived by different codes. Cockran believed in the rule of law, not men. Sullivan didn't. But there were times, Cockran thought, when Sullivan was right. Last year in Germany, dealing with Nazi thugs out to sabotage the factories of a Cockran client, had been one of them. Today was another. Cockran had no moral objection to Sullivan killing Waterman. Indeed, the one thing possibly keeping Waterman from an early grave was the protective figure of Owney Madden. He suspected, however, that even Owney couldn't save Waterman from Sullivan's wrath if Cockran didn't stay his friend's hand.

The problem was Ingrid. Waterman was a public figure, a captain of industry. I.C.E. was one of the country's biggest companies. His murder while undergoing a messy divorce would inevitably involve Ingrid. There would be an investigation. Those photographs of her would be shown to the police and press, their content publicized even if the actual photos were not. Suspicion would be cast upon her. Sullivan, of course, would have an iron-clad alibi but Owney Madden would know better and he might well tip off the police after the fact.

Cockran decided he would talk later to Sullivan and explain it to him. It was not in his client's best interest to have Waterman killed while the divorce was pending. He would tell Sullivan that killing him after the divorce was a different story entirely. Sullivan would be satisfied with that. He was a patient man. Sometimes.

Cockran swung his chair back around to face Ingrid and Sarah. "Ingrid, your husband bought the judge today and probably had Judge Perkins murdered. You're not safe in New York. We'll appeal and win because the law is on our side. Husbands can't legally rape or beat their wives in New York. But that will take several weeks if not months. Meanwhile, even Mr. Sullivan can't keep you safe here twenty-four hours a day. Too many things could go wrong no matter how many guards we hire. Are there people you can go to back in Minnesota?"

Ingrid was calm and cool. Cockran admired that. Another woman might have broken under the humiliation the judge attempted to heap on her in court. But not Ingrid. She shook her head and replied in a firm voice. "No, Bourke, there isn't. My parents are dead. My brother and sister are traveling in Europe. There's nothing for me in Minnesota. Besides, Wesley knows I grew up outside St. Paul. Even if I stayed with friends there, he would be able to find me."

"Is there anywhere else you can go where your husband couldn't find you?"

Ingrid smiled. "How about Europe?"

"You have friends there you can stay with?" Cockran asked.

Ingrid smiled more broadly this time. "You might say that."

"Where will you stay?"

Ingrid paused and closed her eyes. "I'd rather not say. Will you need to contact me?"

"Probably not," Cockran said. "But it would be useful if we had a way of reaching you."

"Okay. Here's what we'll do," Ingrid said decisively. "We'll have a code. I may be traveling in Europe. I may stay with a friend. I may catch up with my brother and sister and travel with them. Do you have some paper?"

Sarah handed Ingrid a legal pad and Ingrid began to write. When she finished, she handed the legal pad to Cockran. "I'll book passage on the next ocean liner to Hamburg. I won't stay there, but you can leave messages for me at the American Express office. I've numbered each city I may visit. I'll send telegrams from each new city. They will contain chatty, "wish you were here" messages. Within each message will be one — — and only one — number. That's where you can reach me next. At the American Express office in that city. Okay?"

Cockran agreed and turned to Sullivan. "Bobby, we'll have our religious discussion later. Meanwhile, take a suite tonight at the Plaza. Register under false names. Stay with Mrs. Waterman twenty-four hours a day until the next ship leaves for Hamburg. Most ships which dock in Hamburg stop in Ireland first. I need you to sail with her at least as far as Ireland. She should be safe after that. If you do all this, I'll pay for a two-week holiday in Donegal. Just keep me posted where I can reach you if I need you. Will you do this?"

Sullivan eyes were cold. "Could I have a wee word with you in the hall?"

Cockran nodded. He stood up, walked outside with Sullivan.

Sullivan spoke in a soft voice. "I'm not daft. Spending twenty-four hours a day with Mrs. Waterman from now on and then accompanying her on a ship as far as Ireland where I'm to spend a two-week holiday means that Waterman has at least three more weeks to live."

Cockran patiently explained to him why the death of her husband prior to the divorce was not in Ingrid's best interest. After that, Waterman's fate was up to Sullivan and his conscience.

Sullivan nodded his acceptance. "By the way," he said, "it wouldn't have worked."

"What wouldn't have worked?" Cockran asked.

"Telling me St. Thomas Aquinas wouldn't approve me rubbing him out."

"Really?"

Sullivan nodded. "Sod St. Thomas. I trust once Mrs. Waterman is asleep tonight you won't object if I pay a visit to the gentleman in question and teach him some manners?"

"No broken bones?"

Sullivan barely nodded. "Ribs?"

"Okay. Ribs."

Sullivan turned to leave and Cockran spoke again. "Bobby?"

Sullivan turned back.

"Hurt him bad, Bobby. Hurt him real bad."

COCKRAN sat in his empty office after the others had left, a lamp on his desk furnishing the only light. He looked out his window and down the island, the lights of skyscrapers twinkling in the twilight. Cockran had left word at Mattie's hotel of his change in travel plans this morning and to call him tonight by no later than 6:30 p.m. He looked at his watch. 7:15.

This wasn't good. Bobby had convinced him Mattie would be safe in Detroit for at least a day because, as of Sunday evening, no one in Madden's gang knew Eddie Monahan was dead. Mattie would leave Detroit for Chicago on Tuesday morning. Chicago would be the place where she might be in peril, not Detroit. Now he wasn't so sure. Late in the afternoon, he had taken a call from O'Hanlon who had traced the laundry ticket to its owner, Frank Templeton. Like the Schmidt brothers, Templeton was a former MID agent. Like them, a black drape was on his file and could only be lifted by former General Van Deman.

He looked again at the time. 7:40. The New York Central's Wolverine No. 17 left for Detroit at 8:30. If she didn't call in the next twenty minutes, he would have to leave. The MID link between the attacks on him and Mattie was disturbing. Was Waterman somehow mixed up in all those murders Mattie was investigating? The three black drapes might be a coincidence but his days with MID and, later, Michael Collins had taught him to believe in coincidence only if all other explanations were tested first and found wanting.

At 7:55, Cockran had picked up his leather Gladstone bag when the telephone rang.

"Mattie! Is everything all right?"

"Of course, why do you ask?"

"My message this morning asked you to call by 6:30. I was worried. Two nights ago, someone tried to kill you. Remember?"

"Oh, that. I'm sorry. I'm still at the newspaper. I got caught up in typing my notes and lost track of time. Anyway, it's just what I thought, Bourke. Twins! I found the birth certificates for two more victims today. Twin brothers! Ted found the same in Denver. Sisters!"

"That's great, but have you found who's responsible? It's not some maniac if he's using muscle from Owney Madden. And it's worse. I found out Frank was an ex-MID agent who likely works for a retired army general named Van Deman. Waterman used two former MID agents just like Frank to attack me. Last night the same two agents held his wife down while Waterman raped her and then beat her unconscious."

"Oh, that poor woman! Is she alright?"

"For now, yes. Bobby's with her. Look, I'm coming to Detroit on the night train. I'll get in at 7:45 a.m. and grab a taxi to the airport. Don't take off without me."

"I agree about the danger. But why not just call Frank Nitti? He did a swell job in '29."

Cockran shook his head. Great. Add a Chicago gangster to the list of people—and not him—Mattie had needed to keep her safe. How many was it? Four and counting. Nitti, Bobby Sullivan, that bastard who seduced her in Europe and, most recently, that colossal jerk Ted Hudson. He let it pass. Hard to argue with facts. "I don't think so. Nitti had a good reason to keep the IRA off our backs in '29. But the Capone mob doesn't run a bodyguard service. For all we know, they may be in bed with

Madden. And they sure don't want to mess with the feds which is how they may interpret the MID connection Listen, I've got to catch the train." .

Mattie got the message. "It's not necessary, Bourke. Really," she said and paused. He didn't reply and she continued, "But I'll wait at the airport. I love you, you know. Forever."

"Me, too," he replied.

"You'd better."

30.

His Holiday Was Over

Norden, Germany
Friday, 20 May 1932

THE waves of the North Sea rolled gently onto the German coast while the sea gulls flew off in terror from an Alsatian that charged down the beach at breakneck speed. The seagulls squawked their protest at the unruly canine as they flapped away to a safer vantage point. The Alsatian turned his head, tongue hanging from his mouth, and barked to his master for approval.

The teenage girl holding the arm of Kurt von Sturm laughed her approval as the Alsatian came running back to celebrate. "He's after the gulls again, isn't he?" she said, turning her sightless eyes toward her big brother. "I haven't taken him for a walk on the beach in months."

Sturm looked down at his nineteen year old sister Franka, still struggling to merge his memory of the gawky adolescent with the beautiful young woman holding onto his arm now. Her hair was blonde, like Sturm's, straight and smooth, tucked under a handkerchief that bound her hair. She was so beautiful, he thought, her eyes so clear. She didn't appear to be blind until she looked directly at him. It was easy to forget her blindness for a moment and then remember it all over again, the pain almost as fresh as the first time.

"How could you torture poor Storm?" he said. "So close to the beach yet not take him?"

"I need someone to take me!" She said, whirling on him. "Torture for Storm would be a walk on the beach where he couldn't run free! Now you are my eyes and Storm can be a dog."

Sturm felt a pang of guilt. He felt it every time he came home to his mother and sister. He felt it the moment he got off the train and saw Franka already smiling with excitement that her big brother had finally come home but the dignified figure of his mother couldn't have provided a starker contrast. She was still thin, her blonde hair gone white, the burden of raising a young daughter alone weighed down upon her shoulders. But she bore it stoically, with strength, like a good German *Frau* .

She knew his mother loved him, but her eyes still seemed to reflect her disappointment that he had never returned home. Their father killed in the last year of the war, Sturm could have provided the father figure Franka needed and helped his widowed mother raise his little sister. For a von Strasser, however, Germany came first, as it always had. His work for Geneva meant that he rarely found time to visit his mother and sister.

His mother had never said so directly, and Sturm was certain she never would, but he often wondered whether she blamed him for what had happened to his sister. Franka had been blinded in a riding accident when she was nine years old. Sturm was away. She had been riding that morning with their mother and, had Sturm been home, he would have been with them, riding as a family as he had done with his parents during his childhood. Because he had not been there, Franka was deprived of such a childhood.

Three ill-clothed, hungry men had attempted to waylay a well-dressed woman and child, easy pickings in a post-war Germany on the verge of anarchy. But his beautiful, blonde mother — her hair color not yet changed — had reacted as the lioness she was, striking the brigands with her riding crop and urging Franka to spur her horse into a gallop. Her mother had done the same and the shots which followed in their wake missed. Franka was a good rider but her horse had been startled by the shots and she could not bring the stallion under control and her mother's mare could not keep pace. A mile from the ambush it happened. Her horse stopped short at a fence and Franka was thrown free, her head hitting a rock, her world cast into darkness.

Sturm and Franka were drawing near the seaside home that Sturm had bought for them five years ago. He could see the outward edge of the long screened porch on the front of the house which rested on the grassy hilltop facing the sea. He had chosen the house because Franka could enjoy the ocean breeze from the porch and listen to the waves roll against the shore. He saw another figure on the hill, standing outlined against the porch. It was his mother and she was waving to them with one hand. The other rested at her side and it was holding something.

Sturm's smile faded at the sight of it as they drew closer. Telegrams reaching him in Norden invariably meant communiqués from Geneva. His mother knew enough to know that telegrams from Geneva were important. Sturm knew enough to know that his holiday was over.

THE telegram was from Berlin. Fritz von Thyssen—not the city. The telephone was located in the sitting room, looking out over the enclosed porch onto the North Sea. Sturm sat down, called the operator and placed a call to the private line he'd memorized years before and waited for the other line to pick up. Through the window, he saw his mother sitting with Franka on the hilltop as Storm sat quietly beside them, resting from his foray on the beach.

"Kurt," a familiar voice answered. "Thank you. I'm sorry to have interrupted—"

"I read the telegram," Sturm said tersely. He didn't have the energy to maintain his usual pretense of deference. "Apologies accepted. Go on."

"Manhattan needs you," Berlin said, taking Sturm's cue. "He wants you to take over."

"Why?"

"I'm afraid Bruno was not successful in New York."

Berlin's words reached him through the telephone like a punch in the stomach. "That's impossible," Sturm said. "What happened?"

"Bruno's primary target fled the country before he could begin his operation."

"Then it was out of Bruno's hands. Let him pursue the target. I'm on holiday," Sturm said, not bothering to hide the edge in his voice. "You told me the Executive Committee of the Geneva Group approved my recommendation of Bruno."

"Manhattan specifically asked that you now supervise the operation. Geneva approved his use of Bruno but he does not consider this assignment as one being conducted under Geneva's auspices," Berlin said. There was the rub, Sturm thought and he didn't like it. He was not hired help to serve at Manhattan's beck and call. "He asked me to appeal to you directly."

"Bruno can handle it," Sturm said, speaking to himself as much as to Berlin.

"If you were just to help Bruno, work as a team as you have for so many years—"

"No."

"But the target has fled to *Germany*," Berlin said. "It would take only a few days out of your holiday and you would be back home by mid-week. And generously compensated."

"I haven't seen my family in over a year and now you're asking me to leave them again," Sturm said. "How will you compensate me for that?"

Berlin exhaled on the other end of the telephone. Sturm could tell he was growing frustrated. Too bad. "Kurt, we must not alienate Manhattan. You know that. Milan is only a few persuasive words away from joining us. With Milan, we would control three fifths of the Executive Committee. That will permit us even greater influence within the Geneva Group to put a real leader in as Chancellor, one who will guide Germany back to greatness. We both know von Schleicher is not that man. Isn't that why you've sacrificed all these years?"

Berlin's voice was almost pleading. "If we lose Manhattan, we lose our most important ally and we are thrown back to the beginning at the most crucial moment. Manhattan is not from Germany. The stakes are not the same for him. We cannot afford to lose him. Please, Kurt, as a favor to your old mentor. I need you to take over. Germany needs you. *Herr* Hitler needs you."

Outside, Sturm saw that his mother had left Franka by herself on the hillside looking out onto the North Sea. She had grown so fast. And she was so indescribably beautiful.

Sturm closed his eyes.

"Who is the target?"

"Manhattan's wife."

Sturm opened his eyes wide. My God! Manhattan's wife! Thank heaven Bruno had failed. Because Kurt von Sturm knew Manhattan's wife. Intimately.

"I'll call you back," Sturm said and disconnected the telephone line.

"Will you be going away?"

He was startled by the voice of his mother, unaware that she had been standing at the entrance to the sitting room, watching him. He looked out the window. Franka still sat outside with Storm, listening to the surf. Sturm rose from his seat and walked over to his mother.

"Only for a few days," Sturm said, taking hold of her arms. "But you will hear from me shortly and I am going to need your help. You must follow whatever instructions I give you without question or hesitation. Do you understand?"

She looked at him with sad eyes, as though seeing a different man than her only son. "Who is to die this time?" she said.

"No one, mother," Sturm said, truthfully. "Not if I can help it."

Kurt von Sturm would not allow the wife of Manhattan to die at the hands of his friend and protégé Bruno Kordt. To do so would not be honorable. And Kurt von Sturm was an honorable man. He could not—and would not—permit Ingrid Waterman to be killed.

PART II

America and Germany

21 May — 28 May 1932

Racial hygiene in Germany remained until 1926 a purely academic and scientific movement. It was the Americans who busied themselves earnestly about the subject.

Reinhold Müller, 1932

[T]he parallel development of political and scientific ideas is not by chance but rather by internal necessity. We geneticists and racial hygienists have been fortunate to have seen our quiet work in the scientific laboratory find application in the life of the people.

Doctor Otmar Freiherr von Verschuer

31.

What List?

ERNST "Putzi" Hanfstaengl's palms were sweaty and he reproached himself for being nervous. After all, he had known Adolf Hitler for over eight years and, unlike the sycophants around him, Putzi was not a member of the Nazi party. Nor did he refer to Hitler as "*mein Fuhrer*," as did everyone else. No, Putzi contented himself with a simple "*Herr* Hitler." Nevertheless, Hitler had summoned him to an audience at the former Barlow Palace, now called the Brown House, Nazi party headquarters. While he was flattered, he was also apprehensive.

Putzi looked at his watch and glanced around the antechamber. He smiled to himself. The gleaming marble, the polished wood and the brass fixtures seemed very much at odds with the "Socialist" and "Workers" portion of the Nazi party's full name.

It well could be, Putzi thought, that Hitler simply wanted his advice. After all, he basically served as Hitler's unofficial foreign press secretary. With an American mother and having been schooled at Harvard, Putzi spoke fluent, unaccented English. Indeed, he had introduced Hitler to the wealthy circles in which Putzi had traveled since childhood. He even introduced him to his own tailor so that the Nazi chief no longer wore ill-fitting suits which made him look like the son of an Austrian customs official. Which he was. Now, Hitler wore white tie and tails with the best of them at the opera or glittering dinner parties.

Putzi knew that other Nazi leaders in Hitler's entourage laughed at him behind his back and, occasionally, Hitler would do so to his face. Putzi took it all in good humor. He was a big man, well over six feet tall, with swept-back black hair and he towered over Hitler and the other Nazis in height as well as class.

Come the fall, however, no one would dare laugh at him again and even Hitler would cease poking fun. Because, by that time, he would be able to casually let it drop that he was a personal friend of the President of the United States as they had been classmates together at Harvard where Putzi knew him as "Frank". Franklin D. Roosevelt's election as president, of course, wasn't a sure thing. First, he had to be nominated but, as governor of America's largest state, he clearly had the inside track. And America's economy was so bad and not getting better that once Frank secured the nomination, he was as good as in. Hoover was a dead duck.

A friend of the American President and a confidante of Germany's next chancellor. No one would be laughing at him then. In fact, when Hitler came to power, as Putzi knew he would, perhaps being named German ambassador to America might well be in his future.

A buzzer sounded. "Yes. At once, *mein Fuhrer*" Hitler's blond, male secretary Friedrich Heinz said. Placing down the phone, he looked across at Putzi. "You may go in now, *Herr* Hanfstaengl. *Der Fuhrer* is ready to see you." There was a note of deference in his voice, which Putzi appreciated. Not only was Hitler's new secretary a poster child for Aryan supremacy, but he was respectful of his betters. Heinz was a good man.

Putzi thanked him and walked through the door into Hitler's spacious office.

Hitler, of course, was not really ready for Putzi. Half-moon spectacles on his nose, he was engrossed in reading the sheet of paper in his hand and did not even look up when his secretary announced *"Herr* Hanfstaengl to see you, *mein Fuhrer."*

Putzi approached the desk and stood there, hands behind his back like a schoolboy summoned to the headmaster's office, and waited. A good two minutes passed before Hitler looked up and appeared surprised to see Putzi in front of his desk. Taking off the glasses, which he never used in public, Hitler smiled and stood up.

"Putzi, my old friend, how good to see you," Hitler said as he grabbed Putzi's big right hand in both of his and held it warmly, his vivid blue eyes locking onto Putzi's. "I am so pleased that you could take time from your busy schedule to come in for a chat."

Putzi preened at Hitler's stroking. "Thank you, *Herr* Hitler. I always have time for the future chancellor of Germany, the man destined to be the Fatherland's savior."

Hitler smiled and, preliminaries over, motioned Putzi over to a sofa covered in leather the shade of oxblood. Hitler took a seat in a straight-backed wooden chair.

Putzi took the proffered seat and once more smiled to himself. Hitler always sat him on that sofa because, with Hitler in the straight-backed chair, his head was now higher than Putzi's whose ample posterior had sunk several inches into the sofa's soft leather cushion.

"Please give me your assessment, Putzi, of where the industrialists and the Conservative and Nationalist parties stand today."

So Putzi began to tell Hitler what he thought the Nazi leader needed to hear. Chancellor Brüning's days were numbered. He had made a big mistake banning the Nazi's military wing, known as the S.A., the brown-shirted Storm troopers. People needed jobs and Brüning had already strangled the economy by raising taxes and tariffs. Sooner or later Brüning was sure to lose a vote of confidence in the *Reichstag* and Putzi believed it would be sooner. While the Nazis were only the second-largest party in the *Reichstag* today, Putzi had no doubt that at the next national election, they would establish themselves as Germany's largest party.

"Who do your rich friends believe will replace Brüning as chancellor?" Hitler asked.

"Sadly, *Herr* Hitler," Putzi replied, "they do not believe President Hindenburg can be persuaded to appoint you. At least not at this time."

"That was not my question, Putzi," Hitler replied softly, with the barest hint of menace.

Putzi strained to hear Hitler and leaned forward. "The most persistent rumors I hear," he replied, "are that either von Papen or von Schleicher will be the next Chancellor and, like Brüning, they will have to rule by presidential decree, leaving the *Reichstag* still as powerless as it has been with Brüning."

Hitler nodded as if he expected Putzi to say that but he made no reply. After a few moments, Putzi continued. "Many think that, once he is Chancellor, von Papen will offer you the post of vice-chancellor. If you accept that, *Herr* Hitler, which I strongly advise that you do, you will become the second most powerful man in Germany."

"Have you expressed this opinion to your rich friends, Putzi?"

Putzi again missed the menace in Hitler's voice because he once more had anticipated the question and his mind had raced ahead to formulate the answer. "Of course, *Herr* Hitler."

"You idiot!" Hitler shouted as he leaped to his feet and threw the papers he had been holding down onto the plush black and gold carpet. "If you know what's good for you, you will refrain in the future from offering your worthless opinion in public about me or the party. It's bad enough that Strasser goes behind my back to talk up the Nazis joining a coalition government. I don't need my foreign press spokesman doing the same! Is that clear?" Hitler shouted once more, flecks of spittle flying in Putzi's direction.

Startled, Putzi nodded submissively. Gregor Strasser was Hitler's right-hand man and more popular with the party rank-and-file than anyone except Hitler himself. "Yes, *Herr* Hitler. Perfectly clear."

"Good," Hitler said, his tone of voice normal now. "Because von Papen visited me today and offered me the vice-chancellorship. He said that he would be Chancellor before the end of the month. And do you know what I told him?"

"You turned him down?" Putzi asked in a timid tone of voice.

"Exactly," Hitler said. "But do you know why?"

Putzi only shook his head dumbly from side to side.

"Of course not, you dimwit! You yourself pointed out why but you were too stupid to recognize it. We will soon be the largest party in Germany and, once we are, no Chancellor, Brüning or von Papen, will be able to govern without our support."

"But what if von Papen governs by presidential decree, like Brüning?" Putzi asked.

Hitler smiled but there was no humor behind it. "We will make the country ungovernable. The streets will run red with the blood of our enemies. And that senile old fool Hindenburg will send for me because he will have no choice. By then, even he will recognize that only I stand between a restored Germany and the anarchy of the Jews and Communists."

"But Brüning has banned the Storm troopers," Putzi said.

Hitler laughed and this time, Putzi realized there was humor behind the laugh.

"He's banned the wearing of brown shirts," Hitler said. "So we won't wear them. The brown shirts don't give the Storm troopers their power. Their power comes from their fists, their clubs, their guns and the deserved fear they strike in the hearts of all those who oppose us."

Hitler walked back to his desk, clearly signaling that the conference was over. Putzi stood up, bent over, picked up the papers which Hitler had thrown on the floor, realigned them, and handed them back across the desk toward Hitler, who had resumed his seat and was looking at another paper he had picked up. Putzi hesitated. He wasn't certain he should bring this up but, through a mutual acquaintance, he had received an inquiry from a German *émigré* in Great Britain. He had known nothing about it and couldn't reply. So he had made several inquiries of his own and ran up against what his American friends would call a stone wall.

Putzi had thought nothing of it at the time, but last week in Berlin, an American reporter had asked a disturbingly similar question. Hitler looked up and noticed Putzi was still standing there. "Is there something more, Putzi?" Hitler asked.

"Yes, *Herr* Hitler. The SS is growing rapidly," Putzi said, referring to Hitler's praetorian guard headed by Heinrich Himmler. "I understand they have even begun acquiring their own businesses."

Hitler waved his hand impatiently, "Yes, yes, Putzi. What of it? Our Heinie is an ambitious man. Good for him."

"Well, *Herr* Hitler," Putzi began, "I have received several inquiries about a new medical facility the SS has opened in the Bavarian National Forest near Passau and, in the event I receive more questions like this, I would like to know how to respond."

Putzi stiffened when he saw Hitler's eyes squint, his lips drawn together in a thin line. His voice was low and Putzi once more strained to hear.

"There is no medical facility at Passau." Hitler said and again began to read the paper.

Putzi turned and walked toward the door. He was halfway there when Hitler once more spoke, his voice soft but clearly audible. "One more thing, Putzi."

"Yes, *mein Führer?*" Putzi asked timidly. He had not missed the menace this time.

"Never mention Passau again unless you wish your name to be placed on my list."

Putzi gulped and then screwed up his courage. "What list?" he asked, feeling his throat constrict.

"The list containing those whose heads will be the first to roll when we take power. Gregor Strasser is working his way onto that list. Make sure you don't end up there with him." Hitler replied and then lowered his eyes once more, again dismissing Putzi from his presence.

Putzi did not need to be told twice.

Chartwell
Kent, England
Saturday, 21 May 1932

WINSTON Churchill placed the telephone receiver down, put his unlit Havana cigar back in his mouth and took a sip from a glass of weak Johnnie Walker Red Label and soda at his right hand on the library writing desk where he sat. In less than two weeks, his god-daughter had made substantial progress. He felt this vindicated his decision to invoke the aid of W.R. Hearst in unraveling the mystery of ten dead bodies in America.

Twins! Who would have imagined it? But there was more work to do. When the telephone rang, he knew the call he had placed moments ago to the Prof was ready.

"Lindemann here."

"Prof!" Winston growled into the phone. "Sorry to disturb you on a Saturday evening but I'm just off a trans-Atlantic call from my god-daughter, the Hearst reporter, Mattie McGary, who is investigating those baffling deaths in America I spoke to you about a few weeks ago. She informed me she discovered some important clues which may assist us in getting to the bottom of these crimes. I would value your input on their meaning."

"What are these clues you refer to?"

"Well, all we knew before was that the bodies were found naked, drained of blood and their eyes missing. But Mattie has found two additional facts. All the eyes were surgically removed and all the victims were twins. What do you make of that?"

Lindemann paused and an uncharacteristically patient Winston waited as the Prof drew on his pipe while he gathered his thoughts. "Twins, eh? I recall monographs I've read from the Kaiser Wilhelm Institute in Berlin on twins and eye color. But that was several years ago and I can't recall the author's name. I'll see what I can find on this."

"Good man, Prof, I knew I could count on you," Churchill replied.

32.

Personal and Confidential

The Cedars,
Sands Point, Long Island
Sunday, 22 May 1932

IT was a beautiful spring day and the sun was streaming in the kitchen window as Mattie brewed a pot of tea. Mattie loved Sundays at The Cedars. Long rides on the beach with Bourke and Paddy followed by a delicious dinner cooked by Cockran's mother-in-law, Mary Morrissey. Mattie had her own bedroom, of course, in order to keep up appearances. Mattie knew that Mary wasn't fooled. But appearances were important and Mattie dutifully followed the rules, carefully mussing up her unused bed each morning. She intended to stay in the good graces of Mary who had even confided on one occasion that she couldn't understand why Bourke hadn't proposed.

Today, however, was special. Her twins story was being published. She and Cockran had spent the last week together. He had met her in Detroit Tuesday morning and they had flown to Chicago. It took her two days there instead of one to track down the marriage certificate of the female victim, Annette Harrison Andrews. She lived in Chicago but had been married in Gary, Indiana. Her maiden name matched the name of the male victim in St. Louis, Anthony Harrison.

The same was true on Thursday in St. Louis where she found the birth certificates for the Harrison twins. Annette had been the oldest, by twenty-seven minutes. Mattie and Cockran had flown back to New York on Friday. She met Ted Hudson on Saturday at *The New York American* and, after her brief call to Churchill, they had spent all day writing the story.

Mattie heard a car outside and saw the green Packard pull in beside the long porch. Moments later Cockran was inside with a big grin on his face. "Here you go, vampire hunter," he said, handing her one of the three copies he held under his arm, the other two being for him and Paddy, who kept his own scrapbook of Mattie's articles.

Mattie frowned. Vampires? Then she looked at the big black headline. TWINS PREY TO UNKNOWN VAMPIRE KILLER. Underneath that, in only slightly smaller type, was POLICE FORCES BAFFLED. Damn it! Ted Hudson! That devious bastard! Once they were both back in New York, Ted had resurrected the vampire angle which he wanted to hype. They had argued for hours yesterday and finally Hearst himself had to intervene. He sided with Mattie. They would not hype the vampire angle. The twins connection was startling enough.

Mattie quickly scanned the story, relieved to see the copy was unchanged.

"What's the matter?" Cockran asked. "You don't seem pleased."

Mattie smiled. "No, I'm pleased. The story is fine. It's just that damned vampire headline. That snake Ted Hudson snuck it in behind my back!"

Cockran grinned. "Heaven forbid that the phrases 'I told you so' and 'I warned you' should ever pass my lips."

Mattie shot him a warning look but the bastard's grin just grew wider and she smiled in spite of herself. "I thought I had won when Hearst took my side in favor of not hyping the vampire angle. It never occurred to me that Ted would do an end run around both of us to the headline writers. Damn it! It makes the story seem less serious. The fact is, it's only one man, not a vampire, and I'll bet Owney Madden knows who this mysterious Dr. V is."

"Why not tell the police about Madden?" Cockran asked.

"For the same reason Madden's name is not mentioned in the article. We have no sources. At least no live sources. Ted Hudson killed them both. Remember?"

"Good point. So what's next?"

"We wait and see what turns up," Mattie replied, directing Cockran's attention to a box set off in the middle of the story.

> ### $500 REWARD
> The Hearst papers are offering a $500 reward to anyone providing information leading to the arrest and conviction of the persons responsible for these crimes. Contact Mattie McGary or Ted Hudson c/o *The New York American*, 50 Broadway, New York, New York.

MATTIE and Cockran had gone for a late afternoon walk on the beach and were just returning when they saw Paddy running up to greet them.

"Mattie! Mattie! You had a phone call from Mr. Hearst. He wants you to call him right away. Here's the telephone number," he said, thrusting a piece of paper at Mattie.

Once inside, Mattie called the operator and had her place a long distance call to William Randolph Hearst's castle-like home in California, San Simeon.

"Hearst residence, Miss Davies speaking."

"Marion! It's Mattie. Answering the phone now, are you? How've you been?"

"Mattie! It's been ages. I'm fine. The staff is off today. How are you?"

"Great! Did you see my new story?"

"I did. It's really scary. Were you calling for W.R.?"

"Yes. I'm with Bourke at The Cedars. The Chief left a message for me to call."

Moments later Hearst was on the phone. "Mattie, I've just had a call from *The New York American*. A letter was received addressed to you 'personal and confidential.' I'm having a messenger deliver it out to Sands Point. Let me know what it says," Hearst said.

"Will do, Chief. You'll be the first to know."

Cockran fixed martinis while Mattie settled down to reread her story. Thirty minutes later there was a knock. Cockran retrieved the envelope and Mattie tore it open and read aloud:

Dear Miss McGary,

I work for the Carnegie Institution at its Station for Experimental Evolution, a biological laboratory at Cold Spring Harbor on Long Island. I read your article today in the Sunday paper. I don't know what to do, but I'm very afraid more people may die. Please meet me tomorrow at 7 p.m. on the observation deck of the Empire State Building. I've seen your photograph. I'll find you.

"What do you think?" Mattie asked.

"Interesting," Cockran replied.

"Do you think I'm still in danger from Madden's men or ex-MID agents ?" Mattie asked.

"Not from Owney. Bobby told me that once the story was out in the public eye, Madden wouldn't dare move against you. As to former MID agents, I don't know. So be careful."

"You want to join me?" Mattie asked.

"I do," Cockran replied. "But I can't. Donovan and I are having dinner tomorrow night with a client who wants to form a German subsidiary for his chemical company."

"Do you think I should take Ted? It's still his story too."

"Ordinarily, I'd say no on general principles. But having him along for protection is probably a good idea. Besides, you and I still will be sleeping together afterwards."

Mattie smiled. "Is that a promise or a proposition?"

"Both."

33.

Three Obstacles

Hamburg, Germany
Monday, 23 May 1932

BRUNO Kordt reminded Sturm of someone else. He sat across from Sturm in the corner of a dark Hamburg beer cellar, the smoke from their Eckstein cigarettes gathering above them in the low stone ceiling. He was seething in frustration, his tie loosened and several buttons of his vest undone, his muscles tensing under his clothes. But it wasn't another man of whom Sturm was reminded. Rather, Bruno's body language reminded Sturm of his family Alsatian after an afternoon spent straining at his chain to chase a field rabbit. His mind understood that he could not chase the rabbit, but his body would not accept it. Yes, Sturm thought, swap the stein of pilsner for a bowl of water and you had the same frustration in the body of his young protégé.

Bruno leaned back, exhaling smoke. "For all the legendary tales of New York gangsters, I expected much more from the Americans," he said. "They are nothing but amateurs!"

"Reputation and performance are not the same." Sturm said.

Bruno took a swallow of pilsner. "I have failed before," he said. "I can handle failure. I am not angry because of my mistakes. But this! My success was entirely dependent on what I was told by these agents of Manhattan! Amateurs!" He slapped his open palm on the thick mahogany table and took another drag on his cigarette.

Sturm let him talk. He encouraged these informal evenings so that Bruno could loosen up and express his frustrations. Sturm enjoyed the casual atmosphere but he never forgot Bruno's purpose this evening: to plan the abduction, interrogation, and murder of Manhattan's wife.

On the short train journey from Norden to Hamburg, Sturm had identified three key obstacles to his plan for Ingrid. The first was that Bruno could not know of the plan. The chance that Bruno would turn on Sturm was high, too high to risk. The ideal outcome would keep Bruno completely in the dark so that their mentor-protégé relationship remained unchanged.

The second obstacle was the most open to chance, the most difficult to control. Sturm must find a way to speak to Manhattan's wife unobserved. But when he did so, would she recognize him? Would she trust him? He knew where to hide her, but how would she react.?

The third obstacle was the most delicate. The actual plan to kill her must be entirely Bruno's idea. If Sturm designed the operation and it failed—as he intended it to fail—Bruno might suspect Sturm. The plan must belong to Bruno so that the failure belonged to Bruno. He must have no time to suspect Sturm. That would afford the opportunity to hide Manhattan's wife.

A crowded public space. Keep Bruno in the dark. Make the plan Bruno's own idea. Those were Sturm's watchwords tonight. But he needed to learn the latest. So Bruno told him everything about New York. The first operation went smoothly. Some local magistrate, a Jew, who needed to be eliminated, which Bruno handled with an automobile accident.

"A woman, too. I couldn't believe it. But they told me she was corrupt, bought out by Manhattan's enemies," Bruno said through a haze of smoke. "But I didn't like that she was a woman. I don't care if she was corrupt, it felt wrong to kill a woman. Excessive."

Sturm listened carefully to a hint of remorse. Might it carry over to Bruno's next assignment? Sadly, no, he thought as Bruno learned forward, clearly intending to impress his mentor. "But an assignment is an assignment and I will not fail however distasteful I might find it personally. Isn't that what you've always told me?" That was, in fact, what he always told Bruno. The assignment came first. Sturm could only nod in response. Keep Bruno in the dark.

"Then they gave me the details of the second operation. Killing another woman!"

"Manhattan's wife," Sturm said.

"Precisely." Bruno had started by following Manhattan's wife, but it hadn't been easy. Manhattan's agents would not reveal her name, in keeping with the Geneva Group's standing policy restricting access to the identities of its members. So Bruno was given only a photograph and a tip on the wife's recent whereabouts. Bruno located her quickly but he could not get close enough. She had protection with her, a hard-eyed and menacing Irishman. Bruno had followed long enough to see the two board the *Bremen* of the North German Lloyd Line.

His mission now compromised, Bruno left word with Manhattan's liaison, contacted Berlin and boarded the next direct ocean liner to Germany which had arrived a full day before his target's ship. Already, he knew she had reservations at the *Vier Jahreszeiten*.

"How do you plan to finish it?"

Bruno put down his empty glass of pilsner. "The room service ploy. I already have a good relationship with the manager and I know the room where she will be staying."

It was unimaginative, but simple and effective. Sturm analyzed the plan, as he would any plan, searching for weaknesses and unintended consequences. "No good," Sturm said quickly. "It will look like a professional hit." He took a sip of his lager. "How would you interrogate? Manhattan wants to know what she's learned about certain confidential matters."

Bruno started to answer but stopped himself. "You are right," he said angrily. "The noise from her screams would be unacceptable."

"We will need an isolated location for her interrogation but, like her death, we must also take her in a way that does not raise suspicion."

"Yes, she must disappear from someplace public," Bruno said.

Good, Sturm thought, he had taken the bait. "Precisely."

Bruno leaned forward on the table. "Could we approach her in an official capacity?"

"Yes, that is possible," Sturm said, pleased at Bruno's ingenuity.

"She is booked on a train the next day, *der Fliegende Hamburger*. I could have the hotel manager inform her that there has been a problem with her ticket, something having to do with her American citizenship," Bruno said, "something that would force her to clear up the problem at the ticket counter in the station. I would be waiting there in a staff uniform. I can innocently guide her down to the offices at the far end of the platform, away from the crowds. There, in private, we can force her into a waiting motorcar and remove her to a secure location for the interrogation. No one will notice. With the North Sea nearby, her body will never be found."

Sturm considered this and took a long draft of his lager to buy himself time. "It might work, but it will require our best efforts. We will have to track her from the hotel to the rail station. She may be with her lawyer. Or her lover. We must prepare for every possibility"

Bruno appeared deflated. "But you think it is a good plan?"

The barman brought over a fresh stein of pilsner for Bruno and another glass of lager for Sturm. Sturm raised his glass. "It is a good plan, Bruno. A good challenge, something to hone our skills for more important operations in the days to come."

"*Ja,* in two days' time, Manhattan will be free of his wife," Bruno said. "Permanently." They each raised their glasses and touched them lightly together in a toast.

34.

Helen Talbot

MATTIE picked up a taxi on Fifth Avenue outside Cockran's townhouse and headed downtown to Grand Central Station. Following Cockran's instructions on how to evade surveillance, she quickly dashed inside and was swallowed up in the crowds of commuters and caught another taxi. If someone were following her, she didn't notice.

Arriving at the Empire State Building, she walked into the lobby and met Hudson.

"Hi, gorgeous. I've missed you," Ted said, kissing her lightly on her cheek. "I take it the boyfriend has more important things to do tonight than be with you?"

Mattie rolled her eyes. "Something like that. Look, Ted, if you want your byline to stay on this story, don't piss me off. One more crack about Cockran and I'm pissed off. *Capisce*?"

"*Capisco*," Hudson replied in correct Italian to Mattie's surprise. Well, she thought, he *was* an intelligence agent.

"Seriously, Ted," Mattie said. "My source is skittish. I don't even know if it's a man or a woman. Make yourself inconspicuous. We don't want to scare off whoever it is."

"Understood," Ted replied as they headed toward the elevators.

At the top, Mattie left Ted behind and moved out onto the observation deck alone. It was an overcast night. She looked up and could see the glow of the lights shining through the cloud and illuminating the art deco spire on top of the building. There literally was nothing to see, so Mattie walked around the perimeter of the observation deck, waiting for someone to approach her. Then she felt a strong hand grip her wrist, pulling her towards the building to a place in the shadows, twenty feet away from the screened enclosure of the outer ring of the observation deck.

Mattie looked down at a small woman, wearing a gray raincoat with a navy blue scarf covering her silver-gray permanent-waved hair. She wore rimless spectacles and kept glancing to her right and left, reminding Mattie of the darting glances of a small bird.

"Miss McGary, my name is Helen Talbot. I sent you the note. Thank you for coming."

"You're welcome," Mattie said. "But tell me. What has you so scared?"

"I'm on the Carnegie Institution's payroll but I actually work at the Eugenics Record Office at Cold Spring Harbor. I'm a private secretary but I also work with the I.C.E. analytical machines and punch cards in data processing. In February, I made a special run with the machines at the request of my two bosses Dr. Davenport and Mr. Laughlin. They wanted me to search through the Cold Spring Harbor data base on hundreds of twins in the United States which they had collected for the past twenty-five years. They wanted twenty twin adults of either sex who lived alone and apart from each other. At least ten of the twins had to be identical."

Eugenics? Mattie thought. Cold Spring Harbor? That was only a short way up the coast from Bourke's place on Long Island. And she had heard the names Davenport and Laughlin before. From Cockran. His court battles against forced sterilization. His dislike for Ted Hudson was exceeded only by his contempt for what he termed the pseudo-science of eugenics and the men behind it like Davenport and Laughlin. But how did twins fit into the picture?

Helen Talbot paused as if to catch her breath, and then continued, the words spilling out and tumbling over one another. "I didn't think it was unusual. I receive all sorts of data base search requests. After all, twins are always visiting the laboratory for tests and interviews. I put together the list for them. Ten sets of twins. I remember the names. But now I'm scared."

"Why is that?" Mattie asked.

"Ten of those names were carried in your article yesterday as victims."

Mattie gasped and struggled to maintain her composure and find her voice. "What about the other ten names?" she finally asked in a halting voice.

"That's what I'm afraid of," Helen Talbot replied. "According to your article, half the names on that list are dead. I fear for the other ten."

"Who are the other ten people on the list?" Mattie asked.

Talbot reached into her purse and handed Mattie a typewritten sheet of paper. "The identical twins. All twenty names and their addresses are listed on this sheet."

Mattie took the sheet and was instantly chilled. The woman was right. Half the names on that list were indeed the victims noted in her article. Mattie looked more closely at the list. There were twenty-two names and addresses, not twenty. She asked Helen Talbot about this.

"Oh, yes. There were two more added early last week. They're the ones at the bottom. It was strange how it happened. Professor Davenport and Mr. Laughlin told me they had a visitor and asked me to fetch the list of twenty twins. I did and when I returned, they had been joined by Dr. Lothrop Stoddard whom I knew from previous visits and someone new—a tall silver-haired man with blue, almost violet eyes. Dr. Otmar von Verschuer."

Mattie froze when she heard the name. Was this Dr. V.? "What happened then?"

"Verschuer was very rude," Talbot said. "He literally snatched the list right out of my hand and penciled in the two names. That's how the list got to be twenty-two."

Helen Talbot pulled Mattie close. "I'm scared, Miss McGary. Really scared. I don't know what's going on. I only know that I used our I.C.E. machine to compile a list of the names and addresses of twenty people, all of them twins. Now half of them are dead. What's going to happen to the other ten? Or twelve? Are they dead too? Or will they end up that way?"

Mattie shook her head. "I don't know, Helen. I honestly don't know. But you've done a good thing. You really have. I'm going to track down these people first thing in the morning. Let's pray they're still alive. But before I go, let me ask you to do one more thing."

Mattie wrote down Helen's address and phone number. Then she wrote down an address on Third Avenue and handed it to the woman. "I'll see you in the morning. Thanks again."

MATTIE said goodbye to Helen Talbot and watched her get into the elevator. Then she walked over to Ted. They rode down alone in an elevator and she filled him in on everything Helen Talbot had told her. Ted scribbled in his reporter's notebook as Mattie talked.

"Where does Talbot live?" Hudson asked.

Mattie gave him the address in the West Seventies and Hudson took it down.

Mattie then gave Hudson his orders for the next day. "I'm going to call the Chief tonight and ask him to have someone start tracking down the whereabouts of the other ten names on the original list. You check out the two handwritten names. Find out what's the story with them."

"What are you going to do?" Hudson asked.

"Me? First, I'm going to have some reporters at the *New York American* check out Davenport and Laughlin so thoroughly we'll know the last time they each slept with their wives or girlfriends."

Hudson smiled. "I'm not certain how useful *that* will be. But what will *you* be doing?"

"I've got other angles to follow," Mattie replied.

"Like what?" Ted asked.

Mattie sighed. "Ted, just check out the last two names. We'll compare notes tomorrow."

35.

She Had a Spare

New York City
Tuesday, 24 May 1932

MATTIE took a booth at the rear of a stainless steel diner on Third Avenue in the Fifties. Cockran had been asleep when she returned home and had left a note for her in the morning explaining that he had an early breakfast meeting with his new German clients. Now she would have to wait until this evening to go over with him the new eugenics angle to the mystery. She ordered coffee and two eggs over easy and waited for Helen Talbot to arrive.

Mattie took a sip of her coffee and started in on her eggs. She looked at her watch. Helen was already fifteen minutes late. This was not good. Mattie finished her breakfast and was certain she had been stood up. She looked at her watch again. 8:40. She decided to wait another twenty minutes, a full hour, before giving up on Helen and starting on the rest of her day.

At ten minutes of nine, Helen Talbot walked in. Mattie caught her eye. Helen smiled and nervously walked over. She slid onto the seat opposite Mattie.

"I apologize for being so late, Miss McGary."

"Please, call me Mattie."

"Mattie. I overslept. I was so distressed last night that I couldn't sleep. So I took a sleeping pill. When that didn't work, I took another."

"That's all right, you're here now. So explain to me. You work at some place called the Eugenics Record Office but your paycheck comes from the Carnegie Institution?"

Helen nodded. "That's correct. Half of the staff are on the Carnegie payroll. Checks for the other half are from the Rockefeller Foundation. Except my bosses."

"Remind me again. Who are your bosses?"

"Dr. Charles Davenport and Mr. Harry Laughlin. Together, they run the Eugenics Record Office. Mr. Laughlin is the Eugenics Record Office's primary spokesman. He spends a lot of his time outside the office meeting with politicians. He travels to Washington a lot."

"What about Davenport?"

"He's more the inside man. He's in Cold Spring Harbor most of the time. He directs all the research we do. He oversees the medical staff as well."

Mattie raised her eyebrows. "Why would a record office have a medical staff?"

"Oh, my, we have a lot more than just the Eugenics Record Office at Cold Spring Harbor. We have a laboratory, classrooms, patient observation rooms. The ERO is the hub, so to speak, but there are lots of spokes. We have six buildings there."

Mattie scribbled some notes on her reporter's pad and ordered more coffee for both of them. Helen declined Mattie's offer of breakfast.

"I don't think I could hold any food down right now," she had said.

"I understand." Mattie said. "Can you tell me more about this Dr. Verschuer?"

Helen hesitated. "Dr. V? I really don't like him. In fact, I'm scared to death of him." she said and shivered, hugging herself with her arms.

"So this was the first time you met Verschuer?"

"Yes, but I knew who he was. He first wrote to us about six months ago. It was a letter addressed to Mr. Laughlin proposing something called Project Gemini."

"What was that?" Mattie asked.

"I don't know exactly," Helen replied. "I wasn't able to read the entire letter. All I know is that it involved the study of twins because that's Dr. Verschuer's specialty. It's something the ERO specializes in as well. We have twins visit us. We take measurements and give them tests."

"How do you know it's Verschuer's specialty?" Mattie asked.

"Oh, it's right there in his *curriculum vitae*, his C.V. he sent to Mr. Laughlin."

"Have you thought of going to the police?" Mattie asked.

Helen shuddered. "Miss McGary, Mattie, something very wrong is going on. I have no proof other than the papers I saw. We're funded by Carnegie and Rockefeller and those two foundations have a lot of influence. I may be an old maid but I'm not stupid. I'm not sticking my neck out with people who have so much power. That's why I came to you."

Okay, Mattie thought. This was probably as much as she was going to get out of Helen Talbot. But there was no harm in asking. "I understand. But will you try and get some proof? A carbon copy of the original list; some other carbons from the file folders of the ten victims?"

Helen vigorously shook her head. "Oh, I couldn't do that, Mattie. I'm too scared. Besides, I'd never get away with it. My desk is right out in the open. Dr. Davenport's office is on one side and Mr. Laughlin's is on the other. Mr. Laughlin keeps duplicates of the Gemini project files but the originals are in Dr. Davenport's office. Dr. Davenport leaves his office door open almost all the time and he would easily see me going into Mr. Laughlin's office."

"What about lunch? Doesn't he go out for lunch?" Mattie asked.

Helen shook her head. "No. Dr. Davenport eats lunch at his desk. Every single day. And he rarely travels or takes a sick day and has never been on a vacation."

Mattie sighed. She needed proof. "Do you have keys to the building and the offices?"

"Sure," Helen said, pulling from her purse a ring with five keys. "They're all marked."

Mattie smiled. "Might I borrow them for an hour?" she asked.

Helen hesitated. "Why?"

"I think it's best you not know." Mattie said. "Do you have a cleaning crew each night?"

"Yes, we do. Why?"

"Again, it's best you not know. How late do they work?"

"From seven to ten. It's in the contract I negotiated with the maintenance company."

"Tell you what, Helen," Mattie said. "How about you meet me in the main reading room of the public library at 11:30 this morning? I'll return your keys to you then."

Helen Talbot bit her lip, deep in thought. Finally, she looked up and held out the keys.

FOLLOWING a quick lunch at the Automat, Mattie was back at her temporary desk which the *New York American* had provided for her while she was in town. After she left Helen Talbot and dropped off the keys at a locksmith so he could duplicate them, she had commandeered a copy editor and gave him instructions that all calls for Mattie from other Hearst reporters around the country were to be routed to him once they found anything about the other ten names on the list Helen had given to Mattie. Then she had picked up the duplicate keys two hours later and delivered the originals to Helen at the library.

Copy editor Tony Molinari was in his fifties. Short and bald, he spoke a mile a minute.

"Any news yet, Tony?" Mattie asked when he approached her desk.

"Plenty," he growled. "It's all here." He handed her a sheet of paper.

Mattie looked at the notes Molinari had made. All ten names she had given Hearst last night were missing persons. Every single one had been reported to the police as missing.

"What about the last two names? The ones that were added recently? Johansson?"

"Hudson got that," Molinari replied. "College students. They're in Europe. Their landlady forwards their mail care of American Express in Munich once a week."

Mattie nodded and tapped her fingernails on her teeth, an unconscious habit. Until that moment, she hadn't decided if she were really going to use the keys which she arranged to be copied that morning. She knew the law. She knew journalists had no more right than the next citizen to break the law. She knew that if she used those keys, she would be committing several crimes including trespass. But people's lives were in danger. She needed a good lawyer.

She also needed back up for what she had in mind tonight. "Is Hudson around, Tony?"

"Nah, Mr. Ivy League is having lunch at the Harvard Club. La dee da," Molinari replied, as he wiggled his pinky finger.

Mattie left Tony and tracked Hudson down at the Harvard Club by telephone. "Ted, are you going to be at Stanhope Hall tonight?"

"I wasn't. I was planning to stay in town. But I can be. Why?"

"I'll let you know," Mattie replied. "I've got research to do and I may need some help."

The Chrysler Building,

COCKRAN was late. Again. Mattie was sitting at the bar in the Cloud Club waiting for Cockran to arrive. She'd finished one martini and started on a second. Already, two good-looking guys had tried to pick her up and a third at the far end of the bar, moments earlier, had paid for her second martini. Mattie raised her glass to him and nodded. The man smiled. Mattie smiled back just as Cockran entered the room. She stood up and they embraced. She could see, over Cockran's shoulder, the other man's smile fade. She gave him a grin and winked.

As she hoped, Cockran noticed. "So who were you making eyes at?"

Mattie shrugged. "Beats me. But he bought me a drink. Strange men always buy me drinks when you're late. As you usually are." Mattie replied.

"And you let them?"

"Sure. Why not? If you never show up, then I've got myself a spare."

Cockran grinned. "So you said you needed legal advice?"

Mattie explained, telling Cockran about her confidential source and the list of twenty twins she had compiled, ten of whom now were dead. She didn't disclose Helen's name.

"You saw the list?" Cockran asked as a waiter brought him a martini.

"Yes, but it wasn't the original. She made a new one."

"It doesn't make sense. Most eugenicists have a highly inflated sense of their own importance and want to run other people's lives. But compiling a list of twins for someone to murder? I don't get it. Anyway, it's one hell of a follow-up story and I can't wait to see Harry Laughlin squirm when it hits the street. How soon will you run it?"

Mattie frowned. "I can't go with it yet. All I have is the woman's story and her list. But I promised her confidentiality. Someone's already tried to kill me over this story. Her life would be at risk if she let me use her name. I can't do that. I need independent proof. Records."

"And how do you propose getting that?" Cockran asked.

Mattie held up the duplicate set of keys she had the locksmith make earlier in the day. "She told me exactly where to find the records I need. I plan to make a visit there tonight."

Mattie paused, sipped the last of her martini, and smiled at Cockran.

"Want to keep me company?" Mattie asked.

Cockran sighed. "I'm your lawyer, Mattie. I'll keep secret your intent to commit several felonies. But I can't become your accomplice. There are some things lawyers shouldn't do."

Mattie smiled and leaned in close, speaking in a whisper. "Like helping Bobby Sullivan kneecap that I.C.E. executive last year in Germany? Or blowing up an L.A. warehouse filled with IRA weapons the summer we met?" she said, ticking off one more finger.

"Those were different," Cockran replied, his voice defensive.

"Really?" Mattie asked, arching an eyebrow.

"Look, Mattie, don't do this. Tell the police what that thug in Cleveland told you."

"I don't think so, Bourke. We've been over that. He's dead. Hudson killed him. I was there. I'm virtually an accessory. It's not going to look good if the police find that out. Also, I can't give them my source's name either. Without that, no judge is going issue a search warrant for some place funded by the Carnegies and Rockefellers. So, are you coming with me or not?"

"Not," Cockran said as he slowly shook his head. "Look, I know I'm not the most law-abiding person. When I'm not, it's usually because the other side is not playing by the rules and the government is either abetting it or doing nothing about it. But, so far on this story, that hasn't happened. Go to the authorities. You have no reason to think the NYPD wouldn't take this seriously, especially after your story on Sunday. I don't think you should risk prison for a story. It's not worth it. But, of course, we both know you're going to do whatever you want. And if you do get caught, it would be better if your lawyer wasn't there with you. So, if you go, please be careful," Cockran said, keeping his voice low and reasonable.

Mattie had half expected Cockran to react this way. He could be so predictable. But it was clear he was avoiding an argument in a way he wouldn't have a year ago. The least she could do was to act the same way.

"Ten people are dead, Bourke. Ten more, maybe twelve, are missing. I can't go to the police and I can't sit back and do nothing. If you won't come with me, I understand. But at least be my lawyer. Can't you figure out a plausible way for me to get inside that laboratory and not be charged with trespass or breaking and entering? For goodness sakes, I'm not going to steal anything. I'm only going to take photographs."

Cockran didn't reply. He took a sip of his martini and stared out the window. Finally he turned back to her. "Okay, here's how you do it. Talk to your source. Have her identify some personal object she keeps at work, it doesn't matter what. She needs it. Have her ask you to pick it up for her as a favor."

"Something like that will work?" Mattie asked.

"Probably not," Cockran replied, "but at least it will give Hearst's lawyer something to argue in your defense after you're arrested. With Hearst's influence, maybe that will keep you from being indicted."

"Thanks, sweetie, I appreciate it," Mattie said as she stood up, leaned over and kissed Cockran on the forehead.

"Where are you going?" Cockran asked, nodding to his unfinished drink.

"I'm off to break the law, sweetheart," Mattie said, smiling at Cockran's frown. "No, that's not it. I'm off to do that favor. I'll spend the night at the Cedars once I'm finished."

Mattie smiled as she took the elevator down to the street. Cockran *was* predictable which is why she had called Ted Hudson beforehand. Cockran had been fine about Ted being with her last night when he couldn't join her. Would he feel the same way about tonight when he *wouldn't* join her? She wasn't sure. If she told him, he might think she was trying to manipulate him into going against his better judgment. She'd never play a game like that with the man she loved. She would have Ted watch her back while she nailed the story. Cockran didn't need to know that tonight, she had a spare.

36.

Tonight for His Client;
Tomorrow for Mattie

The Chrysler Building
New York City
Tuesday, 24 May 1932

COCKRAN finished the last of his martini, staring out at the New York skyline aglow in the setting sun. He was not looking forward to an evening alone. Especially when he hadn't anticipated an evening alone. Damn it, what was the matter with him? He should have gone with her. Eugenics! He had never hesitated to take those bastards on when they were using the legal system to sterilize innocent young women. If you didn't stop eugenicists there, the lethal chamber of state-sanctioned euthanasia was next for the inconvenient souls who didn't fit the perfect genetic profile these people wanted to perpetuate.

But cold-blooded murder? Cockran thought he knew a lot about the science of eugenics. And murdering twins didn't make sense from all he knew. Yet if Mattie's confidential source was telling the truth, the Eugenics Record Office had created a list of twins for what might be a murderous psychopath. Why? Damned if he knew but the woman he loved — and not him — was right now trying to find out. He had spent the last week keeping her safe. And now? Well... the most he could say was that rural Long Island was not an especially dangerous place.

Cockran took the elevator back down to the Donovan firm's offices. He didn't much like being a lawyer right now. Last week, the lawyer in him had kept Bobby Sullivan from killing Wesley Waterman. Tonight, the lawyer in him wouldn't even look after Mattie's safety as she sought evidence which might save the lives of ten, no, make that twelve innocent people.

When he entered his office, Cockran noticed on his desk an unopened envelope marked "Personal" and postmarked Long Island. Curious, he slit it open and removed copies of hotel bills from the Hotel Cleveland and the Phoenix Hotel in Findlay in the name of Mr. & Mrs. Theodore Stanhope Hudson, IV, along with several room service chits signed by Mattie. Cockran laughed and threw the papers in the trash. Just how dumb did Hudson think he was?

Looking back to his desk, he saw the large file folder that Sarah Steinberg had left for him earlier in the day. The file was thick and the label on it read "Waterman — Nonprofit Holdings." Seeing the file there made him feel better. It reminded him that he had a client — a vulnerable client — to whom he also owed an obligation right now. It helped him clear his conscience. Tonight for his client; tomorrow for Mattie. In the morning, he would visit the New York Public Library and find out all he could about eugenics and twins to share with Mattie.

He opened the file and began to read. Two hours later, Cockran leaned back in his chair and rubbed his eyes. One more folder to go. "Leases." He picked it up and began leafing through it. Waterman was the sole member of a string of non-profit corporations dedicated to the science of eugenics. Each non-profit was a subsidiary of the Waterman Foundation and all were headquartered in the I.C.E. building. Moreover, a good 25% of the non-profits' considerable endowment came from the National Institute of Health in Washington. Government money.

Cockran came to the last clip of documents in the lease file and he instantly became alert. All the balance sheets on the non-profits had shown rental income, which was not out of the ordinary. There was no reason non-profits could not own and lease real property. But the actual leases were something else entirely. All the leases were for property in Cold Spring Harbor, Long Island. He quickly scanned through them. American Eugenics Society, Brooklyn Institute of Arts and Sciences Biological Station. Cockran chilled. Wesley Waterman owning anything in Cold Spring Harbor was not good.

Cockran stared in disbelief at the next lease. The Carnegie Institution for Experimental Evolution. The employer of Mattie's confidential source! He picked up the last lease in the folder but he already knew what he would find. The Eugenics Record Office! The place where Mattie's confidential source worked. The place where Mattie McGary would be tonight. The last sheet of paper in the file contained a schematic of Waterman's Cold Spring Harbor holdings. Cockran looked at it. Six buildings on the northeast side of Cold Spring Harbor were all contiguous and all owned by Wesley Waterman's non-profit corporations.

It all fit together perfectly, Cockran thought, as he felt the hair rise on the back of his neck. Waterman regularly hired Owney Madden's thugs and, apparently, ex-MID agents to do his dirty work. More ominously, one of Madden's men and an ex-MID agent had tailed Mattie and attempted to kill her in Ohio. Mattie was going to be trespassing tonight on property owned by a man who didn't hesitate to hire hit men to take out his adversaries. Not good at all.

Cockran looked at his watch. It was 10:05 p.m. Too late for the 10 o'clock train to Long Island. The next train wouldn't get him there in time. Mattie would enter the buildings around 11:00 p.m. after arriving on horseback. That added to her cover story, she had said. A late night ride under a hunter's moon was not an uncommon sight on Long Island's north coast.

It was a long shot but Cockran quickly placed a call to the Cedars and let the phone ring fifteen times before he hung up. He looked out the window. Visibility was good. He called the sky port on the East River below Wall Street where he rented a hangar for his autogiro.

"Joe? Bourke. I'm going to Long Island in twenty minutes. Prepare a flight plan and gas up the *Celtic Princess*."

"Sure thing, Mr. Cockran, but come sooner if you can. There's a front moving in fast."

Cockran hailed a taxi outside the Chrysler building and headed up to his place on Fifth Avenue. In his bedroom, he stripped off his coat and tie but otherwise didn't change clothes. There was no time to waste. He put on his leather flying jacket, his skin-tight leather driving gloves and placed three extra clips for his Colt .45 in the jacket pocket. Then he stopped. Would that be enough? He hesitated, then opened the door to his closet and, using his pocket knife, pried up two floor boards in the right rear of the closet. He reached inside and pulled out a bulky package covered in cloth. A large Webley revolver, a shoulder holster and two cartridge boxes of heavy .455 caliber shells. Michael Collins' parting gift to him ten years earlier. He headed back down to the waiting taxi. He rarely took out the Webley revolver. Only when there might be dirty work at the crossroads. Like tonight.

The wind was at fifteen knots with gusts up to twenty-five by the time Cockran arrived at the sky port. He filed his flight plan and, minutes later, fired up the Wright Whirlwind engine and lifted the autogiro into the sky. He was still kicking himself for not having read the Waterman non-profit folder earlier. It had been there since lunch.

Cockran shook his head at the irony. Earlier that evening, he had been concerned about committing trespass and a technical breaking and entering. Now, armed to the teeth, he was prepared to violate any number of laws in order to keep Mattie safe from harm.

Cockran felt strangely calm yet his adrenalin level was high. He knew that, but for the war, he would never have discovered this dark side of himself. Being his father's son, it always bothered him because it made him feel less like his father, who believed life and death were matters that belonged to God. But his father had never fired a weapon in combat. He had never killed a man. The same could not be said of his son.

37.

The Names Matched

Cold Spring Harbor, Long Island
Tuesday, 24 May 1932

MATTIE pulled in the reins on Heather, her favorite chestnut mare, as they reached the edge of the woods and the open lawns of the Carnegie Institution for Experimental Evolution campus which Helen had described. Mattie had taken the 6:30 train to Sands Point and then had driven the Auburn fifteen miles from The Cedars to Cold Spring Harbor to determine the best way to approach the buildings. Once that was done, she had swung past Stanhope Hall on her way back to the Cedars and briefed Ted Hudson on her plans for that evening. She tied the mare's reins to a tree and, staying in the shadow of the woods, walked a hundred yards.

Mattie was dressed for riding. Dark tan jodhpurs that fit her like a second skin, polished brown leather boots which came up to just below her knee and a dark wool navy blue watch sweater with a dark cotton turtleneck beneath. She had a large leather camera bag slung over her shoulder within which was an electric torch, her Leica camera and a flash attachment.

She sighted Hudson's maroon Cadillac parked on the street, a block away from the main building. The complex looked like a college campus. Brick buildings in a Georgian style, six in all, two stories high, surrounding a four-story administration building where the Eugenics Record Office was located, as well as the Carnegie Institution laboratories.

Hudson saw Mattie and approached her, his smile as wide as ever. They embraced warmly and exchanged a kiss. Against her better judgment, Mattie had reluctantly agreed to Ted's suggestion that, in case someone was watching, it was best they appear to be lovers out for a stroll. She was reluctant because, after that damn nightcap and its aftermath, she sure as hell didn't want to give Ted the wrong impression again.

When they reached the front of the building, they veered away from the main entrance, which had a long, wide expanse of brick stairs. Helen had told Mattie that was not the place to enter the building. Instead, they walked along the left-hand side down half the length of the building until they located the door recommended by Helen. It was a secluded alcove with a stairwell leading down to a basement door. Ted would wait here to provide cover for her retreat if she needed it.

"Wait a minute, Mattie," Hudson said. "What about Cockran?"

"What about him?"

"Your boyfriend didn't want you coming here tonight. What if he shows up? What then?"

"He won't," Mattie replied.

"Maybe. He always was something of a pussy in MID but what if he does? What's your Plan B?"

Mattie frowned. She didn't need this. They were wasting time. She had to get into the building quickly. Cockran wasn't coming. "Look, if Cockran shows up, be civil. Explain you're my back-up and try and persuade him not to do anything foolish."

Hudson grinned. "You got it. I can be real persuasive when I put my mind to it."

Mattie rolled her eyes and headed for the building. Once inside, Mattie quickly made her way to the third floor. By entering the left side of the building, Helen Talbot had assured her, Mattie would pass through the wing of observation rooms where the twin studies were conducted. It was just as Helen had told her. She visited two of the rooms and they were identical. Each room had a long mirror covering half the wall. The wall itself was covered with flowered wallpaper containing colorful, oversized black-eyed susans with the lens of a motion picture camera hidden in the middle of one of the flowers. Helen had explained that the mirrors were one-way and, together with the cameras, permitted scientists to observe their subjects being put through a series of tests where they were in various stages of undress and might otherwise be embarassed by having strangers observing them.

Mattie walked down to the middle of the building and took the main staircase up to the joint offices of Davenport and Laughlin. A large door, its top half pebbled glass, carried the legend in large black letters. "Eugenics Record Office." She got out her copy of the keys, found the right one and unlocked the door. She was in a reception area where Talbot's desk was placed in the middle of the room. On either side of the door through which she had entered were several hard back leather-cushioned armchairs where visitors could wait.

Helen had warned Mattie that both Davenport and Laughlin's offices were locked, as were the file cabinets inside. The originals of the Project Gemini records were all kept in Dr. Davenport's office. The file cabinet would be easy to spot. It was the only unmarked file cabinet in the room. Mattie unlocked Davenport's door and let herself in, keeping the torch by her side, pointed downward to minimize its being seen from outside.

After adjusting the wooden blinds to keep light from escaping, she got out her keys and tried several before she found the one that unlocked an unmarked file cabinet. She opened the top drawer. It was empty. Strange. She opened the second drawer. Empty also. This wasn't looking good. You normally filled a file cabinet from the top down, not the bottom up. The last three drawers were empty also. Had they removed the records after her story?

Mattie walked out to the reception area and stood there. Helen had clearly said that Davenport's office was to the right and Laughlin's to the left. She had gone to the office on the right. Wait a second. Whose right? Her right or Helen's? Helen's desk was in the middle of the room facing the door. Mattie had gone to her right. Perhaps she should have gone to Helen's right. She moved across to the other office, quickly found the key and entered. The two offices were identical. She turned around and looked at the wall beside the door. Several framed photographs and diplomas were arranged there. She apprpoached them and raised the torch. Yes! Dr. Charles Davenport, Ph.D., Harvard University. She walked to the file cabinets.

The unmarked file cabinet in this room was right in the middle. She unlocked it and pulled open the top drawer. Inside were files neatly arranged chronologically. PG-1 through PG-8. She pulled out PG-5, opened it and drew a deep breath. James Roger Miller. The Findlay-born Cleveland engineer. She pulled out PG-6. His twin sister, Elizabeth Ann Miller. She closed the folder and chilled. She hadn't noticed it on PG-5, but stamped across the front of the PG-6 folder was the ominous legend "CLOSED." She quickly skimmed PG-1 through PG-4 and PG-7 through PG-10. They were all stamped "CLOSED" as well. Mattie knew the names. They all had been in her story. The second drawer was only half full and ended with PG-9 and PG-10, the Neumann sisters. She went through the third drawer where there were ten more folders, PG-11 through PG-20. The names matched with the ones Helen Talbot had given her.

The fourth drawer was only partially full as well. PG-21 and PG-22. But the other files contained several sheets with background information on each twin compiled by the Eugenics Record Office. PG-21 and PG-22 were different. No information. Simply handwritten names in ink in the same neat, precise block letters that appeared on the folder. A brother and sister, presumably twins, named Johansson. No addresses, no other identifying characteristics.

Mattie stood up. She had to photograph these files. Not all the papers but the top sheet in each one of the murder victims' files. How in the hell would the E.R.O. and the Carnegie Institution explain *that*? She placed the files on the pristine desk top so that the "CLOSED" was visible on all ten. She took five photographs with her flash, two folders per photograph. Then she took the top sheet out of each file folder and arranged it on top. One photograph per folder now, so that the PG-6 stamp was visible beside the name of Elizabeth Ann Miller. She did the same with all the other folders before she returned them to the file cabinet and relocked it.

Mattie sat back down in Davenport's desk chair and tugged at the drawers of his desk. They were locked as well. She fished the key ring out of her handbag and tried different keys to unlock it. None of the keys fit. Which only piqued Mattie's curiosity. Helen Talbot was allowed a key to the file cabinets but not Dr. Davenport's desk. Why? Mattie didn't want to advertise that she had been here, but the locked desk was too great a temptation. Mattie knew how to pick locks. Cockran had taught her.

In fact, Cockran had once proudly showed her his own set of MID issue lock-picking tools which she had surreptitiously borrowed this evening from his library. She had thought about asking him but, given his opposition to her plans for tonight, she already knew how he would have reacted to *that*. Hell, she knew how the police would react if they found her with lock-picking tools. Wasn't even possession of them a crime?

There was nothing in the center drawer, so she picked open the bottom right-hand drawer where she saw a number of file folders. One was openly labeled "Project Gemini — Bavaria — Correspondence." Intrigued, she pulled it out and opened it. On the left-hand side was a typewritten list with all twenty names. Two more names had been added in ink at the bottom—the Johansson twins. The right side of the folder contained correspondence bound at the top with two prongs. She quickly leafed through it. There it was. Letters between Dr. Otmar Verschuer and Dr. Charles Davenport! What caught her attention most, however, was right on top, a trans-Atlantic cable addressed to both Drs. Davenport and Verschuer:

TEN SUBJECTS ARRIVED SAFELY. STOP. WILL ATTEMPT TO FIND OTHER TWO. STOP. EARLIER SPECIMENS PRESERVED. STOP. ARRIVAL BAVARIA 19 MAY. STOP. EXPERIMENTAL EVOLUTIONI TESTS BEGIN AT CLINIC 20 MAY. STOP. AUTOPSY PROTOCOLS BEGIN 3 JUNE. STOP. REGARDS JM. STOP

They're alive, Mattie thought. All twelve were still alive! But they wouldn't be alive for long. Autopsy protocols? June 3 was less than two weeks away. How the hell do these people expect to explain all this? Leaving the folder open on the table, she took out her Leica and froze when she heard a noise in the hallway outside. She switched off her torch and put it, the Leica, and the correspondence file in her camera bag. She walked softly to the door, stopped and listened. Someone was out there trying to open the locked door to Laughlin's office. The footsteps came closer and the person tested Davenport's door also but Mattie had locked it as well. After a few moments, the footsteps receded.

Mattie waited for several minutes until she could hear nothing more. She stepped into the reception area, locked Davenport's door and was suddenly struck by something hard in the back. She stumbled and fell to the floor. She quickly twisted over in an effort to see who or what had attacked her but all she saw was a big club of a left arm encased from wrist to elbow in plaster of Paris cast come crashing down. She put up her arms in a vain effort at self-defense, but the arm crashed through them and pain shot through her head as the arm hit her in the side of her face, her head bouncing hard off the polished wooden floor.

38.

A Gentlemen Never Tells

Cold Spring Harbor, Long Island
Tuesday, 24 May 1932

COCKRAN feathered the autogiro to a landing at the Cedars around 10:45 p.m. He still might be in time, he thought. He took off the Colt .45 and its shoulder holster and replaced it with the Webley and its holster. He put the .45 inside his waistband in the small of his back.

Moments later, Cockran was in his Auburn speedster headed out of Sands Point, turning left onto Northern Boulevard. He hit the North Hampstead Pike and opened the Auburn up, hitting seventy-five miles per hour until he had to slow down for East Norwich. He slowed again as he passed Oyster Bay Cove. At the end of the pike, he turned left into Cold Spring Harbor.

Off to his right, he came across the grounds of what had to be the Carnegie Institution complex. Georgian style brick buildings, manicured lawns, tall elm trees, all owned by a Wesley Waterman nonprofit. He pulled two blocks past the campus and drove the Auburn into a stand of trees so it was hidden from the road. As he got out of the motorcar, he heard a horse whinny. He walked toward the sound not ten yards away and found Mattie's own chestnut mare, Heather, her reins tied to one of the trees. The mare recognized Cockran and shuffled her hoofs, pleased that Cockran had come to interrupt her boredom. He stroked her mane for a moment to calm her, thinking that Mattie must have been gone for a considerable amount of time if the mare was this restless. He gave her a gentle pat and headed off toward the campus.

Cockran passed under the tall elms surrounding the main building, looking for an entrance. He moved quickly around the front of the building to the right-hand side. The elm trees provided more cover on the left-hand side and he intended to gain entry from there if he didn't find Mattie first.

Mattie was nowhere to be seen as he emerged from behind the back of the building and moved quickly down the left-hand side, looking for a point of entry and finding it. A stairwell that led below ground level. Perfect for breaking a window and gaining entrance.

"Don't move. Hands on your head or I'll blow a hole in your spine," he heard someone say as he felt a pistol barrel jammed into his back.

Cockran froze at the sound of the voice. Ted Hudson! Cockran did as he was told, the pressure of the gun staying firmly in his back while an expert hand patted him down. He kicked himself for his poor tradecraft. He sure as hell hadn't been quiet approaching the stairwell.

"Turn around," Hudson said and Cockran did.

"What the hell are you doing here?" he asked.

"First things first, Cockran. With your left hand, slowly remove your weapon from its shoulder holster," Hudson said, keeping his .45 automatic pointed directly at Cockran's chest.

Cockran did and placed the weapon on the ground. He kicked it away as instructed.

"Next, the weapon in the waistband. There's a good boy. You know the drill."

Again, Cockran did as instructed. Hudson knelt and picked up each weapon, tossing them behind him, then pointed his service .45 Colt at Cockran's chest. He looked at Cockran and flashed him a smile. "What am I doing here? I might ask you the same question. What I'm doing here is taking care of your girlfriend."

"Listen, we don't have time for this crap. Mattie's in danger. She's walking into a trap."

"A trap?" Hudson asked and then laughed. "Come on, Cockran. You can do better than that. Mattie told me what a big pussy you were about her coming here tonight. Same as you always were. Afraid to do what has to be done. Always following the rules. Just like the time with that Bolshevik baker in Brooklyn. You were a pussy then and you still are now."

Cockran didn't reply.

Hudson grinned. "The only danger Mattie faces is you trying to stop her from doing her job and she wants me here specifically to stop you from interfering. Which is just what I'm going to do."

"God damn it, Hudson, we've got to help her. She could be killed."

"Mattie's a big girl, Cockran. She can take care of herself. You know what I think your problem is?" Hudson said, tilting his head to one side. "You're jealous, aren't you? Afraid I'll take her back from you. I saved her pretty little ass in Ohio you know. She tell you about that?" He paused and smiled but Cockran didn't reply. "Guess not given all that happened after that. Let me tell you that girl knows just the right way to show a man she's grateful."

"Listen Hudson. . . ."

Hudson stopped smiling. "No, you listen, Cockran. Mattie and I go way back, long before you ever met her. I know she's told friends in the Hearst organization that she and I only had dinner a few times and that there was nothing romantic between us. She probably told you the same thing, didn't she? I can well understand why she kept you in the dark because we were something of an item, you might say, and she was one hot little number."

Cockran didn't reply, his attention focused on the .45 Colt leveled at his chest. "We had more than a few dates, I can tell you that but that's all I'm going to tell you. The boys at MID used to ask me whether Mattie was one of the many skirts who spread for Ted. But I don't go in for vulgar expressions like that nor do I ever answer questions from others who are curious about my love life." Hudson said and then flashed a smile. "Look at you. You're no better than them. You really want to know, don't you? Did she or didn't she? Well, you'll never hear about it from me. You want to know why?"

Cockran didn't reply.

"A gentleman never tells. That's something you wouldn't understand, you shanty Irish bastard. All you micks nail your round heeled tramps and then brag about it down at the pub with the boys. And later you probably bring her to the pub yourself, don't you? So all the lads can undress her with their eyes and make believe they're all fucking her. That's what you Micks do, isn't it? I'll bet that's just what you did with Mattie, didn't you?"

Again, Cockran made no reply. Hudson was feigning carelessness. That gun might look as though it were held inattentively, but Cockran knew he was waiting for an excuse to fire. Hudson knew all about Cockran's temper and was goading him into making a dumb move.

His only thought, however, was Mattie's safety. Much as he wanted to knock out all the teeth in Hudson's head and let him choke on them, Mattie came first and time was running out.

"But don't you worry about what Mattie and I did before you met her. That's all in the past." Hudson said. "You ought to pay more attention to the present. Did you receive those hotel bills I sent? You know, from where Mr. and Mrs. Theodore Stanhope Hudson, IV, stayed in Ohio? What did you think when you saw all the late night and early morning room service chits signed by Mattie from our suite? Oh, that's right. You were in military intelligence. You should be able to figure it out. Why don't you just run along home now? Mattie's in more than capable hands and she doesn't need you to keep her safe. Or for anything else. Now that she's had a chance to compare the two of us in more ways than one, I'd say she's ready to trade up for a better model. Someone who really knows how to take care of her."

A sharp crack interrupted Hudson's monologue. The sound of a pistol shot from inside the building and, for a fraction of a second, Ted turned his head in the direction of the shot. That was all Cockran needed. He bolted from his position, launched into a flying tackle, and caught Hudson square in his midsection. Hudson managed to snap off a shot just as Cockran made contact and the impact knocked him to the ground, the weapon flying out of Hudson's hand.

Cockran aimed his head at the bridge of the other man's nose, but Hudson moved his head aside and Cockran's forehead only grazed his cheek. Hudson twisted over onto his front and attempted to get to his feet, but Cockran put him in a headlock and began to apply pressure, choking off his windpipe. Hudson rammed his elbow back hard into Cockran's stomach, creating space to twist from Cockran's grasp. He leapt to his feet, spun around and aimed a kick at the still-kneeling Cockran's head.

Cockran wasn't quick enough and his ears rang from the kick, his perspective jarred for a moment as he staggered to regain his feet. But Hudson followed up with a kick to the midsection sending Cockran back down to his hands and knees. A third vicious kick caught his jaw and sent Cockran flat on his back. He felt the warm trickle of blood spreading over his left cheek.

"You're pathetic, Cockran. You never could take it!" Hudson shouted as he dropped onto his chest with the weight of both knees and put his hands around Cockran's throat. "Don't worry about your girlfriend, Cockran. You'll be a dead man soon enough and that sexy broad will soon enough find better men than you to share her bed."

Cockran's air supply was being choked off and the blood from his face was blurring the vision in his left eye — but blurry or not, he saw exactly where Ted was now, hovering above him. He stiffly jammed two fingers of his right hand into Hudson's left eye. Hudson screamed and brought one hand to his face while Cockran slapped the other hand away from his neck. Then Hudson howled with pain when Cockran grabbed his crotch and squeezed. Hard. Cockran used his newly acquired leverage to roll Ted off him and onto his back.

Cockran released his grip on Hudson's crotch and rammed his knee into Hudson's groin once. Twice. Three times. Hudson had no countermoves and groaned as he curled into a fetal position in a vain effort to protect himself. Cockran was in no mind to show mercy. His blood was up and he wanted some teeth. Hudson was helpless and moaning as Cockran grabbed him by the back of his coat, lifted him to his feet and threw him back against the wall of the building. A right cross to Ted's jaw was followed by a left uppercut that snapped Hudson's head against the wall. Cockran grabbed him by his shoulders and this time his head butt didn't miss, striking Hudson on the bridge of his nose. With no fight left in him, he crumpled to the ground.

Cockran moved in to finish him off. Hudson was dazed, his eyes glassy, thoroughly beaten, as the sound of two more shots emerged from the building. Mattie! Cockran looked around for his weapons and quickly found them. The Webley was in his right hand as he tucked the .45 in the front of his trousers and looked down at Hudson who coughed, spat out blood and what looked like a tooth. He was still breathing but his face was a bloody mess.

Damn Hudson! He hoped he wasn't too late Cockran thought as he headed toward the building, holding the Webley straight down at his side. He saw Ted's .45 laying on the ground, paused, picked it up and tucked it into his waistband also as he resumed sprinting towards the building. Another shot rang out. There would be dirty work at the crossroads tonight.

39.

I Work Best Alone

KURT von Sturm dressed slowly and methodically in his hotel room. He had slept little the night before. The fading evening sunlight filtered through the blinds, casting shadows across his bed and illuminating the dust motes that drifted in the air. He focused on the mechanical details of the knot in his blue silk tie to keep his mind from dwelling on the operation ahead. The details had been finalized, the assignments given, the surveillance arranged, the traps set for both *Frau* Waterman and Bruno.

For several years now, Sturm had been betraying the Geneva Group's agenda in large ways and small, a betrayal originally known only to his mentor Berlin and now shared by other powerful members like Manhattan and Munich. But that was to achieve a common goal. Hitler as Chancellor. To achieve his goal of stopping the assassination of Manhattan's wife, he would be alone. Completely alone. Good, Sturm thought. I work best alone.

Sturm reached for two soft caps — one a bright blue, the other a soft green — stuffed them both in the waistband of his trousers before covering them with the jacket of his charcoal gray suit. He topped his head with a fedora and walked out of his hotel room. Outside, he hailed a taxi to take him from his hotel to the *Hauptbahnhof*, Hamburg's central train station.

Sturm's taxi pulled to a stop at the northwestern corner of the station. It was the primary drop-off point for motorcars and it was where Ingrid would enter. The building was a magnificent canopy of glass and steel that stretched along the length of the station, sheltering its passengers from the elements. It was sleek and simple, a house of industry proudly exposing its naked steel girders to the world. The face of the canopy resembled the giant grille of a motorcar, its vertical steel beams reaching their apex at the center and sloping down to the earth in the shape of a spade. Two clock towers framed the *Wandelhalle*, a more traditional bridge building of Prussian style that hung over the tracks below, housing a bustling shopping center.

Sturm stepped out of the taxi and looked up at the clock tower above him. It was just after six o'clock . Her ticket was for a seven forty-five departure. Bruno's plan anticipated that *Frau* Waterman would take a specific path through the train station to the ticketing office so they had placed men at each turn along the route, each within sight of the other, to monitor her progress. But Sturm had carefully nurtured Bruno's anxiety that Ingrid might stray from the expected path. In turn, Bruno had spread his men too thinly over the station to compensate for this which left a narrow gap in the surveillance along her expected route that Sturm intended to exploit.

He made eye contact with the first point in the surveillance, a neatly dressed young man sitting in an off-duty taxi. Sturm gave a slight nod and walked through the entrance near the base of the clock tower. The noise was tumultuous, exactly what he had expected. The early evening crowds of business commuters filled the *Wandelhalle*, rushing to and from their trains.

Sturm noticed the second man in their net standing by the public telephones who by now should have received word of how she was dressed when she left the *Vier Jahreszeiten*. He approached him and asked the time. The man looked at his watch and whispered "Pale yellow dress, white hat."

Sturm thanked him and went back to alert the first man. Then he moved on through the *Wandelhalle*, removing a pen from his coat pocket and jotting the clothing details down on a note card. As he neared his own position, he spotted Jaeger, the third man in the surveillance outside a small café. Jaeger asked for a light and Sturm told him "pale yellow dress, white hat" as he lit the man's cigarette. Sturm kept the note card to himself and walked to his own post. He was the natural choice to cover the most vulnerable point along the route, a blind spot within the corridor leading to the tracks. Blind to all but Sturm. There, on a stool just inside the blind spot that Bruno had unwittingly designed, was a tow-headed, skinny 10 year old boy, a shoe shine box under his arm.

The boy perked up at the sight of Sturm. "You're here!" he said.

Sturm smiled and reached into his pocket to reward the boy as promised. "Good work." he said, handing the boy the note card. "Take this to the tailor and come right back."

"Yes, Sir!" The boy leaped off his stool and navigated the thick crowd to the small dress shop run by a young Jewish tailor, another man Sturm recruited for his counter-op. Meanwhile, Sturm approached Kalb, the last man along the path, the only one between him and Bruno's post at a telephone booth by the ticket counter. "Yellow dress, white hat," he told him.

Back at his own post within the blind corridor, Sturm dumped the green cap in a trash bin. The blue hat would do fine. Now, it was up to the tailor and his blonde sales clerk.

Already, the boy had returned to his stool. "What did he say to you?" Sturm asked.

"Nothing. I gave him the note and he said, 'Yes, thank you.'"

"Good," Sturm said. "Now, do you remember your last assignment?"

An enormous smile filed the boy's small face and he nodded. His next assignment ended with fifty *reichsmarks,* more than he could make in an entire year.

Sturm left the boy and walked towards the *Wandelhalle.* Jaeger signalled that the woman still had not arrived. He checked the clock over the entrance. Six thirty. Time to wait. At times like this, Sturm was cool. Today was no different. And yet it was. He was doing something for himself, not another. A matter of honor. He felt like his father. It felt good.

Finally, Jaeger removed his hat and wiped his brow. She was here. Sturm walked to the other end of the corridor to pass the signal to the fourth man, Kalb, who would alert Bruno. Once back at his post, Sturm could see Jaeger helpfully offering directions to a woman in a white hat wearing a yellow dress. He pointed toward Sturm's location.

Sturm handed the shoe shine boy fifty *reichsmarks* and said, "Go! Now!" The boy headed back toward the boutique to signal the tailor that it was time. Standing within the blind zone , Sturm stared at the crowd until he saw a distinctive white hat over blonde hair flowing with the stream of passengers. He looked past her to the tailor's shop but saw no sign of activity. If the tailor didn't provide the diversion Sturm required, he might well have to abort. Or improvise. He needed the diversion. Now. Or they would both be in danger. As the crowd began to thin, he could see the pale yellow of her dress, the smooth white skin of her collarbone exposed to the air, and then — he saw her face. She was more beautiful than he remembered.

Ingrid.

Her golden hair was bound and wrapped neatly for travel under a broad-brimmed white hat and she carried a small case of luggage. Her expressive blue eyes flitted left and right, seeking the sign that would take her in the right direction. And then she saw him. There was a moment of hesitation at spotting a familiar face. Her face wrinkled in surprise and then broke into a smile at seeing her lover in a foreign train station thousands of miles from home.

Sturm looked to the tailor's shop. Still, nothing.

Sturm's eyes returned to Ingrid. He froze. She seemed on the verge of calling out his name. That would place them in peril and she was too far from him to reach her, to stop her. There was nothing else he could do but vigorously shake his head no and hope she understood. Both their lives were in Ingrid's hands now.

40.

The Street Was Empty!

The Eugenics Record Office
Cold Spring Harbor, Long Island
Tuesday, 24 May 1932

MATTIE heard voices speaking in accented English but she couldn't place it. She lay still, feigning unconsciousness. Both men's backs were to her. They were big men with thick necks. Each had casts from hand to elbow, one of them on his left arm, the other on his right.

"What do we do with the broad?" Righty asked.

"You clubbed her pretty good," Lefty replied. "She's not going anywhere soon. We need to check Davenport's office to see if the Gemini clinical files have been disturbed."

"But what about this folder she had in her camera bag?" Righty asked as he held up the Project Gemini correspondence file.

"Put it there on the desk for now," Lefty replied."I'm not sure where it belongs."

"And her camera?"

"Smash it."

Mattie winced as she saw a heavy boot come down on her Leica twice, three times. Once the two left the reception area and entered Davenport's office, she leaped to her feet, grabbed her bag and the correspondence file from Helen's desk and bolted out the door into the darkened corridor. She heard a shot behind her but she didn't slow down. Then she heard a second shot but it seemed more faint than the first, possibly from outside. She ran the length of the building until she reached the end of the corridor, turned left and headed for the stairwell which would take her down to the basement, her point of entry. To Ted Hudson. To safety.

Mattie took the steps two at a time, clinging to the railing to steady herself in the darkness, the heels of her boots creating a racket as she did so. She reached the second floor landing and was halfway down when she saw a light below her.

"Ted! Is that you?"

She was answered instead by two gun shots that ricocheted off the iron railing above her. Trapped, Mattie turned back up the stairs to the second floor. As she reached the landing, she could hear footsteps coming from the floors above and below her. She sprinted down the pitch-black hallway toward the far side of the building, hoping it was free of obstructions.

There were at least three of them after her. Lefty and Righty from upstairs and whoever shot at her from the stairwell. She had walked right into a goddamn trap!

Mattie was halfway down the corridor when she heard another shot and a voice shouting "She's on the second floor. Get her! Get the bitch!" She stopped briefly, stuffed the correspondence file in her bag, slung it by a strap over her shoulder and dashed down the stairs. pulling her PPK automatic from the small of her back inside the waistband of her jodhpurs just as she heard a volley of shots behind her.

Hudson wasn't on this side of the building but his motorcar was. Plan B. If she couldn't leave the way she came, she had a spare set of keys and would drive the Cadillac down the shore road to her mare. After sounding the car's horn as a signal, she would leave on horseback and Ted would retrieve the motorcar and meet her at Ted's estate, Stanhope Hall.

Mattie reached the basement and she could see moonlight coming in the door which led to the outdoor stairwell and up to the manicured lawn and the tall elm trees which dotted the campus. And, beyond the elms, was Hudson's Cadillac and a clean getaway.

Mattie was out the door and racing up the steps. She had a stitch in her side from all the sprinting, but she couldn't worry about that now. She didn't have time to catch her breath. She ran across the lawn, heard the basement door open and, moments later, flinched as a shot zipped past her head. She raced past the first elm and saw ahead the distinctive double elm beyond which Hudson had parked the maroon Cadillac.

Then her heart sank. The street was empty! The bloody street was empty!

Mattie weighed her options as she ran. A second elm was coming up on her left. Should she take cover behind it and attempt to bring her pursuer down with her automatic? Or should she run an extra twenty yards and do the same behind the double elm?

Mattie chose the double elm. The ground was harder and the grass sparse beneath the great tree but she never saw the exposed root on top of which her foot landed awkwardly. Her ankle twisted painfully as it rolled over until she landed heavily on her right side, the Walther PPK flying from her hand upon impact with the ground.

Winded, Mattie sucked in air and tried to scramble to her feet. She had to retrieve her weapon. Pain shot through her left ankle. It would not support her weight and she collapsed again, the Walther still eight feet away. Painfully, using her arms and her right leg, she began to crawl toward the weapon, but she could hear the man running behind her. She knew she wouldn't make it but still she crawled. She was no more than three feet from the weapon when a heavy boot stepped on her left hand while the man's other boot kicked the Walther further away.

"Lady, sorry about this but you should have minded your own business."

Mattie looked up into Lefty's face and stared helplessly as the big man pulled out a sound suppressor and casually screwed it onto the barrel of his Colt .45 automatic before pointing it directly at Mattie's forehead.

41.

Your Life is in Danger

INGRID'S smile vanished as quickly as it formed, Sturm's name caught in her throat as she read Sturm's body language, his face knotted with intensity. Sturm pushed through the crowd to reach her. "Ingrid," he said tersely. "Your life is in danger." A confused look on her face, Ingrid opened her mouth but Sturm cut her off. "There's no time to talk. Just do as I say ."

"But... how do you know that?"

"Because your husband hired me to kill you."

Ingrid looked stunned. As the shock of his words sank in, Sturm scanned the crowd behind her, looking for a sign that the tailor was finally playing his part, but there was nothing. He turned back to Ingrid and pulled the bright blue cap out of his waistband. "Wear this hat. It will cause my men to lose sight of you. Go to the train on Track 2."

Strum reached into his jacket pocket and removed a train ticket. "Take this train to Norden. My mother will meet you there. You may trust her. She will shelter you."

He looked up again. Still no sign of the diversion.

Ingrid still had not removed her hat, but held the blue cap limply in her free hand. "Kurt," she said. "I don't understand."

"You understand exactly what your husband is capable of." he said. "Get on that train. Don't look back. I'll come to you. I'll explain it then. For now, just do as I say!"

Sturm looked up one last time for the diversion, determined to kill any of his men who got in his way if that was what it took to save Ingrid. Then he saw her. The diversion. The tailor's sales clerk, another young woman with blonde hair, appeared wearing a bright yellow dress and a white hat as she strolled to the newspaper stand. The dress was far brighter and the hat looked nothing like Ingrid's, but the last man in the net before Bruno would not know that.

"Kurt, you're scaring me," she said.

"I mean to. Give me your hat! Now!" Sturm said.

The tailor's clerk had passed them in the crowd. There was no time. If she did not move quickly, he would lose his diversion. Finally, Ingrid pulled a few pins out of her hair and extricated the white hat from her head. She handed it to Sturm and examined the blue one.

"No time to worry about appearance," Sturm said. "You look beautiful." She stared at him with those deep blue eyes and he could tell his tender words had reached her despite the extraordinary circumstances. He leaned in and softly kissed her lips. "Now go!"

Sturm stepped quickly through the crowd, trying to catch up to the tailor's sales clerk. He emerged from the blind zone and made eye contact with Kalb just as the blonde diversion in her bright yellow dress and white hat turned the corner. He tipped his hat back from his forehead and directed his eyes towards the tailor's sales clerk. Kalb caught the signal and scanned the crowd.

Sturm risked a glance towards platform two and saw Ingrid's blue hat bobbing between the taller heads of the men in the crowd, making her way towards the train. Good. Another obstacle cleared. Now for the final hurdle.

Sturm turned his attention back to Kalb and saw that he had taken the bait. He was tracking the tailor's sales clerk intently, no expression of doubt or confusion. Now was the time for Sturm's move. He reached up with his free hand and waved. Nothing. Kalb had his entire attention focused on the tailor's clerk. Sturm pushed his way through the crowd, waving his free hand again, keeping the white hat low by his side.

This time, Kalb noticed the movement. He turned to look at Sturm and recognized the signal: She's on the run. Alarmed, Kalb turned his attention back to the tailor's sales clerk and realized too late that he had been tracking the wrong woman. Kalb turned back to Sturm, but Sturm was pointing past him and towards the ticket counters, gesturing to an imaginary Ingrid. Kalb turned to follow Sturm's gestures. Sturm then stooped to his knees as though to pick up something off the floor. When he rose again, he held Ingrid's white hat high above his head.

Sturm came up to Kalb, brandishing her cap. "You damned fool!" he shouted. "Did you not see her remove her hat? She is on to us! Who were you following?"

"There was another woman with a white hat!" he said. "Was she the wrong one?"

"Yes, damn it! Find the right one! Send the signal to Bruno! Find her now!"

Kalb ran off and began signaling Bruno. Sturm retraced his steps to pass the alert back through the surveillance net to Jaeger. He looked for the shoe shine boy, but found his stool and gear missing. Good. One less witness. He looked to track number two but could no longer see Ingrid's blue hat. It was 8:30. Another fifteen minutes until her train left. She was not safe yet.

It took a few minutes, but Sturm was able to quickly round up their five men. He showed everyone the white hat they had all seen, explaining what they all had been too late to realize. *Frau* Waterman had been tipped off. She knew they were watching her and took advantage of the crowds to disappear. But she was still here, Sturm insisted. Likely hiding on a different train.

"I want you to search every train in this station. Every seat, every sleeping compartment, every toilet on board. I want this woman found! I'll do tracks one and two. You do the rest."

The men spread out wordlessly on Sturm's command. Bruno stayed behind, his face ashen. Sturm turned to him. "Do not blame yourself. I told you this might happen."

"If you do not blame me, then why did you not give me an assignment?"

"I think you have something better to do."

Bruno looked up. "It was the American," he said. "Wasn't it? It was her American lawyer, her lover, who tipped her off. You warned me about him."

Sturm concealed his reaction. Bruno did not suspect. He had taken the bait once again.

"That woman," Bruno said. "The woman that Kalb saw. It is too much of a coincidence that she happened to be wearing a yellow dress and a white hat."

"Yes," Sturm said. Of course Bruno would notice the decoy. "You may be right. Find her and question her. Gently. No need to draw too much attention to ourselves. But she should give you a lead to the American."

"I will find this man, this American," Bruno said. "And I will find *Frau* Waterman."

Sturm nodded solemnly. "I know you won't disappoint me, Bruno.".

42.

What About Ted?

The Eugenics Record Office
Cold Spring Harbor, Long Island
Tuesday, 24 May 1932

COCKRAN grabbed the handrail at the stairwell and reached the bottom in two strides. He smashed the window pane with the Webley, reached inside and opened the door. He could hear footsteps above him as he ascended the steps, making no effort to be quiet. He reached the first landing and headed up to the second when a shot ricocheted on the wall beside him, plaster spraying onto his head. He stopped and cautiously moved up as he heard a shout above him.

"She's on the second floor! Get her! Get the bitch!"

The footsteps on the stairway were moving away and Cockran pushed open the exit door to the first floor. He had to outflank them. Moving up a closed stairwell was suicide.

Cockran stepped into the darkened hallway and was greeted by two shots slamming into the wall above him. Cockran dropped to the floor and fired three shots in the direction of the muzzle flashes, then rolled to his left to change his location. There was no return fire. He moved cautiously along the wall and saw a shape on the floor, a Colt New Service laying five feet away. He knelt, checked for a pulse and found none. Lucky shots but the guy was just as dead.

Cockran quickened his pace down the corridor until he came to a large, high ceilinged vestibule, the building's main entrance. Above him there was another shot and more footsteps. Screw caution, he thought, as he sprinted across the vestibule and up the main staircase, encountering no one as he made it to the second floor. He turned to the right and ran in the direction of the noise and straight into a clothesline in the form of a plaster of Paris cast. It hit his chest and knocked him to the floor, jarring the Webley revolver out of his hand. As he lay sprawled on his back, the bright white cast came crashing down. Cockran rolled out of the way as the cast hit the terrazzo floor with a loud crack. Cockran moved to a crouch and saw the man awkwardly reaching with his left hand for a pistol in his waistband. Cockran caught him with a leg whip and the man fell to the floor, his head hitting hard against the tiles.

He was slow to get up. Cockran took advantage, scrambling across the tiles to find his Webley. It would be near the door. His hand brushed against a hard object and he seized it, fumbling to find the grip. He heard the man stirring behind him. Cockran spun around, long enough to see a gun held unsteadily in the man's left hand. Cockran fired twice from the seat of his pants. The kickback jerked the barrel up but he knew he'd found his mark. He got to his feet and approached the man. Kneeling to check his pulse, he recognized his former MID colleague Peter Schmidt. He had broken the man's wrist last week. He had no pulse either.

Cockran regained his feet and ran down the corridor, going through the exit door and down the stairwell on the other side. Moments later, Cockran was out the basement door and up the stairwell. He reached the top and froze. There, less than fifty yards away, he could see, outlined in the moonlight, Mattie laying on the ground and a man with a plaster of Paris cast on his left arm holding a silenced weapon pointed straight down at her. Wilhelm Schmidt! It would be damn difficult to take him down, a shot worthy of Ted Hudson to hear Mattie tell it, but he had no choice if he was to save her. His only advantage was that the Webley had a longer barrel than a Colt .45, a more accurate weapon in the hands of a more skilled marksman than Cockran.

Cockran steadied the barrel on the metal railing, cupped the butt of the Webley in his left hand as he aimed at the man's head and squeezed once. The first bullet missed. Cockran shifted the barrel slightly to the right and squeezed again and hit Wilhelm's shoulder. He fired a third time and it tore a gash along the back of the man's neck, emitting a spray of blood as Mattie screamed. Cockran holstered the Webley and ran to her.

"Are you all right?" Cockran asked when he reached her and knelt down.

Mattie brushed spots of blood off her forehead. "I'm fine . . . I think. It's not my blood," Mattie said, rising to a sitting position. "Bourke? It's you? How'd you get here?"

Cockran didn't reply and looked at the body sprawled beside Mattie. The man was groaning loudly but the blood from his neck wound was not spurting, nor was it a bright, arterial red. It might not be as bad as it looked. If help came in time, he might well survive. That would not be good. It didn't happen often but sometimes on the battlefield, circumstances dictated you just couldn't take prisoners and the Geneva Convention be damned. Both sides did it and this was one of those times. The ex-MID agent Wilhelm Schmidt may have been a good guy once but now he was a cold-blooded killer who had been seconds from executing Mattie. Alive, he might well try again. Cockran wasn't going to risk it. Mattie watching didn't make it easier.

Cockran reached down to the commando knife strapped to his right ankle and then stopped when he saw the sound suppressor on Schmidt's Colt .45 not four feet from his twitching hand. Cockran reached for the weapon, stepped over Schmidt so that his back was to Mattie, blocking her view of his head. He never liked this part of bloody mayhem but it was easier than he expected. Reminding himself the bastard was about to kill Mattie without a qualm, he placed the suppressor's snout against Schmidt's temple and pulled the trigger. Behind him, Mattie's gasp made a louder noise than the shot.

Cockran turned to Mattie whose face bore an unmistakable look of horror. "Look, we've got to get out of here. Can you walk? I left two more dead bodies inside the building. Someone must have heard all the shooting and called the sheriff by now."

"I think I sprained my ankle," Mattie said in a very small voice.

Cockran helped her to her feet and put his right arm across her back. Together, they began moving slowly across the lawn and down the street. When they reached her mare, Mattie stopped. "Wait a minute, Bourke. What about Ted?" Mattie asked, her voice stronger.

"What about Ted?"

"I left him there on the other side of the building. He was my back-up. Someone must have stolen his car. It's not there. We've got to make sure he's okay."

"Screw Ted," Cockran said. "The bastard tried to keep me from coming into the building after you. Kicked me in the head to make his point. He said you told him to keep me away. "

"That's not true!" Mattie cried, looking directly at him. "He was just my back-up."

"Some back-up," Cockran snorted. "He almost got you killed."

"But can't you go. . . ?"

"No," Cockran said firmly. "If his car's not there, he took it on the lam."

"Even so, he might be hurt. Look at you. You're going to have a black eye soon."

"Oh, he's hurt all right. I can guarantee that. I left him unconscious."

"What? Unconscious? Then we really should check on him."

"Leave it, Mattie. If I went back there and found him, I'd probably kill him too."

Mattie didn't reply and broke off eye contact, her look of horror returning.

"Can you ride?" Cockran asked.

"I. . . I think so. But I'm going to need a hand mounting her."

"Sure thing ," he said as Mattie put her left foot in the stirrup and he helped lift her up.

Mattie looked straight ahead as she picked up the reins, avoiding his eyes. "Do you think I should swing past Stanhope Hall to see if Ted made it there safely? We agreed to meet there."

Cockran exploded. This was really too much. "For God's sake, McGary! Haven't you listened to a word I said? I don't care if he's safe. He pulled a gun on me to keep me away from you. If he had succeeded, you'd be dead. What part of 'dead' don't you understand? The man who was about to kill you was an ex-MID agent. So is Ted Hudson."

"Ted was only trying to help. He just misconstrued what I wanted him to do. Ted would never do anything to cause me harm. I'm sure his intentions were good."

"Bullshit! The next time Ted Hudson has a good intention will be his first." He was really pissed, his face cold and unforgiving. He had barely saved her life. He should never have let her come here alone. He wasn't making that mistake again. Not until this was all over.

"Bourke?" Mattie said in a small voice, obviously sensing the extent of his emotions.

"Yes?"

"Thank you," Mattie said softly, her voice barely above a whisper

"For what?"

"Saving my life. I don't want you to think I'm not grateful. I am. Really." She paused, wiping a tear from the corner of her eye. She pulled her Walther from the small of her back and chambered a round. "I'm glad you were here. But this isn't over."

"I know it's not. It's only beginning." Cockran replied, his face still cold. "I also know you won't walk away from this story and I won't try and talk you out of it. But until this is really over, I'm going to do whatever I think is necessary to keep you safe." He looked up at her profile bathed in the moonlight. "Are we agreed?"

"Yes. Thank you again. I love you."

Cockran's face softened at last and he grinned. "You'd better."

"Forever." Mattie said and blew him a kiss as she headed her mare away.

43.

How Could She Blame Ted?

The Cedars
Sands Point, Long Island
Wednesday, 25 May 1932

MATTIE and Cockran ate breakfast in the Cedars' sun-dappled kitchen. She was surprised at how hungry she was after her late night adventure and Cockran had cooked her a second helping of eggs and bacon. Then they brought each other up to date on what he had discovered about Waterman and what she had found at the Eugenics Record office.

Well, almost up to date. She had stopped by Stanhope Hall on her ride home to check on Ted Hudson and ended up spending half an hour there. It was almost beyond belief. Cockran hadn't been exaggerating. He had given Ted a savage beating. His lips were puffy, there were cuts above both his eyebrows. His eyes were beginning to blacken and one of them was almost closed, a mere slit. And he definitely needed dental work. Thankfully, Cockran hadn't asked why it had taken her so long to ride home and she wasn't about to volunteer where she had been.

What was it with those two? Ted's answer had been plausible enough and Mattie felt guilty. She had told Ted of Cockran's lawyerly aversion to her nighttime trespass at the Carnegie Institution's campus. Maybe she shouldn't have. Just like she shouldn't have told Ted the year before about the tensions in her and Cockran's relationship. So Ted had overreacted last night. He had genuinely believed that Cockran was there to keep her out of the building; to keep her from covering her story; to keep her from doing her job. How could she blame Ted for that? That had been as much her fault as his, just like that last night in Findlay.

"Okay, so they destroyed your camera and exposed all your film," Cockran said. "But what about that file you lifted? What does it show?"

Mattie looked up at Cockran, guilty that she had been thinking about Ted, and passed over a manila folder. "This is the original correspondence file for Project Gemini. On the left is a list of all 22 twins. On the right are letters between Harry Laughlin and Charles Davenport of the ERO and Dr. Otmar Verschuer of the Kaiser Wilhelm Institute in Berlin. The letters are harmless enough, full of scientific and eugenics mumbo jumbo. Nothing incriminating. But the last item in the file, right on top, is scary. It's a telegram from someone with the initials JM. Talks about ten subjects arriving safely in Bremen. It also mentions their efforts to locate an additional two. Something called experimental evolution tests beginning on 20 May. What's worse is it mentions "autopsy protocols" at some clinic in Bavaria on 3 June. Here, look for yourself," Mattie said, handing him the folder.

Cockran took the folder and opened it. "Mattie. There's no telegram here."

Mattie grabbed the folder out of Cockran's hands. "What do you mean? Of course there is. . . .oh my God! It's gone! I swear, Bourke, there was a telegram here."

"I believe you," Cockran replied. "But that's not going to help. If your interpretation of the telegram is correct, more twins are going to die. And soon."

"But where? Bavaria is a big place. Where in Bavaria is this clinic? Do you think we should go to the authorities here with what we've found?"

Cockran shook his head. "Nope. We can't. We left behind three dead bodies in Cold Spring Harbor last night and we don't want the authorities knowing we were anywhere near that place. It was self-defense but we were both inside that building illegally. In fact, it would be wise if you simply burned that correspondence file you lifted last night. Your fingerprints are probably all over it."

"But . . . ." Mattie began and then stopped as she saw Cockran's face. This was no longer the lawyer of yesterday lecturing her on trespass. This was a man who had killed in cold blood telling her how best to cover her own ass. "Okay. I'll do that."

"Next, call Hearst. Have him put his correspondents in Europe to work and see if they can track down any facility in Bavaria where Verschuer has a connection. Also, have him put together a file on everything his people can uncover on the E.R.O., Davenport, Laughlin and Verschuer. And especially anything they can find on eugenics and twins. I don't see how killing them fits together with anything I know about eugenics. Also, track down Winston. Tell him about the clinic. See if he's managed to find out anything more."

"Fine," Mattie said. "It's only 6:00 a.m. in California. I'll call Winston first."

"One more thing. See if Hearst's New York office can book us passage to Germany."

"Us? Germany?" Mattie asked. She had known *she* was going to Germany — Bavaria — ever since she read the telegram. But . . .

"Us," Cockran reiterated. "It's like I told you last night, I know you're not going to rest until you run this story to ground. So I'm not going to try and talk you out of it. But until this is over, I'm going to keep you safe and I'm not letting you out of my sight. In fact, have Hearst put me on the payroll. A dollar a year. I want to know who your source is and anything else you're still keeping in confidence from me. Understood?"

Mattie stood up, walked over to Cockran and kissed him on the cheek. "You bet," she said. Telling him about Helen Talbot was fine with her but Cockran didn't need to know about her visit last night to Stanhope Hall. It *might* be misinterpreted.

"WINSTON!" Mattie said, "How lovely to hear your voice again. I wanted to tell you about some surprising new developments in the story since last we talked and see if you've learned anything new yourself." Mattie proceeded to brief Churchill on all that had happened since they talked on Sunday.

There was a long pause before Churchill spoke, "This is a dangerous business, Mattie, and you should proceed with caution. Whatever this monstrous scheme may turn out to be, whoever is behind it will stop at nothing to preserve its secrecy. I recently learned my original source committed suicide two weeks ago. His wife doesn't believe it but the authorities refuse to do anything more. The case is closed she was told."

"Do you have other sources in Germany who might help us find this clinic in Bavaria?"

"Possibly. I'll ask the Prof to see what he can find. He's already checking some other things out based on your story. This Verschuer fellow you mentioned is one of the names he's come across. Seems he's done a lot of studies and written papers on twins and their eye color," Churchill said and paused before continuing, "What's worse is he's a Nazi," he said in a low growl, pronouncing the last word as "Narzi."

"Really? That's interesting. I'll ring you up once our ship docks whether it's Southhampton or Hamburg. We're taking the first available liner."

Mattie then placed a call to Hearst in California and, fifteen minutes later, was back in Cockran's study. "You are not going to believe this," she said.

"Try me," Cockran replied.

"While we were talking, Hearst had one of his reporters check out last night's shoot-out at Cold Spring Harbor with local law enforcement. It's all very odd."

"What's odd about that? It will be interesting to know how the story's being played. Three murders must be big news for a small town like that."

"That's just it. That's what's odd. Neither the sheriff nor the local police chief knew anything about it. So the reporter called the Eugenics Record Office directly and was told there were no shootings last night on their campus."

"Interesting. Not even the mob cleans up so well," Cockran replied. "I wonder if the Schmidt brothers or that ex-MID guy Hudson shot are temporarily on active duty. It would explain the Black Drape on their MID files." He stood up and walked to the window where he looked out at Long Island Sound. "What's the status on our travel to Europe?"

"The Chief's taken care of it. He's booked us passage. We'll be in Germany Saturday."

"To be in Germany Saturday we would have had to have sailed yesterday."

Mattie grinned. "But we're not sailing, we're flying. The *Graf Zeppelin*. Tomorrow. It was delayed two days because of high winds. Isn't that great? Your first airship voyage." She could could see from the look on his face that he didn't share her enthusiasm.

"How was Hearst able to do that? Aren't seats on the *Graf Zeppelin* hard to come by?"

"Yes," Mattie replied. "But when Hearst sponsored the round-the-world voyage back in '29, he made a side deal with Hugo Eckener that he could have a cabin whenever he asked so long as he put displaced passengers on the next available ocean liner. First Class. And we're the lucky ones who reap the benefit."

Mattie wondered why Cockran didn't reply. Then, it hit her. It was on the *Graf* where she met the man who became her lover last year. No wonder Bourke wasn't excited about a trip on that airship.

44.

It's Still Ted's Story Too

The Cedars
Sands Point, Long Island
Wednesday, 25 May 1932

MATTIE was in a state of high excitement as she usually was when starting on a journey, especially a trip on the *Graf Zeppelin,* not alone this time but, rather, with the man she loved. Her thoughts were interrupted by the loud ringing of the telephone. Cockran picked it up.

"Bourke Cockran," he said. A few seconds later, "Yes, she's here. It's for you," Cockran said, the expression on his face cold and hard as he handed the receiver to Mattie.

Uh oh, Mattie thought as she took the phone from Cockran. This can't be good. When she put the receiver to her ear, she knew why as the baritone voice of Ted Hudson filled her ear.

"What?" Mattie said and then gasped. "Oh, my God . . . When did it happen?"

Mattie listened silently for nearly three full minutes, tears welling in her eyes. Finally she spoke, wiping the tears from her face with the back of her hand. "Look, Ted, Bourke and I are leaving for Germany tomorrow on the *Graf Zeppelin* to try and find the clinic where the autopsy protocols will take place. Churchill is checking with his contacts. So is Hearst."

Mattie paused to catch her breath. She took a sip of tea. "No, Ted. You don't need to come to Germany." Mattie paused. "That's not a bad idea. I agree with you."

Mattie listened and then spoke again. "Bourke and I are booked at the Hotel Rose in Friedrichschafen for Saturday night. After that, Munich will be our base of operations and we'll be at the *Bayerische Hof.* Fine. We'll see you there," she said and then hung up the receiver.

Mattie turned to Cockran with tears in her eyes. "My confidential source—her name is Helen Talbot—has been killed. It's too horrible. They tortured her. Cigar burns on her body. Ted was tipped off by a friend in the police department. He went to the crime scene. Oh, my God, Bourke, he saw her body." She shook her head and hugged herself with her arms, her voice small and quiet. "They cut out her tongue, Bourke, they cut out that poor woman's tongue."

Cockran reached out for her, his big arms warm and comforting as Mattie let herself cry, horrified at the unintended consequences of her story and her visit to the ERO offices. They had been on to Helen and her. Probably followed one or both of them. Oh, God, why didn't she warn Helen? When she barely escaped with her life, she should have known they'd come after Helen. They must have known about the file Mattie took. She should have warned her!

Mattie closed her eyes, drew a deep breath and exhaled. She had to refocus. She pulled away from Cockran's embrace. Too many people had died. They had to get to Germany and the bottom of this before any more people died.

"Bourke, we ought to return to Manhattan now. The *Graf* lifts off as soon as the ground fog clears tomorrow morning. We can't be late," Mattie said and then stopped. "Is something the matter?" Cockran's face was as hard as it had been when he first handed her the phone.

"Yes," Cockran replied. "but we don't need to talk about it now."

"No, something's bothering you. You can tell me. What is it?"

Cockran hesitated and continued cautiously. "Why did you give Hudson our itinerary?"

"Why not?" Mattie replied. "It's still Ted's story, too. Just because he thought you were trying to stop me last night and you two got into a fight doesn't change that."

Cockran shook his head but said nothing. Finally he spoke again and Mattie was relieved as he changed the subject. "What idea of Ted's did you agree was 'not bad'?"

"He knows the military attaches in Berlin and Munich. They might help find the clinic."

"Damn it, Mattie, I still have good friends in military intelligence. They would have put me in touch with the military attachés in Germany. We don't need Ted for that."

"Well, that's news to me. Why the hell didn't you mention it before?"

"You didn't ask. And I wasn't working on your story until now. Look, don't you understand? Your old boyfriend almost got you killed. He tried to kill me. For all you know, he could be working hand-in-glove with the people responsible for the twins' disappearance. After all, the guys who tried to kill you last night and in Ohio were ex-MID. So is Hudson."

"Come on, Cockran! So are you! That means nothing. And Ted was never my bloody boyfriend! Regardless of your fight last night, he saved my life in Ohio. I'm in no danger from him." In fact, Mattie thought, the only thing in danger from Ted was her virtue and she wasn't about to ever give him another opportunity like she had that night in Ohio.

"I'm sorry. Whatever was once between you is not my point. My point is he can't be trusted. And your dates with him are part of it. Don't kid yourself that he doesn't still have a thing for you. He does. Big time. He made that clear to me right before our fight. He can't stand the fact that you and I are together. He's actually told people at Hearst and friends in MID that I stole you from him. Hell, he even mailed me hotel bills and room service chits claiming you registered at hotels as man and wife on your recent trip."

Cockran paused, his voice more calm. "Look Mattie, there's a lot I can't tell you about Ted but we were always rivals, even in MID training. And, yeah, we once got into a helluva fight over a girl. We busted each other up pretty bad too. That you and I are together means he's lost another round to me and it didn't help I had to beat him up last night. Getting you in the sack would be a real trophy for him. Trust me, that guy would be all over you if I weren't around."

You got that right, Mattie thought, hoping the guilt she was feeling wasn't showing. Cockran wasn't there that night in Findlay and Hudson *had* been all over her. Damn it, Hudson! A gentleman would have kept quiet about that hotel mix-up in Cleveland yet Hudson had actually tried to mislead Cockran into thinking it was more than it was. She had misjudged Hudson. She knew Ted had feelings for her but had their wrestling match really been more about Cockran than her? Well, Ted had said he never finished second to Cockran in anything except for her. At the time, Mattie thought that Ted misread the brief exposure of her breasts as a come-on. Unflattering to think that trophy-hunting and not his feelings for her had been Ted's motive.

"He lied," Mattie said, "We never shared a hotel room in Ohio."

"Again, that's not my point. I'm working with you on this story now and that's another reason why Ted can't be a partner whom you can trust any longer. Look, based on some really bad things he did in one case we handled together at MID, I filed charges against him. He beat the rap. The brass swept it under the rug. I was so disgusted I resigned my commission. Score one for Ted. But I'm still ahead on points in his mind both because of you and now that fight last night. You don't know him like I do. He can be a dangerous man. I want to say more but I can't. Please trust me."

Mattie was more angry with herself than she was with either Cockran or, especially, Hudson but clear-headed enough to realize a good offense was sometimes the best defense. Cockran was half-right. Ted *was* a dangerous man. The two thugs he killed were proof of that. But twice in Ohio he had come to her rescue. She wasn't in any danger from him.

"Look Cockran, you can't have it both ways. Yes, ex-MID guys are somehow involved in this mystery and Ted is ex-MID. But so are you. If Ted really is involved, then he might be a threat to me. But if you're right and he just has a thing for me, then he can't be in league with Verschuer. The fact he saved me twice from that ex-MID guy in Ohio proves that. How many of their men does he have to kill to persuade you? He killed two in Ohio; you got three last night. Does he have to kill two more? Is it a ball game with you two where you keep score? You and Ted have a history. I understand that. Whatever Ted said about me last night was intended to get your goat and it's clear to me that he succeeded. But even if he considers me a trophy in a contest with you doesn't make him a threat to me. If there ever were a contest like that—and I don't think there was and there bloody well better not have been on your part—it's over and you've won. For the record, I have never in my life spent the night in a hotel room with Ted," she said, the half-truth coming easily. "I'm going upstairs to pack. Lives are at stake, damn it, and if your paranoia about Ted keeps you from joining me now that I've told him our travel plans, that's your problem. I don't care. I'm going to Germany with or without you!"

Upstairs, having slammed several doors on the way and now packing her clothes, Mattie calmed down. That was really stupid, she thought, with a flash of *deja vu*. She hated it when she and Cockran had a fight on the eve of one of her departures. They had had a fight like this a year ago before she left on her maiden *Graf Zeppelin* flight where the seeds of her affair first had been sown. At least this time she and Cockran would be traveling together, she thought. Unless he took seriously her last comment that she didn't care whether he came with her or not.

That was untrue. She cared very much. She should let him know that. Sooner rather than later. After all, it wasn't Cockran's fault his suspicion of Ted was off base. She was the one who had accidentally sent him the wrong signals in Ohio and she was the one who had asked him along for back-up last night. Cockran had just risked his life to save her. They didn't have to leave for Manhattan right away. They had time. After all, when a man saves your life, a girl really shouldn't seem ungrateful. She had tried not to be that way with Hudson. It was the least she could do with the love of her life. Sure, Cockran could be a bastard but he was her bastard. Her big, beautiful Irish bastard. It was her turn to apologize and, unlike that night in Ohio, the signals she was about to send would not be the wrong ones. She headed for the door, leaving her blouse and brassiere behind.

45.

Emerging From the Mist

Lakehurst, New Jersey
Thursday, 26 May 1932

THE *Graf Zeppelin* was scheduled to lift off after the morning fog had cleared but no earlier than 9:30 a.m. Nevertheless, Cockran and Mattie had arrived at 8:00 a.m., nearly one hour earlier than necessary to board an airship flight. The perpetually tardy Cockran had complained that arriving an hour early for any sort of departure was unnecessary but the ever-punctual Mattie demanded that they take no chances. When they arrived at the *Deutsch Zeppelin Reederie* company's passenger departure lounge, the huge airship could not be seen. Then, as the fog disappeared, the silver-skinned zeppelin slowly materialized, emerging from the mist.

Cockran had seen the world-famous airship the year before, seeing Mattie off, but that had not inoculated Cockran against his involuntary reaction when he once more saw the giant silver ship. Its size was breathtaking as the morning sun sparkled on its shimmering surface.

They boarded the ship by way of wooden steps set up against its side, entering into a vestibule, turning left down a short corridor into the grand salon where he and Mattie took seats at a table beside one of the cabin's bay windows. Champagne was offered and both accepted.

Mattie touched her flute to his in a silent toast. "I'm happy you're here. Thank you."

"You're welcome," Cockran replied. Mattie had been the first to apologize and he had accepted, but he had apologized as well. He should have waited until later to caution her about trusting Hudson, after she had gotten over the shock of Helen Talbot's murder.

Matties's story on the ten dead twins was baffling, a mystery. He had no clue on how they could locate the clinic in Bavaria or stop the autopsy protocol if they did. Getting to the bottom of the mystery and saving the twins was not going to be easy. No matter what Mattie thought, having Ted Hudson still involved wasn't going to help.

The window beside their table was open and Cockran clearly heard the electronically-amplified voice of *Käpitan* Hans Pruss and the command "Up ship!" The giant airship disengaged from the mooring mast and rose silently into the sky, the faces below waving their goodbyes and gradually fading into small dots amidst the low hum of the Maybach diesel engines. Cockran was no stranger to flying but this was far beyond his experience. Better yet, and unlike last year, Mattie and he would be sharing this journey together.

On board the Graf Zeppelin

COCKRAN and Mattie passed the morning in their cabin reading clippings from the Hearst research on eugenics which had been delivered to Cockran's townhouse the night before, occasionally looking out their cabin window to the ocean below. The file contained everything the Hearst organization could find about Charles Davenport, Harry Laughlin and Dr. Otmar von Verschuer.

"Listen to this, Cockran," Mattie said. "It's from Point Eight of the *Preliminary Report of the Committee of the Eugenic Section of the American Breeders Association To Study and To Report On the Best Practical Means For Cutting Off the Defective Germ-Plasm In the Human Population*:

> However much we deprecate Spartan ideals and their means of advancing them, we must admire their courage in so rigorously applying so practical a system of selection.

"My God, Cockran, they're admiring the Spartans who drowned their weakest young boys. And this garbage is published by the Carnegie Institution for Christ's sake!" She passed the sheet over to him and then continued. "Listen to this. It's George Bernard Shaw from a lecture in London at the Eugenics Education Society:

> A part of eugenic politics would finally land us in an extensive use of the lethal chamber. A great many people would have to be put out of existence, simply because it wastes other people's time to look after them.

Cockran nodded. "I'm not surprised. Believe me, I'm not surprised."

Mattie picked up another sheet. "Here's one that's worse. Arthur Treadgold. A professor at Oxford no less. He wrote the *Textbook on Mental Deficiency*. He defends Shaw:

> A suggestion of the lethal chamber is a logical one. It is probable that the community will eventually, in self defense, have to consider this question seriously. There are over 80,000 imbeciles and idiots in Britain. It would be an economical and humane procedure were their existence to be painlessly terminated.

Cockran smiled. "The British always were a bloodthirsty lot."

Mattie laughed. "And Americans are not? Here's a California Ph.D., Paul Popenoe, on the board of the American Eugenics Society and co-author of *Applied Eugenics*:

> From an historical point of view, the first method which presents itself is execution. Its value in keeping up the standard of the race should not be underestimated.

"I never said we weren't," Cockran replied. "Ask the American Indians whom we systematically slaughtered or herded onto reservations as we inexorably moved west. Does Hearst have anything in there about Madison Grant? He's a big time buddy of Lothrop Stoddard, that guy I listened to at Carnegie Hall. They both lectured at the Army War College."

"Just a minute," Mattie said. "Let me check." Mattie rummaged through the file and pulled a sheet out. "I have it." She whistled. "You're not going to believe this."

"Try me."

Mattie began to read:

Mistaken regard for what are believed to be divine laws and a sentimental belief in the sanctity of human life tend to prevent both the elimination of defective infants and the sterilization of such adults that are themselves of no value to the community. Laws of nature require the obliteration of the unfit and human life is of value only when it is of use to the community or race.

"I've read it before," Cockran said. "It's from *The Passing of the Great Race* which is the bible for an entire generation of MID officers, including Theodore Stanhope Hudson,IV."

"Come on, Cockran. Give Ted a break. He's said a few unkind things about Jews and Communists but nothing as vile as this."

Cockran had heard Hudson say lots worse but now was not the time to bring this up. "What's in there about Verschuer?"

"That's what's strange," Mattie said. "For a German, he is constantly being mentioned in American publications. The Eugenical News announced his being appointed secretary of the German Society for Race Hygiene in 1925 and again in 1927 when he was appointed department head at the Institute for Anthropology, Human Heredity and Eugenics in Berlin. What I still don't understand is why they're killing twins. Killing mental defectives is one thing. It's gruesome, inhuman, but there's a twisted scientific rationale. But not the twins. They were all normal. The victim in Cleveland was a brilliant engineer. Why would they want to kill twins like them?"

"I don't know", Cockran said. "I know a lot about racial eugenics but I can't figure out where killing perfectly normal twins fits in. One branch is weeding out the weak. The only other branch I'm aware of is breeding for the best. So either there's a twisted third branch on the eugenics tree or we're dealing with a psychopath."

Mattie nodded. "I vote for the psychopath."

"Maybe. But I don't see the Carnegie and Rockefeller people — or even Waterman — funding a madman. There's got to be more to it. There's got to be another branch to eugenics we don't know about."

Just then, the steward knocked on their cabin door to announce lunch in the grand salon.

"GOOD afternoon, *Fraulein, mein Herr* ," their waiter said. "It is a pleasure to see you again so soon, *Fraulein*. How was your stay in South America?"

"Fine, thank you, Karl," Mattie replied. "I am pleased once more to be in your care."

The waiter gave a small bow and moved onto the next table. Cockran raised an eyebrow. She hadn't told him she had flown to South America on the *Graf Zeppelin*.

"So, was the additional research on twins helpful?" Mattie asked, ignoring his eyebrow.

Cockran shook his head. "Not really. For some reason, eugenicists are bonkers about twins but almost all of their studies revolve around 'nature versus nurture'."

"What about Verschuer? Helen said he was an authority on twins. So did Winston."

"He is," Cockran replied. "His studies don't fall outside the norm."

"Any photos of him?" Mattie asked.

"Nope," Cockran replied. "Laughlin and Davenport, but not Verschuer. But I already know Laughlin and Davenport by sight. They've been state witnesses in my sterilization cases."

The waiter returned and Cockran was impressed. Excellent food served on porcelain with monogrammed silver. They started with vichyssoise, followed by Dover sole and breaded veal. Karl never allowed their crystal wine glasses to be empty.

As Karl was clearing off the dishes, Mattie placed a hand on his arm. "Karl, would you please ask Commander Pruss if he would make an exception and arrange a tour of the *Graf* for my friend and me?" she asked, giving Karl the same dazzling smile that had so captivated Cockran when they first met. "You've got to see this, Bourke. It's incredibly beautiful."

"Certainly, *Fraulein*," Karl replied. "It's not as if this would be your first time."

Mattie actually blushed at that but Cockran wisely said nothing. He knew all about her little adventure risking her life atop the *Graf Zeppelin* the previous year and there was no point in reminding her. Not even a raised eyebrow.

"Idiot! *Dumkopf!*"

The salon was only half full but all eyes turned toward the loud noise. A silver-haired man with vivid blue eyes was berating a steward who had spilled a small amount of the schnapps he was pouring in the man's glass when the *Graf* had hit a mild air pocket. It had barely caused a ripple in Cockran and Mattie's own wine glasses but, apparently, it had been enough to disturb the steward's aim. Beside the silver-haired man sat a young, hard-looking character with a thick neck and closely-cropped skull. The silver-haired man had a patrician air about him and seemed to be in his mid to late fifties. The other man was more thug than businessman.

Right then, Karl returned with the good news that Commander Pruss had agreed to Mattie's request and that he, Karl, was to have the honor of being their tour guide tomorrow.

"Who is that man," Mattie asked Karl, keeping her voice low and gesturing towards the table where the commotion had just occurred.

Karl rolled his eyes. "He has flown with us before but he is using a different name than he has in the past."

46.

I'm Their Big Sister

Norden, Germany
Friday, 27 May 1932

THE muscles in Kurt von Sturm's body protested at every step. His lungs seared with pain, his nerves cried out for mercy, begging him to rest, to stop, to give in. But he ignored their pleas and pushed harder, forcing his body through the final leg of his exercise regimen — running barefoot for ten miles along the shores of the North Sea. The salted sea air filled his lungs and sweat stung his eyes, dripping from the hair over his brow.

As the rhythm of his running pace settled in, the pain and aches took on a steady monotony and fell into the background — an irritation he was aware of but could readily ignore. His mind had won the battle over his body, as it always did. Rewarding himself, he allowed his mind to wander. It had been two days since he rescued Ingrid in Hamburg and so far, everything had gone according to plan. After every train had been searched in the Hamburg *Hauptbahnhof*, and Ingrid was safely on her way to Norden, Sturm advised Bruno to focus his energies on finding this mysterious "American" they suspected was traveling with *Frau* Waterman.

Sturm would handle communication with the Geneva Group from now on. In his call to Berlin, Sturm made it clear that the fault for failure did not lay with Geneva. It was likely Manhattan's own incompetent men who had tipped his wife off to the danger she faced here in Hamburg. Thanks to these errors, there was now a very high probability that *Frau*

Waterman would never be found. Manhattan had no one but himself to blame.

With Waterman and the Geneva Group chastised and Bruno busy chasing ghosts, Sturm's only remaining concern was Ingrid. As Sturm's men searched other trains, he had found her waiting nervously inside her first-class compartment. She had demanded to know what was going on and he told her everything short of the actual truth. The less lies to cover up, the easier it was to keep them covered. He told her he was the Executive Assistant for Fritz von Thyssen, head of the largest steel manufacturer in Germany where companies did not always thrive simply by offering superior products and services. Bribes and blackmail, sabotage and subterfuge were also part of the game.

Sturm had claimed to have come across the plot in the course of his usual work. One of the various "agents" whom he employed on a semi-regular basis told Sturm of a commission to assassinate the wife of a wealthy American businessman. Was he interested? Sturm had said no but, curious, he began checking into the matter and quickly learned the businessman was Wesley Waterman. After that, he had sought out the commission and accepted it in order to save her.

In the adrenaline rush of the moment, Ingrid had accepted his explanation. Sturm had been able to note faint discolorations beneath the make-up around her eyes. He could see that she had been beaten, likely by her husband. That her husband was violent probably helped Ingrid to accept Sturm's story so quickly. Once in Norden, he noted a trace of suspicion. She became more observant, asking questions, clarifying the details in his story, probing beneath the surface. It was clear to Sturm that there was something she didn't fully trust about him. And well she shouldn't.

Sturm shook his head to clear his face of sweat. Beyond all these legitimate concerns, of course, was a more basic question: What to do with Ingrid? But that could wait for another day. For now, he was thankful she was still alive.

STURM returned early from his morning run. Rubbing a towel over his face, he walked into the kitchen for a bite, surprised to find his sister Franka already up and sitting with Ingrid, practicing her English. Franka lifted her head at the sound of his footsteps.

"Excuse me?" she said in strongly accented English. "You are not permitted here."

"I can't make myself breakfast?"

"We are having girl talk."

"Girl talk?" Sturm looked to Ingrid, but she shared Franka's severe countenance, albeit with a playful smile drifting beneath the surface. "Is this your influence?" he said.

"I'm sure I don't know what you mean," she said. "I'm helping Franka with English."

"That is no form of English I've ever heard," Sturm said.

"Then you haven't been spending time with the right girls," Ingrid said.

"Now scram, brother!" Franka said, giggling at the use of her new American slang. She picked up an envelope and spoke in German. "Here, you have a telegram. Go read it in the sunroom."

Sturm took the telegram and left the room. It must have arrived during his run on the beach. It was from Bruno. The message inside was short and cryptic. He sat down next to his private telephone line and hailed the operator. A few minutes later, he was speaking with Bruno.

"What have you found?"

"She never made it to Munich. At least not to the Hotel Continental. At this point," Bruno continued, "I'm not going to waste any more resources searching for her in Munich."

"Perhaps," Sturm said. "But tap some of our Munich agents to keep an eye out."

"I already have," Bruno said. "Now, I am focused on finding her siblings. Her visa application gave some indication of their itinerary, listing some villages along the *Bayerischer Wald*, like Kötzting and Regensburg. I think they provide the best opportunity to find her."

Regensburg. That was unfortunate. That was exactly where Ingrid's brother and sister were staying. If Bruno found Ingrid's brother and sister, hotel phone records would show calls from Norden and a phone number Bruno knew well. It would not take Bruno long to figure out Ingrid's location.

"Keep me posted on your progress," Sturm told him. "I will check messages every day."

After hanging up the telephone, Sturm walked back into the kitchen where Ingrid and Franka were still chatting away like schoolgirls. Ingrid turned to eye him playfully.

"Time for this woman-talk to end," Sturm said. "Franka, I need to speak with Ingrid privately. You can tell her all about your precious boyfriends later."

"Boys?" Franka said, rising from her seat with an air of haughtiness. "Who says we were talking about my boyfriends?" She guided herself out of the room, a wicked smile crossing her lips.

Sturm turned back to Ingrid. "Then who were you talking about?"

"Well, wouldn't you like to know?" Ingrid said.

Sturm didn't understand. "Of course I would. That's why I'm asking."

Ingrid laughed, a delightful sound. "It's an American expression. I know you're curious, but I won't tell you. You'll have to ask Franka. A girl must have her secrets."

Sturm nodded, understanding the joke, but he sat down without smiling. "It's time to call your brother and sister," he said. "I just got off the telephone with one of my agents."

Ingrid visibly stiffened at the words. "What did he want?" she asked.

"The names of a few contacts I have in Bavaria," he said. "They have given up trying to find you directly. Now they have turned their attention to your brother and sister."

"Are they in danger?" Ingrid asked, growing tense.

"No," Sturm answered quickly. "But you are. I do not think the agents pose any danger to your siblings, but they might use them to find you. You need to call them and tell them to leave at once for any town not on their itinerary."

It was her brother Thomas who answered. She spoke calmly at first, explaining what must be done but then she stopped. Something was wrong. Sturm could hear the raised voice on the other end of the phone. "What? What do you mean she's gone? She hasn't come back? Where did she go?"

"What is it?" Sturm asked gently.

Ingrid held the receiver away from her mouth and turned to Sturm. "Tom says they can't leave because Beatrice hasn't returned from her hike yet."

"When did she leave?"

"Yesterday afternoon. Tom stayed behind to work on his senior thesis and she left to hike with some of the friends they've made there. He thinks she just spent the night with them, probably to be near a boy on whom she has an eye. She should have returned by now. This isn't right."

"We can't know anything until he looks for her," Sturm said. "Tell him to get his belongings ready and then go out to find your sister. Whether he finds her or not, he should be in his room by five o'clock when we will call him to confirm if he's found her. If he has, they must leave immediately."

Ingrid nodded and relayed the instructions to her brother. There still appeared to be some disagreement, presumably Tom's objections to a forced change in plans for reasons that Ingrid would not explain. "I don't care what your friends will say!" Ingrid said. "Find Beatrice and be at this phone today at five o'clock! That's all you have to do!"

Ingrid sighed in frustration after she hung up the phone.

Sturm placed a gentle hand on her shoulder. "He is young, as you say," Sturm said. "He will come around. Clearly, they've made friends and we're asking that they leave them behind on a moment's notice. Of course it will be difficult for them."

"I know, I know," Ingrid said with a sigh and straightening in her chair. "I just can't help worrying. I'm their big sister. What if something terrible has happened?"

"You don't know that," he said. "And even if something happened, there is nothing you can do about it until we speak with Tom. The best part of the day is still before us. You shouldn't waste it fretting about something you can't control."

"What do you propose?" Ingrid asked, attempting to force a smile.

"Sailing."

"Sailing?"

"Nothing helps clear the mind more than a few hours at sea."

47.

Cathedral in the Sky

On board the Graf Zeppelin
Friday, 27 May, 1932

COCKRAN and Mattie stood inside an immense circular cathedral in the sky, the thin duralumin girders and bracing wires like a huge spider web extending the length of the airship. The outer skin was translucent so that the light flowing through and around the sixteen huge gas cells lining the ship's interior between the girders and wires made him appreciate the immense sense of space. It was like nothing else he had ever seen, nothing else ever built by man. Cockran and Mattie were walking on a catwalk which ran along the base of the ship. They were wearing shoes made of cotton and canvas that were designed specifically for use on zeppelins so that they would not generate any sparks. Cockran was nervous. The zeppelin's catwalk was barely two feet wide. It formed the base of an inverted triangle of duralumin, thicker than the girders, the duralumin struts flaring out on either side of him and coming back to a point two feet above his head.

The steward took them the entire length of the ship. Cockran was surprised at how many men were at work wherever they walked. The men were high on the framework, adjusting the tension of wires, tending to the large Maybach engines. They even saw men sewing and splicing fabric as if they were making a sail.

"What are those men doing?" Cockran asked.

"You can't see it because the gas cells block the view," Mattie replied, "but there's undoubtedly a small tear in the ship's outer canvas fabric. The canvas is coated with a mixture of resins and aluminum flakes which gives it a silvery appearance. These men are stitching together a patch. Once they have it the right size, they'll climb up the vertical ladder closest to the tear. Then, using harnesses and cable, they will lower a rigger over the outer skin of the ship until he reaches the tear. He will slash the torn fabric away and then, like a seamstress, he will sew the patch into place."

"That sounds dangerous."

Mattie smiled. "Very dangerous. I was taking photographs of the riggers doing the same thing last year when I climbed out too far and almost . . . ," Mattie said, her voice faltering. "Well, you remember."

Oh, yes, he remembered. All too well. She had told him all about it and they had argued over her impulsive recklessness right before she left on the assignment that brought her together again with the man who had saved her life on the airship. An assignment that led eventually into an affair with him as well.

Cockran listened as Mattie resumed her conversation with Karl. "That horrid man at lunch yesterday. What's his name on this voyage, Karl?" she asked.

"Vogel. *Herr* Otmar Vogel."

"And his name before?"

Karl hesitated as if he knew he shouldn't be talking about one passenger with another. "I really shouldn't say but seeing as how this is your fourth trip with us, you're practically a member of the crew. I trust you will be discreet?"

"Of course, Karl," Mattie said.

"Verschuer. *Herr Doktor* Otmar von Verschuer of the Kaiser Wilhelm Institute in Berlin."

48.

Something Has Gone Wrong

Norden, Germany
Friday, 27 May 1932

KURT von Sturm felt the wind pick up, rustling his hair and battering his shirt as his 15 meter sloop glided past the buoys that marked the end of the breakwall into the stronger currents of the *Nordsee*. The water here was relatively gentle, a string of islands and sandbars protecting the shores of Norden from the rougher waves of the open sea, but the wind was strong.

Ingrid had been quiet so far, settled back in her seat in the stern several feet from Sturm at the tiller, pensive as she watched him adjusting the sails.

Now that they were out of the inlet and the sloop was gaining speed, Ingrid moved closer to Sturm. "You were an airship pilot in the war?" she shouted the question over the wind.

Sturm glanced back at her and into the wind. Long tendrils of yellow hair escaped from the scarf wrapped around her head and twisted in the breeze. "How did you know that?"

"I'm living in your family's home," she said, standing beside him now. "It's not very hard to miss the displays of medals or the photographs of you with your father."

Sturm smiled. She had been paying attention. "I flew in the Naval Airship Service. I've sailed since I was young but sky sailors, like those on water, are still at the mercy of the wind.

"A 'sky sailor.' I like that. Do you miss it?"

You have no idea, Sturm thought. "I hope one day to return to the sky as a commercial airship pilot. Until then, my days of sailing the skies are as old as the medals you've seen."

"Yes, about those medals," she said, walking past Sturm's position at the helm to face him. "All of the medals are for men named von Strasser. Why no medals for von Sturm?"

Sturm met her gaze and then turned his eyes back to the sea. He was not used to women being so forward. Intelligent? Interesting? Of course. Pushing where he didn't want to go? No. But Ingrid wasn't so much pushy as slippery. Stop one question and she simply flowed around it like water and asked another seemingly unrelated question. Sturm took his eyes from the sea to look at her and decided there was no great risk in explaining it.

"It was after the war," Sturm finally said. "The 23rd of June, 1919. The Allies had awarded all eighteen of our naval airships as reparations. Two days earlier, the officers of the German High Seas Fleet interned at Scapa Flow in Scotland opened the sea valves of their ships and sank them all. I persuaded my fellow naval airshipmen to emulate the bravery of our seafaring brothers. When the sun rose, most of the naval zeppelins had been destroyed."

He could still picture them in his mind, a twisted mass of blackened duralumin, patches of canvas still smoldering in the warm morning light. That sense of justice washing over him, the sense that he had fought his own battle here and fought it well. He remembered it all. Including the two Allied sentries he had killed with his own hands, his knife slicing deeply across their throats. The first men he had ever killed up close.

The first men, yes, but not the last. "The military awarded me the Blue Max for my actions as well as the whole of my wartime service. But the new Socialist government in Germany did not reward me. They called me a 'war criminal.' They issued a warrant for the arrest of Kurt von Strasser. So I changed my name to Kurt von Sturm and, courtesy of an introduction from Hugo Eckener, went to work for Fritz von Thyssen and his United Steel Works. Germany takes care of its heroes, even if its spineless Socialist government did not."

"So you named yourself after the family dog?"

"Our government would do well to emulate his courage and loyalty." Sturm said as he scanned the horizon for the sand-bar ahead.

"But it's a different government in Germany now, isn't it?"

He turned back to Ingrid. "Yes. The Socialists are no longer in power. The National Socialists are now the second largest party in Germany. They soon will be the largest."

"So why don't you change your name back?"

"I suppose I've grown attached to it over the years," he said. "Mostly it is a promise I made to myself. And to the memory of my father."

"What sort of promise?"

"The Allies seized entire swaths of German land after the war and gave it to our enemies. Our family estate in Pomerania near Posen was part of that land-grab by the Poles. After my own government turned on me, I swore I would not reclaim my name until things had been set right. The von Strasser name died with my father in the war and it will not return until our family estate is restored to Germany and the Versailles Treaty is on the ash heap of history."

"You really loved your father," she said. A statement, not a question.

Sturm noted her change of subject. He had been talking about righting wrongs. Revenge. She talked of love. "Of course. But more importantly, I admired my father." he said. "He taught me the three principles by which a good German must lead his life: Respect, honor, and strength. A good German shows respect to his adversaries and those less fortunate than him. His honor requires that he always keep his word. And strength means he must always be prepared to defend his family, his country and his honor."

"And you think the National Socialists will be the ones to restore these principles?"

"Yes." Sturm said. "They are the only party that knows about honor. They know to whom Germany owes its past greatness. They know how to honor its heroes."

"What do you think about this man Hitler, their leader? What does he stand for?"

"You've already named one thing I admire about him," he said. "Hitler is a leader. He does not beg for votes, or change his principles to pander for popularity. He is popular because he challenges people to cast aside their petty personal interests and unite as Germans.

"Funny, all I heard when my husband talked about him is that he hates Jews."

"No. Only the others. Toads like Goebbels and Himmler blame everything on the Jews." Sturm said. "Hitler never speaks of Jews except as Germans. I've met him several times. He's never displayed anti-Semitism to me. 'A man cannot help how he is born,' is what he said."

"But what does that tell you?" Ingrid said. "People say Hitler is a master politician so he must be well versed at masking his true feelings. He can be all things to all people if men like you are willing to ignore what his associates say about Jews in his name."

Sturm had no answer to that, none that he could voice freely. Sturm was aware of his own ability to manipulate others just as he was also adept at spotting attempts to manipulate him. His life often depended on that ability. Having met and spoken to Hitler on a number of occasions, he had never picked up a hint or sign that Hitler was anything but genuine. It would be disturbing on many levels if it turned out that Sturm had simply missed those signs.

"I don't sense that with Hitler." he said, his eyes scanning the approaching sandbar.

"But then why does he keep people like that around him?"

Sturm ignored the question and in the distance, he saw what he was looking for. "Look," he said, pointing at the sandbar. She shifted in her seat to look in that direction. "Do you see them?"

"Those lumps on the sand?"

"Yes," he said. "Look closer."

"Goodness, is it garbage?" Her sentence died in her throat as what appeared to be a lump of debris leaned its head back and yawned. "Oh!"

Sturm lowered the sails and stood beside her. "I think you call them 'seals.'"

"Yes, that's what we call them," she said in astonishment. Scores of white and gray seals stretched out in the sun, lounging on the thin strip of sand that emerged from the sea. She leaned back into his shoulder and Sturm let her. "What do you call them?"

"*Der seehund.*"

"Sea hounds?"

"Yes, that's quite close to the literal meaning. Sea dogs."

"They're adorable." Ingrid looked at him. "I forgive you for changing the subject."

"It is a time-honored tactic for German men to distract their women."

Ingrid laughed. "I apologize. I can see you don't like to talk about yourself but how else am I to learn what lies beneath your defenses?"

Sturm turned her to face him and kissed her deeply. He pulled back and said, "I can think of a way." He kissed her again and this time she kissed him back. Sturm had wanted to make love to her from the first time he saw her again but he had been inhibited by his mother's and sister's presence. Now he had no such worries. He didn't think the seals would mind.

UPON returning to the house from their sail, Ingrid had been relaxed, comfortable with herself and her surroundings, and especially comfortable with Sturm. She no longer looked like a grateful prisoner. She seemed happy to be hiding from her vengeful husband with her once and future German lover.

When the time came to call her brother, Sturm placed the call and handed her the phone.

She asked for Room 525 and waited. And waited. "No one is answering," she said.

"Try it again," Sturm said but again, no one answered.

"I'll try the front desk," Sturm said. He had the operator place the call and waited.

"*Palast-Hotel* Regensburg," the receptionist said.

"I am looking for a gentleman staying at your hotel by the name of Thomas Johansson. He's in Room 525."

"No, Sir," the receptionist said. "We have no guest registered here by that name."

"When did he check out?" Sturm said, glancing towards Ingrid who was growing more tense by the minute.

"He didn't," the receptionist said curtly. "There has never been anyone here by that name. You are looking in the wrong place and I strongly advise you search elsewhere."

"Perhaps you don't understand," Sturm began, but the receiver clicked loudly in his ear and the line went dead. The man had hung up on him. Slowly, he replaced the receiver in its cradle and turned to Ingrid.

"Well?" she demanded. "What happened? Where is he?"

"Something has gone wrong," Sturm said. "The receptionist claimed your brother was never registered at the hotel."

"That's impossible! He was there this morning! I talked to him," she cried. "What is going on? First my sister. Now my brother. Where are they? Both of them are missing."

She looked up and Sturm could see the anguish on her face.

"The twins are missing."

PART III

Germany

28 May — 31 May 1932

While openly eschewing eugenics with statements and memos, the Rockefeller Foundation in fact turned to eugenicists and race scientists throughout the biological sciences to achieve the goal of creating a superior race.

Edwin Black, *War Against the Weak*

Everywhere in life only a process of selection can prevail. In antiquity, the Spartan constitution was the only one that required and enforced a healthy selection. Today there are still states in the USA which also ... support human self-selection.

Adolf Hitler, 1931

49.

A True Believer

WESLEY Waterman grimaced when he reached for the bottle of champagne as they lingered over a late lunch in the Adlon's dining room.

"Are you all right, my dear?" *Frau* Magda Quandt asked.

"It's nothing," Waterman replied. "Broken ribs. Hurt them in a riding accident the day before I sailed," Waterman lied as he recalled the grim, black-haired, blue-eyed Irishman who had driven his heavy boots into his ribs time after time. And the bastard's next target had been Waterman's groin. He literally had passed out from the pain. He had not had a woman since.

"Has your delightful *schloss* been in your husband's family long?" Waterman asked.

The blonde-haired, blue-eyed Magda Quandt smiled and laughed. "Generations, Wesley, generations," she replied. Magda was an attractive woman. Not a classical beauty like Ingrid but more a pretty farm girl, with short blonde hair, blue eyes and, Waterman noted with anticipation, larger breasts than Ingrid's. Magda was in her early thirties while her husband was well into his seventies. Their estate north of Berlin was a gathering place for National Socialists.

Magda had flirted openly with him the entire weekend once she heard from Fritz von Thyssen about the extent of Waterman's wealth. Not that *Herr* Quandt wasn't wealthy but his oldest son by his marriage to his late first wife would inherit everything and Magda would be at the son's mercy. Clearly, she was looking for another horse to ride. So was Waterman. But Waterman had another reason for cuckolding Gustav Quandt wholly apart from the joy of mounting the man's wife. Heinrich Himmler himself had told Waterman that Magda, through her husband, was one of the National Socialists' largest benefactors. Unlike industrialists who contributed funds to the Nazis because they had no choice but to curry favor with Germany's second largest party, Magda Quandt did so because she was a true believer. Wesley Waterman's kind of woman.

Waterman already had I.C.E.'s accountants run projections on what revenue and profits would accrue to it if an entire country of over 70 million people, and not just the membership of the SS, were to have the genetic qualities of every single citizen cataloged, tracked and updated by the Hollerith calculating machines of I.C.E. going back a minimum of four generations. The profits would be enormous.

With Ingrid out of the way in the very near future, a newly divorced Magda Quandt would be a more suitable consort for an international business leader of his stature. He didn't need her husband's money and she would bear him the perfect children so far denied him by his barren first wife and his adulteress second.

"You seem preoccupied, my dear," Magda said. "Is there anything wrong?"

Waterman shook his head. Yes, there was something wrong but Magda could not be privy to Project Gemini, at least not until the National Socialists took power. The agent's cable he had received on board ship advising him that the damn woman journalist for Hearst had been caught snooping at the ERO in Cold Spring Harbor was not good news. It was bad enough that they had not been able to stop her before she had broken the twins story. Even worse was that her boyfriend, that meddling lawyer for his faithless wife, had managed to rescue her and apparently killed three of their best men in the process while the bitch had made off with a key Project Gemini file. Worst of all, however, was the news that the Hearst journalist and Cockran were landing in Germany today on board the *Graf Zeppelin*. He hoped they would not prove to be as troublesome in Germany as they had been in America. He didn't think they would because Project Gemini's tests and subsequent autopsies were to be complete within the week. There was little chance they could locate the clinic that quickly nor, even if they did, that they would make it past the clinic's SS guards. Their every move in Germany would be closely watched. Still, he was concerned that the Hearst journalist had learned as much as she had in the US. Dr. V's carelessness coupled with a traitorous secretary in the Eugenics Record Office had made it possible. In Germany, she would have no such advantages.

Waterman took a sip of champagne. The only good news he had received lately was that the SS had finally managed to track down his dear wife's brother and sister. Himmler assured him that the twins would arrive at the clinic this evening. He smiled. He was looking forward to letting his wife know before she was killed that her adultery had led to the extinction of what remained of her miserable family—her twin siblings.

"I was only thinking of you, my dear," he said to Magda, "and all the pleasures that await us upstairs in my suite."

Waterman stood up and grimaced once more as a sharp pain shot through the left side of his chest. Magda definitely would have to be on top this afternoon but all the better to see those big beautiful breasts in action.

50.

I Will Find Them

Norden, Germany
Friday, 27 May 1932

TWINS?" Sturm asked..
"Yes. They're twins. My brother and sister mean the world to me. Everything I've done with Wesley was for them. Now they're missing," she had said. She looked up at him, her eyes red and swollen. "I don't understand. How could this have happened?"

Sturm did not have an answer. He turned his back on Ingrid and looked out at the North Sea. Street violence was always a possibility. Caught up in a fight between Nazi and Communist thugs. But their separate disappearances made that unlikely. Kidnapping? It seemed likely given that the hostile hotel clerk obviously had been paid off. But who could have kidnapped them? It wasn't Bruno. He was still in Hamburg this morning.

Had Manhattan hired someone else to kidnap her siblings and lure her out of hiding? Possibly. Likely even. His corporation, International Calculating Equipment, had a growing presence in Bavaria and Waterman himself had great personal wealth. Who would he hire in Germany? The man's money plus his sympathy for the Nazis might give him access to common thugs like the SA. Possibly the SS. But to no one in Sturm's league. Few were.

Ingrid still held her face in her hands. He knelt in front of her and gently pried her hands away, her tears reflected in the afternoon sun. "I will find them. I will find your brother and your sister," he had said. "You have my word."

She smiled weakly. "What will you do?"

"I will travel to Regensburg and make inquiries," he said. "I have some connections."

"Won't you draw attention to yourself?"

"I will be discreet."

Ingrid brushed at her cheeks, wiping away the tears. "Take me with you," she said.

"No," Sturm said firmly. "I work best alone."

"But you need me."

"I will be traveling where my agents will be searching for you," he said. "People in Regensburg will notice a beautiful blonde American. Your risk of being discovered is too high."

"You don't even know what my brother and sister look like," she said. "What makes you think they will trust you? Or follow you?"

She had a good point but Sturm said nothing.

"And if you won't take me, I'll go to Regensburg and look for them myself."

Sturm saw the determination in her eyes. She meant every word. And if she tried to go on her own, making inquiries in English, Bruno inevitably would find her. She'd be dead within days. He had no choice. They were her siblings after all. To keep her safe, he would not be working alone.

51.

We're Going to Need More Guns

On board the Graf Zeppelin
Friedrichschafen
Saturday, 28 May 1932

COCKRAN was mesmerized by the view as they approached low, less than three hundred feet above the waters of Lake Constance at the intersection of Germany, Switzerland and Austria. He and Mattie were sitting at their customary table in the grand salon. He squeezed her hand. "You were right about zeppelins. They're faster than a ship and better than a train because there are no stops. Equally as elegant and, unlike airplanes, there's no noise."

Mattie smiled and squeezed his hand back.

Cockran heard a commotion behind him when the airship was barely a hundred feet from the ground. Multiple ropes had dropped from each side of the great ship and Cockran could see below as many as forty men grasping the ropes and pulling the zeppelin lower still.

Cockran turned and saw that *Herr* Verschuer was standing at the exit leading from the grand salon into the passageway through which all the passengers would debark. His valet was standing behind him, clutching two large suitcases, one in each hand.

Cockran leaned over and whispered to Mattie. "Our boy intends to make a quick exit."

Mattie nodded. "Let's do our best to follow him. If he goes anywhere except Berlin, I vote we take the same train and hope he's headed for the clinic".

"Agreed." Cockran said. He looked out the window and could see the mooring mast as the men below steered the ship toward it. Beside the mast was a long black Mercedes sedan.

Once the ship was securely locked into the mooring mast, Verschuer and his valet were the first through the door, making a bee line for the sedan. Cockran and Mattie were close behind, the third couple down the six wooden steps from the passenger gondola to the ground.

Cockran and Mattie quickly sidestepped the older couple in front of them and were close behind Verschuer, hoping to get a glance at the Mercedes' license plate. Verschuer's valet had a different idea. He turned, as if he had forgotten something in the zeppelin and started back toward the *Graf*. But when he came abreast of Cockran and Mattie, he swung the suitcase in his right hand and caught Mattie squarely in the stomach. She cried out and fell to the ground.

The valet dropped the suitcase and knelt to offer her a hand, apologizing in a stream of German. Cockran wasn't buying it. He shoved the man hard but the valet was a rock. He regarded Cockran with indifference, rising to his feet and stepping back to give them some room.

Cockran helped Mattie to her feet. She brushed off the dirt. The valet was still jabbering in German when he leaned close to Mattie as though to apologize. He switched into accented English: "Be more careful, *Fraulein*," the valet said. "Germany can be a dangerous place."

With that, the valet picked up the suitcase and walked away from the zeppelin. Enraged, Cockran moved to follow, but Mattie put a hand on his arm to stop him. "Let it go," she said.

The diversion had been what Verschuer needed for the Mercedes had turned and sped across the landing field toward the road. Cockran couldn't make out the license plate at that distance but what he could see on the right front fender was chilling. A small, familiar flag whose red background surrounded a white circle inside of which was a jet black swastika.

Cockran turned to Mattie. "That figures. If Waterman's involved, so are the Nazis. They're old friends."

COCKRAN and Mattie checked into the Hotel Rose in Friedrichschafen. They had a small suite which overlooked Lake Constance and the white sails of boats in the distance. They ordered an early room service supper of *wienerschnitzel* and a bottle of *Gewürztraminer*.

"It's still afternoon in Ireland," Cockran said. "After supper I'll call the phone number of a pub in Donegal where Bobby said I could leave messages for him. I thought we'd have a few days in Germany *incognito* until the Apostles arrived to provide you around the clock protection. Given Verschuer's threat, however, I'd feel better if we had more firepower as soon as we can."

"You'll get no argument from me," Mattie said.

The telephone rang and Cockran picked it up. "Yes. That's fine. Send him right up."

"Who was that?" Mattie asked.

"The front desk. Captain David Baker from the American Embassy in Berlin."

Moments later, David Baker was in their room. Introductions and handshakes were exchanged. Baker was a compact, good-looking man, five foot eight, his golden hair slicked back. What was it with MID and blond hair? Cockran wondered. This guy could be Ted Hudson's younger brother, minus a few inches.

"I received Major Hudson's cable yesterday telling me to meet the zeppelin and tail a silver haired man named Dr. Verschuer. I came here as fast as I could. Unfortunately, the only automobile I was able to lease was a small Opel. It was no match for Dr. Verschuer's Mercedes. I lost track of him about five miles outside of Friedrichschafen. Major Hudson said I was to stay with Verschuer as long as possible and then come back and report to you where he went."

"Do you know Major Hudson," Mattie asked.

"Not personally, no, Ma'am. But everyone in MID knows who he is," Baker said in a voice tinged with admiration and awe.

Just great, Cockran thought. The bastard probably had his own fan club of bright eyed, bushy tailed young acolytes like this puppy dog Baker. "Did you get the license plate?"

"No, Sir," Baker replied. "But the Major asked that I deliver this to you, Miss McGary," as he handed a thick manila envelope to Mattie.

"What's this?" Mattie asked.

"It's MID's dossier on Dr. Verschuer. I updated it myself yesterday afternoon."

"Thank you," Mattie replied.

"Captain, is there information here about Verschuer's clinic in Bavaria?" Cockran asked.

Baker seemed embarrassed. "Uh . . . well, no. There's nothing in there like that. I mean, Major Hudson didn't ask me to find anything like that.

He just told me to make a photostat of all the articles in our dossier. He didn't say anything about a clinic."

"Well, is there anything in these articles about any clinics in Bavaria?" Mattie asked as Cockran walked to the other side of the room to refresh his drink.

"Well . . . I don't know. I didn't exactly read the articles myself."

Behind Baker's back, Cockran rolled his eyes at Mattie. The kid probably *was* one of Ted's protégés. Receiving solid intelligence from MID would be a triumph of hope over history.

Baker turned to leave and then stopped and turned back. "Major Hudson said in his cable that he was working on his last story for Hearst and that you were assisting him. Is that true?"

Cockran suppressed a smile as Mattie sighed and said, "Actually, Ted's working for me."

Baker's eyes grew wide. "What's Major Hudson really like?" Baker asked.

He's an asshole, Cockran thought, as Mattie smiled. "He's a nice man but I don't think Ted would appreciate my talking about him."

Baker was duly chastised and began to apologize when Mattie cut him off. "No, don't worry about it, Captain. But, if you don't mind, we need to review the dossier."

Baker apologized again and left them.

Cockran and Mattie walked over and took chairs beside a small table which looked out a pair of French doors onto Lake Constance. Three sailboats were in the far distance. Mattie took half the contents of the envelope and handed the other half to Cockran.

Thirty minutes later, Mattie finished sorting through her pile and went over to the drinks bar in the corner of their suit where she made a small pitcher of martinis.

"I don't know about what you've read," Mattie said, handing a martini to Cockran, "but this confirms my suspicions about American military intelligence."

"What's that?" Cockran asked as he took a sip.

"I'll take a Hearst reporter over an MID agent any day. There was only one article in here that wasn't in the Hearst report and a lot of articles that we saw there simply aren't here."

Cockran smiled. "I saw nothing new in what I reviewed. What did you find that was?"

"A 1929 article by Verschuer from a student-edited journal at Heidelberg. It's called 'Genetics and Race Science as the Basis for Purifying Politics,'" Mattie said. "He wrote that the most important task of Germany's internal politics was their population problem, which he described as 'a biological problem which can only be solved by biological-political measures.'"

"What the hell are 'biological-political measures?'" Cockran asked.

Mattie shook her head." It's like he's writing in a code that only the initiated understand."

"Well, you're right about MID. They can't find their asses with both hands."

"But that's not the right question," Mattie said as she stood up, came over and sat on Cockran's lap, taking another sip of her martini.

Cockran did the same. "What is the right question?"

"Whether an ex-MID agent like you can find *my* ass with both hands."

"Is that an invitation?"

"Consider it more of a challenge."

MATTIE lay on her side facing Cockran, a sheet pulled up to her waist.

"I've been thinking, Bourke, about locating the clinic. I know Winston has the Prof looking into it, but there's another angle I ought to try once we arrive in Munich."

"What's that?" Cockran asked.

"I've covered some big stories in that city over the past ten years. I've made good contacts, including quite a few in the criminal underworld, what you Yanks would call gangsters."

Cockran didn't like the sound of this. "What kind of gangsters?"

"Well, they're fairly scary. Prostitution, drugs, protection, extortion, smuggling."

"And how could these gangsters help?" Cockran asked.

"Two years ago this fall I was in Munich at a fairly seedy bar. The White Mouse Cabaret. I was waiting to meet a contact who was going to help me arrange interviews with some low-end people in a network which was smuggling arms into the Balkans. Anyway, my contact didn't show and a couple of guys with too much beer and too little brains started to display unwanted attention. So when one of them tried to fondle me, I decked his buddy."

"His buddy? Why'd you deck him?" Cockran asked.

Mattie laughed. "Hell, the guy was as big as you and weighed fifty pounds more. His buddy was more my size. He never saw it coming. One punch."

Cockran laughed. Mattie might — hell, she did — take too many risks but he had to admit she could take care of herself. Most of the time. It was the rest of the time that concerned him. "What happened then?"

"The bartender intervened, called over a bouncer and had the two guys thrown out. He took me back to a corner table and introduced me to the owner who apologized for the behavior of his customers. When he introduced himself, I was astonished. Erich Boldt. I knew him by reputation. He's one of the biggest crime bosses in Munich. I knew he smuggled weapons, but I hadn't heard that he was involved in the Balkans. It turns out he wasn't, but he wanted to be. He set me up with several more interviews that pretty much allowed me to expose the people who were running guns into the Balkans. Convictions followed. My guess is that he's already stepped into the vacuum my stories created. I figure he owes me one."

"Okay," Cockran said. "We're both fairly well armed. It shouldn't be that dangerous."

Mattie sat up now. "That won't work, Bourke. I've got to go alone. I'll take my Walther. But you can't go with me."

"Why?"

"If this guy's still around," Mattie replied, "my going there with an armed escort would scare him off. He probably wouldn't see me. I've got to go alone."

Cockran could sense an argument about to begin, one he wasn't going to win. Not yet anyway. But there was no way he was letting her meet with that guy alone. He got up from the bed and walked toward the small sitting room.

"Nice ass, Cockran," Mattie said. "Where are you going?"

"To call that pub in Donegal and try to find Bobby. We're going to need more guns."

52.

Why Are You Working for the Nazis?

WINSTON Churchill was in fine form. Alternately smiling and scowling beneath the sparkling crystal chandeliers of the Hotel Continental's dining room, the United Kingdom's former Chancellor of the Exchequer was guiding his dinner guests, Mattie, his son Randolph and Cockran through the Battle of Blenheim, whose battlefields in Bavaria Churchill had spent the last week touring. Puffing on a long Havana cigar and taking an occasional sip from his flute of Pol Roger Champagne, Churchill had reached the battle's climax when their first course arrived.

Later, after the waiter had cleared their table and brought them brandy snifters and a bottle of Remy Martin, Churchill returned to the subject they had discussed earlier in the day. The inability of Hearst, American MID, or Churchill's good friend Professor Frederick Lindemann, "The Prof", to pinpoint the location of Verschuer's clinic.

"The Prof has come up dry. His source at the Kaiser Wilhelm Institute told him it was highly confidential. In fact, he wouldn't confirm if Verschuer even had a clinic in Bavaria."

"Do you believe him?" Mattie asked

Churchill took a puff of his cigar and shook his head. "Baron von Verschuer's Nazi sympathies are well known. *Herr* Hitler's party will soon be the largest party in Germany and his becoming chancellor is only a matter of time. Courage is in short supply in Germany today."

"Amen!" Randolph said as he poured himself another generous measure of brandy.

"Does the Prof have any other sources?" Cockran asked.

"As a matter of fact, he does," Churchill replied. "A secretary at the Kaiser Wilhelm Institute who is in charge of making travel arrangements for all the visiting scientists. A woman to trust, the Prof says. She converted but her mother is a Jew. She's no friend of the Nazis."

"So she knows where the clinic is?" Mattie said.

"No. But the secretary has frequently arranged train tickets from Munich to Regensburg for scientists who have come to confer with Dr. Verschuer."

"That's close to the Austrian border, isn't it?" Cockran asked.

Churchill nodded. "Yes, it's on the Danube."

"Perhaps we should plan to go there tomorrow instead of Mattie going to a meeting tonight with this Erich Boldt character."

Mattie tensed. On the train from Friedrichschafen to Munich, Mattie had sensed that Cockran was holding back over her refusal to allow him to accompany her to meet Erich Boldt. Regardless of what Churchill or Cockran thought, however, she was going to meet him. Alone.

Churchill swirled his brandy in the snifter. "Who is this Boldt fellow?"

"An old source of mine," Mattie replied. "He's an underworld figure here in Munich. Gambling, prostitution and smuggling. Inadvertently I helped him eliminate one of his competitors two years ago with stories on gunrunning in the Balkans. He owes me a favor."

"And Bourke does not wish you to go?"

"I'm not fond of the idea," Cockran said. "Especially if she goes alone."

Mattie shook her head. "It's the only way. He won't talk to people he's never met."

"Will you be armed, my dear?"

Mattie nodded. "My Walther."

"And it's a place you've been before?"

Again, Mattie nodded.

Churchill took a puff of his cigar and gazed off, finally returning his glance to Mattie.

"The risk seems acceptable," Churchill pronounced.

Mattie smiled. Good old Winston. She knew he'd never say no to an adventure but Cockran's displeasure was written all over his face.

The White Mouse Cabaret

MATTIE wrinkled her nose at the oppressive odor of cigar smoke, stale beer and sweat as she sat at a table nursing a scotch and water and watching what passed for the floor show. The table at which she was sitting had a small lamp with a red fringed shade and a telephone beside it which bore the number twelve, the same as her table. She was wearing the little black dress she had worn on her trip with Ted Hudson. It was fine then in a decent restaurant but here, she felt like a high-class hooker. Already, her phone had rung twice and she had turned down propositions to join prosperous, well-fed Bavarians at their tables. Being Sunday night, the cabaret was only two-thirds full and the aging dancers seemed no more enthusiastic than the crowd as they shed their clothes. All the way. No pasties or g-strings as in America. Mattie found it all to be sad and certainly not erotic.

The telephone rang and Mattie picked it up. A deep voice said '*Fraulein* McGary?'"

"This is she."

"A large Mercedes motorcar is waiting outside for you. Are you armed?"

"Yes."

"At the motorcar, you will be relieved of your weapon. This is acceptable?"

"Yes."

Mattie claimed her evening coat from the hat-check girl and walked out the door to the end of the frayed and tattered red awning which covered the entrance to the White Mouse. Waiting there, its engine idling, was a long black Mercedes. A door swung out as Mattie arrived and she ducked her head and stepped into the car. She felt strong hands pat her down. The man was thorough and professional as he searched for the automatic pistol he soon found in her coat pocket. She turned, and there in the far right-hand corner of the limousine, its windows lined with curtains, was the gleaming bald head and thick neck of Erich Boldt.

"*Fraulein* McGary. How pleasant to see you again."

"A pleasure to see you, as well, *Herr* Boldt." Mattie answered in German.

"So. You are seeking information about *Herr Doktor* von Verschuer. A strangely popular man. Yours is the second inquiry I have received today about him."

Mattie was surprised and she let it show. "Really? Who was asking?"

"All in good time, my dear. All in good time. But first, we are taking a little ride. Somewhere quiet where we won't be disturbed."

Before she knew what was happening, the same strong hands which had patted her down and relieved her of her weapon grabbed her wrists in one deft motion and encased them in a pair of stainless steel handcuffs, ignoring her struggles. A soft cotton blindfold was tied over her eyes. When she began to raise her hands to her blindfold, someone pulled them forcefully down and slapped her face hard. It was Erich Boldt and his voice was cold.

"None of that if you know what's good for you," Boldt said. "Now tell me. Who sent you? Why are you working for the Nazis?"

53.

I Am Spoken For

Night Train to Regensburg
Sunday, 29 May 1932

*V**IELEN Dank*," said an attractive brunette in the dining car on the night train to Regensburg via Munich. The waiter nodded and left the couple to their meal.

Kurt von Sturm sat across from the brunette and marveled that a pair of false eyeglasses failed to dim the brightness and beauty of Ingrid Johansson — the name "Waterman" no longer applied to her as far as she was concerned. The "precautions" he had insisted upon just might do the trick. After his mother cut her long hair in a fashionable bob, he had spent time applying the dyeing chemicals he purchased from his Norden barber as Ingrid sat patiently in the tub.

The twins' disappearance had changed Ingrid. Her life was in danger but finding her siblings gave her a purpose beyond herself. For Sturm, finding them was another matter of honor.

Ingrid was practicing her German over dinner. That was the second layer of her disguise. Ingrid had to appear to be German to anyone with whom she had to interact. The dining car was mostly empty as Ingrid spoke quietly in English. "I think my accent is improving."

"And all this time, you thought you were teaching English to Franka." Sturm replied.

"How do you explain who I am?"

"You are my assistant. My traveling secretary. You are there to take notes. Given your beauty, they will probably assume you're also my mistress. Let them make that assumption."

"But I'm the one who's married," she said. "Wouldn't that make you *my* mistress?"

Sturm frowned. When Ingrid said things he didn't quite understand, she was usually making a joke. He had known another beautiful woman who did the same. Kurt von Sturm. A mistress. That *was* pretty funny. He allowed himself a faint smile.

"Good boy," Ingrid said, "Now, I'm not the only one learning a new language."

"But you are learning fast," he said. "*Meine liebe Fraulein, von wo du bist?*"

Ingrid replied "*Entschuldigen, ich bin sehr beschäftigt.*" Excuse me, I am very busy.

"Excellent," Sturm said. "*Entschuldigen, Fraulein, wurde du mögen etwas Tee?*"

"*Nein, danke. Ich bin fein,*" No thank you. I'm fine.

Sturm responded in a blur of German which roughly translated to, "As you wish, *Fraulein.*You look so beautiful, I should like to introduce you to my mother and sister."

"*Danke sehr, aber ich wurde für gesprochen.*" Thank you but I am spoken for.

Sturm leaned back in his seat with a smile. "You're getting better all the time."

Ingrid laughed triumphantly. "I don't know. The only words I understood were *beautiful, mother and sister.* But you're the kind of man who would make a pass at me after offering tea, let alone wine." She gave Sturm a devilish look. "Can we return to our compartment now?"

"Yes. Why?"

"I'd like to practice my German pillow talk."

Sturm paused, sensing another joke had been made with an American idiom.

Ingrid sighed with impatience. "Think about it for a minute. You're a smart guy. You'll figure it out."

Sturm did. Then he laughed. He really did like Americans. Even their sense of humor.

54.

The Nazis Are Not My Friends

DAMN! Cockran thought, as he slouched low in the front seat of his dark gray BMW 328 roadster parked half a block away from the White Mouse Cabaret. Cockran had watched with rising concern when he saw Mattie come out and step into a Mercedes with its side curtains drawn. He had a clear view through the front windscreen of all that happened once she was inside. The handcuffs and the savage slap was all he needed to know. Meeting Boldt alone was a mistake. As the car pulled abreast of Cockran, its rear interior light was switched off and he strained to see anything out of the shadows inside but he couldn't. Where the hell was Sullivan? He should have been here by now with two more Apostles.

Cockran had tried one last time to persuade Mattie to put off her meeting with Boldt until the following day when Bobby and the Apostles would certainly be there, but she had refused.

"We can't afford to waste a whole day. And I don't want to be followed, Bourke. It will make Boldt suspicious and I must get him to trust me" she had said.

Cockran turned in his seat to watch the Mercedes speed down the street. It turned right at the first intersection and Cockran put the BMW into gear, executed a u-turn and followed the Mercedes. Soon, they were deep within a warehouse district. Lights were on in some buildings but most were dark.

The Mercedes turned left at another side street. Cockran was about to do the same when he noticed that the street was a dead end. Fifty yards away at the end of the street sat a squat, three-story brick warehouse building with fading white paint. It did not look occupied. Cockran drove past the dead end, did a u-turn, parked the BMW on the boulevard, and walked back to the dead end street. He reached the building on the corner and heard a horn sound three times.

Cockran peered down the street and saw a battered overhead metal door rise in the white building and the Mercedes disappear inside. The front of the building was featureless and the only windows were long horizontal ones set eight feet above the ground. The metal door closed and two guards armed with submachine guns returned to their position.

Well, that takes out a frontal approach, Cockran thought. He needed another way to get inside. When he was a captain in the Great War, he would never move a unit forward without reading the latest reports from aerial surveillance to give him a current layout of his own and the enemy's trenches. As he did not have access to a biplane or a reconnaissance balloon now, he would have to get higher up for a bird's eye view.

Cockran looked up at the building that shielded him from view of the guards a block away. It was four stories high which was enough to give him perspective. He began rounding the building, searching for some way to get inside, and stepped into an alley which ran along the building's right side. A rusted metal fire escape zigzagged its way up the side for four stories. Unusual for a German building but fortuitous for him. The fire escape was set ten feet off the ground to discourage what Cockran had in mind — gaining entrance to the roof. A rusting metal oil drum was at the far end of the fire escape, but that still left him a good foot short of getting his hands on the bottom rung. He walked deeper into the alley until he found what he was looking for. Several sturdy looking empty wooden crates with stencils on their sides, *Braun Precision Tools.* Underneath that, *Milwaukee, Wisconsin.* God bless America.

Picking up one crate, Cockran returned to the oil drum and placed the crate on top. Standing on the crate, he hoisted himself onto the bottom rung of the fire escape and made his way up it to the roof. Once there, he walked over to the ledge to get a look at the warehouse. He lay prone on the roof and peered over to see the two guards standing watch outside the entrance. Along the right side of the warehouse, he could see at least two more guards by the telltale lights from their cigarettes. Not a very good chance of gaining entry at ground level.

Directly across, it was difficult to see much detail on the warehouse's roof, the lights from street level not reaching that height. One thing was clear, though. The warehouse was surprisingly close to his building, separated by an alley about ten feet across, although it was at least a twelve foot drop down to the warehouse roof from his building. But if he made it, the odds became better. They would not be expecting an intruder from above.

It was risky, to be sure, but it was the only way he was going to be able to rescue Mattie and maybe commandeer that Mercedes to get them out of there and past those machine gun-toting guards outside. Would the noise of his landing be noticed by the guards? He didn't think so. The sound of the traffic on the boulevard would mask his aerial approach.

Of course, there was the immediate problem of a four story drop to his death if he couldn't clear the ten foot space. He thought he could leap that far, certainly with a running start and the lack of any ledge to impede his progress. But doing it was entirely different than thinking about it. Still, he had no choice. Mattie was in trouble and, just like the idiot he had been about her visit to Cold Spring Harbor, he had let her walk into it alone.

Cockran took a few steps back, steadied himself, waited until he could hear approaching trucks on the boulevard, then started forward. Gradually building his speed, he stutter stepped near the building's edge to time his footing and plant his right foot. He leaped into the air, the roof below soaring towards him but his heart hung in his throat as he saw his legs waving over the four story drop to the pavement below. He landed hard, his right foot and then his knee hitting the roof as he rolled forward and back up to his feet. Ignoring the pain in his knee, he turned around to look up at the other building. It seemed a lot higher and further away than before. He waited, listening for any sign his landing had been heard but there was only silence.

A small padlock hung on the heavy metal door to the stairwell but it was easy work for Cockran to pick. Padlock gone, he had to be careful with the door. It was big, old and looked like it was rarely used. He needed to be quiet. He pulled the door open slowly and squeezed inside the stairwell. He followed the stairwell down two floors to another door.

He opened it and saw a metal stairway leading down to a metal gangway that lined the perimeter of the open ground floor of the warehouse. He could hear voices echoing up from the warehouse floor. He let the door close behind him. Despite his care, it gave out a faint metallic squeak.

Cockran froze. He heard the voices stop at the sound. After a moment, the voices resumed and he made his way carefully down the metal stairway, trying to minimize the noise.

When he reached the gangway, he looked down and then drew the Webley from its holster.

The warehouse floor was mostly dark and three quarters filled with crates stacked two high, nearly eight feet. There were aisles between the crates every fifty feet or so. In a clearing in the middle of the floor sat Mattie, a single overhead light shining down on her. Her wrists were still cuffed in front of her, her ankles bound to the sides of the chair. Her coat was off and all she wore was that damn skimpy black dress with its narrow halter top. Normally, Cockran liked that dress a lot but now it made her seem bare and vulnerable. Beyond Mattie, cloaked in shadow, he could see two other figures bound and gagged in chairs, their features indistinguishable at this distance.

Cockran could not tell what was going on. Mattie was being interrogated and giving her answers in German. Her tone of voice was angry. Four men stood around her, but the man questioning her was large with a gleaming bald head, his tuxedo jacket carefully folded on a chair behind him, his sleeves rolled up, his black bow tie neatly in place. He smacked Mattie with a vicious backhand, followed by an open-face slap with the forehand, blood appearing on her split lip. The bald man was clearly angry and not at all happy with Mattie's answers.

Quietly, Cockran began to move down another metal stairway from the gangway to the ground floor of the warehouse. Four men inside, four men outside. Not very good odds, but with most of the warehouse cloaked in darkness and the crates for cover, he would have the advantage of surprise. He stopped halfway down the stairs and saw the bald-headed man kneel down in front of Mattie and gently dab the corner of her mouth with a handkerchief. His tone was soothing. Then the bald man turned, took a glass of water from one of the other men and offered it to Mattie who held it in her cuffed hands. Good, he thought. A distraction. Time to move.

Cockran started down the rest of the stairway and stopped short, two-thirds of the way to the warehouse floor. There was a man directly in front of him beginning to walk up the stairs. The man saw him and froze, startled. Cockran took one more step and leaped at the man, his shoulder hitting him in the chest and taking him back down the stairs where he landed on his back with Cockran on top. He heard the man's head bounce off the pavement with a thick crack and felt his body go slack. Behind him, the remaining three men began to shout.

Standing up, Cockran could see two of the three men approaching him from the spot of light in the center of the floor. They had heard the impact but it was clear they hadn't seen him in the shadows behind the crates. He'd have to take advantage. The bald man—unarmed, from what Cockran could see—stayed behind with Mattie and watched the others. Cockran moved sideways to his right, trying to outflank the men who were walking from the light into the dark. One of them switched on a flashlight off to Cockran's left. By the time the flashlight swept over to the aisle where he had been, Cockran had moved so far to the right that he'd become even with the aisle leading to the bald man holding Mattie hostage. He inched forward towards the light, Webley held tight in his palm. The bald man was staring after his men, shouting instructions in German, all of them searching in the wrong spot for Cockran who was about to come up behind the bald man. Cockran stopped just short of the light and cocked the Webley, the click echoing through the now silent warehouse. The bald man spun around as Cockran spoke.

"You'd better understand English, Buddy, because it could save your life. Hands up!"

"Cockran!" Mattie yelled, craning her neck to see him.

"Tell that bald asshole to call his men off or I'll kill him where he stands."

"I speak English, *Herr* Cockran," the bald man said in a thick guttural voice. He didn't raise his hands. Instead, he shouted something in German to his men. "But I don't fancy the odds of your leaving this warehouse alive, with or without my death."

"Cockran, what are you doing?!" Mattie yelled, almost angry it seemed. "Coming in here with a gun when you're outnumbered four to one? You could have been killed."

"More like eight to one, actually," the bald man said, rolling his shirt sleeves down and smoothing them out. "But I admire your courage."

"Lunacy is more like it," Mattie said. "Cockran, put the gun down!"

What the hell was going on? What was Mattie trying to pull? Cockran saw the other two guards appear at the edge of the light, their weapons pointed directly at Mattie, the bald man and Cockran who had stepped forward, his Webley no more than three feet from her captor.

"Let her go now or you're dead," Cockran said.

The bald man leaned forward and took the cuffs off Mattie's hands and untied her feet. "There, *Herr* Cockran. She is free. If you put your weapon down, I would be happy to explain."

"Bourke, it's okay," Mattie said,. "It was just a misunderstanding. Put the gun down."

"A misunderstanding? That asshole was using your face for target practice."

"There is an innocent explanation, I assure you," the bald man said, re-fastening his cufflinks. "I am Erich Boldt."

"Do I look like I give a damn?" Cockran replied.

"Apparently you do not," Boldt said. He reached for his tuxedo jacket and calmly put his arm through the sleeve. "But you must understand. The Nazis are not my friends."

"So what? They're not my friends either." Cockran said, impatient at the *non sequitur.* "What's your point?"

Erich Boldt stepped towards Cockran, straightening his jacket. "My point, as you put it, is that I have no patience for Nazi sympathizers. The Nazis frown on my activities and believe that only they may use violence in furtherance of their goals. While I know *Fraulein* McGary has done me a favor in the past for which I am grateful, she is close enough to Hitler to have interviewed him not once, but three times. In my experience, *Herr* Hitler does not so willingly grant interviews to his enemies. So, when *Fraulein* McGary wanted the location of a clinic in Bavaria run by Baron von Verschuer, a well-known party member, I was suspicious. She was the second person to make that inquiry today. I had to make certain she was not, what is it you Americans say? 'Setting me up.'"

"She's not setting you up. She's working on a story which, if von Verschuer really is a Nazi, will bring them a lot of unfavorable publicity," Cockran said.

"Indeed, that is what *Fraulein* McGary told me," Boldt responded, "and I think I now believe her. Frankly, if you would just lower your weapon, I might be fully convinced."

"You first," Cockran said. Boldt nodded to his men and Cockran watched them holster their weapons and then he slowly lowered his Webley and did the same.

"Good. Now we can talk." Boldt said. "As I said, it naturally aroused my suspicions when *Fraulein* McGary was the second person to contact me today seeking information about Baron von Verschuer. Perhaps you can help me identify these other gentlemen."

Boldt snapped out a rapid order in German and his three men crossed to the other side of the warehouse where the other two captives were bound and gagged. Cockran watched as their hands and legs were freed and they were helped to their feet. One of the captives needed two men to lift him up as he could not put weight on one foot. He leaned heavily on one of Boldt's men as he hobbled over to the spotlight.

"Bobby!" Mattie exclaimed. "What are you doing here?"

"And couldn't I be asking you the same question? Our original plan was only to be your bodyguard but we had a wee problem along the way," Bobby Sullivan replied with a smile, or as close to a human smile as he could muster and one he usually reserved for Mattie. Sullivan then turned to his fellow captive who Cockran could see was Rolf Heyden, a young Munich hotel concierge who had helped them last year with the Cockran client who had been the victim of a Nazi extortion scheme.

"Rolf, I know you told me you knew of someone who, for a price, could find anyone. But these two," Sullivan said with a nod in the direction of Cockran and Mattie, "weren't the ones I was looking for."

55.

I Want To Help the Party

Regensburg, Germany
Monday, 30 May 1932

ONCE in Regensburg, Sturm wasted no time. He hailed a cab and headed directly for the local offices of the National Socialist German Workers Party. He was dressed all in black—a turtleneck, slacks, and the hip-length leather coat worn by German naval airship officers.

"Shouldn't we start at the hotel?" Ingrid asked under her breath.

"Not yet. I do not wish to be seen or noticed any more than is necessary."

They arrived at a squat beige two story building with a red tiled roof. Five blocks away, the twin spires of St. Peter's Cathedral towered over the buildings around it. Ingrid adjusted her false glasses, wielding her pale green notebook like a shield and followed Sturm inside. A large flag in colors of red, black and white dominated the lobby, although not in the traditional horizontal bars of Imperial Germany. Instead, the flag was blood red, with a large white circle in the center, enclosing the ancient spiritual symbol of the hooked cross, a black *swastika*.

A young man, a boy really, with short blond hair sat beneath it at a small desk and greeted them both with cold and suspicious eyes. "What is it?" he asked.

"My name is Kurt von Sturm. I wish to speak with the *Gauleiter*."

"Do you have an appointment?"

"No. But it is a matter of some urgency."

"*Herr* Vokhsul sees no one without an appointment," the boy said with more than a trace of arrogance . "Everyone in Regensburg know this!"

Sturm held the boy's gaze. The boy grew uncomfortable in the silence, eventually shifting his eyes away. "I'm going to have to ask you to leave," he said. "Sir."

Sturm reached into his breast pocket for his billfold. He found the badge inside and rested it quietly on the table beside which he placed an ID card. Before the boy had a chance to look at the badge, Sturm placed his hand over it and spoke in a quiet voice. "Give this to the *Gauleiter*. If you are quick about it, I will not mention your impertinence to *Herr* Vokhsul — and more importantly, I will not report to my superiors about the pathetic staff he has hired in this district."

Sturm slowly lifted his hand. The boy took one look at the badge and then the ID card. His face drained of color. "I am sorry *Herr* von Sturm. Deeply and truly sorry. Sir, I…"

"I said to be quick about it."

"Yes, Sir!" the boy said as he stood up, shot Sturm a quick Roman salute and left.

THEY chose to walk the ten blocks north to the main police station, the twin spires of the cathedral towering at their backs. Ingrid tried to keep pace with Sturm's long strides..

"What was that about back there?" she said in a whisper.

"I secured the name of a police detective who will be able to help."

"No, with the boy out front. What did you show him?"

"That? I showed him my credentials as *Herr* von Thyssen's executive assistant."

"From the boy's reaction, you would think *Herr* von Thyssen was Vlad the Impaler."

"He owns the United Steel Works," Sturm said, ignoring her humor. "A man like that has a great deal of power and influence in Germany and his name carries instant respect."

"And the badge of his executive assistant strikes terror into the hearts of little Nazis?"

"Was your wait outside uncomfortable?" Sturm asked, ignoring her question.

"No, it was fine. The boy was too frightened to engage in conversation," she said. "But why did you have to visit a Nazi party office to find a policeman who could help us? Why couldn't we go directly to the police?"

"Little happens in Bavaria without the Nazis' knowledge, certainly not an abduction of two American students."

"How would the Nazis know if the police did not?"

"They are privy to information that is not available to the general public, and that includes the authorities. They have key men and sympathizers placed at all levels of government. They are called 'V-Men,' shorthand for *Vertrauensmänner*, 'trustworthy men.'"

"You mean spies?" she said.

"Sympathizers."

"Why wouldn't the Nazis tell the police about kidnappings? Shielding kidnappers doesn't seem honorable."

Sturm shifted his body to avoid another passerby and answered her stiffly. "Unless you continue this conversation in German, I insist you remain quiet." Ingrid blushed but did not answer. Sturm took her hand and urged her onward, "*Angegangen, hast!*"

At the police station, they did not stop at the booking desk to ask directions. Two stairways on either side led away from the entrance and up to a hallway of offices on the mezzanine. Sturm led Ingrid down this hallway, passing mostly men in muted gray plainclothes, until they reached a doorway that opened into a large open anteroom. The Bureau of Detectives.

Sturm approached a stout woman in her thirties with short brown hair, sitting outside the main office. "Kurt von Sturm for *Käpitan* Bloem, please."

"Yes, Sir," she said. "He's been expecting you." The secretary rose from her seat and knocked on the door, announcing their presence. Then she opened the door and waved them in.

The office was darker than the anteroom outside, blades of light seeping in through horizontal wooden blinds. *Kapitän* Bloem stayed behind his desk and did not rise.

"Good afternoon, *Kapitän* Bloem," Sturm said. "I hope you don't mind that I've brought my traveling secretary with me. She is excellent at taking notes if I need them."

"*Gutentag, Kapitän* Bloem," Ingrid said in perfectly practiced German, adding a curtsy.

"Please sit down," Bloem said. "Let us see whether there is anything to take notes about." Sturm nodded and sat directly before the desk. Ingrid took her seat at the side of the room. "I'm told we have some mutual friends?"

"We may, in fact," Sturm said, and reached inside his breast pocket again for the badge he had shown earlier. He laid it on the detective's desk and let him examine it. Ingrid was too far away to see it and she would not be able to follow their conversation in any event.

"45,250?" Bloem said with astonishment. "You must be one of the "old fighters".

Sturm nodded. "1923. How long have you been a member?" Sturm asked.

"Me? Not nearly so long. I did not join until I saw which way the wind was blowing in 1930. I've never known which politicians to support. But the Depression persuaded me the Nazis had the answers. Even before then, I wanted nothing more than to rid Germany of the Versailles treaty and to hang the traitors of Weimar that burdened us with it."

"I could not agree more, *Kapitän* Bloem," Sturm replied. "Why else become a V-Man?"

Bloem gave a quick sideward glance at Ingrid, but she had not shown any special interest in Sturm's comment about V-Men. Instead, she appeared to be scribbling away on her pad.

"I want to help the party. I like to think I am in a position here in Regensburg to do so."

"Here is how you can help," Sturm said. "My employer has asked me to track down two Americans. They were seen last in Regensburg. They're missing and I need to find them."

"Americans? Is there anything you can tell me about them?"

Sturm went on to describe them each individually from what Ingrid had told him—brown hair, average height, early twenties. Fraternal twins.

"*Herr* von Sturm," Bloem said quickly, "we receive so many visitors here in Regensburg every summer to see our cathredral, many of them Americans. You must understand how difficult it is for us to keep track of every one that comes in and out of our town. I will be happy to make several inquiries."

"I recently sat down to lunch with Heinrich Himmler," Sturm said, conversationally. "Himmler and I joined the Party around the same time in 1923 but he's been a member longer than I have, Number 42,404. The one thing he kept emphasizing to me when we take power was record-keeping. Every police station in every town will keep perfect records of every citizen and stranger in their jurisdictioin. That way, Germany can keep a careful eye on the Fatherland's enemies from *abroad* as well as at home."

Sturm paused for effect. It was true as far as it went. He had lunched with Himmler. But recently? Well, August, 1930 might be considered recent. It was right after the National Socialist breakthrough election that month when the Nazis overnight had become the second largest party in Germany. Sturm had brought much needed funds to the party and he was the apple of Hitler's eye. Himmler tried to recruit him for the SS but Sturm turned him down flat. Few could do that with impunity but Himmler would never insult a man high in the Fuhrer's favor. Hence, the invitation to join the SS remained open and the gleaming black uniform of an SS *Obersturmbannfuhrer* still hung in Sturm's Munich apartment. Unused.

"Now, Regensburg can't be so large that a good Nazi like yourself would not be able to keep track of foreigners passing through your town. I imagine *Herr* Himmler would be most disappointed to learn that I was unable to find adequate assistance here in Regensburg."

Bloem removed a handkerchief from his jacket and patted the sweat from his brow. He turned to Ingrid. "*Fraulein*, please put your notebook away for the moment."

Ingrid looked up with blank eyes, probably understanding only the word "notebook."

Sturm intervened. "It's all right, Heidi," he said, nodding to Ingrid and gesturing with his hand to make it clear that he was asking her to stop taking notes. "You may stop taking notes."

Ingrid picked up the message and put her notebook down.

Bloem stood up from his desk, his nervousness on display, and walked over to a cabinet at the side of the room. "It's difficult to know how one should proceed in situations like these, *Herr* von Sturm, because the chain of command within the party is complicated," he said. He opened the cabinet to reveal a couple bottles of liquor. "May I offer you some *schnapps*?" Sturm shook his head no and the detective proceeded to pour one out for himself.

"Earlier this year, all V-Men in Bavaria were placed under strict orders to identify any twins who registered in hotels with a foreign passport and report them to Dr. Otmar von Verschuer at his biological clinic, fifteen miles north of Passau in the Bavarian National Forest."

The detective glanced at Ingrid who raised her eyebrows perceptably at the name Verschuer. "Frankly, I'm still not sure if I'm supposed to be telling you any of this, let alone in the presence of your secretary," he said and sat back down with his drink in hand. "We were under strict orders not to reveal this surveillance to anybody, so you must forgive my reluctance to divulge it to you. I don't understand to what party member level I am allowed to reveal this information, but I want to make myself clear. I want to help the Party if I can."

Sturm nodded slowly. "I appreciate your candor. I was aware of Dr. Verschuer's activities," Sturm said, the lie coming easily, "but not of the details. This should probably clear matters up, so you were right to tell me. Do you know why he is so interested in twins?"

The man shook his head. "I don't understand why Dr. Verschuer is on the lookout for twins, but perhaps he has simply recruited these American students for his studies?"

"Yes, I expect that is so," Sturm said. "Thank you, *Kapitän* Bloem, for your help."

"You will be sure to mention this to *Herr* Himmler when you see him next?"

"Of course," Sturm lied once more as he had no intention of ever seeing the odious SS chief again.

After they had left the police station and were back on the empty afternoon streets of Regensburg, Ingrid reverted back to English. "What happened? What did he tell you?"

Sturm ignored her question. "You did well in there. But you tipped your hand at one point. You must learn to conceal your reactions."

"What do you mean?"

"Verschuer," he said. "There, see? You reacted again. You've heard of this man?"

"Yes," Ingrid said, turning to look away from him. Sturm often had that effect on people when they realized how easily he could read them. "I met him once at a charity ball in New York to benefit the American Eugenics Society. My husband introduced us. He's one of the leading racial hygiene scientists in Germany. And his specialty is the study of twins." She turned back to look at Sturm. "What did Bloem tell you about Verschuer?"

"He gave me the name, and the approximate location of his clinic in Passau. Party members have been under strict orders since earlier this year to report to Verschuer any foreign twins staying at hotels in Bavaria. I fear your brother and sister may be at this clinic."

"Then we must go to Passau!"

"No, we return to Munich."

"Why?"

"To visit the Brown House, the headquarters for the National Socialist Workers Party."

"The Nazis? Why?" Ingrid asked.

"Verschuer is undoubtedly a Nazi. I need to know for sure. If he is, there may be a way to make our visit to Passau easier."

"You mean anyone can just walk into Nazi headquarters and find out if someone is a member?" Ingrid asked, her voice incredulous.

"Not exactly."

"But you can?"

"I can."

"I'm impressed but I'm not especially pleased to know that you have such influence."

Sturm smiled but said nothing. He had much more than influence with the Nazis. He had a friend. A very important friend. And very soon, he would have the exact location of the good *Herr Doktor* von Verschuer's Bavarian clinic.

56.

Where Is Verschuer's Clinic?

BOBBY Sullivan leaned hard on the walking stick in his left hand and looked down at the thick tape surrounding his left ankle and foot and swore silently. The *bräus* they had entered was smoke-filled and crowded but the dark beer was good. Not Guinness, of course, but good. He had been injured before, even shot once or twice, but never before a broken bone except for his nose which wasn't exactly a bone. It may have been only two small bones in his foot, fractured by the grinding hobnail boots of one of Erich Boldt's thugs but, for Sullivan, it was a professional embarrassment. And it hurt like hell. But at least he was still mobile. Barely.

The two lads with him on his flight to Germany, Sean O'Driscoll and Barry Ryan, were both former members of Michael Collins' squad of assassins nicknamed "the Apostles" in 1921 when their number reached twelve. Their chartered flight was paid for by Hearst and they had arrived early in the afternoon, four hours before Cockran had said his train would arrive.

Sullivan had called on an old friend, Rolf Heyden, the concierge at the *Bayerische Hof* whose acquaintance he had made the summer before. Rolf was not a professional, by any means. He was an ordinary German who harbored a deep grudge against Nazi Brownshirt thugs for what they had done to his sister's boyfriend. He had been easy to enlist back then — hatred was the best recruitment tool there was — but this time around, Bobby had not been sure that Rolf would even be in Germany. When last he had seen Rolf, he had said he was going to take his family and leave the country for good. Something, however, must have caused Rolf to change his mind. Fortunate it was for Sullivan since Rolf still held the same post as concierge and still possessed his position's required breadth of local knowledge.

Sullivan knew he was there to protect Mattie but he had wanted to impress his friend Cockran by being the first to find that mysterious clinic. He figured Rolf might know who to talk to. He was right and that knowledge had led him to Erich Boldt whom Bobby had badly underestimated. That was a mistake. Still, they now had a list of high-ranking SS members at least one of whom, Boldt assured him, was bound to have knowledge of the clinic's location.

Sean and Barry as well as Rolf were with him tonight to follow up on that list. Their order of *salzbrezeln* and white sausage arrived and they tucked in with gusto. The list had only four names, the top two for himself and Rolf, the less likely two for Sean and Barry. Cockran would not be with them. He was a good friend, perhaps Sullivan's only friend in America. But Cockran believed in civilized limits during interrogation. Bobby Sullivan did not.

Besides, in his own way, Sullivan was concerned for his friend's safety. What he had done last night had been foolhardy. Entering a warehouse alone against eight armed men without creating a diversion could have been suicide. Sullivan shook his head. The Bourke Cockran he knew was deadly but a hell of a lot more careful. He didn't know what to make of this new one.

"Let's go, Rolf," Sullivan said and slipped an iron pipe up the sleeve of his blue coat.

THE first man on the list knew nothing. Sullivan had shattered the man's kneecap anyway, savoring the satisfying crunch of broken bone. Sullivan really didn't like Nazis.

The second name on the list, Dietrich Wenger, proved more pliable than the first. As Wenger walked down a nearly deserted street, Rolf drove their Opel sedan up onto the sidewalk and blocked his path. Bobby swung the rear door out and pointed the ugly black snout of a silenced Luger automatic at him.

"*Gutentag, Herr* Wenger," Sullivan said, leaning on his cane. He gestured with the weapon to get into the Opel. Wenger didn't argue.

Rolf had arranged for access to a shipping office near the rail yards and the area was deserted when they parked the Opel and hustled Wenger into the building. Wenger had thinning brown hair in a pronounced widow's peak and close-set blue eyes. He was no more than five foot eight inches tall with a slender build. He was placed in a chair and Rolf tied his hands.

When Wenger refused to answer any questions, Sullivan went to work and when he stopped, Wenger's face was a bloody mess. He motioned for Rolf to come over.

Rolf stepped forward and spoke quietly to the man in German, asking questions that Sullivan had given him. "Where is Verschuer's clinic?" Sullivan knew that Rolf was repulsed by violence and it seemed as if he were pleading with the Nazi to answer and make it stop.

Sullivan was irritated when Wenger shook his head defiantly. The Nazi bastard was making Rolf sit through too much of this ugly business. He'd have to hurt him more.

"Step back Rolf," Sullivan said, as he once more approached Wenger, the lead pipe now in his hand. Rolf stepped away, turning his back to avoid watching any further violence.

Sullivan leaned on his good foot, braced himself on his cane and swung down with the lead pipe on the man's upper arm, connecting with that space between the biceps and elbow that exposes the bone. Wenger howled and Bobby swung again to keep the pain fresh.

"*Herr* Sullivan!" Rolf shouted. "That's enough. Let me try again." Sullivan deferred to his young friend and limped away to give him room. Rolf and Wenger spoke again in German and the Nazi seemed to be more pliant, conversing as best he could with Rolf, trying to catch his breath from the screaming. Finally Rolf leaned back. "Passau," he said. "Dr. Verschuer has a clinic ten miles north of Passau in the Bavarian National Forest."

Sullivan looked at him and smiled.

"DID you tell *Herr* Wenger we would leave him right where we found him?" Sullivan asked once they were back in the Opel.

"Yes, I told him that. He asked me if it were true and I assured him it was," Rolf said over his shoulder to Sullivan who was in the back seat with Wenger.

"Oh, it's true alright. It's true," Sullivan said softly.

The street where they had picked up Wenger was still deserted. Rolf pulled the Opel to a stop and Sullivan reached over Wenger to open the door. He grabbed the Nazi roughly and pushed him out. Wenger landed on his face and gingerly sat up, facing the open car door. The black snout of Bobby Sullivan's silenced Luger coughed once and a third eye appeared in the Nazi's face, centered above the other two. He fell back, his head splashing into a puddle of water which rapidly grew darker.

Sullivan saw the shocked look on Rolf's face and reached over the seat to pat his shoulder reassuringly. "Lad, he was a Nazi. I had no choice. Too many lives are at stake. Wouldn't it be a shame now if the bastards knew we were coming? "

Hotel Continental
Munich

CAPTAIN David Baker looked into the dining room of the Hotel Continental and saw in one corner a round table where Bobby Sullivan had just taken a seat beside Cockran, the female Hearst journalist and a pink-faced cherubic-looking man with thinning red hair whom the head waiter had assured him was the British statesman Winston Churchill. Baker stepped into a nearby telephone booth and placed a long-distance call to the American Embassy in Berlin. It took a few moments but at last the person he was calling was put on the phone.

"Major? Baker here. I followed the Irishman as you requested. At 10:15 this evening he shot and killed a German national named Dietrich Wenger. According to the police report, Wenger is a member of the SS. The police are attributing the shooting to Communist violence."

"Yes, sir. Of course I've bribed the waiter at their table. The head waiter also. I'll have a full report of their conversation for you by morning."

"Yes, sir. I'll meet your train when it arrives tomorrow. Don't worry. No, the pleasure is all mine. I'm looking forward to working with you, Major Hudson."

Baker couldn't wait to actually meet Major Ted Hudson. He was a living legend among MID agents, the scourge of Bolsheviks everywhere. And here he was, David Baker, trailing Nazis and IRA terrorists, all at the great man's bidding. He remembered one story he had heard about Hudson. After an interrogation where he had broken all the fingers in both hands of a Bolshevik agent who was posing as a baker in Brooklyn, Hudson had sliced off the man's ear. "Let us know if you hear anything more" Hudson had joked as he stuffed the Bolshevik's bloody ear firmly into his mouth. What a great story.

Hudson hadn't told him what this new assignment was all about but Baker didn't care. He'd learn about that soon enough. What was more important was that he was working with Ted Hudson and America's enemies better be afraid.

57.

Other Undesirables

THE Barlow palace, now known as the Brown House, beckoned across the *Königsplatz*, its khaki-colored exterior standing out against the white buildings in the square. It was a large, four-story rectangle, the blood red swastika flag of the party atop it all flying high in the breeze.

Kurt von Sturm ascended the short steps alone. He had left Ingrid safe in his apartment where they went upon their arrival in Munich late last night. She wasn't happy to be left behind but Sturm had persuaded her that he would get more done, more quickly if he did this alone.

Earlier that morning, Sturm had gone to the main reading room of Munich's public library where he had reviewed books, monographs and articles by Dr. Otmar Verschuer. Sturm had been astonished to find that three-quarters of the periodicals were in English. *The Biological Bulletin, Eugenical News, American Breeders Magazine, Eugenics Review,* and *The Journal of Heredity*, all published in the United States. Sturm was no scientist but Verschuer's monographs had seemed unremarkable, written in dense scientific jargon with charts and learned conclusions.

Sturm's opinion of the good *Herr Doktor* had abruptly changed, however, when he picked up a bound volume of *The Journal of the American Eugenics Society* and began to read Verschuer's monograph on involuntary sterilization as a practical method for improving Germany's racial stock by eliminating the ability of the feeble-minded, the criminal class and other undesirables to have children. His blood ran cold when he read the passage in one monograph that made clear Verschuer included blind people among the "other undesirables":

> For the good of all mankind and in the interests of strengthening the race, we must ruthlessly implement the involuntary sterilization of all fertile blind people in order to eliminate hereditary blindness. There should be no exceptions because even those whose blindness is supposedly the result of an illness or accident may not be telling the truth.

The old Germany whose greatness Sturm sought to restore would never have stopped his sister Franka from having children. Verschuer's new Germany apparently had other plans.

Inside the corridors of the Brown House, Sturm gave his name to a young man dressed smartly in the khaki uniform of Ernst Rohm's SA — the "brownshirts." Unlike Regensburg, he was immediately ushered in to see Friedrich Heinz, Hitler's appointments secretary, who gave him a stiff-armed Roman salute followed by "*Heil*, Hitler!" and a warm handshake.

"Kurt, how good to see you again," Heinz said. He was a young man in his late twenties with neatly combed blond hair and a mustache to match. "The *Fuhrer* is in Berlin, I'm sorry to say. He will be disappointed to have missed you."

"That's fine, Friedrich," Sturm said. "I did not wish to impose on his busy schedule."

"What brings you to Munich?"

"A personal matter. I need to look at party records," Sturm said. "As you know, my sister Franka was blinded in a horse riding accident. I've just read of a new surgical procedure that may be able to cure her, but it is impossible to secure an appointment with the physician who pioneered the technique. He is primarily a research doctor and does not see patients. But he may be a party member, and if so, he may give preference to me and agree to an appointment."

"Of course, Kurt," Heinz said. "Anything for an old friend of the *Fuhrer*. You're welcome to look at party records anytime you like, even if all you need is the name of a good dentist! Come, I'll escort you myself."

Sturm was guided by Heinz through long marbled hallways lit by sunlight pouring through floor-length windows to a staircase to the basement. There, he was led through tight bunker-like corridors with low ceilings until they reached the door to the records room.

Heinz stopped at the entrance. "Take as long as you need, Kurt."

"Thank you, Friedrich."

The records room was a cavern of row upon row of filing cabinets, each holding three-by-five-inch file cards. Sturm made his way towards the back of the room, searching for the file cards under letter "V". Within moments, he found it: "Verschuer, Otmar." Verschuer had been a party member since 1923 also but he had joined before Sturm. His badge number was lower. 43,487. Sturm noted further down on the card that Verschuer was a member of Himmler's SS, having joined in 1928. That meant Dr. Verschuer was an old fighter like Sturm and, as an SS member, a fanatic as well.

Sturm shook his head in disgust. He knew Hitler had to appeal to all Germans for the good of the Fatherland. But people like this Verschuer? Or Himmler? Surely the party could do without the likes of them.

"Did you find what you were looking for?" Heinz asked upon his return.

"Yes, thank you, Friedrich. Dr. Verschuer is a longtime member of the party. I wonder if I could impose on you further," Sturm continued. "Would you mind giving me a letter of introduction to Dr. Verschuer? Something that could attest to my own party membership? Perhaps with a reference to the high regard in which I am held by the *Fuhrer*?"

"Of course," Heinz said. Within minutes, Heinz returned from his office and handed Sturm an embossed heavy sheet of cream stationery bearing the swastika in the upper right-hand corner and Adolf Hitler's name on the bottom, signed by his private secretary, Friedrich Heinz.

STURM returned to his apartment shortly before noon to take Ingrid to lunch. He told her what he found at the Brown House and about the appointment he arranged with *Herr Doktor* Verschuer for later that afternoon in Passau. All of which gave them the opportunity to enjoy a pleasant meal together. He took her to a large beer garden, the *Löwenbräu-Keller*, where they ate a light lunch of *salzbrezeln* in a quiet corner, safe in the anonymity of the crowd.

Afterwards, they headed back toward his apartment in Munich to prepare for their trip to Passau. On the way, they neared Café Heck, one of Hitler's favorite haunts. It was easy to see why Hitler spent so much time at the Café Heck as the luncheon crowd lingered over their steins at the tables spilling onto the sidewalk in the afternoon sun, greeting friends who passed by on the street. Sturm remembered the occasion a few years ago when Hitler had spotted him walking past the Café Heck and called out to him from his customary outside table, inviting him to join his luncheon party. He could see that table now, unoccupied for the moment, and he began to direct his eyes back to the street.

As Sturm did so, he came to a sudden stop. Ingrid was not by his side. He looked back. and saw her standing beside one of the outdoor tables. She appeared to be talking to a café patron who had risen from his seat. He quickly walked to her and heard the patron speaking rapidly to her in German. Ingrid looked back at Sturm for help as it was clear she didn't understand a word that was being said. As she did, Sturm chilled when he saw the patron's face for the first time.

Bruno Kordt

58.

I'm No Gentleman

Hotel Continental
Munich
Tuesday, 31 May 1932

SULLIVAN joined Mattie and Cockran in Churchill's suite Tuesday morning for breakfast. It seemed to his eye that Sullivan had more mobility and was able to put more weight on his left foot than he had yesterday. His cane seemed different also. Slimmer than the one he had before. "New cane?" Cockran asked.

Sullivan smiled. "Rolf found it for me. Dual purpose." Cockran watched as Bobby grasped a metal band at the top of the cane and with his thumb and forefinger turned it a quarter-inch to the left. He flicked his wrist to the right and the cane dropped away to reveal a gleaming two-foot long stainless steel stabbing blade, its edges honed, its tip deadly. Cockran leaned down, picked up the cane and handed it back to Bobby who reinserted the sword into its sheath.

Cockran shook his head. "I once read that sword canes were an indispensable part of a nineteenth-century gentleman's wardrobe, but I've never seen one."

"I'm no gentleman," Sullivan replied.

No, you certainly are not, Cockran thought. And, right now, he was glad of it.

Churchill arrived in a maroon silk dressing robe and Cockran spread out a map of the Bavarian National Forest. Sullivan had briefly advised them of the clinic's location last night in the hotel's dining room and now Cockran asked him to pinpoint the location on the map.

Using a grease pencil, Sullivan had marked the location with a black X. "Ten miles due north of Passau is what Wenger told me," Sullivan said as he ran his fingers along the map. "This is the only road leading out of Passau to the north. Give or take half a mile, it ought to be somewhere within this circle." Sullivan then used the grease pencil again to draw a six-inch diameter circle around the X he had previously placed.

Churchill stepped forward, put a cigar in his mouth and took the grease pencil from Sullivan. He then erased the X and the circle. "I believe we can be more precise than that,' he said and proceeded to place a smaller X approximately an inch outside the circle Bobby had drawn. Then, he drew a small square around the X.

"How can you be so sure?" Cockran asked.

Churchill smiled and took his cigar from his mouth. "After we finished last night, I talked to the Prof and told him what Mr. Sullivan had discovered. This morning, the Prof placed a telephone call to a medical supply company in Regensburg and asked them when the last shipment of test tubes had been sent to Dr. Verschuer's clinic near Passau. Two weeks ago he was told. The Prof said it never arrived; read the riot act to the man; and ordered more test tubes. Then, he had them repeat the address. The clinic is 18 kilometers outside of Passau on the Regensburg road."

"Great. But time's running out. Only three days. So what's next?" Mattie asked.

"Reconnaissance," Churchill replied. "I suggest Mr. Sullivan and his two colleagues travel by motorcar to Passau and check out the security up close. They should be back by early evening. The rest of us," Churchill said, nodding to Mattie, "will head out to the aerodrome this afternoon for a flight to Passau where we will take aerial photos of the clinic. We'll compare notes this evening and decide how best to effect a rescue."

Cockran shook his head in admiration. Winston didn't waste time. "You chartered a plane this morning?"

"No , my dear boy," Churchill replied, "I delegated that to Randolph. And not one plane but two. I specified he engage autogiros like you used last year. Quite remarkable aircraft. I was most impressed by their versatility. Perfect for aerial photography with their open cockpits."

"Why two?"

"Why not? I assume Mr. Hearst will cover the expense. You will pilot one of the aircraft and Detective Sergeant Rankin the other. Mattie and I will take photographs. What one of us might miss, the other hopefully will not."

"Rankin is here in Germany and not Inspector Thompson?" Mattie asked with surprise.

Churchill paused, put his cigar down, and took a sip from his ever present weak scotch and soda. "Tommy is on holiday with his family at Beachycliff and Scotland Yard kindly offered the services of Sergeant Rankin to serve as my bodyguard in his place."

Cockran smiled. Robbie Rankin was a giant Scot, easily 6' 4" with a flaming red beard and hair to match. He had been with them the year before in their pursuit of Mattie into the Austrian Alps and her subsequent rescue. Not only could he fly autogiros, but he was rated on multi-engine planes from his days flying Vickers bombers in the Great War. As a fellow Scot, he had a soft spot for Mattie and was as protective of her as he was his own sisters.

Churchill continued, "There's another reason as well for two aircraft. Verschuer's clearly gone to a lot of trouble to keep his clinic's location confidential. A single aircraft flying low and slow over the clinic might attract too much attention. Two aircraft, especially autogiros, are more likely to be considered a pleasure trip."

"And you're determined to do this yourself? Take photographs?" Cockran asked.

"Well, I could fly one of the aircraft myself and have Sergeant Rankin take the photos. I was once a seaplane pilot, you know. These autogiros don't seem that difficult."

"Really, Winston?" Cockran said. "When was the last time you flew an airplane?"

"1913," Churchill replied. "But it's no different than riding a horse. Once you get the hang of it, you never forget."

Cockran chuckled and looked over at Mattie who gave him a knowing smile. They both knew that in the dictionary, right under the word "irrepressible," was a smiling photograph of Winston Churchill.

59.

The Other Man Was You

GOOD afternoon, Kurt," Bruno said. "Under most circumstances, I would be happy to see you. But these are not ordinary circumstances."

No, they were not, Sturm thought. This was no chance encounter on the street.

"I see you've colored your hair, *Frau* Waterman," Bruno continued in German, confirming Sturm's suspicion. "It does nothing to hide your beauty, but much to disguise your identity. Your German, however, could stand some improvement. Am I right?" Bruno took in Ingrid's uncomprehending stare and continued. "But of course I'm right."

"That's enough, Bruno."

Sturm had been careful to hide Ingrid when he was not with her so Bruno must have followed Sturm without his mentor spotting him. That was disconcerting. But Bruno did not intend to kill at this point. He had something else in mind. Bruno wanted to talk.

"If you have something to say, speak to me. Leave the woman alone."

"She is safe for the moment," Bruno said. "You have my word."

Sturm turned to Ingrid. "Go to the apartment, lock yourself in and wait for me."

"Why? What is happening? Who is this man? Why are you so tense?"

"Please. Do as I say. I'll explain later."

Ingrid released his hand, reluctantly, and continued down the street to his apartment.

Sturm watched her leave and then turned to join Bruno at the table. He caught the waiter's attention and ordered a coffee. Then he waited for Bruno to break the silence.

"I still can't believe it was you," Bruno said at last. "I wanted to be wrong."

Sturm's coffee arrived and he took a sip.

Bruno took a long pull on his cigarette and exhaled. "Why are you doing this?"

"I do not believe in killing innocent women. There is no honor in such an act."

Bruno laughed. "You mean to say you haven't killed innocent people?"

"Killing is never clean," Sturm said. "Sometimes good people die, I accept that — but that does not mean they were innocent. Ingrid Johansson is innocent."

"Innocent? She was fucking another man, betraying her marriage vows."

"Germany is not a Moslem country. Adultery does not deserve a death sentence."

"The other man was you."

"Even less of a crime," Sturm said with a smile. "Ask Juliette."

"You expect me to believe that you're not in love with her?"

"Yes, I do" Sturm said. "But I do not expect you to understand." He paused and took another sip. "My aim was to spare her life, yet keep both you and me in Geneva's good grace."

"And make me look like a fool for my failures," Bruno countered.

"If necessary, yes," Sturm said. "You have only yourself to blame for being deceived. In truth, however, I deflected most of the blame from you onto Manhattan."

"I must kill her," Bruno said. "Otherwise, Geneva will never make me your successor." Bruno put his free hand down, his cigarette still in the other. "I must kill Manhattan's wife."

"You can try. But you will have to kill me first."

"I know."

Sturm couldn't help but smile again. His hair was darker and he was slightly shorter, but Bruno reminded Sturm of himself years ago. Willing to do whatever must be done no matter how personally troubling. And he could see plainly on Bruno's face how troubling it was for his young protégé. He felt a twinge of regret. He was the very man Sturm had trained him to be.

"Who else knows about this?"

"No one," Bruno said. "I kept these suspicions to myself."

"Why?"

"You are my friend, Kurt," Bruno said quietly, "and my mentor. I owe you that much."

"You owe me nothing."

"I owe you a fair chance. I don't want to kill you, but I will. I won't reveal your treachery until after you are dead. If, by chance, I don't survive, I won't have deprived Geneva of your services. I know you will keep working for what we both believe just as I will."

They said nothing for a while. Finally, Bruno broke the silence.

"If you and *Frau* Waterman leave Munich, you have my word of honor that I will neither follow nor monitor you for the next twenty-four hours. Those are my terms."

"I accept." Sturm said and stood up, extending his hand. Bruno took it and the two friends shook hands. For the last time, Sturm thought. Once he rescued Ingrid's brother and sister and left all three safely in Vienna, he would return and kill his protégé, his friend. If he did not, Bruno would one day succeed and Ingrid would die.

STURM stood outside the door to his bedroom and listened. He could hear Ingrid crying inside. He knocked softly and spoke in English.

"Ingrid? It's Kurt."

There was no answer from inside, only more crying.

"Ingrid? I'm coming in."

Sturm unlocked the door and pushed it in slowly. He saw her lying on the bed, his Luger on the floor. She looked up when he stepped in the room, got up from the bed and ran to him.

He held her tightly against his chest as she cried. "Don't worry, you're safe now," he said, cradling her head in his hands. "He's not going to harm you. I will not let him harm you."

Ingrid pushed back from him suddenly, furiously flailing her hands at his chest, then slapping at his face. "You're a liar! A liar! You've been lying to me this whole time!

Who are you?!" she demanded in a loud voice. Then, more softly, "Who are you?"

He took hold of her hands. "Listen to me and I will tell you," he said calmly. "Please. We don't have much time."

Still angry, she broke her hands free, and she sat down. "You lied to me."

"I did not lie to you," Sturm said. "But I did not tell you the entire truth."

"Who was that man? Why did he speak to you like that?"

"He is an agent of mine," Sturm said, honestly.

"He's a killer, isn't he? Just like you," she said. "You're not an executive assistant to a major industrialist. Tell me the truth."

"I *am* the executive assistant to Fritz von Thyssen," Sturm said quickly before Ingrid could object, "but that is not my primary work. I am an assassin. That man is my protege."

"And now he's trying to kill me?"

"Yes," Sturm said. "That's his job."

"Then why didn't he try to kill me just now?"

"That's difficult to explain."

"Try me."

"I am his mentor," Sturm said. "And his friend. As a courtesy, he warned me that he's discovered I am hiding you and that next time, he would not be coming to talk."

"Why does he want me dead?"

Sturm took a moment before answering. "Because your husband hired both of us to kill you. And I could not let that happen. By sabotaging his operation against you in Hamburg, I have placed myself directly in his path to you. He knows he must kill me if he is to complete his mission. But I will *not* allow that to happen. I promise you."

Ingrid took the news quietly. She tried to look away, but Sturm reached out to her.

"I am sorry I deceived you," Sturm said. "I lead a life of necessity, not preference. I do not take great pride in what I do. It is not the unambiguous heroism of a soldier but the duty amounts to the same thing. I am involved in a secret fight for the future of Germany. It requires me to do unpleasant things. I could not be sure you would understand. I do not know even now if you understand but I hope you understand at least one thing. I will not let that man harm you."

Ingrid nodded, too tired to argue anymore. "I believe you," she said, wiping the tears from her cheeks. "I don't know how German women do things here, but in America, we don't tolerate secrets from our lovers. No more, understand?"

American or not, the statement was naïve in the extreme. Lovers *always* kept secrets from each other. But that was not what a woman whose life was in danger needed to hear. If he were to keep her safe, she had to believe in him. "Of course," he said.

"What next?"

"I keep my promise. We find your brother and your sister."

60.

A Fine Day to Fly

Passau, Germany
Tuesday, 31 May, 1932

THE 90 minute flight from Munich over to Passau was uneventful. It was a fine day to fly with sunshine and fleecy cumulus clouds high above them. At Winston's suggestion, the autogiros would make two, and only two, passes. The first pass would be at 500 feet at a slow speed, fifty kilometers an hour. After the first pass, they would fly due north fifteen minutes and then head back. The second pass would be at two hundred feet but even slower, no more than thirty-five kilometers per hour. Churchill and Mattie would use a telephoto lens for the first pass and a standard lens for the second.

Once they reached Passau, the autogiros banked left and followed the Danube River north. Off to their right was the two lane highway which wound through the Bavarian National Forest on its way to Regensburg. They had flown from Munich at an altitude of 1000 feet but once they were ten minutes outside of Passau, Cockran descended to 500 feet and began to scan the terrain below looking for a clearing. 15 minutes later, they found it.

"Robbie, up ahead at ten o'clock" Cockran said into the two-way radio which connected the autogiros. "I think that's what we're looking for."

Rankin agreed and, as they passed over the clinic the first time, Cockran could see it was truly isolated. Except for a few scattered cottages, it was the only substantial man-made structure they had encountered since passing over Passau. It was a large triangular compound, probably a good five acres all told, inside of which was a low whitewashed building in the form of a large H and a smaller adjacent building which resembled a barracks. The triangle of the perimeter was formed by a high fence with coiled barbed wire on top. There were watchtowers at two of the three corners of the triangle — the two corners facing in the direction of the highway — and a large gate between them. There was no watchtower in the rear at the third point of the triangle, facing the forest. A long winding dirt road extended from the gate approximately a half a mile to the highway. Neither the fence, the gates nor the whitewashed structures would be visible from the highway.

On the second pass, Cockran could see Mattie snapping pictures rapidly. The autogiros were much lower now, flying side by side only two hundred feet from the ground, and he could see something which had escaped his notice in the higher pass. Half-way down the entrance road and not visible from the highway was a swinging gate manned by two sentries in black SS uniforms, submachine guns slung over their shoulders.

Two sentries posted at the road looked up as both autogiros passed low over them. Mattie and Winston waved gaily and the sentries smiled and waved back. As they passed once more over the compound, Cockran noticed a large grey Mercedes touring car, its top down. A woman with short chestnut brown hair was in the driver's seat and a blond-haired man had just opened the door to step in.

Hotel Continental
Munich

CAPTAIN David Baker found that the lock to Churchill's hotel suite posed no challenge to the lock-picking skills he had learned during counter-intelligence training at Fort Holabird in Baltimore. Once inside, he immediately spotted the map on the table with the X in the small square. He brought a lamp from a nearby side table, placed it beside the map and turned it on, directing it at the X. He took several photographs and then returned the lamp to its original position.

Baker had been skeptical at first when Hudson gave him this new task. "I don't understand. Didn't you tell me your partner Miss McGary was working with Mr. Churchill to find this German clinic where some kidnapped Americans might be held?"

"I did, kid." Hudson had replied. "But the broad and Churchill are both Brits. It's the same as if we were working with a friendly foreign intelligence service. Trust but verify. We need to know everything they know as soon as possible, not when they're ready to spoon-feed it to us. I'm working on my own angle to find the clinic but every piece of information is critical."

Hudson had been right, of course, and Baker still couldn't believe his good fortune, working on a top secret assignment with Major Ted Hudson. A black drape even. This was really going to look good on his record.

61.

For The Good of All Mankind

The Verschuer Clinic
The Bavarian National Forest
Tuesday, 31 May 1932

THE roaring engine of the open-top Mercedes touring car echoed off the towering pine trees that stood sentinel along the side of the road as it carried Sturm and Ingrid north of the border city of Passau. Ingrid sat pensively watching the scenery, her brown hair protected from the wind by a scarf and her eyes protected from Sturm's view by sunglasses. She had been quiet during most of the trip from Munich and difficult to read.

Around another twist in the highway, they saw what Sturm had been looking for. The first road they had encountered since leaving Passau, the dirt entrance road leading to Verschuer's clinic. Sturm downshifted and turned left into the road and 500 yards later came to a white barrier with two armed SS guards in black uniforms carrying submachine guns with full ammo clips. Ingrid reached over to hold his hand, the tension in her body rising at the sight of the weapons. He squeezed her hand.

"Everything will be all right," he said.

Sturm pulled to a stop outside the barrier as one armed guard approached his door. Sturm handed him the letter from Hitler's secretary. The first guard signaled to the second guard to call the compound. In a moment, the barrier arm was lifted and the guards waved them through.

The main gate of the compound was set in the middle of a fence between two high watchtowers, each manned by an SS guard and containing a fixed heavy .50 caliber machine gun. The arrangement seemed strange. The two guards in the towers faced inward as though focused on a threat from within rather than without.

Once through the gate, they pulled to another stop outside a one-story, whitewashed building several hundred meters wide. A tall man in a white lab coat stood just outside the entrance, his silver hair brushed back tightly against his scalp.

"Heil Hitler!" the man said, raising his arm in a Roman salute. "*Herr* von Sturm. *Herr* Heinz told us to expect you. I am *Baron Doktor* Otmar Freiherr von Verschuer."

"Kurt von Sturm," he said, limply raising his arm in the same fashion he had seen Hitler employ and then shaking Verschuer's hand. He gestured to Ingrid. "My traveling secretary."

Ingrid held out her hand and Verschuer took it gently, gazing at her intently for a moment, a smile forming on his lips as he leaned forward to kiss her hand. "Welcome, my dear."

Ingrid smiled demurely, but she remained quiet. Sturm could feel the anxiety radiating from her body.

Verschuer motioned for them to follow him. "Come, let me show you our facility."

"I understand you are interested in my work on hereditary blindness," Verschuer said.

Sturm did not expect this and briefly wondered what else Hitler's private secretary had had told the man over the phone. "It's a subject of some personal interest," he said.

"The work we're doing here could make human blindness a thing of the past," Verschuer said. "In fact, all physical misery that afflicts the human race may become history when our work here is finished, I truly believe it."

"And what is this miracle procedure, *Herr Doktor?*"

"Oh, it's no miracle," Verschuer said. "We're simply taking a page out of nature's book. Many of these diseases and weaknesses, like blindness, are passed on from generation to generation by the people who are afflicted with them. Our work here will enable us to identify the afflictions that are passed on genetically."

Verschuer led them into a room with a two-way mirror that looked in on another room where two identical twins were being examined. The two women had brown hair and hazel eyes and appeared to be in their late twenties. They were both very attractive and completely naked. The two white-coated male attendants were using calipers to measure various parts of their bodies, one measuring, the other writing figures down on a clipboard. Both men seemed oblivious to the women's unclothed condition. The women also appeared indifferent to their nakedness, a distant, vacant look in their eyes. Sturm thought they had been sedated.

Ten minutes later, Verschuer led them back out of the two-way mirror room and down the opposite corridor to another examination room where two naked men were being measured. "What do you do to heal them, once you've discovered these genetic defects?" Sturm asked.

"We can't heal anyone with defects. None of our subjects today have any apparent defects but if they did, we simply would sterilize them," Verschuer said. "They could live out long and happy lives, but we essentially quarantine their genetic defect to their own lifetimes. We prevent them from spreading their affliction to succeeding generations."

"I wasn't aware German law permitted this."

"It doesn't without consent but the subjects we examine have signed consent forms. Should defects be present, they have agreed to sterilization. But soon, once *Herr* Hitler assumes his rightful place as Chancellor, I'm confident that we will no longer need to bother with consent forms. Any German with genetic defects will be sterilized just as they are in the majority of American states. A nation has a right to protect its gene pool for the sake of future generations."

"*Herr* Hitler agrees with you?"

"Read his book. The weak have no right to force their deficiencies on the rest of a healthy German race. If we can make these difficult choices, we can conquer human frailty for good."

"Come now, *Herr Doktor*," Sturm said amiably, maintaining a light air to keep Verschuer talking and remembering the monograph he had read in Munich. "How can you expect to conquer all of human frailty? Not every ailment is passed from mother to child. Many people develop blindness because of an accident, not because of any birth defect."

Verschuer stopped. "For the good of all mankind and in the interests of strengthening the race, the involuntary sterilization of all fertile blind people will be necessary in order to eliminate hereditary blindness," he said. "There should be no exceptions, because even those who claim their blindness is the result of an illness or an accident may not be telling the truth."

Sturm recognized the line almost word for word from Verschuer's monograph. "Doesn't that strike you as a little cruel, *Herr Doktor*?"

"No," Verschuer said. "Perhaps to the person involved but patriotic Germans will put individual concerns aside and focus on what is best for all the German people. It will require men of strong will like Hitler to accomplish this. I pray he takes power before it is too late."

Sturm checked his tongue and nodded his head, as though agreeing. He glanced at Ingrid, but she had of course understood none of their German. Her face was still tense, each set of twins examined being another source of hope extinguished. All of the twins appeared drugged like the first two and spoke little but when they did speak to Verschuer's staff, it was in English and they appeared to be American. But none of them were Thomas or Beatrice.

After visiting a fourth examination room, Verschuer led them back to the entrance and seemed to have no intention of extending the tour any further so Sturm decided to wander down the corridor to a closed door with a large sign that read: "Authorized Personnel Only".

"I'm sorry, *Herr* von Sturm," Verschuer called out from the entrance where he appeared ready to lead them back out. "That wing is off-limits to visitors."

"Why is that?" Sturm asked without turning around.

"The twins in that wing are quite ill and possibly contagious," Verschuer said. "They are in quarantine for your own safety. My protégé, *Doktor* Josef, looks after them personally."

Sturm stopped, close enough now to see the three sets of dead-bolts in the doors from top to bottom. It had the look of a door that was rarely opened. The kind of door that opened only to receive new subjects, not release them. Thomas and Beatrice had gone through this door. Sturm was sure of it. He was just as sure that he soon would be walking them back through it. He had a plan, courtesy of Heinrich Himmler and his gift of a black SS officer's uniform.

"*Herr* von Sturm?" Verschuer called again. Sturm turned around and followed him.

Sturm let Ingrid climb into the driver's seat, as he walked around the front of the car to get in the passenger side. Verschuer followed him to the door and held out his hand.

"I'm sorry we couldn't show you more of our facilities, but I hope you have come away with a sense of the great importance of our work here."

Sturm reached out and shook Verschuer's hand. "I've no doubt that the fate of Germany hangs on the outcome of your work."

As he moved to step into the Mercedes, Sturm heard an unusual sound—something he had heard before. When he turned his head skyward, he saw the familiar blurring pattern of two autogiros, their large rotary blades spinning directly overhead. He once had flown in such an aircraft, almost losing his life. It was not a pleasant memory. Neither was losing a woman he loved.

62.

That's Suicide

Hotel Continental
Munich
Tuesday, 31 May, 1932

STANDING at the table in Churchill's suite, Cockran looked at the blown-up photographs Mattie and Winston had taken of the compound. To his surprise, Winston's photos were every bit as good as Mattie's. They overlapped and complemented each other and showed that, in addition to the two SS guards on the road and the two in the watchtowers, there were also two others stationed at the gate itself as well as two more walking the perimeter of the compound. All of them had the same submachine pistols slung over their shoulders.

"The forest is fairly close to the tip of the triangle at the back of the compound," Sullivan said. "Would it be possible to drop down from the trees and land inside the fence?"

Cockran shook his head. "The branches extend over the fence but I don't think they're that strong. I think heavy-duty wire cutters at that same spot will do the trick."

"I agree with Bourke," Churchill said. "How do you propose to align your forces?"

"Including Bobby, there are four of us. They appear to have eight on duty during the day, not counting any personnel inside the compound that we didn't see. We can't know how tight their security is at night, so we have to assume it's the same as during the day. If they're pulling twelve-hour shifts, that's sixteen men to our four. Twenty four if they have three shifts."

"My lads and I didn't see a changing of the guard," Sullivan said, "but there's a barracks-like structure and we saw several men walk in and out. Sean had a good view from a tree."

"So what's your plan?" Mattie asked.

Cockran turned. "I'm going in alone at the rear of the compound. Sullivan's men will take out the two sentries at the road. I'll create a diversion once I'm in the compound and by that time Bobby, Sean and Barry should be ready to storm the front gate."

"Diversion?" Mattie asked in a skeptical tone of voice. "What kind of diversion?"

"I'm working on it. Don't worry, I'm good at this. I'll think of something."

"Like what?"

"Right now, I'm partial to lobbing two incendiary grenades into the barracks. That will draw the attention of the guards at the gate as well as the two in the watchtowers."

Mattie shook her head. "And you call me reckless? What about the two perimeter guards? Won't they have something to say about this?"

Cockran shook his head. "Not if they're dead."

"So let me get this straight," Mattie said. "You're entering alone into the rear of that five-acre compound where you will be outnumbered anywhere from sixteen to twenty-four to one and you hope that a few incendiary grenades will even the odds?"

"That's the plan," Cockran said.

"That's not a plan. That's suicide."

"You got a better idea? It's Tuesday. Autopsies begin Friday. There's not much time."

"Isn't there were some way we can take this to the authorities and get their help?"

Cockran took a deep breath. How many times did they have to go through this? He could hear the irritation in his voice as he began to speak. "For starters, we have no proof that there are kidnapped twins in that compound. We only know its location because Bobby tortured and killed an SS agent. But even if we had proof, it wouldn't help. We know it's an SS operation. The Nazis have too much influence here. They'd be tipped off long before any police raid and the twins would just be hidden elsewhere. So, I repeat. Do you have a better idea?

"I do," Mattie replied. "Ted Hudson should be in Munich by now. Let me go over with him what we've found. If he agrees, then we'll leave for Berlin in the morning and show everything to the American ambassador and get him to intervene with the Bavarian authorities."

Cockran shook his head at the irony of Mattie being more cautious than him. But her plan really *was* a triumph of hope over experience and he didn't mean Ted Hudson. Cockran had met the American ambassador a year ago, a career politician and personal friend of President Herbert Hoover. He was *not* going to stick his neck out on something he would consider an internal German problem.

Still, Mattie made a good point. Cockran didn't like the odds either. He preferred a sure thing also. But, with only three days left, they had little choice. You played the hand you were dealt. Mattie might not know it based on his last two efforts to rescue her—which in some ways *had* been suicidal—but he was really good at this sort of thing. With her life not at stake, he would be more cautious. The sentries were there to keep people in. They weren't expecting bloody mayhem from outside. His odds weren't great but the sentries' odds were worse.

Better yet, Cockran thought, sending Mattie and Ted off on a fool's errand to Berlin had its merits. She would be out of harm's way while he and the Apostles attempted to rescue the twins. Otherwise, knowing Mattie, she might demand to accompany him into the compound. And that was *not* going to happen.

Cockran shrugged. "Talk to Ted. Get his opinion. Bobby and I met the ambassador last year. He's a political hack. He wouldn't lift a finger to help my client whose companies were being terrorized by the SS. I can't imagine he's any different today." Cockran grinned. "But go ahead, see what you and your old…"

63.

Trigger-Happy Boyfriend

DAMN it, Cockran, " Mattie said cutting him off in mid-sentence, "he's not . . ."

Cockran raised his hand as if to stop her, but he never had a chance.

". . . my old boyfriend!"

Cockran grinned. "But I was only going to say 'your old partner on this story'. Honest."

Mattie arched an eyebrow. "Sure you were." Hell, Cockran was probably right. But what was the downside? Cockran going in alone really *was* suicide. The men were ignoring her now as they pored over the photographs, refining their plans. Winston was talking about hiring a motorbus to take the rescued twins to Regensburg where a tri-motor he chartered would be waiting to fly them out of Germany. Mattie was by nature an optimist herself but Winston was in a league all his own. She wanted to save the twins as much as anyone but nothing was worth Cockran's life. Mattie walked over to Cockran, put her hands on his shoulders, and kissed him on the neck as she whispered into his ear, "I'm going back to our suite and call Ted."

MATTIE noticed, as she opened the door to their suite a white envelope which had been slipped beneath it, "M. McGary" printed on the envelope in neat block letters. Mattie tore it open and read the message inside.

New developments. Call me in Room 525. Ted.

Intrigued, Mattie picked up the telephone and the switchboard connected her to room 525. "Ted? Mattie. What's up?"

"Not over the phone. But it's important. What's your room number? I'll come there."

"Room 820. But we shouldn't meet here. How about the lobby?" Mattie asked. Having Cockran return to find Ted Hudson in their hotel room was not a good idea.

"Too many people around," Ted said. "Why don't you come to my room?"

"Okay," she replied. It wasn't much better going to Ted's room but at least she had her knickers on.

Mattie knocked on the door to Ted Hudson's room but there was no answer. She rapped louder and heard a muffled voice from within, "It's open."

Mattie tried the knob and the door opened. She stepped into the room. A sofa was on one side of the room with a long low table in front of it. Two silk-covered armchairs were placed opposite the sofa, creating a conversation area. A dusty pair of khaki pants hung over the arm of one of the silk chairs, the rest of Ted's clothes marking a trail to the bathroom where she could hear a shower running behind it. Mattie smiled. Well, she thought, at least one of them would be fully clothed. Nice to know Ted hadn't changed.

He hadn't. Moments later, Ted Hudson emerged from the bathroom, a heavy white terrycloth towel knotted loosely at the waist, seemingly ready to fall off at any moment as he rubbed his blond hair with another towel, the golden curls on his chest glistening with water.

"Good to see you, Mattie. As beautiful as always. Excuse my appearance but I had a dusty afternoon," he said as he leaned forward and kissed her cheek.

Mattie was annoyed and unflattered. Get to the point, she thought. "What's so important we couldn't meet in the lobby?" she asked in an impatient tone.

"I found the clinic."

"What do you mean?"

"Just that," Ted replied. "Verschuer's clinic is located in the Bavarian National Forest approximately 18 kilometers north of a small border town named Passau."

"I know that, Ted. I flew over it today and took photos. But how did you find it?"

Hudson shook his head. "Confidential sources. I can't reveal MID secrets to a civilian. But if you were there too, you know they're good sources. While you were flying over it, I was inside the compound," he said, pointing to his pants on the arm chair.

"You were inside? How'd you arrange that?"

Ted shook his head. "It's not only Top Secret. It's MID Black Drape Top Secret. I can't tell you more, but I can tell you this. Everybody has their price, even the SS."

"So, we both found the clinic. What do we do now?" Mattie asked.

"What's your plan?" Ted replied.

"Right now, the only option appears to be a forced entry by night."

"Who? When?"

Mattie hesitated. Cockran, Bobby and Winston were planning this assault, not her. Hudson had given Mattie no reason for her to mistrust him but Cockran did not feel the same way. Better to be cautious. "We're still working out the details. Things are still up in the air."

"But Cockran's involved. Correct? So there's bound to be more gunplay. You and your trigger-happy boyfriend. It wasn't enough he killed three people at Cold Spring Harbor?"

"That's what I wanted to talk to you about. You've been inside the place. I've got aerial photos. Don't we have enough to go to the U.S. ambassador and get him to bring in the German authorities? Aren't you always telling me to have a Plan B? Well, this is my Plan B. I don't want more people to die but if we do nothing, those twelve twins may well be doomed."

"It won't work. I didn't see any twins when I was inside. They may be there, but I can't prove it. Without proof, there's no way to persuade the ambassador. He was a big financial backer of Hoover and he's not the sharpest knife in the drawer. He's not a risk taker."

"You're certain?"

"Positive," Ted said. "But look. Cockran doesn't need to act like a cowboy on this. I do have a Plan B. I can get us in there. And, with a little luck, we can get the twins out with nobody the wiser. At most, we'll leave a few orderlies behind, bound and gagged. By the time they're found, we and the twins will be long gone."

"How?"

"The same way I did," Ted said, picking up his khakis and shaking the dust from them. "There's an escape tunnel beneath the compound which opens up in the woods approximately a half mile from the fence. My source indicates that's not an uncommon feature in SS facilities."

"Bourke needs to know this. Can you join us for dinner tonight?"

"Sorry, sweetheart. I don't think Cockran and I are destined to break bread together anytime soon. Besides, I have a previous engagement."

"How about if we meet on neutral territory tomorrow morning? Churchill's suite."

"With witnesses?" Hudson asked. "So your boyfriend won't sucker punch me again?"

Mattie smiled. "Sure. With witnesses. I'll leave a note with the time at the front desk."

MATTIE let herself back into their hotel room. Cockran had still not returned. She thought over her conversation with Hudson. Cockran was not going to be happy, but at least she had tried to explore a political solution. Maybe the fact that Cockran and Hudson had the same low opinion of the ambassador might count for something with Bourke. But Hudson's knowledge about the escape tunnel ought to count for more. That might be just what they needed. Safer than Cockran's suicidal plan, that was for sure.

Still, something nagged at her. How did Hudson know that Cockran had killed three people at Cold Spring Harbor? Mattie was fairly sure she hadn't told Ted that night when she stopped by Stanhope Hall to check on his condition. But that had been a traumatic night and her memory of it was uncertain. Still, that wasn't the biggest mystery on Mattie's mind at the moment as she picked up a folder from the table in their sitting room. The folder contained three photographs she had taken that day in their second pass over the compound, photographs which she hadn't shared with Cockran or the others.

The first two photos had caught Mattie's attention because of their disturbing resemblance. At first, she thought it might have been Ted Hudson with the blond hair but the profile was more angular, the jaw line firmer, the nose longer. The third photograph was the one that sent a shiver through her body and she felt herself flush as her mind went back to a tent and a cot and two naked lovers in the Austrian Alps.

If Ted Hudson had been inside the compound that day, he wasn't the only person Mattie knew who had been there. Because, sitting in the open touring car beside the H-shaped building at the center of the SS compound, looking up at the autogiro, his face unmistakable, was another man she knew. A kind man. A ruthless man. A man who loved her. A man who twice had made love to her. A man to whom she still was magnetically attracted. Kurt von Sturm.

PART IV

Germany

31 May — 6 June 1932

For decades, American eugenicists had stressed the research importance of twins' eyes, and the German movement naturally adopted the precept. In addition to eyes, Verschuer wanted blood. Litres of it.

Edwin Black, *War Against the Weak*

The twins had died at the same time and were now lying beside each other on the big dissecting table. It was they who had to resolve the secret of the reproduction of the race. To advance one step in the search to unlock the secret of multiplying the race of superior beings destined to rule was a noble goal.

Dr. Miklos Nyiszli

64.

A Favorite of the Führer

Castle Wewelsburg
Westphalia, Germany
Tuesday, 31 May 1932

WESLEY Waterman shook his head. Customers came in all shapes and sizes but Heinrich Himmler, the head of the SS, took the fucking cake. Part of the man was living in the middle ages with Knights of the Round Table dancing in his head. The ghastly castle in which the two men sat was its concrete manifestation. Yet Himmler was also a modern man, a man of science, dedicated, as was Waterman, to the improvement of the human race and, more specifically, assuring that the Nordic peoples would contribute more than their fair share to the human gene pool in the future. Here, Wesley Waterman was doing his part as well. After all, hadn't he volunteered his wife's brother and sister to further the groundbreaking experiments being undertaken at this very minute at the SS Clinic near Passau? It served the bitch right.

Better still, Waterman carried in the breast pocket of his gray flannel Brooks Brothers suit the biggest contract I.C.E. Europe had ever received. Scores of electronic computing machines and punch cards to feed them, cards on which I.C.E. held a monopoly. And, of course, the service contracts to keep the machines running smoothly as they tabulated and compiled the genealogy of every single member of the SS back ten generations, insuring that no Jewish or Slavic blood would ever defile Adolf Hitler's Praetorian guard, the Black Knights of the SS.

Himmler led Waterman into his personal study, the walls lined with books and tapestries and lit by electricity. Large chandeliers hanging from the beamed ceiling and brass lamps between overstuffed brown leather armchairs cast a warm glow over the room. A teetotaler like his leader, Hitler, Himmler sipped from a cup of herbal tea while Waterman had a large brandy. He studied Himmler's face. Round, a weak chin, pince-nez glasses, his brown hair shaved on the sides in a futile attempt to make his face appear narrower, closer to the Nordic ideal. But those muddy brown eyes gave it all away, Waterman thought. A distinct contrast to Waterman's own blue eyes, fair brown hair and aquiline nose, his face naturally long and narrow. And, of course, at six feet four inches, Waterman towered over the smaller Himmler. In fact, Waterman wondered from time to time how he would look in a black SS uniform. Certainly more imposing and more like the Aryan ideal than the SS chief himself.

But if Waterman was feeling smug and superior to Heinrich Himmler now that he had that contract safely in his pocket, Himmler managed to swiftly change all that. "It would appear, Wesley," he said, taking a sip of tea, "that your wife has located those two siblings of hers whose names and location you so generously furnished to us."

Waterman was instantly alert. That bitch had found her brother and sister? How the hell had she done that?! Bruno Kordt's latest report was that she couldn't be found. "Excuse me?" Waterman asked.

Himmler picked up a brown manila envelope. "Take a look at these."

Waterman knew the game. He unfolded his large frame, walked across the room, took the proffered nine-by-twelve envelope and returned to his seat. He picked up his brandy snifter, swirled the liquid around, and took a sip. He wasn't going to give Himmler the satisfaction of showing any concern. That was not how Wesley Waterman had climbed to the top of the greasy pole. He opened the envelope and pulled out four glossy photographs. Her hair was brown and cut short but he would recognize his wife anywhere. Ingrid. That bitch!

Waterman's jaw almost dropped when he saw the next photo. Standing beside his wife, dressed in black, was the blond hair and arrogant face of Kurt von Sturm! But Waterman wasn't going to let on that he knew Sturm. While he and a few other members of the Geneva Group were allies of the Nazis in their effort to achieve power, they never took the Nazis into their confidence. The Geneva Group used politicians. They didn't trust them. Nor confide in them.

"That's my wife. She's cut her hair and dyed it. Who is the man with her?"

Himmler smiled. It was a tight little smile. Waterman didn't like this man. Which was not unusual. Waterman disliked most of his customers.

"An old party member. We joined in the same year. 1923."

"These photos were obviously taken at the clinic." Waterman said. "Is the man SS?"

Himmler shook his head. "I'm afraid not. He is a favorite of the Fuhrer who turned down my invitation to join the SS. Do you know why he would be with your wife?"

Because he's fucking her, you sexless toad, Waterman thought, and I've got the goddamn photographs to prove it. The man's face had never been visible in the photographs but his blond hair had been unmistakable. It was all too painfully obvious now that the man who had fucked his wife and made a cuckold of Wesley Waterman, III, was the Geneva Group's own executive director.

"I have no idea," Waterman replied. "Do you know where they are staying?"

"No," Himmler replied. "The SS guards are not permitted to leave the compound."

"Why were they there? Why were photos taken of them?"

"Dr. Verschuer recognized your wife. Because of your generous support of our work at the clinic and the fact that she was disguised, he thought I would find it of interest. I did."

The little toad was evading the question. "What was the purpose of their visit?"

"A tour of the clinic. Surm had a letter of introduction from the Fuhrer himself."

"Did they see her brother and sister?"

"Of course not," Himmler replied. "They were allowed to see a few of the rooms where some of the twins were being examined. Nothing more."

Himmler motioned that Waterman was to return the photographs to him, which Waterman obediently did. As if he had a choice. Waterman knew what Himmler was doing, letting the silence build until Waterman had no choice but to fill it which, in the event, he did.

"My wife and I are estranged. We are in the middle of rather messy divorce proceedings. It would be unfortunate if she were able to locate her siblings. Can you find where she's staying?"

"Possibly," Himmler replied. "What do you propose to do if we locate her?"

Have the fucking bitch killed once and for all, Waterman thought. "Perhaps I can appeal to her better side." Waterman replied. "There is no reason we can't be civilized about this. But I would be most appreciative if you could locate her."

Kurt von Sturm! No wonder Bruno Kordt botched the kill in New York and Hamburg. The man clearly was beholden to Sturm. Indeed, according to von Thyssen, Sturm was pushing Kordt as a possible successor to him as executive director. Well, that was never going to happen.

Meanwhile, Waterman would have to have a quiet chat with Dr. Verschuer. It was intolerable that Verschuer had passed information about his wife to Himmler and not to him.

The Hearst reporter and that lawyer Cockran no longer seemed such an imminent threat to the project that they once had been. He had been assured they were both under control and under close surveillance. His wife, however, was another matter entirely. The project was still in jeopardy. But he knew what had to be done. The twins would have to be moved; his wife still would have to be killed. And for the latter, he knew just who to call.

65.

Ted Agrees With You

Hotel Continental
Munich
Tuesday, 31 May 1932

SOMETHING was bothering Mattie. Cockran could tell that from the minute he returned to their room. She seemed preoccupied, distant. Winston, the Prof and Randolph were dining at the home of a German history professor while Bobby and the Apostles were touring the beer cellars of Munich. Cockran suggested room service and Mattie agreed. He made martinis and they sat opposite each other in wing chairs beside the suite's small fireplace.

"A penny for your thoughts," Cockran said. "You seem quiet."

"Sorry," Mattie said. "I just don't have a good feeling about your rescue plan."

"I'll be fine," Cockran said. "Bobby's already bought the bolt cutters. He brought four new Thompson submachine guns with him from Ireland. All with Maxim sound suppressors. And plenty of ammunition. I'll go in after midnight. The guards won't know what hit them."

"Sound suppressors for Tommy guns? You're either drunk or dreaming."

Cockran didn't reply. She was right. The sound suppressors weren't that effective. But he had faced worse odds. Killing the first two SS sentries would not be a problem. The rest was dicey but doable. But what else could he do? He had to try and rescue the twins. He had used his skills as a lawyer, so far unsuccessfully, to fight what he considered to be the evil of eugenics and its state-sanctioned sterilizations. He didn't know why twins were being murdered and mutilated in the name of eugenics but the SS was involved and, from personal experience, that told him a lot. They talked of honor while they murdered innocents. Thanks to Mattie's skill as a journalist and her dogged perseverance, he now had a unique opportunity to use his government-acquired skills in bloody mayhem to save the twins' lives and strike a blow against the evil of both eugenics and the SS. It may have started as Mattie's story but it had become his fight. He rarely picked fights but he never backed down once they came. Never.

Room service arrived and the thin potato pancakes, asparagus and sauerkraut Mattie had ordered went very well with their medium rare rack of lamb. They ate in silence and Cockran waited. Either Mattie would tell him what was troubling her or not.

"What if there were a safer way to rescue the twins? Would you consider it?"

"Sure but I don't think there's a better way, let alone a safer one."

"I talked with Ted today. He knows the clinic's location also."

Cockran frowned. He hadn't expected her to actually tell Ted the clinic's location.

"Why did you tell him that?"

"I didn't."

"How'd he find out?"

"He wouldn't tell me how, but he implied he bribed an SS guard."

"And?"

"Ted's found a tunnel underneath the compound that leads directly into the main building. He says we can get all the twins out that way."

"What about you and Ted talking to the U.S. Ambassador?"

"Ted agrees with you. The ambassador is too political to stick his neck out."

Cockran listened as Mattie relayed what she had learned about the tunnel. It seemed too convenient. But, he told himself, keep an open mind. It might be a safer way with less gunplay.

"Okay. I'll meet with Ted and hear him out. Want to come along and referee?"

Mattie laughed and it was the first time this evening that she seemed like herself. "Ted doesn't want to meet you alone either. He said he wanted witnesses in case you tried to sucker punch him again. I suggested Winston's suite tomorrow morning."

Well, Cockran thought, she had a point. Meeting on neutral territory was better. He couldn't stand the sonofabitch but he would try not to let that affect his judgment as he heard what Hudson had to say. A tunnel? It almost seemed too good to be true.

66.

Is It Really You?

MATTIE had been pleased when Cockran returned from his meeting with Ted and Bobby in Churchill's suite. The three of them were now flying to Passau to check out Ted's tunnel. Cockran had been taking far too many risks lately but at least he wasn't being stubborn about Ted's discovery.

Maybe Sullivan's presence had something to do with it, she thought, for Bobby had told her, off the record , that he agreed with her about the dangers of their plan. "It's more risky than I prefer," he had said. "But Bourke is determined and I see no other way if the twins are to have any chance at all."

Restless, Mattie decided to take a long walk before lunch. The sky overhead was clear and blue, another fine day for flying. The air was brisk and Mattie zipped her brown leather jacket up to her neck. As she walked, she realized that her route would take her past the Brown House, Nazi party headquarters. Mattie still had not shown Cockran the photographs she had taken yesterday afternoon of Kurt von Sturm. She saw no upside to it and plenty of downside. Regardless of why Kurt had been there, it wouldn't help them rescue the twins.

Mattie looked at her watch. It was nearly 1:00 p.m. and she was feeling peckish. The Brown House was still four blocks away and she decided she didn't want to continue on that route. The photo of Kurt filled her Nazi quota for the day. She turned left and soon found herself at a large beer garden with outside seating. She ordered a stein of pilsner with bratwurst and kraut, pulled out *Brave New World*, the book she was reading which Hearst had included in their eugenics research file. Test tube babies! Huxley sure had an active imagination.

She was halfway through her stein and had finished off the wurst when a shadow blocked the sun. This had happened before as people passed by her table. But this shadow was not moving. She put her book down to deliver a stern frown to the rude person standing above her.

Suddenly, the shadow spoke. "Mattie, is it really you?"

Oh, my God. Mattie thought. It can't be. She turned her face up at the shadow to see a smiling Kurt von Sturm. She started to rise but Sturm motioned her to stay seated.

"May I join you?"

"Please do," Mattie said, extending her hand. He grasped it and his lips softly brushed the back of her hand . Her pulse quickened, her body's invariable reaction to the touch of this man.

Sturm settled into the chair opposite her and ordered a large stein of lager.

"What are you doing in Germany?" Kurt asked.

"Working on a story," Mattie replied.

"Really? May I inquire as to its nature?"

"I'd rather not say. Ten murders in America and the trail has led me here," Mattie said.

"You believe the killer is a German?"

Mattie nodded. She had wanted to ask the question the minute she saw Kurt but she had refrained. Kurt, however, had opened the door wide and Mattie walked right through it.

"Kurt, why were you at *Doktor* von Verschuer's clinic outside Passau yesterday?"

Sturm had been raising his stein to his lips as Mattie asked the question and he stopped midway there and returned the stein to the table, unable to hide the surprise in his face.

"How . . . ?"

"I took your photograph as we flew over. You were in a large open Mercedes motorcar ."

"You were in one of those two autogiros?" Sturm broke eye contact, turning to watch the street traffic. "I was reminded of you the moment they appeared in the sky. You were flying out of my life. I thought. . ." he turned back to face her . "I never expected to see you again."

Yeah, well, same here, she thought, but you're evading my question. She waited.

"*Herr* Cockran is with you?" he asked. Mattie nodded. "So what were you doing flying out there?"

Mattie smiled and shook her head. "No, Kurt. I asked first. Why were you there?"

"May we speak in confidence?" Kurt said, and then quickly added, "Lives are at stake."

Mattie shook her head. "If it involves my story, no. Whatever you tell me I will share with Cockran. The clinic is key to solving these murders so we can't speak in confidence."

"It's a long story," Sturm said and looked away. "Last year, before we met, I was involved romantically with an American woman. Her husband was away. . . ."

"A married woman?" Mattie asked and waited. She wasn't about to make this easy.

"Well, yes. In fact, almost all of my romantic liaisons are with married women." He paused and once more looked her in the eye. "You were the exception."

Now it was Mattie's turn to feel uncomfortable as she looked away and felt the color rise in her cheeks. It served her right. Then the similarity struck her. Cockran was just the same! Before he met Mattie, his "romantic liaisons" were with Gold Coast socialites eager to get even with their straying husbands. Mattie was the "exception" for Cockran as well. The similarities didn't end there. Both could kill in cold blood. Both were in love with her. Both had made love to her. But that last thought was one best not to dwell upon in this captivating man's presence. She turned her head back. "Go on. I didn't mean to interrupt."

Mattie listened with growing amazement as Sturm told how he had briefly resumed his affair with the American woman two months ago; how he had saved her from being killed; how her twin siblings had disappeared; and how they came to be on the trail of Otmar von Verschuer. Mattie repressed a shudder when Sturm told her about the introductory letter from Adolf Hitler. It reminded her that she really had slept with a Nazi. But the journalist in her quickly recovered.

"We're after the same guy, Kurt," Mattie said, as she pulled a sheet of paper from her handbag. "What are the twins' names?"

"The girl is named Beatrice and the boy . . . ."

"No," Mattie said, cutting him off, "their last name."

"Johansson."

Mattie handed the paper to Kurt. "There. The last two names. We're after the same guy."

"Please explain," Kurt said.

So Mattie did, from her first meeting with Hearst right down to her meeting that morning with Cockran about the tunnel. She wasn't certain Cockran would approve but it didn't matter. She wasn't holding anything back now because she fully intended to recruit her former lover to help them. Why? Because it would immeasurably improve Cockran's chances for safely rescuing the twins. And Cockran's safety was more important to her than the twins or the story.

Once Mattie reached the point in her story where Wesley Waterman's nonprofit corporations were involved, Sturm raised his hand to stop her.

"Wesley Waterman? The chairman of I.C.E.?"

"The same. Why do you ask?"

"My friend, the woman I'm helping, is Waterman's wife, Ingrid."

Mattie felt her face drain of color.

67.

Hudson's Tunnel

COCKRAN pulled his goggles down over his leather flying helmet and watched as Bobby Sullivan and Ted Hudson climbed into the autogiro's front cockpit. The meeting in Churchill's suite had gone surprisingly well. Hudson had not revealed his sources but had otherwise told them everything he had learned about the escape tunnel. Cockran was impressed. Hudson's story had even persuaded Bobby Sullivan, a man who could smell a liar a mile away.

Hudson had produced a hand-drawn schematic of the clinic's interior which he claimed to have been given by his source. He said he had explored the tunnel yesterday but had not gone into the clinic itself. The door from the tunnel into the clinic was locked but Hudson said he had easily picked the lock open. The existence of the tunnel and its location were known to only a few senior medical staff. If the political winds favoring the Nazis suddenly shifted, the top medical staff would escape to conduct experiments another day.

Cockran's own days in MID, however, had taught him that conducting any operation without advance intelligence was unwise. Usually, if one member of the team had been on the ground learning the lay of the land, that was sufficient. But not if that person had been someone you didn't trust. Like Ted Hudson. Once Cockran made the suggestion that he, Bobby and Hudson fly out to Passau for a first-hand inspection, however, Hudson had readily agreed.

Had he misjudged Ted? No, he thought, Hudson was still an ends justifies means types of guy who still had a problem with Mattie and Cockran being together, the Ohio hotel bills and the Cold Spring Harbor brawl being Exhibit A. But the situation with the twins just might be different. Or so he hoped. Hudson and men like him believed themselves to be American patriots whose methods could be quite ruthless and their interrogations excessive if not bordering on torture, the latter a lot like Bobby Sullivan if truth be told. But intelligence was a tough business and Cockran had never doubted Ted's competence in the field. If it took Hudson's help to save the American twins, this could be just the break they needed.

And time was running out. The autopsies would start on Friday. Cockran pressed the starter button and the cylinders in the Wright Whirlwind engine rumbled into life. Whether the tunnel proved viable or not, they would have to try and rescue the twins tomorrow night.

The Verschuer Clinic
The Bavarian National Forest
Wednesday, 1 June 1932

TWO miles from the compound, Cockran cut the autogiro's engine and made a silent dead stick landing, floating gently to earth in a flower-filled clearing early in the afternoon. After putting camouflage netting over the autogiro, they hiked through the forest and approached the clinic's compound from the rear, the point of the triangle with no watchtower. Within 30 minutes, they were at the tunnel's entrance. No effort had been made to conceal a plain, gray metal door built into the side of the hill with a lock but no door handle. Hudson easily picked the lock and the door swung open on well-oiled hinges. Weapons in hand, they entered the tunnel and 15 minutes later, they reached steps up to a second door which opened into the clinic. Hudson again picked the lock.

Cockran motioned behind him for Sullivan and Hudson to switch off their electric torches. Then, he carefully opened the door a crack and peered inside. There was a long white corridor brightly lit with a floor of white tile. He heard voices. He watched as a white coated orderly walked past the door. He was followed by a procession of what appeared to be patients. They walked slowly past the door, clad only in hospital gowns, tied at the neck but open in the back. They were paired off as they walked past, two women, two men, two more women, two more men, followed by two more women, and then a man and a woman. It was difficult to tell their ages when all he could see were their bare backsides, their naked flesh fairly firm. Behind the twelve was another orderly but, he noted, both orderlies were unarmed and he saw no guards.

Cockran silently closed the door and switched on his torch. "Twelve people walked past in hospital gowns. Two orderlies were with them, both unarmed. It looks like the twins are all here."

"How do they look?" Hudson asked.

"Difficult to say," Cockran replied. "I could only see the back of them. But they were walking slowly, almost shuffling. Possibly sedated. Let's watch for another hour."

Cockran switched off his torch and once more opened the door a crack. He watched an empty corridor for nearly thirty minute before he heard voices again and watched as the twins returned in the same order as they had left. Two women, two men, two women, two men, two women, all followed by a man and a woman. Cockran could see their faces now. Five sets of identical twins ranging in age from, as best Cockran could tell, mid-twenties through late-thirties. All the women were fairly attractive. Two of the six women were blondes; two had light brown hair; and two were brunettes. As before, the a man and a woman brought up the rear and were the only fraternal twins. Now that he could see their faces, Cockran could tell that they certainly had been drugged. Vacant stares and a listless demeanor were proof of that. They did not look well. Another thirty minutes passed and Cockran saw no more activity in the hallway. No armed guards patrolling.

Cockran hated to admit it but Hudson might be right. Ted's tunnel might work.

68.

I Wish Luck to You Both

MATTIE gasped. "Your lover is Ingrid Waterman?"

Sturm put his finger to his lips. "All of Munich does not need to know this, Mattie."

"Do you know she's getting a divorce?" Mattie asked.

"Yes. I assume that is one of the reasons her husband is trying to have her killed."

"Well, hang on to your hat, buster. Guess who Ingrid's lawyer is for her divorce?"

"I'm sure I don't know but . . . ." Sturm paused. "*Herr* Cockran?" he asked tentatively.

"Yes. Bourke is her lawyer. I haven't seen them but I'll bet you're the blond mystery guy rogering Ingrid in those naked photographs her husband introduced in the divorce case."

"Photographs? Of Ingrid and me? I don't need to guess what 'rogering' means . . . ."

"An old English expression but, yes, you know what it means."

Sturm said nothing. If he were embarrassed, it didn't show.

"What is Verschuer doing with those twins?" Mattie asked.

"I don't know," Sturm said. "He has long specialized in the study of twins. But, judging from what happened to the ten twins on your list in America, it doesn't look good for the others."

"I know," Mattie replied. "But you've seen the twins there. You said they spoke English and appeared to be drugged. Can't you go to the authorities? Won't they do something?"

Sturm shook his head. "Sadly, no. I was only able to learn the clinic's location from a Nazi sympathizer in the Regensburg police department."

"If the authorities won't help, will you help us?" Mattie asked. "Me. Cockran. And Bobby Sullivan. You remember him?"

Sturm smiled. "I remember *Herr* Sullivan very well."

"Well, June 3 is the day after tomorrow. Bourke and Bobby and two of Bobby's friends from Ireland are planning an assault to free the twins, probably tomorrow night."

"That would not be wise," Sturm said.

"Why?"

"Many SS guard the place and they are well armed."

"If you would help, that would improve their chances," Mattie said.

Sturm shook his head. "I work best alone."

Mattie's heart sank. "But how do you plan to rescue Ingrid's brother and sister?"

"I cannot say. You have made it clear that you will repeat whatever I tell you to *Herr* Cockran. Suffice it to say I will secure their release."

"But not the other ten?" Mattie asked.

"No."

"Do you know about the tunnel?" Mattie asked.

"Tunnel? I know of no tunnel."

Mattie explained about Ted Hudson and the tunnel. "If they decide the tunnel is a viable option, will you help them then?"

Sturm shook his head. "My first obligation is to Ingrid's brother and sister."

"What can I say to persuade you to change your mind and help us?" Mattie asked. There was an icy calm about Sturm that she had to break through. He couldn't be that cold. "What if Ingrid weren't involved? What if it were just me asking you to help? What would it take?"

"It still wouldn't be my fight."

"What would make it your fight?"

"Something my honor forbids me to ask and yours to answer." There was a softness in Sturm's eyes and Mattie knew exactly what he meant. Mattie couldn't imagine many woman saying no to Kurt von Sturm. Ingrid Waterman certainly hadn't. The same had once been true of Mattie McGary. But no more. It wasn't her honor, however, it was her love for Cockran.

The problem of Cockran's safety, however, was still unresolved. She wanted to save the twins every bit as much as he did. With one exception. It was not worth Cockran's life. Kurt von Sturm would have gone a long way toward improving their odds for success. Without that, Mattie knew she had only one card left to play. She was going in with Cockran. Whatever happened, they would face it together. He could complain all he wanted. And if Mattie's threatened presence caused Cockran to call it off? Did she want that? Perhaps. She wasn't sure. But she was finally beginning to understand how Cockran felt when she took unnecessary risks.

Mattie knew she had to persuade Kurt to reconsider but she could not think of anything that would convince him. "Is there some way I can contact you?" she finally asked. "In case I need your help on something else and you're in a position to give it?"

Kurt took a drink of his lager as he considered her request. His eyes watching her over the rim of his stein betrayed his continuing love for her. "I cannot say whether I will be in a position to help you, but if you must reach me, ask for *Herr* Boettman at the *Bayerische Hof.*

Sturm stood up from the table and took her right hand in both of his. "I'm happy we met again," he said. "I'm sorry I cannot help you or *Herr* Cockran. He is a good man whom I both admire and respect." He smiled. "I envy him as well and I wish luck to you both." With that, he turned his back on her and walked away.

69.

Speechless

Hotel Continental
Munich
Wednesday, 1 June 1932

BOURKE Cockran was speechless. He sat there in stunned silence as Mattie recounted her meeting with Kurt von Sturm. He couldn't believe it. That damned Nazi was back! Worse, the man who had seduced Mattie had also done the same to his client, Ingrid Waterman! The studio-quality photographs now resting in a court file took on an entirely new significance for Cockran who had torn himself up a year ago with his fevered imaginings of Mattie and Sturm making love. Over time, that wound had begun to heal, the images fading. No more. No more imagining, either. The images were there again playing over and over in his mind like a motion picture, Mattie's face and body all too easily substituted for Ingrid's.

"Bourke, are you listening to me?" Mattie asked.

Cockran blinked. "Uh, yeah. Sure."

"Well, what do you think of my idea then?" Mattie asked.

Cockran grinned sheepishly. "Maybe you should run it past me one more time."

"I didn't think you were listening," Mattie said. "Kurt is only willing to rescue Ingrid's brother and sister. I urged him to coordinate his plans with you and Bobby but he refused. Will you talk to him? If you both attempt a rescue, I'm afraid you both might fail."

Cockran closed his eyes and massaged his temples. He needed a drink. He walked over to the sideboard and mixed himself a martini. How to put this delicately? *I don't need his help and I have no desire whatever to talk to your old Nazi lover.* Probably not a good idea.

Cockran took a long sip and turned back to Mattie. "You're right. We may jeopardize our chances if two different efforts are made. But let's face it. You have a lot more influence over the man than I do." After all, he thought but did not say, you were the one who slept with him. "Besides," he added, "Sturm is still a Nazi. He may be able to retrieve Ingrid's brother and sister but, for all we know, he supports whatever Verschuer is doing there to improve the race."

Mattie's eyes flashed. "That's not true! He doesn't support the SS. He may be a Nazi party member but he's not like them. He's an honorable man."

Cockran didn't reply. He took another sip. An honorable Nazi was an oxymoron.

"When the SS held me captive last year at Castle Wewelsburg," Mattie continued, "Kurt helped you and Bobby rescue me. There were no SS survivors."

"That proves my point," Cockran replied "Sturm was willing to help because it was personal, not because he had anything against the SS. He was in love with you. I accepted his offer to help for the same reason. I'd make an ally of the devil if that's what it took to keep you safe. And teaming up with a Nazi is just about the same thing. He's doing what he's doing to help Ingrid, his current lover, just as he was willing to do the same when you were his lover."

"He's not like that, Bourke," Mattie said softly. "I can't explain how I know. I just do."

Cockran stayed silent for a long time. A statement like that couldn't be cross-examined. How did she know? How could she? Had Sturm's semen supplied her with insight into his soul? But he would not voice that bitter thought. Regardless of the obvious feelings she still had for Sturm, Cockran knew she loved him as much as he loved her. He was not going to jeopardize their future together by angry words he might later regret. He knew now exactly how he was going to secure their future but, for the moment, he needed to address more immediate concerns.

"Maybe. But if he wouldn't listen to you, he's a lot less likely to listen to me."

Mattie nodded. "I understand," she said, her tone of voice resigned. "But it's going to complicate things and jeopardize the lives of all the twins, not just Ingrid's brother and sister."

"I don't know if it will do any good but I'll track down Ingrid and see how she feels. I can't believe she would knowingly sacrifice the lives of ten other people"

"You'll do that?" Mattie asked, her voice suddenly brighter.

Cockran nodded.

"Thank you. Thank you so much," Mattie said as she embraced Cockran. He held her tight. It felt good. By the time he let her go, the motion picture images were no longer playing.

Yes, he knew what he was going to do to secure their future and he was damn well going to find the right time. And the right place. And soon.

Early Wednesday evening

BOURKE Cockran paused in front of the mirror in their hotel suite and adjusted his black bow tie. Behind him, reflected in the mirror, a stark naked Mattie McGary scurried about, holding up clothes in front of her, deciding what to wear for that evening's dinner party. Cockran loved that about Mattie, her lack of inhibition at appearing naked before him but especially as she was getting ready to go out. It took his breath away how drop-dead gorgeous she was.

Cockran had met Ingrid in the bar off the *Bayerische Hof's* lobby late that afternoon. She had been appalled to learn of the twins who had been killed in America and that the twins they had seen at Passau had also been kidnapped. She promised Cockran she would take care of it with Sturm. Would she be able to persuade him? Cockran hoped so. It was clear to him that Ingrid had fallen in love with Kurt von Sturm. He only hoped the Nazi sonofabitch reciprocated.

70.

Fight for Me

KURT von Sturm walked into the *Bayerische Hof* lobby with a singular purpose. He was leaving for the clinic at Passau. Tonight. Running into Mattie McGary was troubling on many levels, but his most immediate concern was the presence of a parallel—and possibly suicidal— attempt to raid the Passau facility with the aim of freeing all the twins held captive.

Sturm knew his plan might be as dangerous and reckless in its own way as Cockran's. But it was dangerous to him and to him alone. He still had Heinrich Himmler's gift of which he intended to make use—the silver-trimmed black uniform of an SS *Obersturmbannfuhrer*. The SS at Passau were well armed but they possessed a weakness common to all hierarchical outfits. Invariably, they would respond to orders from a uniformed authority figure. Him. And, after claiming they had Jewish ancestors, he would walk out with the Johansson twins.

Sturm stepped off the elevator and hurried down the hall to their room. He had asked Ingrid to stay behind ostensibly to reduce the possibility of another encounter with Bruno. In reality it was because Sturm did not want Ingrid to see him packing an SS uniform into a valise at his apartment. His membership in the National Socialist Workers party was one secret he intended to keep from her as long as possible.

Sturm knocked twice on the door so that Ingrid knew it was him. He opened the door himself and quickly moved to the closet to put the small suitcase away. Once he closed the closet door, he noticed that he hadn't heard any of the telltale sounds of her presence.

"Ingrid?" No answer. "Ingrid?"

Still no answer. He swept through the suite's sitting room and past the archway leading to the bedroom, calling her name. The covers remained pulled back from the bed, an open magazine resting on the bedside table as though she'd just been here. But she was nowhere to be found. He checked the tables and writing desk, searching for a note. She had left none. She was gone! Could it have been Bruno? Had he become too careless?

As his mind raced, he heard the sound of a key inserted into the door to their suite, then the lock being turned. He reached inside his jacket for his Luger. He positioned himself behind the archway between rooms in their suite and leveled his gun on the entrance. The door opened.

Ingrid appeared in the doorway and uttered a short scream she stifled with her hands.

Sturm lowered his gun in relief. "Where have you been?"

Ingrid closed the door, her temper rising. "Don't you *ever* point that thing at me!"

Sturm replaced his Luger in its holster. "Where have you been?"

"I was in the bar off the hotel lobby."

"You left me no word of these plans. Why did you leave the room?"

"I left to meet my lawyer. Not that it's any of your business," she said.

"*Herr* Cockran?"

"Yes," she said, a look of surprise on her face. "He's here for the same reason we are. More twins have been kidnapped by people associated with my husband and ten of them have already been killed. He's asking for our help to save the others."

"I know," Sturm said. He should have known better than to underestimate Mattie. Once she knew she couldn't persuade him to help, she had given their hotel information to Cockran so that he might be able to succeed with Ingrid where Mattie had failed with him.

"So you know about the other twins?" Ingrid said.

"Yes," Sturm said. "I ran into his girlfriend, the Hearst reporter, Mattie McGary."

"And?"

"And I said 'No.' The safety of your brother and sister are what matter most, and Cockran's plan would jeopardize their lives"

"No," Ingrid said. "It's just not right to save my brother and sister at the expense of ten other human beings."

"But they all can't be saved."

"We don't know that and never will unless we try."

"Never stretch a mission beyond its original scope unless you have the means and the time to adjust," Sturm admonished her. "We have neither."

"Stop thinking like one of your agents, Kurt. Act like a human being!"

Sturm was stung by this but tried not to show it. "We must be rational about what we can control and what we cannot and limit our efforts to what we can realistically accomplish."

"But when have you ever done that yourself?" Ingrid leveled at him.

"I don't understand."

"You put away your dreams of flying airships and for what? To be a hired thug, a paid murderer for men you despise. How is that rational?"

"Ingrid, one man can do only so much. I must place my support behind imperfect men who can implement the changes that I cannot. Attempting to rescue all of the twins will place your siblings in danger."

"That's a false choice, Kurt and you know it," Ingrid said. "My brother and sister are already in danger, the same danger as the other twins you refuse to help. I don't understand how you can think this way. You have more power over the fate of the twins in Passau than you ever will have over the fate of Germany yet you're refusing to act on that power! What would your father say? Honor. Respect. Strength. Is saving two lives at the expense of ten deaths honorable? You have the power to possibly rescue them all and I want you to use that power. Stop wasting it on men who do not deserve it. Fight for yourself. Fight for your honor. Fight for me."

Her last words lingered between them. "Fight for me," she said, her voice a whisper.

Sturm did not know what to say. She had turned his own values—his father's values—against his natural instincts and better judgment. She had not spoken with cold calculation to manipulate him. She meant every word. And he knew she was right. He knew his father would want him to try. It was a matter of honor. To fight for himself. For his father. For his honor. And, yes, for her.

"You may be right," Sturm said, relenting. "I will meet with your lawyer, *Herr* Cockran, and hear him out. But I will make my own judgment on the matter once I have heard precisely what he has in mind. Saving two lives at the expense of ten is better than all twelve dying." But Sturm suspected that he and Cockran would work something out. He admired and respected the man. They were alike in more ways than loving the same woman.

Ingrid's face lit up with a smile and she rushed to him, hugging him tightly. "Oh thank you, Kurt!" she said. "I knew I was right about you. I knew it." She kissed him deeply.

Sturm kissed her back until he couldn't help but laugh at her exuberance. It was the first time she'd been this happy since their encounter with Bruno. He leaned back from her. "Now tell me when and where I am to meet *Herr* Cockran."

"That's yet to be determined." Ingrid said. "But we're both having dinner with Bourke at the Continental along with Miss McGary, the new U.S. military attaché in Berlin, and Winston Churchill. Hitler's Foreign Press Secretary, Putzi Hanfstaengl, is the guest of honor."

Sturm raised his eyebrows. "So this is to be a dinner party of sorts? Am I expected to discuss our military strategy for Verschuer's clinic with *Herr* Hanfstaengl as well as your lawyer?"

"No, silly," Ingrid said, walking towards the water closet attached to the bedroom. "That's just the cover for you to meet Bourke and arrange a meeting with him for the next day. I could have made the arrangements myself but I thought you'd prefer to make them directly."

"I see," he said, following her to the door of the bathroom where she began to unwrap several packages of hair dye clearly designed to return her hair color to its original blonde. "Is that wise?"

"The hair dye? Now that your protégé Bruno has seen me as a brunette, I see no reason to continue that disguise. I'm not afraid of him. Not when I have you to look out for me. Besides I want to look my best when I meet Mr. Churchill and *Herr* Hanfstaengl and I'm at my best as a blonde."

"All that for an out-of-office English politician and a German who speaks for Hitler to the foreign press?"

"Perhaps not only for them," she said, her voice carrying from the bathroom. He heard the rush of the shower and Ingrid now had to shout over the sound. "If it all works out as Mr. Churchill hopes, your hero, *Herr* Hitler, may well be joining us later in the evening. That's the real purpose of the dinner. Churchill wants to meet Hitler."

71.

My Weakness for a Pretty Face

Hotel Continental
Munich
Wednesday, 1 June 1932

MATTIE'S first thought when she and Cockran arrived at Churchill's table was that she might well die of embarrassment. Ingrid, stunning in a strapless blue silk gown, took a seat directly across from her at the round table set for eight. Winston and Randolph took their seats on either side of Mattie while Hudson was seated to Ingrid's left. Sturm sat between Winston and Ingrid, directly across from Cockran. Looking up, she saw the tall, lantern-jawed dark-haired figure of Hitler's foreign press secretary, Putzi Hanfstaengl, approaching the table. Introductions were made and Putzi took his seat.

Mattie shook her head, inwardly ashamed. What were the odds? Except for her godfather Winston and his handsome twenty-one year old son Randolph, she had been to bed with all four of the other men at the table and, given the attention Randolph was paying her breasts as he downed his third martini of the evening, he was eager to be number five. Mattie took a sip of her own martini. If you only knew, kid, if you only knew. She sighed silently. Three former lovers and her current lover all at the same table. She didn't think she could look Cockran in the eye right now. On the one hand, it was all so very civilized. On the other, there was a lot to be said for monogamy.

The guest of honor, Hanfstaengl, was the only source Mattie had ever taken to bed. Once. It was a rookie mistake she never made again but the story had been sensational. Literally a front-row seat at Hitler's so-called Beer Hall *putsch* in 1923. It had made Mattie's reputation and led directly to her current position with Hearst. She owed her career to that story.

Dinner turned out to be surprisingly pleasant. Everyone, even Cockran and Hudson, were on their best behavior. It was indeed all so very civilized, made more so by the fact that not much conversation was required at a table with Winston Churchill who rarely permitted more than a sentence or two from someone else to interrupt his monologue of the moment.

"If you'll excuse me, gentlemen," Ingrid said, rising from her chair after the waiters had cleared the table. "I'll be right back." Instantly, all six men rose from their chairs.

Mattie stayed seated but Ingrid imperceptibly but definitely motioned with her eyes for Mattie to join her. She rose before the men resumed their seats. "Excuse me also, please."

Once in the ladies' room, Ingrid checked the stalls to see that they were alone. "I didn't have a chance to tell Bourke before dinner, and I obviously couldn't say anything at the table so I thought this would be the best opportunity. Tell Bourke that I've talked with Kurt and he has agreed that we must make an effort to save all the American twins at the Clinic."

Mattie didn't reply but inwardly was elated. Cockran now had a fighting chance.

"Until Bourke told me, I didn't realize that you and Kurt knew each other or that he had refused to help you. Please don't hold it against him. He was just trying to keep his word to me."

Mattie nodded, silently relieved that Kurt had kept their affair secret. "I understand. So what's the plan?"

"Kurt hasn't said. I told him about the tunnel your friend in military intelligence found and he said he would arrange with Bourke to meet tomorrow morning to discuss logistics."

"Has Kurt said anything about how he intends to work with Bourke?"

"No. He told me not to worry. But I'll learn the details whether he tells me or not."

"Really?" Mattie asked. "How do you propose to do that?"

Ingrid smiled. "I intend to be beside him every step of the way," she said. "I've always been a big fan of your articles, Miss McGary, and you strike me as the kind of girl who feels the same way I do. It's my brother and sister after all. I'm not going to let the men take all the risk and leave me behind to worry."

Mattie had known she was going to like this woman. "Please, call me Mattie," she replied with a smile. "You're right. We definitely are not going to let the men take all the risk and we certainly are not going to let them leave us behind."

MATTIE returned to the table and immediately noticed that Hanfstaengl was nervously glancing at his watch. It was quarter past 10 p.m. and Mattie realized she and Ingrid had been in the loo longer than she thought. Hitler was to have joined them at 10 p.m. He was late.

If Churchill noticed, he didn't let on. Rather, he kept badgering Putzi about the Nazis and anti-Semitism. Putzi was embarrassed and with good reason. Mattie knew Putzi was a snob and an anti-Semite but not like the Nazis. His social anti-Semitism was no different than what you found in any American country club or most men's clubs in London. Churchill, by contrast had long been an ardent Zionist. Even some of his friends said he was too fond of the Jews.

"Tell your boss from me that anti-Semitism may be a good starter, but it is a bad sticker," Churchill said, concluding his monologue. Churchill relit his cigar, took a sip of champagne and directed his attention toward Ted Hudson. "So, Major, when do you take up your new post as U.S. military attaché in Berlin? I'm half American, you know."

By 11 p.m., Churchill was showing no signs of slowing down but it was becoming ever more apparent that Hitler had stood them up. Mattie had heard enough. Churchill was explaining, for at least the third time that night, why France should not disarm until a general treaty on European disarmament had been reached where Germany agreed to limit its military in the same manner as the French. Sturm agreed but each time reminded Churchill that the Versailles Treaty already forbade Germany from equality of arms with the French.

Mattie caught Cockran's eye and signaled they should leave, the two of them rising together. To her surprise, Kurt and Ingrid had promptly done the same, leaving Hanfstaegl and Hudson behind, hostage to the Churchillian monologue. After thanking Winston for his hospitality, the two couples excused themselves and walked to the lobby where Mattie spotted a medium-sized man in a green fedora and a tan Burberry trench coat on a wide staircase talking to an overweight man in his late fifties with close-cropped white hair and a triple chin. The man in the trench coat shook hands with the fat man and turned to walk down the stairs. Adolf Hitler.

Mattie turned to Cockran. "Oh, my God! You see who that is? Come on, wouldn't you like to meet him?" Mattie said, grabbing his hand and heading toward the staircase.

"Not especially," Cockran mumbled, but he didn't let go of her hand.

"*Herr* Hitler! *Herr* Hitler! It's Mattie McGary. Remember me?" she asked in German.

Hitler paused and frowned, as if he were displeased to have been recognized.

In a moment, Mattie was on the steps, blocking Hitler's way, her hand extended. She sensed Cockran was still behind her and she noted with surprise that both Kurt and Ingrid had followed as well, the four of them facing Hitler. Hitler's frown turned into a smile. He took off his fedora and grabbed Mattie's right hand in his. "*Fraulein* McGary! How nice to see you again," he said as he raised her hand and lowered his face to kiss it gently, his bright blue eyes a contrast to his limp brown hair.

Mattie turned and placed her hand on Cockran's arm. "*Herr* Hitler, may I present my friend from America, Bourke Cockran?" She watched their perfunctory handshake but was amazed when Hitler shifted his focus to the right. To Kurt von Sturm.

"Kurt!" Hitler cried, grasping Sturm's hand in both of his and shaking it vigorously. "How very good to see you. Friedrich told me you stopped by the other day. I regret I was not there to receive you. I trust he took good care of you? The letter he gave you was satisfactory?"

"Yes, *mein Fuhrer*," Sturm replied. "Most satisfactory. Please thank Friedrich for me."

"Think nothing of it," Hitler replied. "And who's this beautiful woman?" Hitler asked. "With *Fraulein* McGary on one side and her on the other, I hardly know which way to turn."

Mattie watched as Kurt introduced Ingrid to Hitler who bowed and kissed Ingrid's outstretched hand in the same way he had done with Mattie. Mattie wasn't exactly speechless but she was bemused. She and Kurt had spent two weeks together last summer in daily contact. While

Kurt had expressed admiration for Adolf Hitler, he never admitted to her that he was a Nazi. Someone else had told her that. Moreover, while Mattie had told Kurt that she had interviewed Hitler on three separate occasions, he had never disclosed that he and Hitler were well-acquainted, let alone that the Nazi leader had genuine affection for him. Either that, or Hitler was one hell of an actor, something Mattie did not entirely discount.

"We were most disappointed," Mattie said, "that you could not join us after dinner tonight at Mr. Churchill's table. *Herr* Hanfstaengl said that you were unavoidably detained."

Hitler's startling blue eyes flashed in a clear display of anger. Mattie knew it well. She had been the object of that anger during her second interview with him in the days before the Beer Hall *putsch* in 1923. She had raised a subject from Hitler's days as an artist in Vienna before the war which he clearly did not want to address.

"Putzi did not tell me that there would be two such beautiful women at Mr. Churchill's table tonight. Of all people, *Fraulein* McGary, you know my weakness for a pretty face."

Mattie smiled at the compliment. She had interviewed Hitler the year before and had negotiated on behalf of Hearst to have him write exclusive articles for Hearst, just as Mussolini and Churchill were already doing. She had struck a favorable bargain—less than the new Hearst deals with Winston and the Italian dictator—and Hitler had made Mattie promise not to discuss their negotiations with others. "My enemies must not learn how easily I can be swayed by a pretty face," the Nazi leader had told her.

"An evening with two charming and beautiful women is something else entirely than listening to Putzi translate the tired bromides of an aging English politician who has fallen from power." Hitler narrowed his eyes. "I shall speak to Putzi about this. Mistakes like this will not happen again. You may be assured I will not again miss such a delightful evening."

Mattie thought about defending Putzi but decided not to. She owed him nothing. They each had gotten what they wanted. Mattie her story. Putzi his shag. Besides, Putzi had been cheating on his wife during his brief interval in Mattie's bed. She had charmed Hitler once again. That was enough. Putzi could defend himself to his boss.

Hitler bade farewell to the quartet, shaking hands with both men, patting Sturm on the shoulder with an affectionate gesture, and then once more kissing Mattie's and Ingrid's hands before putting on his slouch hat, pulling it low on his forehead and heading down the stairs.

"I knew you'd interviewed Hitler several times," Cockran whispered in a deadpan voice as they walked down the staircase and made their way to the elevators, "but I had no idea he was one of your old boyfriends as well."

72.

I Do Care For Kurt

Hotel Continental
Munich
Wednesday, 1 June 1932

MATTIE turned on him. "Damn it, Cockran, he's not . . . ." and then laughed as she saw Cockran grinning at her. That bastard! Still it was good that Cockran could joke like this after an evening spent at the same table with one man he knew was a former lover and another he suspected of being one. Thank God he knew nothing of Putzi. It *was* better to be lucky than good, she thought, and squeezed Cockran's arm as they stepped into the elevator.

"I saw you and Kurt talking before dinner with Ted. Does that mean he's going with you two when you try to rescue the twins?"

Cockran didn't reply. He fished out his key and opened the door to their room. Once inside, he turned to her. "I don't know. Probably. I intend to break several federal laws tomorrow morning when I tell Winston, Rankin, Bobby and Sturm all I know about Hudson. It's probably OK to trust Ted on this. I'm willing to take the risk but the others deserve to know the kind of man with whom they're going into harm's way."

Mattie turned to him, placing both her hands on his arms. "I'm not sure I understand. I know you don't like Ted and I'm fairly certain you don't like Kurt."

"True. But Sturm's not one of my favorite guys for a different reason."

"I know why you don't like Kurt. He's a Nazi and . . . .."

Cockran nodded. "That's not the only reason…"

Mattie blushed. "Okay, I understand. But you never told me anything specific about Ted's past. Yet you're going to tell Winston, Robbie, Kurt and Bobby what you won't tell me? Why"

"Look, Mattie, everything which makes me dislike Ted Hudson occurred before we met. Almost all of it is classified information under the Espionage Act of 1917. You've got a history with Hudson and it's bound to color your views of what I say. I mean, would you believe me if I told you that it sure seemed to me Hudson tried to stop me entering the Eugenics Record Office that night specifically to make sure you were captured or killed?"

"No," Mattie said, shaking her head. "We've been through this before. He simply took something I said and blew it out of proportion. That plus the bad blood between the two of you explains everything. He's saved my life. Ted would never do anything to bring me harm."

"You prove my point. The golden boy can do no wrong in your eyes. If Winston, Bobby and Sturm agree with you or believe the risk is minimal with Hudson, then we'll take him along. Personally, now that we have the tunnel as well as Sturm, I don't think we need Hudson."

"But here's what I don't understand. You don't like Ted or Kurt, but you obviously trust Kurt enough to take him into your confidence. Why's that?"

"I don't like Sturm for the reasons I told you. But I both respect and trust him. From the first time we met, he's never given me reason to doubt his word. Also, you don't talk about Hudson the same way you do about Sturm. If you did, I might be jealous of Hudson the way I am about Sturm."

"You're not jealous of Ted?" Mattie asked, surprised that Cockran had just admitted he *was* jealous of Kurt. He had never admitted *that* before. Maybe that Irish bastard was vulnerable after all or, at least, he didn't always have to hide it behind humor. It was a start.

"Hell no. I've never sensed you held tender feelings for Hudson. Sturm is different. You know why." Cockran walked to the sideboard and poured them both a short nightcap from their bottle of Johnnie Walker Red and handed a glass to Mattie. Yes, she knew why and she still carried the guilt.

"Take Ingrid," Cockran began. "I had a long talk with her. She says many of the same things about Sturm that you do with the same kind of look in her eyes that you have. I think she's in love with him just like I know you still care for him. I can't change that."

"Ingrid? Really?" Mattie asked, ignoring his comment about her feelings for Sturm.

"She may not know it yet, but it's clear to me. In any event, Sturm obviously listens to her. He turned down your request because he had promised to rescue her brother and sister and trying to rescue all the twins would have jeopardized that. It was a matter of honor that he keep his promise to Ingrid. She had to release him from that and once she did, he agreed to help us. So, do I trust Sturm? Sure. He's a man of honor. His word means something to him. In my experience with Hudson, honor doesn't play a part in his decisions. Once he decides on an objective, the ends justify almost any means."

Mattie drew back and looked into his eyes. "You're right. I do care for Kurt. The two of you are alike in so many ways. He's a strong and caring man who's not afraid to occasionally express his feelings. Like you. But it's you I love, not him, and you're stuck with me," she grinned, " Forever."

"I can live with that," Cockran replied with a small smile.

"You'd better."

73.

Growing Up in Passau

Munich
Thursday, 2 June 1932

KURT von Sturm inspected the four Schmeisser submachine guns the warehouse manager had produced for him. Five hundred rounds per minute without sound suppressors. Four hundred rounds with suppressors.

"I need four sound suppressors for each one." Sturm said. "Eight boxes of ammunition. Four Lugers also. Sound suppressors and ammunition for them as well."

"At once, *Obersturmbanführer*," the manger replied, his double chin wobbling as he virtually came to attention, turned smartly on his heel and scurried off.

Sturm smiled. His black SS officer's uniform, the silver trim and polished knee-high black leather boots, often had that effect on people, especially in Munich. He had worn the uniform to Churchill's suite this morning as well if only to show them how its appearance might buy them time tonight upon confronting any SS guards.

Together with the Irishman's four Thompson Model 1921 SMGs with 100 round drums, the Schmeissers and Lugers would give them all the firepower they would need. Sullivan's two men would function as a strategic reserve or as a diversion depending upon what happened when the four of them entered the Clinic. Sturm shook his head. The four of them. The American MID Major Hudson would be joining them. It was not Sturm's choice. After listening to Cockran describe the man's background, he instinctively shared Cockran's reservations. For whatever reason, the bloody fool had almost gotten Mattie killed.

Yet the minute Mattie arrived with Ingrid, she had promptly argued against them, backed by Churchill, Rankin and Sullivan who all wanted the extra firepower Hudson would furnish. Sturm hadn't agreed. In his experience, trusting all the members of your team was more important. He knew both Cockran and Sullivan. He trusted the Irishman just as he trusted Cockran whose timely tourniquet had saved his life a year earlier.

Strangely, he also trusted the Englishman Churchill, his former enemy in the Great War. The man was clearly a warrior, a leader. Cockran may have planned the initial assault, since modified by the discovery of the tunnel, but it was Churchill who had orchestrated the logistics of the twins' extraction by motorbus from the clinic and by air from Regensburg. He even trusted Churchill's bodyguard Sergeant Rankin, a British bomber pilot from the war for goodness'sake.

Still, he kept coming back to Cockran. Sturm knew he and Cockran had more in common than loving the same woman. He was honorable, courageous and coldly efficient in a firefight, qualities Sturm valued and thought he possessed as well. Yet each of them had gone along over including Hudson just as they had when Mattie and Ingrid insisted upon making the flight with them to Passau. The aircraft take-off time was about all the two men had agreed upon which their women had not changed.

Their women. The thought brought Sturm up short. Mattie was Cockran's woman. No matter how much he loved Mattie McGary, he knew she would always be Cockran's woman. But did he consider Ingrid to be *his* woman? True, they were lovers but did he *love* Ingrid? Until now, the thought had never crossed his mind. Like all Sturm's lovers, she was married and love was not part of the equation. By design. He had deviated from the design only once. And had fallen in love. With Mattie. Had he done so again? He wasn't sure but the two women were disturbingly similar. Mattie was British but to Sturm, she talked and acted like an American. Irreverent. Opinionated. Free. Like Ingrid. Was Sturm in love? Again?

Forget the women, he thought, as he closed the boot. Focus on the immediate future. Tonight's raid. He felt no more emotion now than he had the night he killed Reynaud. Killing him had been an obligation he owed to the men who employed him. The obligation to do so tonight would be different. Owed not to his employer, but to himself. To his honor. To his father's values. To all that Germany once stood for and, he hoped, would do so again.

Back in his hotel room, Sturm stripped off the *Obersturmbannführer* uniform and thought about his visit to the clinic yesterday. Passau. Why was the SS Clinic located near Passau, a town on the border with Austria? Adolf Hitler had lived there as a child from age three to six when his father had been stationed nearby as an Austrian customs inspector. It was less than two years ago when Hitler and Sturm had talked together outside the Cafe Heck. Sturm couldn't remember how it came up but Hitler had talked of his childhood, growing up in Passau.

"I thought of myself as a German, not an Austrian, because I was living in a German city and playing with German children," Hitler had told him. "My German today bears the traces of the Bavarian dialect of my youth. Whenever I hear it, it reminds me of my childhood in Passau."

Did Himmler or Verschuer locate this clinic dedicated to perfecting and multiplying the Aryan race near Hitler's childhood home to curry his favor? Did Hitler know of the so-called science being conducted there in his name? Did Hitler realize that twins were being killed in experiments and that Verschuer wanted to cleanse the race by sterilizing the weak — the feeble minded, the lame and even the blind? Was it Hitler's will as well? He didn't know. He wished he did. He hoped it wasn't. The old Germany whose greatness he wanted to restore would never have done that. What would the new Germany do? Sturm wanted to know. He *had* to know.

74.

Just Like Your Wife

The Bavarian National Forest
Thursday, 2 June 1932

THE autogiros lifted off early in the evening at the same time Sergeant Rankin and Churchill took off for the Regensburg airfield in a leased Ford tri-motor. Rankin, of course, was in the left-hand pilot's seat, having flown multi-engined bombers before but Winston was in the right-hand co-pilot's seat despite never having flown an aircraft since 1913. Cockran just shook his head. Churchill's regular bodyguard Inspector Tommy Thompson, had once told him that Winston so much enjoyed danger that they rarely told him when his life was in peril. Which it very much was tonight. The plan was for the two men to refuel the plane upon landing in Regensburg; spend the night at the airfield; and be ready to take off as soon as the rescued twins arrived in the motorbus Rolf had hired.

Cockran flew the lead autogiro, Mattie and Ingrid in the front cockpit. Sullivan piloted the second with Sturm and Hudson in front. The sky was overcast and a line of thunder squalls lay between them and their landing zone in the Bavarian National Forest. There was one drawback to open cockpit aircraft, Cockran thought, and that was rain. When it happened, you got soaked and there was not a damn thing you could do about it except wear a rain slicker over your leather flying jacket and hunker down. Which they all did.

In deference to Sturm's and Cockran's reservations, the others had agreed Hudson would only be advised of their departure for the clinic thirty minutes before take-off. Cockran had expected Hudson to complain about the short notice he had given him over their departure time and he did. Too fucking bad, Ted, Cockran thought with some satisfaction. So far as they knew, all the twins were still there at the clinic. The two Apostles Sullivan sent to watch the clinic had phoned that, as of 6:00 p.m., no one had entered or left the clinic gates. The Apostles also had a surplus army field telephone and, once in position at the tunnel's entrance, Sullivan would use his own field telephone to once more verify whether anything had occurred since their last communication.

By 8:00 p.m. the autogiros had reached the landing zone, feathering silently to the ground as he had the day before. Once more, camouflage netting was produced. As the gloom of the evening settled in, enhanced by the low cloud cover, Cockran knew the camouflage was less necessary than it had been in the bright sun yesterday but there was no reason to take chances.

Cockran listened as Sullivan cranked up the field radio. Earphones on, Sullivan spoke in a low voice. After a moment, Sullivan looked up and took the earphones off so that they dangled around his neck. He gave Cockran a thumbs up. "All twins present and accounted for."

Cockran returned the thumbs up gesture. "Game on," Cockran said, as he swung a Schmeisser and a Thompson submachine gun over his shoulder and headed off into the woods. Armed the same way, Hudson and Sturm fell in behind him. The two women and Sullivan followed, the Irishman leaning heavily on the sword cane. Mattie carried the field radios.

Once at the tunnel, Ted Hudson picked the lock to the exterior tunnel door for the second time in two days. Surprisingly, Mattie had agreed with Cockran that she and Ingrid should wait at the tunnel entrance until they had secured the clinic. Cockran led the way into the tunnel and the others followed. Sullivan limped along behind Cockran, followed by Hudson. Sturm, electric torch in his left hand, Luger in his right, brought up the rear.

After the four men had traversed the half-mile long tunnel and were again at the door leading into the clinic, they switched off their electric torches and Cockran opened the door a crack. The corridor was silent and empty. Still, Cockran waited. There would never be a good time to enter the clinic. Anyone could come along. But he was determined to wait at least thirty minutes to make sure that, as before, there were no patrolling guards, armed or otherwise. After twenty minutes, he heard a noise, the sharp click of leather heels on the tile floor. Two guards walked by clad in a black SS uniform, submachine guns over their shoulders.

Cockran closed the door and switched on his electric torch. Armed guards were new. This was *not* going to be a walk in the park. He found some humor in the truth he'd learned over a decade before in the Great War. It was easy to plan an operation. He no more considered the possibility of his own death while doing so than he did when he was a child playing with the toy soldiers Churchill had given him. It was only when he reached the precipice of action, trapped at the bottom of a trench and staring at a wall of mud, that he would consider the peril into which he had deliberately placed himself. The waiting was always the hardest. Once over the top, adrenaline kicked in and his body took over. He knew what to do.

Cockran passed back the news of the armed guards and Sturm volunteered to spell him at the door and wait for the next set of guards to pass by. Cockran almost declined and then caught himself. Sturm, wearing the uniform of an SS *Obersturmbannfuhrer*, was going to be the first in harm's way. He deserved a first-hand look.

Waiting, Cockran reflected on how loyalty to your unit transcended personal differences. Sturm was Mattie's former lover and yet, instinctively, he had agreed to Sturm's request to spell him at the door because he knew it would increase the German's chance for survival and the unit's chance for success. He had learned that lesson in the war. Men didn't fight and die for their country; they fought and died to protect their mates in the unit. Officers who didn't understand that didn't live long in combat. If the enemy didn't kill them, their own men would.

STURM'S thoughts at that time were less philosophical. Waiting was indeed difficult, but easy to master if you had disciplined your mind. Sturm focused on nothing but the details of the mission, clearing his mind of any emotions that might weaken his resolve. He knew precisely what he must accomplish but how he did so depended on many unknowns.

The timing of the guards' rounds clear, he closed the door, then switched on his torch. "We'll wait for the guards to make their next round. When they do, I will elmininate them. Wait for my signal."

Twenty minutes later, the footsteps of the guards returned, echoing off the metal door which led into the tunnel. As they passed by, Sturm made his move but the door betrayed him. As he opened it and stepped into the hall, it emitted a soft squeak which sounded as loud as thunder to Sturm.

The two guards, both *Untersturmfuhrers,* spun around at the sound, their submachine guns aimed directly at Sturm. It was apparent someone had placed the entire clinic on a high alert. As if the Nazis had known they were coming. And the two junior lieutenants looked both nervous and inexperienced. If this didn't work, he would be dead and Cockran would have to abort the mission.

Sturm slammed shut the tunnel door and and stepped into the hall, rising to his full height which was several inches above the two blond-haired SS guards who appeared barely out of their teens. "Idiots! Lower your weapons! Now!"

The guards lowered their weapons but Sturm could see the suspicion in their eyes. They recognized the uniform but not the man wearing it. "This facility is on high alert and were I an intruder, you would both be dead. I watched you twice walk by an external entry point," he said pointing to the tunnel door "and you never once checked to see if it was secure."

"You're both being placed on report for dereliction of duty." Sturm said as he closed the distance between them. "So shoulder those damned weapons; stand at attention; and salute a superior officer!"

The two guards slung the leather straps of their machine pistols over their shoulders and sprang to attention. "*Heil* Hitler!" they said in unison, their arms raised in the Roman salute. It was all Sturm needed. No time to think. Sturm pulled the silenced Luger from the black leather holster on his belt and shot the guard on the right in his forehead at point blank range, the .9 mm bullet exiting through the back of his head with a spray of blood and bone.

Reacting to the faint cough of the silenced shot, the guard on the left barely had time to lower his extended arm and look over and down at his fallen comrade when Sturm shot him in his right temple, his head exploding in a similar way. He went back to the tunnel door and knocked to signal all clear. Cockran opened the door and, followed by Sullivan and Hudson, stepped into the hallway and saw Sturm's handiwork.

"Put the bodies in there," Sturm ordered, pointing to the open tunnel door. Cockran and Hudson did so. Sturm and Sullivan followed them into the tunnel.

"*Herr* Cockran and Major Hudson, strip them of their tunics and caps and put them on. The three of us will clear the clinic. Kill any guards. As for the orderlies, bring them back to *Herr* Sullivan who can bind them and can keep them under guard in one of these rooms."

As Cockran put on one of the dead guards' tunics and Hudson did the same, Sturm motioned for Sullivan to hand him the field radio: "Ingrid? Do you read me? Over."

The radio squawked and he heard Ingrid's voice. "Advance through the tunnel until you reach the clinic and wait there," he told her. "*Herr* Sullivan will meet you. Over."

Sturm turned to Sullivan. "Wait for the women inside the door. I'll keep this radio. We'll call you once we have secured the facility."

Cockran pulled out a floor plan of the single story clinic—two parallel wings joined at the center by a corridor and forming a crude H—and laid it out on the ground. "We're in the bottom right-hand leg of the H," he said to Sturm. "You and Ingrid were shown the top two legs. The bottom leg on the left was the locked one. We'll clear the top and bottom of the right side first and then the top of the left side. We'll save the locked leg for last."

Sturm gave Cockran a curt nod and headed for the door. Hudson followed and Cockran fell in behind. In clearing the entire right or north side of the complex, they only came across two unarmed orderlies who were taken back to a room where they were bound and gagged by Sullivan who then rejoined the women just inside the tunnel door.

The trio proceeded across the bar of the H to the left side of the building when Sturm heard voices in conversation coming from the direction of the locked wing. He stopped suddenly as he reached the corner and motioned behind him for Cockran and Hudson to stay low. He was on the near side of the corridor wall while Hudson and Cockran crept along the far side of the wall. Hudson in the lead, Cockran behind. Hudson would be the first to see whoever it was coming up from the locked wing, Cockran the second.

There were four voices, joking and laughing in German. Three SS men and an orderly in white whose name apparently was Gunter.

"Tell me Gunter, how did yours compare to the two blondes we poked three days ago?"

"Much better. Like riding an unbroken young mare. Did you see how she bucked when I mounted her? Did you hear her moans after I brought her to heel? Don't try to renege on our bet. I know I brought her off. Much more spirited than those blondes who lay there like dead fish."

"Just like your wife, Olga, right Gunter? Shagging a dead fish should be nothing new for you. " the first man said, followed by more laughter.

"Olga is never like that with me," a third voice chimed in. "She always flops around like a trout you speared with a pike and keeps begging me to stuff her more. She says Gunter's pike just doesn't measure up to mine or any of the other SS." More laughter.

"We'll see who's laughing tomorrow." the man named Gunter replied "I'm only an orderly but you'll have to pay off our other bet when *Doktor* Josef publishes his pathology report on those two blondes and we learn whose seed was successful."

More laughter and the first man spoke again. "We don't need to wait. Just ask your wife. She's practically an SS mascot. Whenever you're on duty, she's over at our barracks in a flash, naked as a newborn. We all take turns. She's insatiable and that body of hers keeps a lot more than our spirits up. Face facts, Gunter, do you really believe her two blue-eyed blond children could possibly have been sired by a brown-eyed mongrel like you?"

Gunter's life would not last long enough for him to reply to the renewed laughter.

75.

Ask Him His Name

The Verschuer Clinic
The Bavarian National Forest
Thursday, 2 June 1932

COCKRAN was concerned when he and Hudson stepped out from the corridor because he could see the fourth man was an unarmed orderly. It would be difficult to take out the three armed SS guards without harming the orderly. Hudson apparently didn't care as he stepped out and squeezed off six rapid shots from his silenced Schmeisser grouped in a tight target over the orderly's heart.

"Why kill an unarmed. . . ?" Cockran began as the dead orderly pitched forward on his face but he never finished as Sturm turned the corner and joined Hudson in unleashing a deadly hail of .9 mm bullets from their Schmeissers at the three guards. Cockran then did the same. Like the first two guards Sturm had executed, all three wore the uniform of an SS *Untersturmfuhrer*, young lads all, who never stood a chance, their weapons still slung uselessly over their shoulders as the bullets hit them.

Both Cockran and Sturm fired short, controlled bursts and between them took down two of the guards with head and chest shots. Hudson had a different method. Unlike the orderly whom he killed quickly, there was now no danger. Hudson ran a line of bullets across the third guard's stomach who cried out, his hands clasping his middle, blood streaming through them. Having gut-shot his target, Hudson approached within five feet and ripped off another burst in the same place, almost as if he were using the man's hands as a target. This time the man did not cry out but merely gasped, coughing up blood as he sank to his knees, his body nearly cut in half. Cockran watched as Hudson approached the man, flicked the lever onto semi-automatic, stuck the barrel of the sound suppressor into the helpless man's mouth, forcing his lips to form a wide "O" around it, and pulled the trigger, blowing out the back of the man's head.

Hudson was still grinning, his eyes bright with the thrill from a kill as he looked at Cockran and Sturm and gave them both a thumbs up. Sturm regarded Hudson coolly and finally said "I was told you were a marksman. Hard to miss when your weapon is in his mouth."

Hudson's smile faded quickly. "Fuck you, Kraut."

Sturm ignored the insult. Behind them, the main entrance to the clinic was halfway up the top leg of the H. "I'll check the entrance," Sturm said, "to make sure more guards aren't on the way. When you've cleared the hallway, head for the locked wing."

Cockran nodded and began checking the rooms on one side while Hudson did the same on the other. As expected, they found no twins. If they weren't in this leg, Cockran thought, then it meant they were all under lock and key in the fourth wing. He walked back across the center of the H to the north side of the building and down to the door leading to the tunnel entrance to help Sullivan escort Mattie and Ingrid to the final wing. They had cleared three wings but he was taking no chances. Mattie came out of the door from the tunnel with her Walther in her right hand, held high beside her face. Ingrid was unarmed.

"Thank God you're all right," Mattie said as she embraced Cockran.

"Kurt, is he . . . .?" Ingrid began to ask, her voice halting.

"Von Sturm is fine," Cockran said. "He and Hudson are taking care of the three SS guards we just killed. That's a total of five. Our odds are improving."

A few minutes later, the six of them gathered around the metal door leading to the last wing of the Clinic. In bright red letters were the words, "Authorized Personnel Only. Do Not Enter." The locks looked more sophisticated than anything he had practiced on in his advanced training at Fort Holabird. Perhaps Hudson, still being in the military, had taken a more recent refresher course. "Ever see one like this before?" Cockran asked.

"Not really," Hudson replied. "But I've seen ones by the same manufacturer. This is their latest model but maybe it works on the same principles. Let me see what I can do."

Cockran and Hudson had doffed their SS tunics by now. Hudson reached into the inside pocket of his leather flying jacket and extracted his tools. He knelt down in front of the locks and set to work, a look of concentration on his face as he did so. Two minutes later he stood up.

"Damn! It feels like an older model, but what I just did should have opened it. Wait. Did we check the SS tunics to see if of the guards had a set of keys?"

"We did," Sturm said, "the dead orderly also." Sturm's eyes narrowed. "But now that you mention it, perhaps we should question the other orderly."

"Let me do it," Bobby Sullivan said. "I have a natural affinity with Germans. For some reason, they simply can't stop talking once I begin asking questions." Sullivan smiled, twisting the handle on his sword cane and pulling the two-foot blade out of its sheath. Light from the overhead fixture glinted off its stainless steel surface as Bobby inspected it carefully.

Two minutes later, they all could hear a piercing howl come from that direction. Thirty seconds passed and another howl split the air. Then, silence. Finally, they heard the tap, tap, tap of the metal tip of the sword cane as Sullivan limped down the tiled hallway.

"Well?" Cockran asked.

Sullivan didn't reply. He pulled the sword cane from its sheath, its sharp tip bright with blood. He reached into a pocket, fished out a ring of keys and lobbed them to Cockran who inserted them one after the other until he found one that fit and unlocked the door.

"Sturm will go first and intimidate any clinic personnel we encounter while Ted and I secure the wing. Then Mattie and Ingrid can search for the twins."

Cockran opened the door and stepped aside for Sturm. A dark haired man in a knee-length white lab coat was standing at a high table halfway down the corridor. He turned at the sound of the door. His face was clean shaven and matinee idol handsome, maybe in his late 20s.

"*Heil* Hitler!" Sturm shouted, startling the young man who recovered enough to bark something at them in German, protesting the intrusion, but Sturm interrupted him with a stream of harsh sounding German. The man appeared to be thoroughly intimidated.

Ten minutes later, they completed their search of the wing and found only two patients, identical twin sisters named Andersen, one from

Milwaukee, the other from Minneapolis. They had light brown hair, blue eyes and appeared to be in their early 30s. Both were heavily sedated.

"There were twelve twins here yesterday," Cockran said. "Where are the other ten?"

The doctor professed ignorance and smiled nervously. At this, Bobby Sullivan extracted his sword cane from its sheath and approached, its tip still bright with blood.

"He doesn't know where eight of them have been taken," Sturm translated. "But he says we'll find another pair of twin sisters in there," pointing to the nearby steel door.

Cockran looked over at the door the man had pointed to and felt a chill. He didn't need a translation. "Pathology Laboratory/Library"

"Ask him what his duties are in the clinic". Cockran said.

The man straightened his shoulders, puffing his chest with pride as he answered Sturm's question. "He says he runs the laboratory. That he is Verschuer's principal assistant."

"Ask him his name" Cockran said.

The man hesitated , then he clicked his heels. "Mengele. *Doktor* Josef Mengele."

76.

We Have No Guidelines

The Verschuer Clinic
The Bavarian National Forest
Thursday, 2 June 1932

WAIT here," Sturm said to Mengele and then walked back to Cockran, who was speaking in a low voice with Ingrid and Hudson. Mattie was standing apart from them with Bobby Sullivan at her side.

"*Herr* Cockran? May I have a word?" Sturm asked politely. "This wing is virtually soundproof. It's possible that Mengele did not hear our silenced weapons. He believed my story that Ingrid and Mattie are my personal assistants. He also believes that you, Major Hudson and *Herr* Sullivan work for me in a plain clothes capacity. Shall I continue to be the *Obersturmbannfuhrer* and see what he will tell us voluntarily about the twins? Or would you prefer *Herr* Sullivan's more direct methods?"

"Just a second," Cockran said. "Ingrid, while Hudson stands guard, you need to look after the Andersen twins and get them dressed and ready to travel." Then he turned back to Sturm. "String him along," Cockran replied. "Let's see what your honey can accomplish before we use vinegar."

Mattie smiled as she saw Sturm's momentary confusion. His English was excellent, his accent barely noticeable, but she remembered that English idioms had always posed a problem.

Sturm approached Mengele and gave a hand signal in Mattie's direction. Mattie stepped forward, uncertain of what he had in mind.

"Take notes *Fraulein!*" Sturm snapped and Mattie promptly pulled out a pencil and notepad.

"What is the purpose of your research here?" Sturm asked. 'We understand you have one set of American twins who are outside the acceptable guidelines for the study."

Mengele looked confused. "Guidelines? We have no guidelines. Of course, the subjects must be twins. Preferably identical twins because they are the most efficient method by which we ascertain inherited human traits. But we use fraternal twins as well. There are no guidelines. We can do anything we want with them."

Sturm's eyes narrowed. "You mean you use Jews as subjects for your study?"

"No," he said immediately, and then reconsidered. "Well, it really doesn't matter so long as they are twins. We are scientifically testing the theories of Sir Francis Galton, the father of eugenics. He believed inherited traits of individuals and humanity as a whole can be perfected. Our work here consists of identifying and then finding ways to improve positive traits and suppress negative ones. It makes no difference if we use Jewish twins or Aryan twins."

"I beg to differ, *Herr Doktor*," Sturm replied. "I am certain it was a mistake, an honest mistake on your part, but there are two twins here, Johansson by name, whose maternal grandparents are Jews. I have come to remove them so that their blood may no longer defile the inspiring work you are doing here."

Sturm paused, a hint of menace in his voice. "Where are they?"

"They're gone."

Mattie chilled. "When? Where?" she asked.

"Yesterday," Mengele replied, pointedly ignoring Mattie and directing his words to Sturm. "I don't know where. Dr. V said he would keep them safely on ice and then send for me."

"And the other twins?" Sturm asked. "I have had my men watching the clinic. No twins left yesterday. We only found two here plus the two you say are in the pathology lab."

Mengele laughed nervously. "Twins never leave through the front gate. They use one of the subterranean tunnels."

Tunnels? Mattie thought. More than one?

"Usually only their bodies, of course. But yesterday, I was instructed to have the orderlies dress eight twins and make them ready for travel."

"Let me see the other two twins," Sturm said, nodding towards the pathology lab door.

"Of course, *Obersturmbannführer*, at once," Mengele replied.

"Why do you use twins for your experiments?" Mattie asked.

Again, Mengele refused to look at her, not breaking his stride. "As I said, they are the most efficient method to ascertain inherited human traits. We have three goals in our studies on hereditary biology and race hygiene here at the Verschuer Clinic. Most importantly, we wish to find ways to guarantee that valuable genetic material can be transmitted unaltered through the generations. That is, undamaged by environmental influences. Naturally, we also wish to insure that inferior genetic material will be excluded from any further transmission. That is another reason why it is so helpful to study disease and hereditary defenses of twins. Finally, if we can, we wish to learn how to improve mediocre genetic material before it can be passed on to future generations."

Mengele reached into his pocket for a set of keys and opened the door to the pathology laboratory. He continued talking while he walked as if he were giving a university lecture. "The advance of science depends upon carefully controlled experiments. Twins are ideal for this. They are the key to the future. Bringing them together here for evaluation was a master stroke by Dr. V. After all, once twins become adults, they typically lead separate lives. Locating them and persuading them to rejoin their siblings for an extended period of testing was virtually impossible. Indeed, it was only the Americans who had such extensive records for twins, going back decades. Once we received their full cooperation and access to their records, we were able to track down our subjects, select the most appropriate ones and assemble them here. Then the true experiments could begin."

Mattie leaned close, her lips to Sturm's ear. "Ask him about the other ten twins."

"Our records indicate there were twenty twins originally identified in America. What happened to the other ten?" Sturm asked.

"They weren't brought here," Mengele replied in a matter-of-fact voice. "They weren't identical twins. After we drew their blood and extracted their eyes, they were painlessly terminated."

The wide hallway into which they walked was dark. Mengele pulled a lever and it was bathed in light from fluorescent fixtures. The walls were white but the floor was concrete, not tiled, and it was painted dark red. On the left side were four examination rooms with clear glass running from waist height to the ceiling. In the distance beyond the examination rooms, the hallway opened into a much larger room. Mattie could see a large table in that room on which there appeared to be two shapes.

Meanwhile, Mengele continued to talk. "Over here," he said, pointing to the left, "is where we conduct our anthropological exams."

Mattie looked and saw that each room contained several chairs, what looked like an examination table, and a wall gleaming with stainless steel measuring instructions. "Every other day, we measure each of the twins together. Every part of their bodies, including the shape of the mouth, nose, color of eyes, color of the skin."

"How long do the anthropological exams take?" Mattie asked.

"Several hours at least," Mengele replied, keeping his eyes on Sturm. "We often conduct x-rays, dental and ophthalmologic examinations as well as psychiatric evaluations. We also photograph them as well as have an artist make comparative drawings of the individual body parts. Color photography simply cannot capture all the possible colors and shades of skin."

"So the twins are naked throughout the entire examination?" Mattie asked.

Mengele had answered Mattie's previous questions without actually looking at her. Now he turned his head slightly, locked his eyes with hers, and then ran his eyes appraisingly up and down her body. Mattie had been mentally undressed by men in the past and she never enjoyed the experience. But Mengele's gaze was different. Chilling. Clinical.

"Of course, *Fraulein*. One cannot capture natural skin color while a subject is clothed. Depending upon what part of the body is being examined, skin color can change dramatically," Mengele said, his eyes, clinical no longer, now staring directly at Mattie's breasts,

"Isn't that rather exhausting, standing naked like that, being prodded, fondled, measured and photographed?" Mattie asked.

"I suppose," he said, "but more difficult for the men. Unlike them, the women all receive a reward when their examination is over. Entertainment for our staff as well. Everyone watches and, while they watch, wagers are made. Our subjects are often exhausted after receiving their rewards but many eventually find it enjoyable as well. Take those two we just saw back there."

"Yes, they seem confused, dazed almost," Mattie replied.

Mengele laughed. "I rather think they were simply satisfied at having fulfilled their obligation as women to science. I know all our men approach their duties enthusiastically but with a comparable devotion to science. Mating with our SS guards is one of the more pleasant experiences our female subjects receive. I observe them all. It is a critical part of our work. We employ only the most virile specimens among the SS. All twins advance our studies but we consider it crucial to impregnate as many fertile females as possible. During mating, each female will service at least two men, sometimes more. It depends upon how attractive they are. Tonight there were four men who did the honors. All of them took a second turn. Perhaps being serviced by four eager young men in one night might account for the two women appearing dazed. "

Mengele laughed again. "The more the merrier. In any event, we believe we are on the cusp of unlocking the secret on how to conceive twins. Each mating advances us one more step. We are like the philosopher kings in Plato's *Republic*, preparing the way for a future utopia. Look," he said and reached to a nearby wall and removed a small frame.

Mattie took the small six by eight inch frame and began to read:

> It would be a sin for mating or for anything else in a truly happy society to take place without regulation. We must, if we are to be consistent, and if we're to have a real pedigree herd, mate the best of our men with the best of our women as often as possible, and the inferior men with the inferior women as seldom as possible, and bring up only the offspring of the best. And no one but the Philosopher-Kings must know what is happening.
>
> Plato, *Republic*

Mattie stifled a gasp and looked at Cockran, Sturm and Sullivan. She handed the frame to Sturm and asked him to translate from the German for Cockran and Sullivan. As he did, she could see that all three were equally appalled. If looks could kill, Mengele was a dead man walking. The casual way that Mengele had described rape as clinical "matings" was more than enough for any of the three to kill the handsome doctor once they had extracted from him all useful information. Sturm had a younger sister and Sullivan's sister had been raped by IRA irregulars during the

1922 Irish Civil War as had Cockran's young wife who was killed afterwards by the same IRA men.

But Mengele was too absorbed in his story to notice their looks. "Each of the men we use — mostly SS but occasionally an orderly if he is of good genetic stock — have different blood types. It is important that each of the men who service the subjects have different blood types."

Mattie wanted to ask why but she couldn't bring herself to speak. Sturm did. "Why is that?" his voice flat and cold.

Mengele laughed. "So we can determine the father, of course. Naturally, science has to be served but we can't overlook determining the winners for our wagers, can we? They're quite popular you know. The more intense the mating, the more bets are placed as to which one will turn out to be the father."

Mengele chuckled and shook his head. "One of the women you saw who was serviced this evening is already pregnant but we don't let that stop the progress of science. Matings within 24 hours before a subject's death permit us to perform sperm migration studies. Not the same as impregnation but it's still useful. I conduct most of them myself. It's a specialty of mine. Seeing how far those little fellows can swim."

Mattie was tempted to kill him herself and reached behind her to make certain that her Walther was still tucked in her waistband. Then she stopped. First things first, Mattie thought, because none of this was getting them any closer to finding where the other eight twins, including Ingrid's brother and sister, had been taken. Mattie hated herself for what she did next but her reporter's instinct took over. She had to know. She had to make sense of this insanity. She cleared her throat.

"You mentioned drawing blood from the other ten in America. Do you draw blood samples from these subjects as well?" she asked.

"Oh yes," Mengele replied. "Twenty cubic centimeters for each examination. More if the subject seems healthy. We do that after the matings so I suppose that might account for their apparent confusion as well."

"Why draw blood?"

"Blood is the key. It can answer everything. Our genetic heritage, for good or ill, is present in our blood. We don't have the answers yet but, as scientists, we can never have too much blood to study. Don't you agree?"

No one replied.

"Are eyes important also?" Mattie asked, breaking the silence. Again, she didn't want to but she had to ask. This whole story had started with eyeless corpses, drained of blood. What was so damned important about eyes to these madmen?

"Eyes are very important to Dr. V, especially heterochromes — different colored eyes in the same person. We also like to experiment with changing eye color. One of our colleagues in Berlin has written a draft report based on studies we've done here: '*On The Relationship Between Iris Color, Histological Distribution Of Pigment And Pigmentation Of The Ball Of The Human Eye.*' A remarkable work. You seem interested in eyes, *Fraulein*. Would you like to see our collection?"

77.

We Are Not Monsters

The Verschuer Clinic
The Bavarian National Forest
Thursday, 2 June 1932

COLLECTION? You have a collection of eyeballs?" Mattie asked.

Mengele smiled. "Over there, *Fraulein*," he said cheerfully, pointing to the right to a room on the other side of wide hallway. "Go ahead. I'll take the others into the lab where my colleague *Doktor* Gustav Kramer will be performing a comparative dissection of the two subjects who expired earlier today. Then I'll come back here and answer any questions you may have."

Mattie chilled. Two more twins had been murdered. She watched as Cockran, Sturm and Sullivan followed Mengele into the large room, hoping it was the last she had seen of *Doktor* Josef Mengele; that one of the three men would kill the little monster before she had to hear his voice or that laugh again. Regrettably, she could still hear him as she opened the door to the room he had directed her towards — the medical library.

"We do our most important work here, gentlemen," Mengele was saying. "The comparative examination of twins from a pathology viewpoint. We compare the twins healthy organs with those functioning abnormally. As it is necessary to simultaneously evaluate any anomalies, the twins must die at the same time so that we can perform a dual dissection. "

MATTIE shivered as she tuned Mengele out and stepped into the room, turning on the light. There were three comfortable leather arm chairs and a large table in the middle of the room on which were stacked several books and periodicals. Three green-shaded reading lamps were in the middle of the table. Three walls were lined with books. But the fourth wall opposite the door? That was different. Very different.

Mattie recoiled in horror. In place of books, there were five shelves of neatly labeled clear glass half-liter flasks, each with two inch wide cork stoppers. There were six flasks to a shelf, filled with a clear liquid. Resting on the bottom of each flask were two human eyeballs.

All the flasks were labeled and Mattie walked over to the shelves for a closer look. She was not a squeamish person. She had seen more than her share of blood and gore, from trenches to field hospitals but, truth be told, it was impersonal. This was different. She could see that the flasks were organized alphabetically. She scanned quickly to the third shelf and her stomach turned when she saw the two names. Elizabeth Miller Adams and beside that, James Roger Miller. On each label was their date of birth. November 3, 1895. The dates of their deaths were identical as well. Mattie had never met James Miller but she knew all about him from his personnel folder. His electrical engineering degree from Case Institute of Technology. His job with General Electric at Nela Park. His scientific articles. His annual evaluations. She could still hear the praise from the Nela Park plant manager. "Jimmy was one of my finest engineers."

Mattie couldn't help it. Her stomach heaved and she turned away looking for a waste basket where she emptied the remains of her last meal. Then, with the sour taste of vomit in her mouth, she got to work. She took her Leica out and methodically began taking photographs of each flask which had the name of one of the twins on Helen Talbot's grisly list. Annette Harrison Andrews of Chicago. Anthony Harrison of St. Louis. Elizabeth Neumann Sanders of Denver. Nancy Anne Neumann of Los Angeles. Helen Talbot was dead but Mattie still had the list she had been given that night in New York on the cloud-covered observation deck of the Empire State Building. That list plus these photographs were all she needed for her follow-up story. Screw Carnegie and Rockefeller. She was going to make them and those people at Cold Spring Harbor pay. The careers, if not the lives, of Verschuer and Mengele were finished as well.

Mattie removed the spent film cartridge from the Leica, put it in its container and slipped it into the small pouch on the back of her vest where she regularly stored all of her exposed film. Habitually, she loaded a fresh roll of film, left the room and hurried to rejoin the others. She could see Cockran, Sturm and Sullivan gathered around a white marble dissecting table on which were two naked female bodies. A tall blond-haired man in a blood-stained white smock was standing at one end of the table. Apparently this was Dr. Gustav Kramer.

"That is my usual routine," Dr. Kramer said. "They expired this morning and I started on the twins this afternoon. I got as much done as I could before dinner. As always, I recorded each phase of my work."

"How did the twins die?" Sturm asked.

"Painlessly, I assure you. We are most humane," Kramer replied.

"Answer the question," Sturm said, his voice tight, "and tell us who was responsible."

"Dr. Mengele and Dr. Verschuer personally perform most of the termination procedures. Five cc's of Evipal is injected intravenously in their right arms. Once they're asleep, ten cc's of chloroform is injected directly into the left ventricle of the heart. One twitch and they are gone. Death is both instantaneous and painless. We are not monsters. We are scientists."

"What causes death?" Sturm asked.

"The chloroform causes the blood in the ventricle to coagulate and deposit on the heart's valves which leads the heart to fail."

Kramer turned back to the dissecting table and placed one hand on each woman's head. Mattie reached the end of the marble table and stood behind Cockran, pressing her body into his back. She gasped. Like a waiter removing the silver dome from a dinner plate, Kramer grabbed the blonde hair of each woman and simultaneously pulled off the top half of their skulls which rose up with their hair, revealing the empty cavity beneath. Reflexively, she turned from Cockran and dry heaved as Kramer casually dropped the half-skulls onto a metal pan beside the table.

"I apologize," Kramer said, acknowledging Mattie's discomfort. "Science is not always pretty. I have already removed the brain pan. Together with the cerebellum, I extracted each brain and examined them. Then I opened the thorax, followed by the removal of the sternum. Next, I separated the tongue by an incision beneath the chin. With the tongue came the esophagus and with the respiratory tracts came both lungs. Then I made a transverse incision across the pericardium and removed the fluid. After that, I took out the heart. I washed all the organs and examined them more thoroughly. The tiniest spot can furnish valuable information. Dr. Mengele does not tolerate the slightest deviation from these standard procedures."

Mengele? Mattie didn't see him. He never came back to the library as he promised.

"Bourke!" she said, breaking back into English. "Where is Mengele?"

It was as if a trance had been broken. All three men, who had been transfixed by the horror on the table in front of them, regained their senses and scanned the room.

"I don't know," Cockran replied. "I thought he was with you."

"He didn't come to the library," Mattie said. "I never saw him."

Cockran didn't hesitate. "Bobby! Sturm! Cover the main entrance."

Cockran turned to face Mattie, placing both his hands on her shoulders, his face as cold as it had been that night in Cold Spring Harbor. "Let's move! We've got to get the twins out of here now! If Mengele tipped them off, more SS guards could be here any minute."

78.

Burn in Hell

The Verschuer Clinic
The Bavarian National Forest
Thursday, 2 June 1932

DAMN! Cockran thought as he raced for the door leading to the corridor. How could they have let Mengele escape? His apparent subservience had caused them to take him for granted. The consequences could prove fatal. He opened the door and spotted Hudson.

"Have you seen Mengele? Did anyone come out this door?"

"Nope," Hudson replied. "Everything's been quiet out here. What's up?"

"Mengele's escaped. The rest of the SS may be here any minute. You and Mattie take Ingrid and the two twins to the tunnel door. I'll get the others and meet you there in a minute."

Moments later, with Kramer left bound and gagged in the Pathology Lab and Sullivan and Sturm in tow, Cockran was back at the tunnel entrance.

"Mattie, you and Ingrid take the twins out through the tunnel. The road where Rolf is waiting with the bus is a half mile due west of the tunnel entrance."

Cockran faced Sullivan. "Bobby, you ride shotgun on the bus. If you and Ingrid think the twins need medical attention, take them to the hospital in Regensburg. Otherwise, take them to the airfield where Winston and Rankin are waiting. Once we're clear of here, Bobby will send the two apostles there also. We'll meet you at the airfield after we see if Kramer knows the other twins' location. If you're not there, we'll try the hospital"

Sullivan frowned. " I'll do it but I'd rather be the one to question Dr. Kramer."

Cockran paused. He had intended to use Hudson to interrogate Kramer. Finding the twins was important and Cockran wouldn't mind for scum like like him to have his severed ear shoved into his mouth. But a shattered kneecap might prove more effective than a severed ear.

"Okay," Cockran replied. "I left Kramer in the Pathology Lab. Find out what he knows."

Cockran then turned to Hudson. "Ted, go with the women to the airfield. We'll follow shortly."

Cockran could see that Hudson didn't like taking his orders but he didn't object.

"Piece of cake," Hudson said as he opened the door to the tunnel and swept his arm toward it in a grand gesture, grinning as he did so. "After you, ladies."

Cockran knew the tricky part was how to buy Sullivan enough time to complete his interrogation. He assumed Mengele had escaped by using a subterranean tunnel. But where did it lead? To the woods? Or to the SS barracks? If it led a half mile into the woods like the one they had used, Bobby would have his fifteen minutes with Kramer before the guards arrived.

Just then, even through the steel door to the Pathology Lab, Cockran could hear a muffled but unmistakable scream. He smiled. Maybe Sullivan wouldn't need all those fifteen minutes.

Cockran turned to Sturm. "The SS barracks is roughly fifty yards west of the Clinic. If there is a tunnel leading from the barracks to the Clinic, we're screwed."

Sturm said nothing but nodded his assent.

"You stay by the clinic's front entrance in case reinforcements come that way. I'll check the doors in this wing. The tunnels should be located in the same spot in each wing. If there isn't a tunnel in this wing, then Mengele probably took a tunnel that led into the forest."

Again, Sturm nodded, his eyes focused on the entrance. "I'll be outside. The field of fire there will be more favorable."

"Right," Cockran said. Sturm had guts. He'd be more exposed that way but more effective. Cockran would have done the same. He then checked every door on both sides of the corridor but there were no entrances to tunnels. Sullivan would have his fifteen minutes.

Cockran saw Sullivan emerge from the lab wiping blood from the edge of his sword cane.

"Did you make any progress with Kramer?"

"A little. He speaks English, you know. I don't believe he's high enough up the food chain to really know where the other twins have been taken. Where's Sturm?"

Just then, Sturm entered through the front door and swung his Schmeisser in a wide arc toward Cockran and Sullivan. "All quiet. No guards yet."

"Are you certain?" Sullivan asked.

"I'm certain."

"Good," Sullivan said. "Come with me. There's more to do."

Cockran and Sturm followed Sullivan back into the Pathology Lab. He could see that Sullivan had draped sheets over the twins' bodies on the dissecting table. Beside the marble table, lashed to a hospital gurney, his mouth gagged, was a very frightened Dr. Gustav Kramer.

Sullivan's blue eyes were as cold as Cockran had ever seen them. "I realize," Sullivan said, "there isn't time to give these two girls a proper Christian burial. But doesn't it seem wrong to leave them here for whatever other use these bastards might find for their remains?"

"What do you propose?" Cockran asked.

"Burn down this bloody shop of horrors." Sullivan replied, as he took a large bottle of isopropyl alcohol and began dumping its contents over the two bodies. "More bottles are over there," Sullivan said, pointing to a shelf. "I'll do this room; you two the observation rooms."

Cockran and Sturm looked at each other and silently nodded their assent.

"This will be a good diversion," Cockran said to Sturm as they began dousing the rooms with alcohol. "The SS guards will be too preoccupied with fighting the fire to worry about finding the ones who committed all the mayhem here."

Sturm did not reply but looked him in the eye and nodded his agreement.

Ten minutes later the two men returned to the main room where Sullivan was just emptying the contents of a bottle onto some drapes. Sullivan fished in his pocket and brought out a box of matches.

"What about Dr. Kramer?" Cockran asked.

"And aren't you a grand fellow to be reminding me?" Sullivan said as he took down one more bottle of alcohol from the shelf, walked over and emptied its entire contents on Gustav Kramer's bound and gagged body. Even though the gag, Cockran could hear the man's muffled screams.

"For what he's done here, we know where this one will be spending eternity," Sullivan said. "'Tis only fitting in the last moments of his life that we give him a wee taste of all that he has to look forward to."

With that, Sullivan undid the gag, lit a match and tossed it on the drapes. Already doused in flammable liquid, they burst into flame which quickly spread across the room, inexorably coming closer to the helplessly bound body of *Herr Doktor* Gustav Kramer. The three men turned on their heels and made their exit amid the unearthly screams of Kramer as he watched his approaching death.

"Burn in hell, you bloody bastard. Burn in hell," Bobby whispered.

Sullivan was a hard man, Cockran thought, as he looked back at the flames, but who would have imagined a cold-blooded killer like him would have such a biblical sense of justice?

79.

SS Ambush

The Verschuer Clinic
The Bavarian National Forest
Thursday, 2 June 1932

THE fire in the Pathology Lab quickly spread to the only path open for its voracious appetite—across the bar of the H leading to the north corridor. Cockran reached the door to the tunnel and looked back. Sullivan was limping down the corridor with Sturm behind him. They were still twenty feet away when he saw the flames leap out into the corridor.

"Hurry, guys! The fire is right behind you."

Sullivan looked to the door on his right where they had placed the orderlies. "Would we be setting those boyos free?" Sullivan asked Sturm. "They aren't SS, after all."

Sturm shook his head. "*Nein.*" His voice was cold. "There are no more innocent people left in this building."

With that, the German put his arm across Sullivan's back and underneath his armpit, helping him quick march the last twenty feet to the tunnel's entrance. Once in the tunnel, Sturm volunteered to take the point with Cockran and Sullivan following.

"What did Kramer say about where the other twins were taken?" Cockran asked.

"Regensburg," Sullivan replied.

"That's a fair size city. Where in Regensburg?" Cockran asked as they moved down the tunnel, following Sturm's electric torch.

"Kramer didn't know. They were moved through the same tunnel Mengele used to escape. Mengele told Kramer he would take him there after they finished the autopsy of the two twins."

"Why weren't the Andersens taken out yesterday as well?"

"They were scheduled to be 'serviced' by the SS. Kramer admitted that, which is why I believed him when he said he didn't know where in Regensburg the twins had been taken."

"You're right," Cockran replied. "If Kramer would admit to that, then he probably didn't know where the other twins were taken. Did he say anything else? Anything at all?

"Aye, and sure it was strange. Both Verschuer and Mengele speak English, just like Kramer. 'Don't worry, Gustav,' they told him. 'We'll keep them safely on ice until you arrive.'"

"On ice?" Cockran said, recalling that Mengele had said the same thing when he professed not to know the other twins' whereabouts. "Did he tell you what that meant?"

"No. His English is passable, but his vocabulary is limited. He was genuinely confused when I asked him what he thought it meant."

Cockran nodded. "Once we get to Regensburg and meet the others, we can ask the Andersen twins. One of them may be able to tell us.

As they exited the tunnel, Cockran could see Kurt von Sturm silhouetted against the dark forest, his face bathed in the light from a raging fire not a half mile away.

"Is that the clinic or also the forest?" Cockran asked.

"I believe only the clinic, but possibly the barracks as well. Perhaps even the guard towers," Sturm said. "But the fire authorities will have been notified . We need to move quickly. It would not be good if two strange aircraft as distinctive as your autogiros are reported in the area by the fire brigade. As you Americans say, someone might put two and two together."

The three men headed north toward the landing zone and the road where Rolf's bus had been parked. As they neared the road, Cockran was surprised to see the dark shape of the bus still there. Something was very wrong.

"You take the left and approach the bus from the front," Cockran said to Sturm. "I'll come from the right. Bobby, keep us covered."

Sullivan nodded, unslung his Thompson and put in a fresh clip while Cockran and Sturm did the same with their Schmeissers. In the light, Cockran could see the rounded rear end of the motorbus, green with gold trim on the bottom half, cream colored on the top. He reached the rear of the bus and listened. There was nothing to hear except the sounds of the forest.

Then Cockran heard a soft moan. It was not far away. He cautiously peered around the corner of the bus and saw a figure on the ground slowly crawling towards the open door of the bus. The man's progress was achieved only by his left arm, the right arm tucked underneath. Cockran saw no one else and stepped into the open and moved toward the figure. If he drew fire, he hoped Bobby and Sturm would be able to suppress it.

The man had stopped all movement when Cockran reached him. In the moonlight, the left side of his face exposed, Cockran could see it was Rolf Heyden. Cockran checked for a pulse and found it, faint but there. Cockran gently rolled him over and immediately saw why he had been crawling with only one arm. Machine gun bullets had ripped across his front. His right hand was tightly clenched against his stomach, vainly trying to hold his intestines in place.

Rolf's eyes opened as Cockran rolled him over. "Rolf! What happened? Who did this?"

Rolf tried to move his lips but no sound emerged. Cockran bent his head down until his ear was only inches away from Rolf's face. He took a canteen of water from his web belt and tipped it up to pour a little into the man's lips which only caused Rolf to choke and cough up blood. Cockran once more bent his ear down to Rolf's face.

"SS ambush," Rolf whispered, barely audible. "They took the women."

"What about Hudson? The other American?"

The question seemed to energize Rolf who lifted his head up from Cockran's hand. "He, …he was. . . " Rolf said and then his head fell back into Cockran's hand. He coughed once and was still. Cockran felt for a pulse, faint but there. They had to get Rolf to the autogiros. The first aid kits there were his only chance of making it alive to the hospital in Regensburg.

"Sturm," Cockran whispered loudly, "Rolf has been shot and the SS took Hudson and the women." Before Sturm could respond, the forest erupted in machine gun fire. Sturm ducked behind the front of the motorbus and Cockran rolled beneath it. From a secure position behind several fallen trees, Sullivan laid down suppressing fire with his Thompson.

Cockran and Sturm joined up behind the bus. "There are at least four of them," Cockran said. "They'll try and outflank us. We've got to do it first. Bobby will keep them pinned down. The noise from the Thompson will cover any sounds we make. You go left. I'll go right."

Sturm nodded.

"Kill silently if you can," Cockran said, drawing a commando knife from its leg holster.

Sturm nodded again and drew his own.

Cockran moved quickly through the woods. He had done this before. His Schmeisser was slung over his shoulder, his knife in his hand. He heard the SS man before he saw him, crashing through the underbrush, intent only on making it far enough to the right to catch Cockran's team in a cross-fire. He could tell the man had never been in combat. Cockran had.

Waiting behind a tree, Cockran moved silently behind the SS man as he passed, wrapped a hand around his mouth, and plunged the knife deep into his kidney. His cry of surprise was muffled and his body went into shock as Cockran let the man fell to the ground, his blood pumping out and spreading over the forest floor. Cockran moved on, his approach masked by the sounds of Sullivan's Thompson. His next victim would not be so difficult to find.

He wasn't. Cockran circled behind him. Sullivan had switched his position and was now far to the right of the two SS shooters. Cockran approached from the left but a sudden cessation in gunfire from both sides allowed Cockran's target to hear him. The man turned to look back just as Cockran launched himself forward, his right arm extended, knife in his hand. Too slow to bring his weapon to bear, all Cockran's victim could do was cry out a second before his throat was impaled on the point of the knife, his hot blood gushing over Cockran's hand. The warning was all the dying man's comrade needed, however, to line Cockran up in his sights.

Cockran rolled over behind his victim's body as bullets intended for him hit the shooter's teammate instead. But Cockran was on his back and could not free the Schmeisser. He reached in his shoulder holster for his Webley but he knew that it would be too little and too late.

Still firing, the other SS man rose up and, as he did, his body danced and jumped from Schmeisser rounds ripping into his back. Cockran watched as Sturm grasped the dying man's hair and sliced the knife blade across his neck, blood spurting from his severed carotid artery.

Cockran lowered the Webley he had brought too late into play. "Thanks. I owe you."

Sturm shook his head. "No. I am only repaying a debt."

"What debt?"

Sturm smiled. "Last year. Castle Wewelsburg. You and I were alone. I was bleeding out. You could have done nothing. No one ever would have known."

"You're wrong. Someone would have known."

"Who?"

"Me."

"You're a remarkable man, *Herr* Cockran."

"Not really. An average American actually."

"I doubt that. But if you are, I hope our countries never go to war again."

"I'm sorry we ever did."

"No more than me, *Herr* Cockran. No more than me."

Cockran nodded. The brief affair with Mattie notwithstanding, he was finding it increasingly difficult to maintain his dislike for the German. This had been Cockran's show and, to his credit, von Sturm hadn't second-guessed him despite his initial reservations. Yet the raid was essentially a failure because Rolf was wounded, perhaps fatally, and the SS still had all the twins as well as Mattie, Ingrid and Hudson. All in all, not much to show for someone who thought himself quite good at organizing bloody mayhem.

Worse, once they were in Regensburg and got Rolf to hospital, he had no fucking clue as to what to do next. And, unless he came up with a plan quickly, the initiative would, by default, belong to Sturm. He wasn't sure how he felt about that. All he knew was that from Cold Spring Harbor to Boldt's warehouse to Verschuer's clinic, he hadn't kept Mattie out of harm's way. Based on what Mattie had told him, Sturm had been a lot more successful doing that a year ago. And, he ruefully reflected, it was hard to see how Sturm could do worse than Cockran now.

Tearing up Rolf's shirt, the two men bound up Rolf's wound as best they could and carried him to the autogiro as Sullivan followed, providing a rear guard.

80.

On Ice

Regensburg, Germany
Friday, 3 June 1932

COCKRAN flew the first autogiro with Rolf in the front compartment, followed by Sullivan and Sturm in the second as they cruised at a thousand feet and headed northwest, following the silver ribbon of the Danube which ran from Passau more or less on a straight line into Regensburg. The pink light of dawn had begun to appear on their right when they saw the lights of Regensburg.

Cockran passed low over the city and saw the twin spires of the Regensburg Cathedral—St. Peter's—which the aerodrome manager in Munich had told him was Regensburg's most prominent feature. To the left was the city center. Further up the river, Cockran spied several modern office buildings, most of them three or four stories high, due to Regensburg's tradition that no building be higher than the cathedral. Then he spotted a modern steel, granite and glass structure on the river directly down the street from the cathedral. It was five stories tall and technically not as high as the cathedral. But on top, a good 50 feet above the cathedral, was a huge, black revolving globe displaying the illuminated, blood red letters of I.C.E. flanked on either side by double red lightning bolts disturbingly similar to the silver ones used by the SS.

Cockran looked to the left where the red tile roofs of houses had faded away and saw the long macadam runway of Regensburg's air field. There were no lights but Cockran didn't need them. As long as there were no trees or electric wires, autogiros could land anywhere, from macadam to grassy fields and everything in between. Cockran switched on the air to air microphone and spoke to Sullivan.

"The airport is a half mile to the left. Set her down, Bobby, right where I do." The wind had died down again as Cockran feathered the autogiro smoothly down and taxied over to the Ford trimotor Winston had hired. Sullivan did the same.

Churchill and Rankin came over as Cockran stepped down from the cockpit. "Where are Mattie and the twins?" Churchill asked. "We expected them hours ago."

"It's a long story but Rolf's been badly wounded." Cockran said as he enlisted Rankin's aid with easing Rolf from the front cockpit and into the back seat of a long Mercedes touring car. When that had been accomplished, Rankin and Sulllivan volunteered to ferry Rolf to hospital while Cockran and Sturm stayed behind to brief Winston on all the previous evening's events.

Churchill had more or less set up camp beneath the shade of the trimotor's huge overhead wing and the three of them sat in a semi-circle in canvas field chairs. Winston produced a wicker hamper filled with ham sandwiches prepared by the *Vier Jahreszeiten* hotel kitchen, a coffee thermos and a bottle of Remy Martin. Thus fortified, Cockran began the briefing, occasionally asking Sturm to add his view point. When he concluded, Cockran confessed he had been puzzling for the past few hours over what Kramer had said about the twins being kept "on ice" in Regensburg. What did it mean? Cold storage lockers? Warehouses?

No one had any answers. They had landed at 5:00 a.m. By 6:30 a.m., Sullivan and Rankin returned to say that, an hour after the critically wounded Rolf had been admitted to hospital, a young surgeon advised them that, while he had removed half of Rolf's badly damaged small intestine, he had a better than even chance for survival unless infection set in. At 7:00 a.m., Bobby's two Apostles arrived from Passau with an ample supply of ammunition in their motorcar for the Schmeissers, Thompsons, Lugers and even Cockran's Webley revolver.

In the distance, the Danube glistened as the rising sun shown off the twin towers of the Regensburg Cathedral. The black glass exterior of the I.C.E. building sat between the river and the church. A Council of War began beneath the large wing. Ironic, Cockran thought that their rescue aircraft was built by a man—Henry Ford—whose photograph adorned

Hitler's desk and whose own anti-Semitism was second to none in the Nazi party.

Churchill took a puff on his cigar and a healthy sip of brandy. "Bourke, you're a lawyer as was your father. I know the continental system is not based on the common law but do we now have enough facts to go to the authorities in Regensburg for their help?"

Cockran didn't know the answer and was about to say so when Sturm intervened. "It will be risky to contact the authorities with any inquiries about the clinic," Sturm said, "given the fire there last night and the men we killed. But I don't see anything else we can do." Sturm paused, took a sip of coffee, and continued. "There is a certain police detective, a *Kapitän* Bloem, who might prove useful." He shrugged. "Or, after last night, he might arrest me. I'll wear the SS uniform for whatever advantage it affords but there are no guarantees."

Cockran nodded. On ice…He had never doubted Sturm's courage and his willingness to go to the police over an SS kidnapping took a lot. But what the hell would they do if going to the police didn't work? Visit all the cold storage warehouses in town?

On ice. . .on ice. . . Why would Germans like Verschuer and Mengele use an American idiom with Gustav Kramer? Why? Then it hit him. English was not an easy language to learn. Idioms and metaphors were always the most difficult, almost an initiation rite for foreigners. Outsiders need not apply until they had mastered them. Mengele and Verschuer spoke English but that was not sufficient to make them insiders. Yet both he and Verschuer had used the same idiom. Germans might understand the "on ice" idiom — if it were explained to them — but coming up with it was a different story. Only an American would have done that. Not a German. Not an Englsishman. An American.

Cockran sat straight up in his chair. Of course! What an idiot he had been! It all became clear. An American! Wesley Waterman! I.C.E.! "On ice." *Just tell them we'll be keeping the twins safely on ice.* Mengele and Verschuer had been parroting what they had been told. The I.C.E. building! If he was right, Mattie, Ingrid and the other twins were being held captive in the I.C.E. building sitting right there less than a mile distant in front of them, across the Danube and next to the Regensburg Cathedral and the City Center.

Cockran turned to Churchill and Sturm. "Let's hold off on Bloem. I have an idea."

Cockran then briefly explained to the assembled Council of War the basis for his conclusion which was met with uncomprehending stares from Sturm, Sullivan and the other two Irishmen. But Churchill only smiled and took another puff on his cigar. "*Herr* Sturm, you may not be aware but my mother was an American and I am the product, so to speak, of an English-speaking union. As such, I can assure you that Britain and America are two nations divided by a common language. I believe my young American friend is correct and I urge you to act accordingly. Sgt. Rankin and I will re-fuel our aircraft at once. We will be ready to depart for Vienna on a moment's notice when you return with the American hostages. God speed, my young friends and dread naught. All will be well."

81.

You're Alive!

I.C.E. Building
Regensburg, Germany
Friday, 3 June 1932

MATTIE McGary sat in the darkness, a black hood over her head, her hands and ankles bound. They had brought her to this room only a few minutes earlier. She had no idea where she was or how long the hood had been on. It seemed like hours, but she couldn't be sure. The SS had been waiting for them when they emerged from the tunnel with the Andersen twins. Mattie had no chance to bring her Walther automatic into play—and it was just as well, for all the good it would have done her. She and Ted were quickly disarmed and they had taken her camera also. They had been outnumbered by the four SS who captured them and bundled them into two dark Mercedes motorcars waiting beside the bus Rolf had hired.

That had been the last time that Mattie saw Hudson and Rolf, their hands bound behind them, before the hood was put over her head. The same had been done earlier to Ingrid and the Andersen twins who were pushed into the back seat of one Mercedes before Mattie and Ingrid were placed in the other. Mattie could not see but she heard the laughter when Hudson had said "I'm a U.S. Army officer. I demand to see the American Consul." Ted's demand had been cut off by abrupt burst from more than one submachine gun followed by the cries of their helpless victims Rolf Heyden and Ted Hudson. After the SS had killed them, Mattie was in shock as the Mercedes had rolled onto the road. Despite Ingrid being seated beside her, they weren't allowed to talk. And, once they reached their destination — wherever that was — she and Ingrid had been separated after they had been taken into an elevator up several floors. Mattie couldn't tell how many.

Just then Mattie heard a door open and someone else entered the room. She heard the scraping of a chair on the floor and somebody sitting down. The door closed and the room once more grew silent. The door opened a second time and Mattie again heard someone enter and, as before, there was the scraping of a chair and the sound of someone sitting down.

She felt hands on her wrists and then the cool metal blade of a knife as it severed her bonds. "You may remove your hoods now," a German-accented voice said in English.

Mattie did so and gasped at the bound figure seated beside her, the handsome, all-American face of Ted Hudson. Beyond him she could see the drawn blonde features of Ingrid.

"Ted! You're alive!" Mattie said. "I thought they had killed you. Where's Rolf?"

"Dead. The Nazi bastards gut shot the poor kid." Hudson replied, his face grim.

Mattie took in her surroundings. The chairs she, Ingrid and Hudson were sitting in had straight backs and no arms. Their feet were all bound as were Hudson's hands but Ingrid's hands, like Mattie's, were now free. They were lined up in front of a large, immaculate walnut desk. Behind the desk were large plate glass windows which looked out over a cityscape Mattie did not recognize. Behind her were two SS guards, each holding a submachine gun.

"Where are we?" Mattie asked.

"Beats me," Hudson replied. "Judging from all the red tile roofs, I'd say we're still somewhere in Germany."

"Regensburg," Ingrid said in a dull, low monotone. "This is my husband's private office. This building is the headquarters of I.C.E. for all of southern Germany. The first and second floors contain a manufacturing facility where I.C.E. produces punch cards for use in the I.C.E. calculating machines. The next two floors contain offices for white collar workers, anywhere from engineers, to accountants. The fifth floor contains only my husband's office."

"Not so, my faithless wife. Not so. Dr. Verschuer, please explain."

Mattie watched in amazement as the tall, bulky figure of Wesley Waterman walked into the room. Freshly shaved, he was clad in a Saville Row dark blue chalk stripe suit, crisp white shirt and a blood red tie. A small white enamel pin with a black swastika, adorned the left lapel. Verschuer, two paces behind Waterman, was followed by an enormous, bald SS guard bringing up the rear, 300 pounds of muscle over a black-clad frame easily four inches over six feet.

Verschuer stepped forward and stood beside Ingrid. "Most of the fifth floor was vacant the last time you visited Regensburg some six months ago. Now, it duplicates all of our facilities at my clinic near Passau. The scale is much smaller but we can comfortably house ten patients here."

Mattie watched as the silver-haired, violet-eyed Verschuer walked past them and stood facing them behind the large desk. Before seating himself, he bowed to Mattie. "*Fraulein* McGary, I presume? We've not been formally introduced although we were shipmates on the *Graf Zeppelin*. Allow me," he said, with a sweep of his hand. "I am *Doktor* Otmar Freiherr von Verschuer, Director of the Institute for Hereditary Biology and Race Hygiene in Berlin."

Sitting down in the desk chair, Verschuer smiled, leaned back and steepled his fingers. "Whatever are we to do with you, *Fraulein* McGary? You do seem to pop up at the most inconvenient times." Verschuer opened a desk drawer and pulled out Mattie's Leica. "Cold Spring Harbor and now Passau. Always with your trusty little camera." He stood up and walked around the left side of the desk to where Mattie was seated. "I understand you showed interest in my collection of eyeballs, *Fraulein*. Is that correct? Probably took photographs of them with this little toy, didn't you?"

Mattie said nothing.

Verschuer stepped forward and, without warning, slapped Mattie in the face with the open palm of his right hand and then swung just as hard with the back of his hand, her head rocking from side to side with the force of his blows, blood trickling from a split lip.

"Answer me when I speak to you! Or would you prefer I have the SS teach you some manners?" Verschuer said, pointing to the SS giant who had accompanied him.

Mattie watched the bald giant nod his head and grin. She could taste the copper flavor of her own blood and felt it trickling from her split lip. "Develop the film yourself, you bastard."

"I'll do better than that, bitch," Verschuer replied, venom in his voice, as he once more slapped Mattie hard across both sides of her face. Then he dropped her Leica to the floor and smashed it with his heel, picked it up and unrolled the spool of film. He then reached over to Mattie's photographer's vest and began roughly removing the film cartridges.

Mattie watched as he unrolled and exposed all her new film cartridges, none of which had been used. Verschuer then walked behind his desk and over to Ingrid where, without a word of warning, he slapped her even harder than he had Mattie. Like her, Ingrid did not cry out.

"And you have caused us problems as well, *Frau* Waterman. You betrayed your husband and caused him a not insignificant amount of worry."

"Aren't you going to slap me as well, you punk?" Hudson said through gritted teeth. "Or don't you pick on people your own size? Is hitting helpless women more your style?"

"Slaps are for women only, Major Hudson. Men deserve steel." Verschuer opened the desk drawer again and pulled out a small leather case which he opened. Mattie could see the glint of sun off surgical steel in the array of razor sharp scalpels which lay before him. He picked up a scalpel and held it up to the sun. "You are still a man, Major Hudson. For now."

He snapped his fingers peremptorily and signaled the two guards to come forward. "Take *Frau* Waterman and *Fraulein* McGary to Observation Room B and strip them. Follow the usual procedure for Dr. Josef's sperm migration studies for twins. Make it quick. Four men only. Two different blood types to service each woman. Bind them securely. They're not sedated."

"Wait, Otmar," Waterman said as he gestured toward the giant SS guard who had followed Verschuer into the room. "Let Max be one of the two for my wife. Mengele said Max has never lost a sperm migration contest. My money's on him."

Verschuer laughed. "So is mine."

Mattie watched as Max's face broke into a broad smile and Waterman turned to Ingrid. "Max won't disappoint, my dear. Since you prefer fucking Germans, I'm sure you'll find him to be more than a match for your last German lover."

Ingrid lifted her chin and gave Waterman a withering stare. "I doubt that very much. Men with bellies like you and Max invariably have trouble seeing their small dicks without bending over. Perhaps that's why you prefer teen age girls. They have no basis for comparison."

The two guards freed their feet and lifted Mattie and Ingrid up from their chairs and prodded them in the back with their Schmeissers as they pushed them from the room, Max following behind. Mattie took one look back over her shoulder and shuddered as she saw Verschuer beside Ted, his scalpel poised above him, the sunlight glinting off its shiny surface.

"As I was saying, Major Hudson, whether you remain a man depends upon you." Verschuer paused. "And, of course, how satisfying—and truthful—I find your answers to my questions. Don't disappoint me."

82.

Are the Twins There?

I.C.E. Building
Regensburg, Germany
Friday, 3 June 1932

ENGLISH is a strange language. *Herr* Churchill is correct. Its idioms are a mystery to me." Sturm had said on their way into town. If Cockran's idea didn't prove correct, Sturm said, he would visit *Kapitän* Bloem. And failing that, he promised that a Nazi *Gauleiter* by the name of Vokshul would be receiving an unpleasant visitor.

It was 7:45 in the morning. As they paused at the bridge in the Mercedes Churchill had hired for them, the Apostles behind them in their Opel, the I.C.E. Building began to stir to life. The building took up most of the block. It was a modern design, the corners of the building curving around, no sharp edges. It had a dark gray granite trim running in wide bands beneath the large windows. The glass was tinted gray also. The front entrance faced away from the river and opened onto a small square. The rear of the building faced the Danube. The loading docks there looked designed to do triple duty—trains, trucks and boats. A freight car, its doors open, was on a rail spur adjacent to the loading docks. Thirty yards further up, a truck backed into the dock and men started to unload.

As lights began to go on in the building, Cockran quickly scanned the windows. "The first and second floors look like some sort of light manufacturing space. The third and fourth floors appear to be offices. What I can't figure out is the fifth floor."

The fifth floor was essentially an oval like the rest of the building but it was set back a good fifteen feet from the building's edge, a three-foot high stainless steel railing encircling it.

"With the sun at our backs reflecting off the glass, I can't see in the fifth floor unless someone turns on a light," Cockran said. The fifth floor's windows curved around at either end but the rest of the fifth floor had no windows of any kind. Strange because that meant most of the fifth floor had no direct view of either the Danube or the cathedral, the city's most well-known landmarks.

"If they're in there," Sturm said, "it will be on the fifth floor. The rest of the building is devoted to commerce. How do we proceed?" he asked, once more deferring to Cockran.

"Let's get you dressed up again," Cockran said, referring to Sturm's SS uniform, stowed in the boot of the motorcar. "We'll drive past the main entrance and have you pull another surprise inspection. If you see SS in the lobby, let's hope no one tipped them off about you."

"And if there are no SS in the lobby?" Sturm asked.

"Hell, dress down the receptionist anyway. Demand to see the man in charge of building security. If they don't have one, that will tell us a lot."

"Yes. The twins are not there," Sturm said.

"Exactly. But if there is security . . . ," Cockran continued.

Sturm nodded in agreement and went to retrieve his SS uniform. "If the twins are there," Sturm said, once he had the uniform on, "we can decide whether it is prudent to seek the assistance of that *Kapitän* Bloem I mentioned moments ago or even the local party *gauleiter*, *Herr* Vokshul. Once they hear from me that Verschuer is using a pair of Jewish twins in his experiments and that I'm here to stop it, we may see some cooperation." Sturm paused and looked both men in the eyes. "It all depends how this uniform is received and how I assess the building's security. We must proceed as if time were of the essence. Because it may well be." Sturm then lowered his voice and spoke almost confidentially to Cockran. "The Nazis will soon be the largest party in Germany because Hitler is not like other politicians. He does not pander to narrow interests like other parties.He does not appeal to them as farmers or laborers, middle class or intellectuals. He urges them to rise above their personal interests and think first of Germany." He shrugged. "Unfortunately, anti-Semitism is prominent among some of those people around Hitler. Himmler is one of them. Goebbels is another. I regret this. I wish it were not so. I do not share their beliefs and there are many party members who feel as I do. Even Hitler once said to me 'A man cannot help how he was born'."

Cockran didn't reply. He wasn't so sure about Hitler but Sturm seemed to be seeking understanding from him for having joined the party, apologizing for the ugly underside of its more prominent members. Cockran didn't know what to make of it. Why did Sturm care? Whatever the reason, he was beginning to see the complex side of this poster boy for Aryan manhood which had so attracted and still fascinated Mattie. He already knew about the man's ruthless side. Had that also fascinated Mattie? It didn't matter. It just felt good to have someone as ruthless and competent as Sturm by his side as they set out to rescue the woman they loved.

Fifteen minutes after dropping Sturm off in front of the building, Cockran returned and pulled the big Mercedes up beside the main entrance. With a soft cap over his forehead and Sullivan in the back seat, he could pass for a chauffeur as they waited for Sturm to appear. The other two Apostles were waiting for them at a café in the next block. Ten minutes later, Cockran began to be concerned. Both Apostles could speak German, but no one would mistake them for natives. They needed Sturm as much for his language abilities as they did his skill with firearms. Five minutes later, Sturm strode out of the building as if he owned it.

"All the guards are on the fifth floor.' Sturm said. "It's accessible by a passenger elevator but a key is needed to unlcock the elevator controls to make it to the fifth floor. There's also a freight elevator to the fourth floor and a stairwell from there to the fifth floor. But the door to the fifth floor is locked. No one makes it to the fifth floor without a key."

"Damn!" Cockran said as he ran his hand through his hair. "I have no idea how to pick a lock on an elevator. That leaves all five of us bunched up in the stairwell while I pick that lock."

Sturm smiled, reached inside his black tunic and pulled out a ring of keys. "The office manager was very helpful. This is the key for the passenger elevator; this one for the freight elevator and this one for the fifth floor door off the stairwell. The freight elevator only goes to the fourth floor so I suggest, *Herr* Cockran, that you take the freight elevator to the fourth floor and the stairwell to the fifth. The rest of us will use the passenger elevator. If we synchronize our watches, the focus of the SS will be on the passenger elevator opening while you attack from their flank.

"Only two guards?" Cockran asked.

"Six, actually, but they pull eight-hour shifts. Two will be sleeping and the two who just went off duty will be having breakfast in the small fifth floor cafeteria."

"Are the twins there?" Cockran asked.

"It seems likely. The receptionist said the night clerk's log showed that five people signed in to the fifth floor in the middle of the night. "

Bingo! Cockran thought. That would account for everyone. Mattie, Hudson, Ingrid and the Andersen twins. "Silenced weapons?" he asked.

Sturm said nothing but Cockran caught his eye and gave him a crisp nod.

"So we don't visit local party headquarters or call in the police?" Cockran asked.

Sturm looked at Cockran, his face still cold as he slowly shook his head from side to side and slowly drew his thumb across his neck, its meaning unmistakable..

83.

Because We Are Patriots

I.C.E. Building
Regensburg, Germany
Friday, 3 June 1932

"WHEN will you kill the two women?" Hudson asked as he rubbed his wrists with his hands after Verschuer's scalpel had severed his bonds.

Verschuer shrugged. "Tomorrow at the latest. It's not my choice alone."

"It's not?" Waterman asked.

"The women are useless to us but Mengele will claim they should be kept alive until he has performed his sperm migration studies. I have serious doubts as to his scientific motivation. Don't get me wrong. Sperm migration studies when impregnating twins helps to unlock the secret of multiple births. But studies on woman who are not twins? I'm not so sure. Still, our Josef rarely passes up an opportunity to insert a speculum inside attractive women."

Verschuer watched closely to see how Waterman and Hudson reacted to this. After all, they were important men. Hudson was the liaison between the Gemini Project and the U.S. Army's MID, the primary government sponsor of his clinic near Passau. Waterman was the conduit for Rockefeller and Carnegie money as well as untraceable funds from him and MID itself.

"Otmar, my people are not pleased at how this entire project has been handled," Hudson said as he pulled out a long cigar and lit it. "Leaving ten bodies scattered around the United States is not the smartest thing you Germans have ever done. Our people, after all, were only following your orders. May we assume that at least the SS ambush in the forest has taken care of Cockran and the Irishman as well as that nosy kraut von Sturm?"

"I've received no report as yet because the telephone lines are down at the clinic. I expect Josef will have a full report for me when he arrives. I have no doubt as to the outcome."

"Nor do I," Hudson said, "which means these two women are the only loose ends. I want those ends tied up and tied up this morning. Permanently. Screw the sperm studies. Got that?"

Verschuer was nervous and his eyes blinked rapidly. He didn't like being ordered about by this arrogant American but what could he do? The German Army had turned him down flat when he requested funds for his twins study. Had Harry Laughlin not gone to Wesley Waterman who in turn led them to the U.S. Army's MID which organized the non-profit funding, well, perhaps there would be no Gemini Project.

"Let's face it, Otmar," Waterman said. "You are the one who directed this operation in America. We were successful in locating twenty subjects yet you couldn't even kill one female journalist. And in Germany, you couldn't even keep the clinic's location from her or my wife."

Verschuer stiffened at the criticism. But his dear wife—may she rest in peace—had never made a cuckold of him like Waterman's wife had done with Sturm. But he said nothing.

Hudson paused and blew a perfect smoke ring. "Nothing is more important to the future of America than weeding out the mongrels and misfits who have swarmed into our country since the turn of the century. Thank God we locked the door with immigration reform in 1924. Now, we must make sure that we outbreed all the inferior scum—wops, micks, polacks, slavs and kikes. America must again look like America. Like our Army officer corps has always looked. We're the only ones willing to stand up to the godless Bolsheviks and the Christ-killing Jews."

"Please, Major Hudson, do not be concerned. Our facilities here at the I.C.E. building equal those at the clinic. While their capacities differ, the equipment is identical. This has been only a momentary setback. Our autopsy protocols will continue here uninterrupted."

"What about the bodies?" Hudson asked. "You couldn't even keep ten bodies from being discovered in the United States. How will you do it in Germany?"

Verschuer smiled. How naïve and unimaginative these Americans were. "Quite simple, actually," Verschuer replied. "As *Herr* Waterman knows, there is a furnace in the sub-basement. Made in America. A regular crematorium. After the autopsy protocols are concluded and their blood and eyeballs preserved, all our subjects will be reduced to ashes and scattered to the wind as human smoke."

Hudson stood up and retrieved from the floor beside him a long, narrow canvas bag which he slung by a strap over his shoulder and walked to the window, where he looked out over Regensburg to the Danube River in the near distance, glitering in the early dawn.

"Heed my words, Otmar. MID helped arrange financing for the Gemini Project and supplied American twins for you to study because we are patriots. Wesley agrees with me that all Americans owe a higher duty to their country than to themselves. But the twenty two Americans we provided for the project must not have died in vain. We need your research. We are involved in a long twilight struggle against the Jews and the Bolsheviks, and it will not end with this generation."

"Have no fear," Verschuer said. "MID will have my research. I guarantee it."

Hudson said nothing and turned back from the window as the light from the rising sun began to fill the window and highlight the American's blond hair as if there were a halo behind him. Verschuer was frightened by that proud and handsome face. The Americans were vital, even critical, to his science. At least until Germany had a new government.

"We know our jobs," Verschuer continued. "Once our research is concluded, the twins and the other two women will all be reduced to ashes. What could be better than that?"

"The red-haired journalist and the blonde Manhattan society broad dead *now*, not tomorrow. Like that loose-lipped secretary in New York whose tongue I cut out before I slit her throat. With Cockran and the other two men dead, those women are the only witnesses who have seen everything. Don't wait for Mengele. Kill them now. If you don't have the stomach for it, I do. But that would make me unhappy." he said to Verschuer, staring coldly into the man's eyes. "Trust me. You don't ever want to make me unhappy."

Hudson turned back toward the window, looked at his reflection in the glass and ran his fingers through his blond hair. Then he reached inside his breast pocket and pulled out a pair of gold-rimmed aviator sunglasses, put them on and left the room without saying another word. Verschuer suppressed a shiver. He couldn't stand the American officer's arrogance but he sensed the man meant every word he said. He didn't want to think about the consequences of displeasing that cold-hearted killer.

"I suggest you take Major Hudson's advice to heart, Otmar," Waterman said. "No need to keep my wife alive any longer on my account."

"As you wish, *Herr* Waterman."

Waterman took a pocket watch from his vest and looked at it. "Wait until Max has finished fucking her and then kill the faithless bitch. Mind you, don't cause her unnecessary pain. Use the same stuff you did at the Clinic. What's its name?"

"Evipol as a sedative injected in the arm. Then chloroform directly into the heart."

"Yeah, right. Use those." Waterman said as he pulled on his gray herringbone Chesterfield coat topped by a velvet collar. "Send me a copy of all the twins' autopsy protocols as soon as they're ready. Don't bother with one for my wife. Just make her into smoke."

84.

They're All Dead

I.C.E. Building
Regensburg, Germany
Friday, 3 June 1932

COCKRAN glanced at his wristwatch as the freight elevator lumbered slowly up to the fourth floor. The elevator lurched to a halt, and Cockran, Schmeisser slung over his shoulder in a ready-to-fire position with his finger on the trigger, reached with his left hand and pulled the protective scissored gate open and, after that, the heavy elevator door itself.

Cockran's eyes went wide as he stared into the equally startled face of Ted Hudson, a long canvas bag slung over his back alongside a Schmeisser which was not ready to fire.

"What the hell are you doing here?" Cockran asked.

"The SS captured us in the forest and brought us here. I just escaped."

Cockran kept his Schmeisser trained on Hudson as he watched the man move into the elevator and place the canvas bag down on the elevator floor.

"What about them? Mattie, Ingrid, the twins?"

Hudson shook his head. "I'm sorry Cockran. They're dead. They're all dead. There were just too many of those SS bastards. I'm lucky I got out alive."

Hudson turned to pull the elevator door closed but Cockran stayed his hand. Something in his voice told him the man was lying. "Follow me, Ted. We're going back up. The odds have changed. Sturm and three others will hit the SS in," Cockran paused and looked at his wrist watch. "Four minutes and fifteen seconds."

"No way, Cockran. Keep out of it. I told you they're all dead. Besides, while I was up there, I learned that what Verschuer is doing here and at the clinic is a matter of national security. American national security. You and that ball-busting bitch of a girlfriend have caused America enough problems. Quit now while you're still ahead. And alive."

"Fuck you, Hudson!" Cockran said as he shoved past Hudson and out of the elevator. He felt Hudson's hand grab his shoulder and he spun to knock it away just in time to see the flash of a knife blade as it thrust forward, aimed at his kidneys. He slashed his arm down, deflecting the blow and knocking the knife from Hudson's hand. Unable to use the Schmeisser, he leaped at Hudson and with a flying tackle took him back into the elevator.

Locked together, they rolled from the elevator and out into the hallway. Cockran was taller but Hudson outweighed Cockran by a good twenty pounds and it was all muscle. Fists flew as each grappled for control. Cockran pounded Hudson beneath his ribcage but the blows did not have enough force at such close quarters. He forced Hudson back against the hallway wall when he heard excited shouts and voices from down the hallway. He looked to his left and Hudson took advantage, delivering a clean blow to Cockran's jaw. Dazed, Cockran toppled over. Hudson disengaged and crawled into the elevator. Prone on the elevator floor, he propped himself on one arm as he slowly reached up to close the elevator's scissored gate. The fight had taken as much out of him as it had Cockran.

Groggy from the solid blow to his jaw, Cockran leaned against the wall and helplessly watched Hudson's face behind the scissored gate as the elevator door slowly began to close.

"Hey, Cockran!" he gasped, his breathing ragged. "About your girlfriend? Just so you know. Our last trip together? I did stuff that horny broad six ways to Sunday. The same way I did in Paris. Ask her. She took it anywhere I put it quicker than a high class hooker." Hudson shouted, his voice rasping through a small space as Cockran watched the elevator door close.

Cockran's eyes narrowed. Fuck you, Ted. His lies meant nothing. What was more important was that he had just admitted Mattie was alive. But if she were harmed in any way, Hudson was a dead man. There was nowhere he could hide. That was a promise.

By now, four men in shirtsleeves and ties had arrived and were standing around him, all talking at once. In German. He had no idea what they were saying but they weren't armed. Cockran pulled the Webley from its holster, pointed it at the Germans and shouted, "SS! SS!" They backed off and he inserted the key into the door to the fifth floor. He opened it and raced up the stairs, glancing at his watch as he did so. Damn! He was forty five seconds late.

Cockran inched the door open at the top of the steps and moved into the corridor.

"*Halt!*"

Cockran was startled. He turned to see two SS submachine pistols aimed directly at him.

"*Der handwuffe!*" the taller of the two men, the blond-haired one, shouted.

Cockran slowly knelt down and laid the Webley carefully on the floor. While the blond kept his weapon pointed at him, his dark-haired companion came up to Cockran, patted him down and removed the .45 automatic tucked in the back of his waistband. His commando knife on his left calf was not touched.

The two SS each grasped one of Cockran's arms and marched him down the corridor toward the elevator banks. He and his captors had not advanced more than ten feet when two loud bursts of submachine gun fire from around the corner caught all three men by surprise.

As the SS released his arms to bring their Schmeissers to bear, Cockran reached for his commando knife.

85.

We Will Build a New Clinic

I.C.E. Building
Regensburg, Germany
Friday, 3 June 1932

VERSCHUER exhaled. He had not been conscious of holding his breath while the Americans were there. But now that they were gone, he felt a sense of relief. He pulled a white linen handkerchief from the breast pocket of his suit and patted down his perspiring forehead. To hell with Josef and sperm migration. These women weren't twins. They were of no use to their studies. He would present Mengele with a *fait accompli*. By the time he arrived, the women would be dead. Hudson and Waterman were too important to ignore.

Verschuer opened the drawer to his desk and pulled out a Luger. He reached inside the drawer again for a sound suppressor which he proceeded to screw into the barrel of the weapon. He chambered a round, rose from the desk, and jammed the Luger into his waistband. To hell with Waterman and syringes also. With their bodies burned, no one would know how the women had died. He was halfway across the room when the telephone rang. He went to the desk to answer.

It was Mengele! "Josef? Where are you? How soon will you arrive?" Verschuer chilled at what he heard next and gripped the edge of the desk to steady himself. "The clinic destroyed? All our specimens gone? But what of the SS ambush in the forest? Dead? All of them dead?"

Verschuer was no longer able to stand and sat back down at the desk. "Calm yourself, Josef. Calm yourself."

Holding the telephone receiver in his left hand, Verschuer pulled open the bottom right-hand drawer of the desk and pulled out a half-empty bottle of schnapps. Gripping the cork in his teeth, he extracted it and brought the bottle to his lips and took a healthy swallow of the fiery liquid. "No, Josef. Don't come here. I will meet you in Munich. Those men who burned the clinic may be coming here. Yes, I realize Kramer didn't know where we had taken the remaining twins but several of the SS did. I'll have to place this facility on high alert at once."

Verschuer picked up the schnapps bottle and once more raised it to his lips, taking an even longer pull on it than before. "I have a minor task given me by *Herr* Waterman and Major Hudson. After that, I'll join you in Munich and we'll go to Berlin. We'll lay low there until the dust settles. Don't worry, Josef. We will build a new clinic. A bigger one. We can always find more specimens but we must keep ourselves safe, my young friend. The science of hereditary biology and race hygiene, indeed the future of eugenics itself, depends on our research."

Verschuer pushed himself up from the desk with unsteady hands but he froze in panic when he heard the unmistakable sound of two short bursts of automatic weapons fire. He had to get out of here! Too late to kill either woman. Let Waterman and Hudson do their own dirty work. But, he thought, the women might come in handy as hostages. Gun in one hand, he picked up the bottle of schnapps with the other, drained it, and headed straight for Room B.

Inside Observation Room B, he saw the SS had wasted no time. Before him was a familiar sight—the bodies of two women bent face down over two metal tables, feet on the floor, wrists firmly bound in leather restraints. He smiled as his gaze lingered on Waterman's faithless wife and that *verdammt* journalist. The fate of the women who ruined his research was set to be sealed as the SS had begun to tug at the women's trousers. Alas, however, he needed hostages and saving his own skin was more important. Still, he was disappointed. He would have enjoyed placing a wager and watching the rugged knights of the SS do their duty. His money would have been on Max. "Release the women," he said.

86.

Bourke Cockran!

I.C.E. Building
Regensburg, Germany
Friday, 3 June 1932

BOTH SS guards released their grasp on Cockran's arms at the same time, bringing their Schmeissers up, focused only on the gunfire ahead. Cockran reacted instantly, muscle memory taking over as he reached for the knife on his left leg. He plunged the blade up to its hilt into the side of the dark-haired man on his left, the blade entering just below his rib cage. Not a killing strike, but Cockran didn't need that. Not yet.

The guard cried out and his blond comrade looked over, momentarily frozen between the gunfire in front of him and the new threat to his left. The moment's hesitation was all Cockran needed to grab the wounded guard's Schmeisser. He fired and a vertical line of bullets went up the blond guard's torso from below the belt to his chest and head, his lower face torn away.

Cockran released the Schmeisser, picked up his discarded knife and drove its point up into the underside of the wounded guard's jaw, piercing his brain. Returning his blade to its sheath after wiping it on the dead man's uniform, he retrieved the Webley and Schmeisser and started down the corridor towards the elevators. Two down and, if Mattie were hurt, it was only the beginning. He'd kill them all.

Cockran stopped short when he turned the corner and reached the bank of chrome and wood elevators. Six bloody SS bodies were sprawled there, all of them dead. The walnut paneling halfway up the marble-clad walls was pockmarked with fresh bullet holes. An eerie silence prevailed. There was no one in sight. "Sturm? Bobby?"

Cockran waited. No response.Wait. He could hear voices from the corridor opposite. Low voices, one of them a woman. Mattie? He drew his Webley and cautiously moved ahead.

MATTIE and Ingrid had resisted, clawing and kicking, as they were forced face down onto the metal tables and their wrists firmly strapped but all four SS were too strong. Now, they could do nothing. Their proud struggles had come to nothing. Mattie shook her head. She couldn't believe this was about to happen. Not in a dark back alley in Cleveland or on a battlefield but in a modern German city inside the marble floored Bavarian headquarters of a major American corporation.

Mattie twisted her head and looked around the room, but could see nothing except the two SS who had pulled off their knee-high black leather boots and silver trimmed trousers. Though the padded door of the well-insulated room, Mattie thought her practiced ear heard automatic weapons fire but no one else in the room seemed to notice, intent as they were on unbuckling the belts on the women's own trousers. Her spirits soared nonetheless. Cockran? Sturm?

The door suddenly opened and Mattie turned her head and saw the ugly black snout of a sound suppressor attached to a Luger held by Otmar von Verschuer. The bastard just stood there, seemingly mesmerized as she felt her trousers tugged down. Finally, he spoke. "Release the women. They are needed for more interrogation in *Herr* Waterman's office."

The two fully dressed SS men started removing Mattie's restraints while the third began to pull on his pants. Max did not. He just stood there, glaring at Verschuer. Once Mattie was free, she pulled her trousers up and rebuckled her belt as the two men moved on to release Ingrid.

Max held up his hand to both and then turned to face Verschuer. He placed his hands on his hips. "Leave the other woman with me. I will deliver her later. When I'm finished."

Verschuer started to object and then appeared to think better of it once he saw the determined look on Max's face. "Fine. You men stay with Max and draw lots to see who goes first. Each of you can take a turn with her for all I care."

"You will come with me, *Fraulein* McGary," Verschuer said, pointing his gun.

As she left, Mattie saw Ingrid's khaki pants pooled around her ankles and heard the beginning of a heated argument between the four SS men. Max loudly proclaimed that the rest of them could draw lots but that he was going to be the first. The others were voicing their disagreement as the door closed.

Once outside the room, she felt Verschuer's hot breath on her face as he spoke into her ear. "I have need of a hostage, Miss McGary. Cooperate and I'll let you live."

Mattie's spirits rose when she heard another machine gun burst. It hadn't been her imagination! Please let it be Bourke or Kurt, she prayed as Verschuer placed his left arm around her neck and pressed the silenced Luger squarely into the middle of her back. He moved down the hallway, using Mattie as a shield, pushing her forward.

"Over here," Verschuer said and roughly shoved her in the back. "We have a private elevator which will take us directly to my motorcar. You and I will be traveling together, *Fraulein*." He pushed again.

"Hold it right there, Verschuer!" an unmistakable voice boomed, one which Mattie had never been happier to hear. Bourke Cockran!

COCKRAN watched as Verschuer spun to his right, keeping Mattie in front of him. Cockran had the Webley pointed directly at Verschuer, still steadying it with his left hand under the butt of the gun, just as he had done that night in Long Island. But this was a stand off. Not like Cold Spring Harbor. Having found Mattie alive, he was not going to shoot. But he also was not going to put his weapon down. Not now. Not ever.

"Let her go, Verschuer. I don't care about you. You can leave. All I want is the woman."

Verschuer didn't answer. Instead, he just stared at Cockran, like a rat trapped in a corner. Sweat was beading on his face. There was unmistakable hatred in his eyes. Verschuer began walking backwards, pulling Mattie with him. He fumbled behind him until his elbow hit a black call button beside a door in the wall. Through the glass at the top half of the door, Cockran saw a light go on and the familiar scissored gate behind the door of a small, personal elevator. The door slid open once the light went on and Verschuer reached behind him with his foot to lever open the scissored gate, keeping his eyes on Cockran as he did so.

"Leave the woman, Verschuer!" Cockran said, raising the Webley level with his eye, sighting along its barrel. But he knew he would not pull the trigger. Not yet.

Verschuer pulled Mattie back until she was standing in the open door, his weapon still pressed into her back. Then, in one motion, Verschuer kept Mattie in Cockran's line of fire while he pulled the door closed with Mattie inside as the elevator began its descent.

Cockran ran toward the elevator. Damn! Okay, he wasn't a Ted Hudson with a sidearm. But he sure as hell was good at bloody mayhem and there was no way he was allowing that fucking Nazi doctor to keep Mattie as a hostage. Cockran tugged at the elevator door. Locked! Screw that, he thought as he stepped back and fired two shots from the Webley at the door's lock. He tugged again at the door and it slid open to reveal the narrow chasm beyond. He was surprised to see how little the elevator carriage had descended in the few seconds which had elapsed. It was barely three feet away and dropping ever so slowly.

Cockran didn't hesitate. He holstered the Webley and leaped into the narrow elevator shaft; flexed his knees for the impact; and wrapped his arms around the car's cables as he did so. He flinched as he landed when a wild shot from the elevator car came through its roof. Gripping the panel on the ceiling of the elevator's carriage, he ripped it off with his left hand and thrust the Webley through.

"Drop it or die Verschuer!" Cockran shouted.

Verschuer tried in vain to reassert his control over Mattie but she instinctively had fallen to the floor and curled into a ball to minimize exposure to Cockran's line of fire. He fired once and missed. Damn! But it was close enough for the German to drop his gun and raise his hands.

"Grab his gun, Mattie."

As Mattie did so and aimed it at Verschuer, Cockran dropped into the elevator car and decked Verschuer with a right cross to his jaw. Verschuer crumpled to the floor and Cockran kicked him in the gut several times before turning to embrace Mattie.

"We've got to get back to the fifth floor and rescue Ingrid!" Mattie said, pulling back. "The SS have her and they're going to do to her what they've already done to the twins!" Mattie leaned around him to press the "5" button. "Let's go. Observation Room B. Hurry!"

The elevator reached the fifth floor and Cockran opened the elevator door to a silent hallway. Then he heard a bell ring up the hall signaling the arrival of the passenger elevator car.

"Wait here," he said to Mattie, "The SS may be sending reinforcements. Keep your gun on Verschuer and don't let him move."

87.

No One's Going to Extradite Me

I.C.E. Building
Regensburg, Germany
Friday, 3 June 1932

COCKRAN moved quickly down the hall until he reached the corner around which the elevator bank was located. He peered cautiously around the corner and breathed a sigh of relief. Kurt von Sturm was there and behind him, leaning on his sword cane, was Bobby Sullivan.

"Where the hell have you been? Are you responsible for this mess?" Cockran asked, pointing to the SS bodies.

"Not entirely. I had a wee bit of help from Kurt and the lads," Sullivan replied. " We got all six of them as soon as the elevator doors opened but one of them was able to get off a shot which hit Sean," he said, referring to Sean O'Driscoll who was standing beside Barry Ryan, the other Apostle. "T'was just a scratch but it knocked him into the elevator controls, sending us back down. By the time I was able to reverse that, we were on the ground floor. Kurt assured the receptionist that it was official SS business and we came right back up."

Mattie came round the corner holding Verschuer at gunpoint.

Sturm saw her. "Where's Ingrid?" he asked immediately.

Mattie looked at Cockran. "She's why I couldn't wait at the elevator, Bourke. We've got to find her. When I heard no shots, I thought it was safe." She turned to Sturm. "She's in Observation Room B with four SS goons. Bobby, here's Verschuer's Luger. Watch him. Come on," she said to Sturm as she began to run. He followed immediately as did Cockran. They reached the door to Observation Room B but it was locked.

"The room is sound proof. I barely heard gunfire. I don't think they did." Mattie said.

Sturm hurried to the door and took out the keys. He found the right one and quietly opened the door to angry voices and four SS men, two of them clad only in their black, silver-accented SS tunics. One of them was sprawled on the floor, blood streaming from his nose. The other was a bald headed giant who had turned away from his fallen SS comrade and moved behind Ingrid who was bent over a metal table. Her khaki pants were around her ankles as the giant yanked her silk briefs down.

Two shots rang out as Cockran and Sturm simultaneously fired. Cockran's shot ripped through the man's throat while Sturm's blew out the back of his head. The giant staggered back from Ingrid and, like a large tree felled in the forest, flopped down onto the floor, his head bouncing once before coming to rest, his eyes wide, blood pooling beneath his shattered skull.

The two fully clothed SS men reached in vain to unholster their Lugers but Cockran put two bullets in the middle of first man's forehead while Sturm did the same with the second.

The last SS man, now struggling to pull his trousers on, raised his hands in surrender. Sturm shot him twice in the groin. The man shrieked in agony, falling to his knees, his hands reaching for his ruined private parts. Sturm slowly walked over, placed the snout of the silenced Luger between his eyes and fired. He fell forward, sprawling across the bodies of the other two.

Meanwhile, Cockran had raced to Ingrid whose white blouse was splattered with the SS guard's blood and brains. He removed her restraints and she stood, pulling up her briefs and then her pants.

Sturm rushed to Ingrid and embraced her. The German held her close, stroking her back and holding her head to comfort her. "Thank God, you're all right," Ingrid said.

"Me? It's you I've been worried about. Your safety is very precious to me. No one will ever hurt you again. You have my word." Sturm replied, as he began to softly stroke her hair and gently kiss her forehead.

"We've got to go." Cockran said as he approached them. "Before the police arrive. Mattie, gather all the twins. Get them dressed for travel.

Meanwhile, I'll take Verschuer into the office with Waterman's name on it. Meet me there."

Cockran found Verschuer and Bobby where he had left them. "I'll take him now."

"Here," Sullivan said, handing Verschuer's Luger to Cockran.

COCKRAN pushed open the frosted glass door on which were stenciled in big letters, "Wesley Waterman, Chairman and President." Once inside the office, Cockran shoved Verschuer into the chair behind the desk. He ripped the telephone cord out of its socket and used it to tie Verschuer's hands tightly behind him. Cockran sat on the edge of the desk, facing Verschur. He placed the Luger on the pristine desk.

"Kidnapping and murder are serious crimes in America, Verschuer," Cockran said, "and Germany has extradition treaties with the U.S. With twelve of the twenty two twins you kidnapped from America now dead, the odds are you're going to be facing the electric chair."

Verschuer's violet eyes blazed and he showed no signs of fear. "Murder? Kidnapping? Where's your proof? I have signed consent forms from all twins at the Clinic. And murder? Where are your bodies? I talked to Dr. Mengele and he told me the Clinic burned to the ground last night. If there were bodies inside, you can't prove who they were. As for that journalist and Waterman's wife, my guards detained them because they were trespassing on Clinic grounds."

Cockran could see Verschuer straining at his bonds, testing their strength. "So, *Herr* Cockran, you're the one in trouble, not me. You and your gangster friends have murdered a large number of our best young men in cold blood. We Germans don't take kindly to that.

"If you know what's good for you, *Herr* Cockran, you will leave my patients with me. If you don't, I will have the authorities track you down and arrest *you* for kidnapping and murder. The police in Regensburg and, for that matter, the police all over Bavaria, are controlled by us, by the National Socialists. Soon, all of Germany will be under our control and we will build more clinics like the one you destroyed last night."

Verschuer laughed again. "We can always find more twins. All we have to do is ask the Americans. Passau was only a trial run. Many more will follow. We must save the future!"

Cockran was livid. "Ask *which* Americans? I don't think the folks at Cold Spring Harbor are going to be giving you much help. Not when the story of your liquidation of American twins is published."

"Really, *Herr* Cockran? You Americans can be so naïve. Do you actually believe your government will allow such a story to be published? Why do you think your Eugenics Record Office was so helpful in our endeavor? *Your* War Department, *Herr* Cockran, is as much interested as we are in saving the "Great Race," the Nordic and Aryan strains which have created the best within modern civilization. The American Army Officers Corps, especially its Military Intelligence Division, made the initial investment in our project from their secret contingency funds. Then MID arranged for permanent funding from the Carnegie, Rockefeller and Waterman foundations."

Verschuer smiled. "We are the cutting edge of scientific progress. The Americans couldn't write their bank drafts fast enough. But it's not only your government and the American Officer Corps. Their German counterparts are equally aware that we must constantly seek new ways to improve our race while we relentlessly weed out the weak — the morons, the blind, the cripples, not to mention the Jews and Bolsheviks who seek to bring our civilization down. Unfortunately, the German Army had no contingency funds, secret or otherwise, for our critical endeavors. The Americans did and the SS provided the final element that was missing."

Cockran heard the door open behind him and looked back over his shoulder to see Sullivan, Sturm and Ingrid enter the office, followed by Mattie. Ingrid's face was hard and set. He had seen that look on her face before, the morning after she had been raped by her husband.

"What did the SS provide?" Cockran asked.

"Manpower, *Herr* Cockran, manpower. Who do you think furnished the construction workers who built our beautiful clinic? Or the young Teutonic guards you savagely murdered? "

Verschuer paused and licked his lips as if they were dry from talking so much. "Soon, *Herr* Cockran, very soon, the SS will be an authorized arm of the German government. Already the SS have many friends and even allies in your Army's MID. So you should free me and leave my patients here. In America, as in Germany, the future belongs to us!"

Cockran sat on the front edge of Waterman's desk and caught movement in his peripheral vision. While Cockran focused on Verschuer,

Sullivan had moved behind him and given Verschuer's own Luger to Ingrid. The weapon in her right hand, Ingrid moved toward Verscheur.

"Ingrid! No!" Cockran shouted and lunged across the desk, the "us" of Verschuer's final sentence still hissing from his mouth as Ingrid placed the snout of the Luger's sound suppressor on the scientist's left temple and pulled the trigger. The spray of blood and gray matter from the exit wound spattered onto the curved glass window of Wesley Waterman's immaculate office.

Ingrid stood there, smoke still curling from the barrel of the Luger, tears streaming down her face. "They raped her! Verschuer and my husband had that Nazi bastard Max rape my little sister!" Ingrid choked back a sob and continued, her voice trailing off. "My little sister…"

Ingrid released the weapon and it fell to the carpeted floor as she stood there, convulsed in sobs. Sullivan silently walked over to the weapon and wiped the Luger clean of prints with his handkerchief. Then he placed it in Verschuer's left hand, closing his fingers over it. Cockran watched as Verschuer's lifeless fingers opened and the weapon once more fell to the floor. Then Sullivan looked at Sturm and gave him a thumbs-up gesture and Sturm nodded in return.

"*Herr* Cockran, I suggest we depart quickly," Sturm said. "The Irish have disposed of the orderlies and we located clothes for the twins. You are correct. No one else is alive on this floor. We need to move the twins immediately to the airfield and *Herr* Churchill's aircraft. We must take them out of Germany before the SS can invoke the aid of the Nazi V-Men in the Bavarian government."

Cockran smiled. Why was he not surprised that Sullivan and Sturm had recognized kindred spirits in each other? "Let's haul ass, Bobby."

88.

I Hope She Was Worth It

Regensburg
Friday, 3 June 1932

KURT von Sturm stepped out of the I.C.E. building into the early morning sunlight with an arm wrapped tightly around Ingrid's shoulders. Ingrid, in turn, had an arm around her sister Beatrice whose brother Thomas held her hand. Mattie followed with the rest of the twins while Cockran, Sullivan and the two apostles provided a rear guard.

Cockran motioned for Sturm and Sullivan to join him. "Bobby, take six of the twins with you, pack them into the Opel and head for the airfield. Move them onto the trimotor and make sure Winston has filed a flight plan for Vienna." He paused and turned to Sturm. "Go and bring the Mercedes here. Take Ingrid, her brother and sister and the last two twins to the airfield. Mattie and I'll grab a taxi with the other two Apostles and meet you there."

Sturm appreciated Cockran's decisiveness. They did not have much time. *Kapitän* Bloem might have been alerted to the gunfight by someone inside the building and soon could be sending reinforcements. Ingrid's sobbing had ceased, her face still wet from tears, but her body seemed drained of energy. Sturm thought back to the numbness he felt after he first killed a man up close—a natural response to an unnatural act. Ingrid was no killer but she did not need to be one in order to do what she had done. He didn't think Ingrid would ever fire a weapon again.

Sturm left Ingrid in the arms of her brother and sister, Cockran protecting them and ready to provide cover fire, if necessary. He walked around the side of the building and back towards the city center at a brisk but controlled pace. At *Brückstrasse*, he saw their canvas-topped Mercedes touring car where he had left it on the narrow side street in the shadow of the twin-spired cathedral.

Sturm quickly took stock of his surroundings, alert to anything unusual but he saw nothing except the bookstore, the electric streetlamps, the empty vestibules of residential entrances. He moved towards the Mercedes, crossed the narrow street and reached for the driver side door. He did not hear a sound, not even the scrape of a shoe sole on pavement but, as he placed his hand on the door, he saw movement. A blur of color moving behind the reflection of his own face in the window. Without thinking, he threw himself to the pavement, hearing the cough of sound-suppressed gunfire, the glass shattering, as his right shoulder hit the ground.

Sturm rolled beneath the car's undercarriage, gunshots chasing him but missing. Sturm reached the other side on his back and heard his attacker's footsteps sprinting around the car to gain a killing angle. Still on his back, he had seconds to act and reached into his holster. Above him was a streetlamp just behind the car. He aimed his Luger and fired, shattering the glass of the streetlamp just as the gunman cleared the back of the car. His attacker flinched as the glass shards pelted his neck and shoulders. Sturm fired three times, each shot landing in a tight circle in the man's upper body.

It was only then, as his assailant staggered back from the killing shots delivered by Kurt von Sturm that he saw his attacker. His friend. His protégé. Bruno Kordt.

Bruno stood there and looked at him with sad, regretful eyes—almost apologetic. His fingers opened and his gun fell to the ground. He sank to his knees and fell forward.

Sturm rose and went to him. He knelt at his side and gently turned him over.

"How did you know I was behind you?" Bruno whispered.

"I didn't know it was you," Sturm said. "I reacted. I was lucky."

"And I was unlucky," Bruno said. "I thought I'd stayed out of the reflection angle. But then I hesitated. It's not an easy thing to shoot Kurt von Sturm in the back."

"It's not an easy thing to shoot Bruno Kordt," Sturm said, reassuring his protégé.

"You're a lousy shot, you know that? It takes you three shots to kill me? You're slipping in your old age." Bruno smiled.

"Four, if you count the street lamp."

"Bastard," Bruno said and tried to laugh but he spasmed with pain instead.

Sturm heard footsteps and raised his gun, but it was only the others running to offer support after hearing the shots. Cockran was in the lead, gun drawn and ready to fire. Sturm held up his free hand to indicate that everything was fine. He saw them all, Cockran, Mattie, the Andersen twins, the two Irishmen, Ingrid's brother and sister…and Ingrid. She was taking the scene in, saw the man that Sturm knelt over. Then she met his eyes. She recognized what had happened. He could tell she understood.

"Kurt," Bruno whispered, straining through the pain. Sturm turned back to look at him and noticed that Bruno had turned his head to see Ingrid as well. Bruno turned back to Sturm, now. "Remember what I asked you in Munich? When I asked you why you had done this for the woman? If you had fallen in love with her?"

Kurt smiled. "I do, Bruno. I remember telling you that I hadn't."

Bruno managed to smile back, as if to say, *I never believed that.*

"I hope she was worth it," he said.

"She is, Bruno."

"Good," Bruno said. "Good. I would hate to have died for nothing"

"You haven't my friend. Believe me you haven't."

Bruno's eyes lost their focus and his breathing grew weak and faint. Then it stopped, his eyes still open as though hoping for one last look at the world of the living.

Sturm reached out with his free hand and closed Bruno's eyelids. Killing was a necessary part of the life he had chosen. But in that moment, while he had kept his promise to Ingrid, it had just become too much to accept.

Sturm looked up and saw Ingrid had separated from the others and was walking toward him. A sad smile washed over his face. He no longer wanted that life. He wanted a life with Ingrid. Bruno had been right. He loved her. As Sturm stood up to go to her, something caught his eye. He looked up at a spot of light drifting across the beige stucco walls of the buildings surrounding them. There was something familiar about its shape, the quality of its movement. It was like a reflection of sunlight off the glass covering of a timepiece. But there wasn't any direct morning sunlight at that early hour. The reflection had to be coming from somewhere else, from a much higher vantage point . . . . A rifle scope!

"Ingrid!" Sturm cried and raced to cover the ten feet that still separated them, reaching out for Ingrid who stopped at his sudden shout, frozen in place. "Get down!" He had to get to her in time. Sturm saw the shot hit her before he heard it as the bullet ripped through her body.

"Ingrid!"

89.

Plan B

COCKRAN, Mattie and the others had been ten yards behind Ingrid. Blood spurted from Ingrid's left shoulder and she lurched forward from the impact. Sturm caught her before she hit the pavement and carried her behind a motorcar. "Get down!" Cockran shouted as he took Mattie off her feet in a flying tackle just as another shot rang out, missing her by inches.

Two more shots were fired, one slamming into the motorcar where Sturm had taken Ingrid and the second hit the automobile where Cockran had taken shelter with Mattie. Ingrid's brother and sister had taken cover with their sister behind the first motorcar while the Andersen twins and the two apostles were huddled beside Cockran and Mattie. The sniper's element of surprise was over but their peril was not. They had to move before the police or, worse, the SS arrived on the scene.

"Sturm!" Cockran shouted, "The shots are from the Cathedral! The left tower! You and Bobby's boys give me cover fire. I'm going in but you stay here! There may be others!"

Up ahead, the narrow street twisted to the right. The rooftops of the buildings directly ahead might block the sniper's line of fire. At best, the sniper would have one clean shot, at worst two, until Cockran had covered the 30 yards of open ground from the last building to the cathedral's wide plaza where the angle would be too steep to hit him. He waited until he heard Sturm fire a shot followed by several more from the two apostles. Then he dashed from behind the motorcar and across the narrow street, his eyes focused on his goal, the twin gray spires of the gothic Regensburg Cathedral. He reached the edge of the last building and made an all-out sprint for the cathedral. A bullet cracked into the pavement behind him spraying splinters of brick. He abruptly changed his direction and headed off at an oblique angle to the cathedral as the sniper fired again hitting the plaza stone in Cockran's former path.

Cockran knew it had to be Hudson. He didn't need to see the sniper's face to know that. The long canvas bag Hudson had thrown on the elevator floor hadn't registered at the time but now it did. A sniper's rifle! Cockran didn't know how badly Ingrid had been hit, but he knew that, had Sturm not reacted as quickly as he did, Cockran wouldn't have either and Mattie might have been hit as well. Both she and Ingrid had been sitting ducks. Instinctively, he knew why Hudson had tried to take them out first. They were credible witnesses to the horror of Passau in ways the drugged twins who had signed consent forms were not.

The shots clearly had come from the left tower's fourth level, just below the spire. Reaching the cathedral, Cockran took the steps three at a time and slammed open the heavy wooden door. Inside, he quickly found the stairs to the left tower. He pulled out the Webley and headed up the curving stone stairs. Hudson was trapped!

At the second level, Cockran paused to catch his breath. There was no need to hurry. Hudson wasn't going anywhere soon. As Cockran moved up, he heard nothing. No more shots. He paused again upon reaching the third level. Again, no sound. He knew they didn't have much time. If Hudson didn't want to be trapped in the tower by the police, he would have to leave. Soon. And Cockran would be waiting.

But, as he waited for Hudson, he heard no sound from the fourth level. Did Hudson know he was there? Cockran knew he couldn't wait. Hudson had to be taken out now. How should he ascend? Swift or silent? He wanted swift but he chose silent and crept up the stairs slowly, his left hand on the inside wall, right arm extended, the Webley in his hand. He paused on the last two steps before his head would be visible from the landing. Now was the time for speed, not stealth. He charged up the remaining steps, firing one shot as he hit the fourth level.

Empty! The fourth level was empty! Where the hell had Hudson gone? Cockran walked to each of the four sides of the tower. On the far side of the tower nearest the river, a crowd had gathered around the place where Ingrid had been shot but, surprisingly, there were still no police. He completed a tour of the tower and came to the side closest to the twin tower on the right and his heart sank. A catwalk! Between the towers. A goddamn catwalk! While he had been coming up one tower, Hudson had been making his escape down the second.

Two could play that game, Cockran thought, and it might be a good idea. It wouldn't do to have the police find him up here alone. Cockran climbed out the window onto the catwalk and walked across in quick strides. Inside the second tower, he stopped. There was a Springfield M1903 sniper rifle with a Warner & Swasey scope lying on the tower floor, its canvas carrying case discarded as well. The same canvas carrying case Hudson had in the I.C.E. building. Both the rifle and the canvas case would have hampered the sniper's getaway. Cockran walked to the far wall of the second tower and looked down. No sign of Hudson. He walked to the south side and looked out. Wait! There, in the distance, barely two blocks away was a blond haired man in a leather jacket scurrying down a deserted side street. Hudson! The bastard who had just tried to kill Mattie and Ingrid!

Cockran quickly calculated the distance at less than one hundred yards. Cockran retrieved the Springfield. At five hundred yards, Cockran had been a mediocre shot in his MID training. At one hundred yards, he was not half bad. Not in Hudson's league, of course, and, unlike now, it had been a stationary target. Still, a shot from a hundred yards or even one hundred fifty yards was worth a try. He might get lucky. Cockran locked in the rifle to his shoulder, wrapped his left hand through the strap and onto the stock, the hard rubber of the Warner & Swasey scope compressing as he pressed it against his right eye. He found the fleeing Hudson with the scope and brought the crosshairs to bear on the back of his head. He tried to hold steady but he felt his knees begin to weaken and it was more difficult to breathe. The crosshairs were shaking. Hudson was still moving, maybe a hundred thirty yards now. Then he stopped, as if deciding which way to turn. Cockran moved the crosshairs up to a point barely a fraction above Hudson's wavy blond hair.

Remembering his MID instructor's mantra, he took a deep breath, let half out and held it. Cross hair. Cross hair. At this range, he knew the bullet would only drop a few inches below the cross hairs. He squeezed the trigger slowly. He remembered it was a three pound trigger pull. He gave the last pound a gentle snatch. The rifle bucked slightly, the shot deafening in the tower's close quarters. Cockran kept his eye on the scope as it settled back a split second later in time for him to see the results of the bullet's impact on the upper half of Hudson's back as blood spurted and his body fell forward. Not half bad, Cockran thought. Tough luck, Ted.

Cockran knew he had no time for a second shot. He had to get out of there. His ears were ringing. Unlike most snipers, he had worn neither ear plugs nor shooting gloves. He pulled a handkerchief from his pocket and carefully wiped the rifle clean of prints. He figured the police would be coming up the first tower and not the second. Cockran would make his way out much as Hudson had done.

As he walked quickly and quietly down the steps of the second tower, Cockran carefully reassessed Ted's role in all this. The I.C.E. Building had been neither the time nor the place to tell Mattie about his fight with Ted Hudson at the elevator or Verschuer's implication of MID in the twins' kidnapping. He had thought there would be time for that later. Now, he wasn't so sure he wanted to do that. If he did, he would leave out the rest of the story—that Hudson had been the Cathedral sniper and Cockran had probably killed him. Since he could not prove that Hudson had been the sniper in the cathedral, he would be admitting to Mattie that, without any proof and acting only on his intuition, he instinctively had shot her old boyfriend in the back in cold blood. Mattie didn't need to know that. It had been bad enough when she had to see him execute the MID thug at Cold Spring Harbor. At least she knew that guy was going to do the same to her. Nope, no one else needed to know he had killed Hudson. Certainly not Mattie.

Cockran stepped out a side door of the Cathedral and walked back to where he had left Mattie and the others. Sturm, Ingrid and the others were nowhere in sight. Good, he thought. He hoped Sturm had them headed for Winston's leased tri-motor and freedom.

"Where are the others? How is Ingrid?" he asked Mattie.

"Kurt's on the way to the airfield. Ingrid's alive. The bullet passed cleanly through her shoulder. He thinks Ingrid's wound can be treated for now with the first aid kits in the autogiros. He didn't want to risk taking her to hospital here. He wants Winston and Robbie to get her and all of the twins out of the country before any Nazi V-men can alert the authorities."

"Thank God," Cockran said. "Ingrid's a tough girl and Vienna has excellent hospitals. And the twins will be safe enough in Vienna as well. But we need to get out of here also and back to Munich. You've got a helluva story to write and Hearst is gonna owe you one big bonus."

TED Hudson watched impassively from an alcove in the narrow, cobblestone street as the twitching body of Captain David Baker grew still, the blood from the gaping wound in his skull forming a growing circle around his head. Plan B, Hudson thought, it was always good to have a Plan B.

Once he saw Cockran at the I.C.E. Building, he knew he could no longer depend upon Verschuer to eliminate the two women who knew too damn much about the Gemini Project. Cockran too but the women came first. So he had set himself up in the Cathedral tower close to the I.C.E. Building and waited patiently. An MID trained sniper, he had been prepared to wait all morning but the two broads had come along like sitting ducks. He still could not believe he had missed that first head shot but he hit her pretty good anyway. With any luck, the bitch would bleed out. When, improbably, his next shot missed Mattie and he failed to stop Cockran from reaching the cathedral, he had turned to Plan B. If the Gemini story broke, Ted Hudson was not going to be there. He was going to be a martyr to Bolshevism. At least until things calmed down.

David Baker had been waiting for him a block from the cathedral as instructed. They had switched leather jackets so that Baker was carrying Hudson's credentials as he stepped into the street and sprinted away as ordered. Hudson had raised his silenced Luger, intending to put two rounds into Baker's head when the man's back suddenly erupted in blood at the same time he heard the sharp crack of a rifle. His MID sniper rifle. He had smiled. Thanks to Cockran, he only had to fire a single bullet into Baker's head. Maybe Cockran wasn't such a pussy after all.

Speaking of pussy, since the fickle Scottish bitch was still alive, Hudson was even more annoyed than before that he hadn't managed to hump Cockran's girlfriend again as he had boasted to him in the elevator. For old times sake. What's an assignment for without fringe benefits? Especially since nailing her again really would have stuck it to Cockran.

After the ambush he had planned for her in the night club parking lot went south and he had to kill those two incompetent ex-MID agents, the

428 Michael McMenamin and Patrick McMenamin

sexy twist had held him so tight that he was certain she was all but begging him to take her in the backseat of their motorcar and drill her right there. That night in Ohio, however, he had been looking for more than an adrenalin-induced quickie. Something more like their last alcohol-fueled night in Paris in '29 where he showed that ungrateful broad everything that she would be missing by having turned his marriage proposal down.

A reprise in Findlay of that night in Paris had appeared promising once they were back in her hotel room from the road house. Especially with all they had drunk earlier combined with both of them finishing an entire bottle of brandy and her stark naked beneath that flimsy gown, flashing those delicious freckled tits in his face. He smiled at the memory. Boy, she had been a handful. *Two* handfuls. A real stand-up double. He thought it was all down hill.

Hell, after he ripped her robe wide open, he hadn't even bothered to touch third. With both her headlights firmly in hand and home plate left unprotected, he knew that once he scored, she would have melted like any other woman. Paris had proved that. A four bagger had seemed his for the taking. And it certainly was, right up until her knee, twice driven hard into his groin, had persuaded him otherwise. Cock-teasing bitch! He had been sore for a week. He owed her one. And Ted Hudson always paid his debts. Until then, they would always have Paris.

Hudson swiftly walked away in the opposite direction from Baker's body. Tomorrow, he would call at police headquarters as Captain David Baker; identify the body as Hudson; and arrange for its cremation. In the meantime, he would make sure General Van Deman knew that it was Cockran who had killed Baker just as he had the unfortunate Schmidt brothers on Long Island. Then he would book passage back to Washington and await his next assignment, either under his new persona as Captain David Baker or whatever other identity MID chose for him. It was not the first time he had forsaken his own identity to defend America against her enemies, domestic or foreign. It would not be the last.

BOBBY Sullivan was worried as he supervised the loading of the twins into the Ford Trimotor, its engines idling, ready to take off once they were aboard. He breathed a sigh of relief when Sturm's Mercedes touring car roared onto the field carrying Ingrid and her twin siblings.

"The police may be on their way here," Sturm said as he stepped down from the big motorcar. "Ingrid's been wounded. I'll give her first aid but she needs real medical attention. In Austria, not in Germany." In the distance, the sound of a siren was growing louder.

"Make haste!" Winston Churchill shouted as he approached the two, a Colt .45 automatic in his right hand. "*Herr* Sturm, after you see to Mrs. Waterman, secure our passengers and ask Sergeant Rankin to bring the plane about for a prompt takeoff. Mr. Sullivan and I will deal with the intruders."

Churchill turned to Sullivan with a grin. "Bourke tells me you're the best shot he's ever seen with a Colt .45. Let's see if he's right."

Sullivan and Churchill settled in behind Sturm's Mercedes, Sullivan with a .45 in both hands, Churchill with one. To his surprise, the approaching siren was not on a police car but rather a large Nazi staff car with swastika flags flying on each front fender. The motorcar was approaching at a rapid speed and Bobby intended to wait until it was 50 yards away as, in his experience, that was the maximum range for a .45 if it was to have any real stopping power.

Sullivan was surprised once more when Churchill fired three quick shots at a range of 75 yards, all of which were tightly grouped squarely in the center of the oncoming Mercedes radiator. Steam began billowing immediately from the radiator and the car slowed its approach, coming to a halt 40 yards away. That was all Sullivan needed as he stood up from their perch behind Sturm's car. He fired a shot from each of his .45s through the windscreen of the Nazi vehicle, both finding their target in the heads of the Mercedes driver and his passenger.

Jesus, Mary and Joseph, Sullivan thought, that old Englishman had just displayed the best shooting he had ever seen. After Churchill's three shots at a moving target, Sullivan's two shots at the stalled vehicle had been like shooting fish in a barrel. He once had heard his chief Michael Collins say about Churchill in relation to Irish independence "Tell Winston we could have done nothing without him." He wondered if Collins had known about Churchill's marksmanship.

The trimotor took off without incident thereafter with Churchill in the co-pilot's seat, earphones over his head. Once airborne, Sullivan approached the cockpit. "Mr. Churchill, I was impressed by your shooting back there. Where did you learn to shoot like that?"

Churchill, an unlit cigar clenched between his teeth, growled back over his shoulder "Sandhurst. India. The Sudan. South Africa. Ypres."

"But sir, that was a long time ago."

"You asked *where* I learned, young man, not why I can still shoot so well today. I can answer in one word. Practice. I have a shooting range at my country home in Kent where I spend several hours once a week keeping up my skills. You can never tell when it will come in handy. I have many enemies who wish me ill. Sinn Fein. Hindus. Muslims. And now, undoubtedly, the Nazis."

"But to hit a speeding motorcar going 40 miles per hour three times at a range of 75 yards with only a .45 automatic hand gun is remarkable."

"Nonsense," Churchill growled again over his shoulder. "How could anyone miss a target as large as a Mercedes radiator? Try hitting the brain of a charging bull elephant, a white rhino, a cape buffalo or a black-maned lion with one shot. Because frequently you only get one shot. Now *that's* remarkable." Churchill paused, took his cigar from his mouth, turned his head, and smiled. "Of course, I've done all that as well."

90.

Brandy and Cigars

Waterspiel Restaurant
Munich
Sunday, 5 June 1932

"TED Hudson is dead!" Mattie McGary exclaimed as she sat down at the table, signaled the waiter to fill her wine glass and then proceeded to drain half the glass.

Winston Churchill was bemused. His god-daughter was 30 minutes late for their dinner and his other guests—Cockran, Ingrid and Sturm—reluctantly had agreed with his suggestion that they begin in her absence. They had just finished their soup and were awaiting the fish course when she arrived.

"That's terrible," Ingrid said. "How? When? Was it the SS?"

"I don't know," Mattie replied. "It's why I was late. A press release came in from the U.S. Embassy over the AP wire. It said that Hudson had been killed in a hunting accident yesterday in Bavaria and that he had been scheduled to become the military attaché to the embassy in Berlin effective July 1."

"But no details on the circumstances of his death?" Ingrid asked.

"No. I talked to the U.S. embassy in Berlin but I couldn't get a straight story out of them. I called the U.S. consulate in Munich and tried to talk to Captain Baker to see what he knew but I was told Baker was no longer there and had been transferred back to the states. Damn it, it's a cover-up! Hudson was with both of us in the I.C.E. Building and we were all bound to chairs."

Ingrid nodded her agreement.

"When the SS took us away, Verschuer had pulled out a scalpel to torture Ted and we never saw him again. Verschuer and the SS must have killed him and for some reason the American embassy is covering it up."

"That's quite possible," Cockran said. "MID could just be covering its tracks. Verschuer claimed MID was backing the Gemini Project and, if that's true, then they won't want it known that one of their own was killed in the process. You realize there's been no publicity at all about what happened at I.C.E. even though we left at least seven bodies behind. The same thing happened at Cold Spring Harbor."

"Well, it's just wrong," Mattie said, "that Ted's death should be passed off as some hunting accident when he was actually killed attempting to save innocent American lives."

Ingrid nodded her head in agreement again but Cockran did not reply and neither did Sturm. Churchill found this curious but said nothing as the conversation changed to other subjects. For his own part, Churchill found it strange that the tunnel into the clinic had been discovered by Hudson and that the SS had been waiting in ambush when their party emerged. Coincidence? Possibly. But a more likely scenario was that Hudson's SS source for the tunnel's location had betrayed him. That was the benign answer. But, if the American MID had supported Verschuer, it was also possible Hudson had been the one to betray them. That thought must have occurred to Cockan as well so his silence on this point was telling.

For his part, Churchill didn't care. He had more important things on his mind. The former German naval airship officer seated to his right was one of them. When the table arose upon the dinner's completion, he laid a restraining hand on Sturm's forearm. "*Herr* von Sturm, I realize you may have other plans for the rest of the evening but if you could possibly join me in my suite at 11:30 p.m., there are several matters of potentially mutual interest which I would like to discuss with you."

Sturm nodded and bowed. For a moment, Churchill feared he was going to click his heels. But he simply said "I am at your disposal. Since last we met, I have become familiar with some of your military exploits in South Africa and elsewhere and I have questions about them which are best not discussed in mixed company."

"Splendid," Churchill replied with a smile on his face. "I'll see you then. I'll furnish the brandy and cigars."

CHURCHILL set out two crystal snifters and a bottle of Hennessey VSOP on the low table between the two burgundy leather club chairs which flanked the suite's firplace in which newly set coals glowed. He had not decided the best way to approach Sturm with his proposition. While he had been briefly introduced to the man during his stay with William Randolph Hearst at his estate near San Simeon, California in the summer of 1929, he hadn't had any prolonged exposure to him until a year ago in Germany.

Churchill had been impressed. Though Mattie had told him Sturm was a dedicated Nazi, she also told him he was no anti-Semite. The man had turned down an invitation to join the SS in 1930 and had crossed swords with them last year and a week ago, both times in concert with him and Cockran. Such a man was formidable but opposing anti-Semitism and the SS as he did scarcely put him in a position for what Churchill had in mind. Or so Churchill had thought.

That all changed on the first day of June when Adolf Hitler failed to stop by Churchill's table as Hanfstaengl had arranged. He had followed Sturm and his attractive blonde companion when they retired for the evening and had watched from afar as the two of them as well as Bourke and Mattie had been greeted by Hitler. When he saw the genuine warmth in Hitler's eyes as he grasped Sturm's hand in both of his, Churchill immediately changed his mind about Sturm. His opposition to Himmler, the SS and anti-Semitism notwithstanding, such a man was worth cultivating. Which is what Churchill intended to do.

The door bell to his suite rang and Churchill rose quickly to open it. "*Herr* von Sturm, thank you for agreeing to join me. May I offer you some brandy?"

Sturm accepted the brandy but declined a cigar as the two men sat down.

"Tell me about Hitler," Churchill said after a brief puff on his cigar. "My son covered his election campaigns for president this year and my god-daughter has interviewed him on several occasions including one as recently as last year. Mattie says that you know Hitler also and, judging from his reaction to you a few days ago, you appear to be in his good graces."

Sturm's eyes momentarily registered surprise, Churchill thought, but he quickly recovered. Still, Churchill wondered if it was his mention of Mattie having talked to him about Sturm that caused the reaction. Well, young man, he thought, there's a lot more Mattie has told me about you—and her—which would surprise you even more.

"Why does he interest you?" Sturm asked.

"Randolph believes there will be another war if Hitler comes to power," Churchill replied. "I'm not in government right now and I may never be again if some people have their way. Still, I will have the ear of those who are in power and, some day, I may be in a position to advise them about *Herr* Hitler and his intentions. I hope Randolph is wrong about a war but I fear he is not."

"I also hope there will not be war but if the enemies of my country do not return that which was stolen from us at Versailles, the fault will lie with them and not Hitler. He is not like other politicians. He urges us to rise above our petty individual interests. He does not pander to us as farmers, laborers, shopkeepers, office workers or even as Catholics or Protestants. He appeals to us as Germans to put our country first and not ourselves."

"Randolph has told me as much based on his coverage of Hitler's campaign," Churchill said. "But I am more interested in Hitler the man and his 'struggle' as he termed his memoirs. The story of that struggle cannot be read without admiration for the courage, the perseverance, and the vital force which enabled him to challenge, defy, conciliate, or overcome all the authorities or resistances which barred his path. He and the ever-increasing legions," Churchill paused for a sip of brandy, poured more into Sturm's snifter, and looked again at the young German "who worked with him—which I daresay includes you—certainly showed, in their patriotic ardour and love of country, that there was nothing they would not do or dare, no sacrifice of life, limb or property that they would not make themselves or inflict upon their opponents."

"There is much truth in what you say and I am impressed that, as an Englishman, you have such insight into those of us who support Hitler. But he is not yet in power." Sturm said.

"He will be, young man," Churchill replied. "One way or another, by constitutional or other means, he will be in power and soon. I hope it is by the former but a man with such popularity cannot be denied. So, tell me more about him."

"He is widely read and knows a lot about history, especially German history," Sturm replied and drained his brandy snifter, prompting Churchill to pour him another. "He is most articulate in private conversation as well as in public speeches. But what really attracts you about him—what attracted me almost eight years ago—are his eyes. Hitler's physical appearance is not especially distinguished but when he's talking to you, his eyes are focused only on you and he makes you feel you are—at that moment anyway—the most important person in the world to him. When he's addressing a crowd, he gives the impression of growing anger as he continues to talk but he is always in complete control of himself. He is in many ways a consummate actor on stage. In private—at least with me—he is always cool and calm, never at a loss for words. And he often displays a sense of humor." Sturm smiled. "Something we Germans are not especially known to possess."

Churchill raised the snifter to his nose, swirled the brandy and took a swallow. "I've been told much the same thing by others who have met him but they were not German like you. I'm told by them Hitler has an agreeable manner, a disarming smile and a subtle personal magnetism. Would you agree?"

Sturm merely smiled and wordlessly nodded his assent.

"And would you not also concur that *Herr* Hitler's party platform, so to speak, has two goals: to cure unemployment and, through rearmament, regain Germany's place in Europe that it had before the Great War?"

"That is a fair assessment of Hitler's primary goals. Do you find fault with them?"

"No, young man, I don't. I think Germany has many legitimate grievances beginning with the absurd French delusion that they could extract vast indemnities from the Germans in order to compensate them for all the devastation the war had cost them. After all, they were the ones who mobilized those vast armies first, not the Kaiser. Moreover, the territorial arrangements in Europe insisted upon by the French at Versailles also created many racial injustices among the German-speaking peoples which need to be corrected. While minor progress has been made on reparations, no efforts have been made by the Western powers to address these racial anomalies whether they be in Poland, Czechoslovakia or Lithuania."

Sturm's eyes narrowed at this as he said in a tight voice "Posen. My family's estate in Pomerania was confiscated by the Poles. The farm families who had looked to us for four generations to protect and provide for them were forced off our land by the Polish Army. I will not rest; Hitler will not rest; and Germany will not rest until our land is returned."

"That is my point precisely which I repeatedly make to those who advocate disarmament, the United States especially." Churchill paused and gave Sturm another measure of brandy. "I have always believed in the doctrine that the redress of the grievances of the vanquished should precede the disarmament of the victors. Until you and *Herr* Hitler are prepared to rest after your grievances over places like Posen are redressed, disarmament is folly and will only lead to another war. But enough of politics. What about the Jews? *Herr* Hanfstaengl seemed positively tongue-tied when I mentioned them the other evening. Yet Mattie tells me that you hold no ill-feeling towards the Jews and that, despite all the evidence to the contrary in *Mein Kampf* and elsewhere, you don't believe Hitler is an anti-Semite either. Pray tell me why."

Again, Sturm seemed a bit off-put by the mention of Mattie having confided in Churchill about him but, again, he quickly recovered. "It is true Mattie and I have discussed this. I don't know many Jews but the ones I do are good Germans, honorable and patriotic. Perhaps Hitler may have had a different experience. This could explain the undeniably negative attitude towards Jews which he displays in *Mein Kampf.* But what I find more significant is that since 1930 he no longer attacks the Jews in his public speeches. Or privately, for that matter, at least with me and Mattie as well. What that says to me is that Hitler may have used the Jews as scapegoats in his early days for political reasons but no longer does. He once told me that no man can be held responsible for the circumstances of his birth."

Churchill paused, took a small sip of brandy and then poured Sturm another generous measure. "*Herr* Himmler and *Herr* Goebbels do not show a similar restraint."

"I agree. They are true anti-Semites."

"But they are both very close to Hitler. Doesn't that give you pause? Especially given Himmler's sacrifice of that English girl at Castle Wewelsburg last year? And their attempt to kill Mattie as well? You saw what the SS are capable of even before this abomination of the SS murder of the American twins."

Sturm stood up and downed the rest of his brandy, running his hands through his blond hair as he began to pace. Helpfully, Churchill refilled Sturm's snifter. Sturm saw this, stopped pacing, and returned to rescue the snifter from which he took a grateful gulp. "Yes, Mr. Churchill, it does give me pause. Very much so. Which is why I will be resigning from the party. As I mentioned to all at dinner tonight, I have been offered command of a new airship by my father's good friend, Hugo Eckener of *Zeppelin Reederei*. Hugo is not political and declined to run for president against Hitler and Hindenburg this year even though he is the most popular man in Germany, thanks to the world-wide voyage of the *Graf Zeppelin* in 1929. That will provide a convenient excuse for my doing so."

"Ah yes, I recall that voyage very well *Herr* Sturm. It is when we first met at Mr. Hearst's home in San Simeon where the zeppelin had been scheduled to land. I later listened with great interest to *Herr* Eckener's speech in Los Angeles about the peaceful nature of airships. But pray explain why this would cause you to leave the Nazi party when it is on the cusp pf power?"

"Eckener hates the Nazis. So does the woman I love. That plus what I know of Himmler is enough for me." Sturm once more drained his brandy snifter.

Chuchill paused and refilled Sturm's glass. Was he referring to Mattie? Or the American woman who had assassinated Verschuer? Best not to inquire, he thought. "Is that entirely wise?"

"What do you mean?"

"I do not share your benign view of *Herr* Hitler. That is why I asked to meet him on this trip to Germany. To assess him for myself and not through the eyes of others. But, alas, it was not to be and thus Hitler has lost the chance of meeting me. But suppose you are correct about him? Suppose that, once German grievances are appeased, we may yet live to see Hitler a gentler figure in a happier age?"

Churchill watched with approval as Sturm took a sip from the brandy in his newly refilled snifter before resuming his monologue. "If that is to happen, Hitler will need men around him to whom honor and integrity are the values which guide their lives rather than the duplicity and hatreds which inspire the likes of Himmler and Goebbels and the other thugs around them. He may be a consummate actor as you suggest but I sense that Hitler both likes and respects you. Much as he does Hermann Göring. Perhaps it is the Blue Max you both wear? In any event, while Mattie has made me appreciate your desire to once more command an airship, I don't think it should also be the occasion where you abandon *Herr* Hitler to the tender mercies and advice of the likes of Himmler and Goebbels. He will need help to offset and restrain excesses like the ones you have witnessed at Verschuer's clinic."

Sturm shook his head in resignation. "I understand but, like Hugo, I am not a political man. What could I possibly do to offset the advice of a Himmler or Goebbels?" Sturm raised his blond head and looked up at Churchill expectantly. 'I want to help Hitler but what could I do?"

Churchill smiled. The hook had been well-baited and the fish was now on the line. The battle was about to begin. He liked his chances. "Let me explain," he said as he once more refilled Sturm's glass while taking a small sip from his own and a puff from his cigar. Would he land the fish? He didn't know. The last time had been off Catalina Island in California on the yacht of William Randolph Hearst. The marlin had been tough. He had been tougher. Then as now, he relished the challenge.

AN hour later, Churchill closed the door of his suite on the departing figure of of the former Imperial German naval airship commander *Kapitänleutnant* Kurt von Sturm, *nee* Strasser. Had he succeeded? He really didn't know. He hoped so. But Sturm hadn't let on, despite numerous opportunities to do so, who was the woman he loved who had prompted his tentative decision to leave the Nazi party. Mattie? Or the American? He hoped it was the latter. If it were not, he feared for the future of his old mentor's son with his god-daughter. Mattie loved Bourke, that much he knew because she had told him so. But, though she hadn't said so, he strongly suspected she loved Kurt von Sturm as well even if she was not yet aware of it. But he thought she was.

Was Churchill surprised at this? Not really. Most people, hopefully including his dear wife Clemmie, would be but he knew better. His first love had been Pamela Plowden about whom he had once improvidently written from India to his mother that she was the only woman with whom he could ever live happily everafter. His worldly-wise mother had kept his confidence and Churchill was to learn, in due time, that he had been wrong. Thanks to his beautiful Clemmie. Five children had been proof of that. But the fact remained that he and Pamela had remained the closest of friends and still corresponded when apart, Winston carefully destroying her letters today just as he had promised he would do when he was a young subaltern in India.

The point, Churchill well knew, was this. You could love more than one person. Had Pamela said "yes" and ignored her parents' importuning that she marry a much wealthier Earl, Clemmie would have remained a "might have been." As it was, he still loved Pamela even though Clemmie was undeniably first in his heart. It wasn't quite the same with Bourke and Mattie but it was close. Whoever was the first to propose to her had the inside track. Much as he admired the young German with the Blue Max, he was rooting for his American mentor's son with the Silver Star. Why hadn't that boy proposed before now?

91.

An Unusual Proposal

Hotel Continental
Munich
Monday, 6 June 1932

A big help you've been!" Mattie said back over her shoulder, slamming the door to their hotel suite as she left. Mattie usually didn't feel guilty after fights with Cockran because, invariably, he was wrong and she was right.

This morning was different. They had fought last night but that was about Ted Hudson and the U.S. Embassy cover-up story that he had been killed in a hunting accident when in fact the damn Nazis had probably done it. To her, Ted was a hero for having attempted to rescue the twins at the Clinic. Bourke hadn't agreed and suggested that Ted's confidential source in the SS had been a double agent who had duped Ted. Telling Cockran that she was keeping Ted's by-line on the story hadn't improved things. But that wasn't why she felt guilty now.

As she waited for the elevator, she nervously fingered the cream-colored envelope in her jacket which had been slipped underneath the door to their suite during the night. Thank God she had been up to retrieve it before Cockran awoke. Would they have had the fight this morning if she hadn't read the message in the envelope? She thought so. But maybe not. Had she over-reacted to Cockran's critique of the first draft of her story? No, damn it! He was wrong! Laughlin and Davenport ought to be indicted as accessories to murder! Why couldn't she just say so? She sighed. Lawyers!

Still, Mattie's guilt was there and the message in the envelope was the reason why. As she stepped into the elevator, she opened the envelope and re-read the message:

> *Dear Mattie,*
> *Ingrid left early this morning to rejoin her brother and sister in Vienna. I must talk to you as soon as possible. Bayerische Hof, Room 825. There are personal matters on which I urgently seek your advice.*
> *Until then, I remain,*
> *Yr most obedient servant,*
> *Kurt*

What gave Mattie pause—and guilt—was that a recovering Ingrid had planned to spend all week with Kurt before joining her brother and sister next weekend in Vienna. Now, Ingrid was unexpectedly gone and Kurt had invited her to his hotel room to discuss "personal matters". She had told Cockran that she was going to the Hearst bureau office to finish her story. True. But she was stopping first to meet her former lover in his hotel room. Alone.

How would that look to Cockran? Not good. Not good at all. So why hadn't she told him? Cockran seemed more tolerant of Sturm than before but this message wouldn't help. Kurt was a *former* lover, emphasis on former, but he was still a friend who was asking for her advice. Prelude to a seduction? Maybe. But, unlike that nightcap in Ohio with Ted Hudson, she couldn't be sure. For that reason, Kurt deserved the benefit of her doubt.

Would she tell Cockran at some point? Perhaps. It all depended on exactly what the personal matters were on which Kurt wanted her advice.

Mattie knocked on Sturm's door and he opened it immediately. He was dressed in a suit and tie, but the circles under his eyes signaled that he hadn't had much sleep while the redness suggested he had too much to drink the night before. Cockran had mentioned to her Churchill's invitation last night to Sturm—and no one else—for brandy and cigars in his suite. Mattie was just as curious as Bourke as to what that was all about. Maybe that—and not the two of them—would be what they discussed. She hoped so.

Sturm extended his hand and Mattie took it, giving him a quick kiss on the cheek, which he returned. Should she have done that? Was it warm in here or was it her? Why kid herself? She was alone with an attractive man who once had been her lover and probably loved her still.

"You look like you had a rough night, Kurt. How late did Winston keep you up?"

Sturm grinned and the hard planes of his face softened in much the same way Cockran's did. "I admire Mr. Churchill's, ah. . . . capacity for alcohol. He seemed none the worse for wear when I left his rooms at 3 a.m. But, as for me," Sturm said and shrugged, "not even the coldest of showers this morning could disguise my condition."

"Did Ingrid leave suddenly?" Mattie asked. "At dinner last night, I had the impression she was going to spend the week here and meet her brother and sister in Vienna next weekend."

Sturm turned away and walked to the window. "Well…her plans have changed."

"What happened?" Mattie asked.

"As I mentioned at dinner, I have a new job offer from *Zeppelin Reederie* to command an airship. I told Ingrid first thing this morning that I was going to accept the offer. But I also told her that I had reconsidered my earlier decision to resign from the Nazi party. She demanded to know why but I told her that it was not something I felt comfortable discussing with her. She demanded I stick to my original decision and, when I refused, she left for Vienna."

"I don't understand. I think you should leave the Nazis also. Why did you reconsider?"

Still looking out the window, Sturm spoke in a soft voice. "Mr. Churchill has made an unusual proposal which, if I accept, requires me to remain a party member in good standing."

92.

Who Knew?

Hotel Continental
Munich
Monday, 6 June 1932

COCKRAN hated arguments with Mattie, especially when he was right and she wasn't. Which was most of the time. He was alone in their hotel suite, finishing the remains of a late breakfast. Their arguments usually involved her work and this one had been no exception. But, on this occasion, it hadn't been about her risk taking. Or about the dangerous nature of her assignments. Nope. Cockran had long ago added those to the short list of forbidden subjects.

Who knew giving your lover legal advice on libel should have been added to the forbidden list? After all, *she* had asked him to read a draft of her article and tell her what he thought. True, libel was not his specialty — — that was international commerce — but his father had represented Joseph Pulitzer and the *New York World* in quite a few libel lawsuits. He had read briefs and trial transcripts in those cases while writing his father's biography and had a fairly good handle on the law of libel. That hadn't been good enough for Mattie.

"A big help you've been!" were her last words as she headed toward the door, turning to look back at Cockran. "We'll see what W.R. has to say about all this. I thought you were a better journalist than that. I really did." With that, Mattie had slammed the door.

Well, Cockran thought, he *was* a better journalist than that. Mattie had written a great story. Unfortunately, she had asked him his opinion as a lawyer, not a journalist. As a lawyer, he knew the gist of the story carried the plain implication that the Waterman Foundation, the Rockefeller

Foundation and the Carnegie Institution were up to their elbows in blood, having compiled a secret death list of twenty twins, twelve of whom had died horribly. The article also implied that Wesley Waterman, Harry Laughlin and Charles Davenport were either idiots or accessories to murder. He actually agreed with the accessories to murder part but Cockran the lawyer had offered a few revisions, deletions mostly, to make the article more defendable.

Mattie the journalist, of course, had intended every single innuendo to which Cockran objected and had taken extensive pains to make sure that the reader would draw the correct conclusion from her otherwise true facts. Cockran could see that and, as a writer himself, he had nothing but admiration for how cleverly Mattie had done so. Cockran had been about to tell her that when her patience reached its limit and she went out in search of a higher authority. William Randolph Hearst himself. The Chief.

Cockran was disappointed but he thought he knew how to make things up with Mattie. Before their fight, he would have done so this evening at dinner. The time was ripe. Now, he couldn't risk it. He was perpetually tardy but this was one time he dare not be late because he never could explain where he had been. Other tactics would have to be employed.

Cockran looked at his watch. 12:45 p.m. He didn't have much time. He placed a paper bag on the bed, sat down at the room's desk and pulled out a sheet of hotel stationery. Twenty minutes later, he finished at the desk and began placing the folded sheets of stationery at strategic locations in the room. He pinned the last sheet to the paper bag on Mattie's pillow.

The buzzer to the suite rang at that point and Cockran rechecked the Webley in its leather holster under his left arm and placed his Army Colt .45 in the waistband in the small of his back.

He opened the door to greet the unsmiling faces of the new Irish-German alliance: Kurt von Sturm and Bobby Sullivan.

93.

No Luckier Than Me

IT had been nearly 12:30 p.m. when Kurt told her he was late for an engagement and bade Mattie goodbye. She headed for the Hearst bureau office and hoped that Cockran had not called her in the interim. She wasn't ready to explain where she had been. She hadn't decided how much she was going to tell Cockran about her meeting with Kurt. It wouldn't be everything. Ingrid leaving Kurt? Probably. He'd learn that anyway. That Ingrid left Kurt because he refused to resign from the party? Maybe, but probably not. If Ingrid explained that to Cockran, fine. But she didn't think Cockran would ask and that was okay with Mattie.

Mattie stopped, caught in her thoughts, and realized she was approaching the Barlow Palace, purchased a few years ago by the Nazis and now known as the Brown House. Really, Mattie thought, parties who proudly carry the label "socialist" shouldn't reside in marble palaces.

Mattie's dilemma, as she looked up at the blood-red flag flying high above the pillars of the old palace, was whether Cockran would ever need to know Kurt's secret, what she had promised him to keep in confidence from everyone except Cockran.

Mattie shook her head again. She still found it dificult to believe. That Kurt had refused Ingrid's ultimatum to leave the Nazi party because he was seriously considering Winston Churchill's "unusual proposal" that he stay close to the Nazis and become an informal agent in Churchill's unofficial European intelligence network. To send Winston information when Kurt learned of anything happening or about to happen which he did not believe was in Germany's best interests and which the outside world should know.

Mattie had been astonished at her godfather's boldness in attempting to recruit a ruthless assassin like Kurt von Sturm. She would never forget the conversation that followed.

"Did you accept?"

"Not yet."

"But you intend to?"

"Possibly. It depends."

"On what?"

"You."

"Why?"

"Mr. Churchill told me he has many contacts and friends in Germany and other countries in Europe. Patriots. Men of principle. Of honor. Of peace. Tell me about Churchill. I was impressed as much by him as any man since my father."

"Even Adolf Hitler?"

Sturm smiled. "What do the Americans say? You certainly know how to press the right buttons. But yes, even Hitler. Still, you would be surprised at what they have in common. Churchill talking to me of the inequities of the Versailles Treaty sounds much like Hitler. But is Churchill an honorable man? Can his word be trusted?"

"He is," Mattie said, "one of the most honorable men I know. It's not a long list. Only five."

"Five?"

"Hearst, my boss. Bobby Sullivan. Cockran…"

'Including Churchill, that's four." Sturm said, sitting back in his chair, whiskey glass on his right, both hands on his knees.

Mattie had leaned forward, took both of his hands in hers and looked directly into those clear blue eyes. "You. You're the fifth."

Sturm had held on to her hands for a long time, maintaining eye contact before finally drawing his hands away and almost shyly averting his eyes. "Thank you. What you think of me means more than you can ever know."

But Mattie knew that and had known for over a year. "So, because of Winston, you told Ingrid you weren't resigning from the party and that's why she left?"

"Yes."

'You realize that if Ingrid knew why you were staying in the party, she would stand by you. Both Cockran and I believe she's in love with you. She's a strong woman. A good woman."

Sturm, clearly agitated, stood up. "I know. I love her too. But you can't tell her about this. Too many Nazis are dangerous people and I can't expose her to that. She's been through enough. I vowed to her that I will personally see that she's never in danger again. Promise me."

"I promise. I think you're wrong. You should let Ingrid decide for herself. But I promise."

Sturm's face softened. "Thank you. Your Mr. Cockran is a lucky man."

Mattie smiled. "He is, but…"

"What?"

"No luckier than me."

Mattie kept walking until she had passed the Brown House. The fact was that Hitler soon was going to be the head of the largest party in Germany. As a practical matter, the Nazis could bring Germany to a standstill if the powers that be did not recognize Hitler's undeniable popularity and reward him with the chancellorship of Germany. In Mattie's mind, that was inevitable and a revolution would follow if backroom politics kept him from power.

Mattie knew Hitler. She had met him socially. She had interviewed him three times. He had been charmed by her. If Mattie was correct and Hitler came to power, Hearst would insist on exploiting that. And she knew she couldn't say no to Hearst. Face facts, McGary, she told herself. Germany was going to be a fertile field for her stories for some years to come. That meant spending considerable time in Germany. And that, inevitably, meant Kurt von Sturm was going to continue to be a part of her life if only because of his relationship with Hitler and his stature in the party.

With Ingrid out of the picture for the moment, that could complicate things with Cockran. She hadn't promised to keep Kurt's secret from Bourke and he hadn't asked. But she had made it clear that she would tell him if ever she believed Cockran had a need to know, also making it clear to Kurt it was her call alone. It would be a lonely call, one she hoped she would never have to make. Especially if it would place in peril either the American she loved or the German who loved her.

Mattie looked back at the Brown House. Clouds were gathering for an afternoon thunderstorm but the sun still shone brightly on the Nazi headquarters and its blood-red flag with the crooked black cross waving in the wind. As the clouds darkened, it was apparent that the pleasant scene would soon vanish in the storm that followed.

Adolf Hitler about to take power. Kurt von Sturm an agent for Winston Churchill. Mattie McGary keeping another secret from Bourke Cockran. She shook her head. The old Chinese saying "May you live in interesting times" was not a blessing. It was a goddamn curse!

94.

Your Contribution to the Next Generation

Vier Jahreszeiten Hotel
Munich
Monday, 6 June, 1932

WESLEY Waterman, III looked up into the cold, unforgiving eyes of the man who had made him a cuckold. Beyond him, he could see the equally unforgiving eyes of his wife's lawyer. But the eyes which chilled him the most were those of the black-hearted Irishman with the broken nose who had beaten him so savagely in New York.

Waterman was bound hand and foot to the posts of his hotel bed. Rage rose along with the blood in his face, making his head pound. He tensed at his bonds, furious at being rendered helpless. It was a new experience and he didn't like it. Not one little bit. Only sixty minutes ago, he had felt like a young bull servicing the fertile *Frau* Magda Quandt, sending his seed forward for the next generation, blissfully unaware of Magda's diaphragm. Then, he had talked with Himmler, arranging for SS assassins to kill his faithless wife before she left Vienna. The one cloud on his horizon was explaining Gemini's failure and the death of Ted Hudson to General Van Deman. But that was a minor problem compared to this.

"What do you want? Why are you here?"

"Why? Your wife. You tried to kill her. I intend to see your widow will live in peace."

At the word "widow," Waterman chilled. He understood. Sturm was an assassin by trade and he was going to kill him. "I'll call them all off. I'll leave her alone. You have my word."

"Your word means nothing," Sturm said, turning to equipment at the foot of the bed.

"Please, Sturm," Waterman said. "Kurt. This business over Ingrid can be settled between us. She's only a woman. Yes, it upset me that you slept with her. Surely, you can understand that. I overreacted. Can you blame me? Can't we just bury the hatchet."

Waterman winced internally at the poor choice of words. For the first time, he looked more closely at what Sturm was doing. "Kurt, what has happened to you? We share the same vision. Germany strong again, a superior race restored to its rightful place in the world."

"That is where you are wrong, *Herr* Waterman. We do not share the same vision for my country. We never have. The abomination at Passau you helped conceive and fund is a stain on German honor. I intend to begin cleansing that stain."

Sturm paused. "Starting with you. Are you aware of how the American twins were killed?" Sturm lifted the metal tray he had been working at so that Waterman could see the objects on it. There was a clear bottle beside a small, one-inch needle along with a brown bottle and a large syringe with a four-inch needle.

Waterman squirmed against his bonds. "No, I'm not. That was all up to Verschuer and Mengele. I had nothing to do with that."

"Well, *Herr* Waterman," Sturm said. "You are about to find out. Unlike with them, I will not slowly drain your body of blood or remove your eyes while you are still alive." Sturm lifted the syringe with the smaller needle. "The SS doctors first sedate their victims by injecting 5 cc's of Evipol. Once they are asleep, they inject 10 cc's of chloroform directly into the heart, killing their victims instantly." Sturm paused. "I do not believe in using anesthetic."

He slowly lowered the syringe with the small needle back to the tray. "I believe a man's inner strength should be sufficient to withstand any pain inflicted by a mere needle. This injection of chloroform into your heart may be painful. But you're a man and I'm certain you can take it. Trust me. The pain won't last long."

Sturm raised the large syringe high. Waterman stared at the long needle, glinting in the late afternoon sunlight that filtered through the white curtains. Oh my God, this can't be happening! Sturm stood up from his seat at the foot of the bed and inserted the needle into the brown bottle, drawing a clear liquid into the cylindrical tube of the large needle. Then he squirted the liquid within in a short burst.

Waterman felt heat flush to his face and his throat constrict. He heard his own voice leak out in a whimper. "Oh God, please, Sturm, don't kill me," he said. "Please. I'll liquidate my assets and give them to you. Or Ingrid. I'll do whatever you want. Just please, oh God, please don't kill me!"

Sturm ignored him. "When the medical examiner looks at your body, his diagnosis will be cardiac arrest. Unless he is looking for it, the injection of chloroform will be completely undetectable. Upon noting your age, your less than fit physique, and the circumstances in which your body will be discovered, he will make the obvious conclusion that you died of a heart attack, overcome in the aftermath of passion with a younger woman you were in no condition to handle. No one will mourn your passing. No one will care. At best, they will laugh."

"Oh God, Sturm, please. Not like this," Waterman begged, tears rolling down his face.

Sturm walked calmly around the side of the bed. "Your life will end as it deserves. You thought you could sacrifice innocent lives in the name of a greater good. You thought you could decide which souls would be permitted to procreate and live on through their children." Sturm spoke again. "You were wrong. I am here to tell you. Your line ends now. The world will be a better place without you or your issue. Consider it your contribution to the next generation."

Waterman tried to scream, but Sturm's hand was clamped firmly over his mouth. The last thing Wesley Waterman, III, saw were the unsmiling faces of Kurt von Sturm, Bourke Cockran and Bobby Sullivan looming over him. The last thing Wesley Waterman, III, felt was the searing pain in his chest as the needle plunged into his heart and filled it with fire.

AS Sturm watched the life fade from Waterman's body, he knew his life serving the men of Geneva was fading with it. Now, as he had learned from Ingrid, he would serve only himself. And his honor. He would control his own destiny. In the sky, his father's spirit to guide him.

Would the new Germany have a place for him? For his sister Franka? He hoped so. He had skills which would help, skills which a fellow Blue Max recipient and war hero like Hermann Göring would appreciate. But

Passau had taught him that many of those building the new Germany did not share his values. His father's values. The values of the Germany Bismarck had formed. He knew the course he had chosen was not an easy one. Nothing in life worth having was easy. His father had taught him that. Churchill had said much the same and he had heard the echo of his father's words in the Englishman's voice. But could he trust a man so recently his enemy? Mattie thought so and her opinion meant as much to him as Ingrid's.

Ingrid. The pain of her rejection was still fresh, worse in many ways than the pain he felt the summer before when Mattie chose the American over him, a man she had loved before she met Sturm. He found strength in the knowledge that now he was fighting his own battles for however long it took. Someday, he hoped Ingrid would understand. He hoped that Ingrid would be waiting for him when his work was finished.

He knew he would wait for her.

95.

Read Me Last

MATTIE McGary was not in a good mood as she stuck her key into the door of the suite she shared with Cockran. She wasn't looking forward to seeing him again. She had finished her final draft of the article, making *none* of the changes Cockran had recommended. Nevertheless, in her teletype to Hearst, she had carefully noted each of Cockran's suggested revisions and her reasons why she hadn't made any of them. She was confident the Chief would back her up but she did accurately summarize Cockran's rationale.

Mattie was still smoldering as she remembered Hearst's reply by teletype. "Story fantastic. Front page for certain. Above the fold. Incorporate all—repeat, all—Cockran changes." Would Cockran resist telling her "I told you so?" Not bloody likely! There were some days she hated all men. This was one of them.

Inside the suite, Mattie swung the door shut behind her. "Bourke, I'm back. Are you here?" Mattie called out. Then she noticed a white sheet of hotel stationery folded in half on the floor with the legend,

"Read me first."

Curious, Mattie stooped, picked up the note and opened it.

"Find the next note."

Halfway to the bedroom, Mattie spied another folded piece of stationery. She picked that one up as well.

"Closer. But look for the next note."

Mattie looked around the room and noticed another sheet of stationery in the middle of the doorway leading to the bedroom. What the hell was this all about, she thought, as she bent down to pick up the third note.

"Take off all your clothes and climb up on the bed."

Mattie smiled. Her mood was improving. "Cockran, are you here?" Mattie called out again. But there was no response. Bloody hell! He must be here, she thought.

Mattie walked over to the bed and saw a fourth note, another folded over sheet of hotel stationery. Without climbing onto the bed or taking off her clothes, Mattie reached for the sheet and opened it.

"I don't believe all your clothes are off. Get that way before you read the next note."

Cockran was definitely in the room, probably watching her from the closet, the sexy bastard, Mattie thought as she undid her belt buckle and slipped out of her trousers, panties and blouse. Her mood was getting much better. Was she really that predictable? She walked over to the bed and dutifully climbed up and picked up the last folded over sheet of paper left on top of the pillow. Like the first, this had writing on the outside:

"Read me last."

She opened the note and read it.

"Lift the pillow on your side of the bed."

Mattie did so and saw a small brown paper bag to which was pinned yet another note. Smiling even more now, Mattie unpinned the note, opened it and read:

M — I apologize for our argument this morning. Your story is great. So are you. Write whatever you want. Those rich assholes deserve what's coming. W.R. can afford the legal fees.

Let's make up this evening. Before or after dinner. Your call. But you shouldn't be entirely unclothed while you wait. Look inside the paper bag. It's yours if you want it. I hope you do.

I know I'm not a prize. After all, you know you're not the first woman to call me a thick-headed Irishman. That would be Nora. And, of course, Paddy's sainted grandmother. But I want you to be the last. A stubborn Scot and a thick-headed Irishman. Imagine what our children will be like.

It's your call but, either way, it would be ever so nice if you were (mostly) naked when I arrive. I will have had a difficult but interesting and satisfying day. I already have someone—you—to love. Now, to make my happiness complete, I also need something to look forward to…

I love you—Forever.

B.

Mattie picked up the paper bag, opened it, reached inside and pulled out a pale blue box with the legend "Tiffany & Company" on top. She opened the box and pulled out a small blue velvet box within. Opening the smaller box, she found herself staring at a very large diamond in a stunning setting on a plain gold band, the facets sparkling in the sunshine.

Mattie began laughing as the tears started streaming down her face. That bastard! That big, beautiful Irish bastard! Maybe that Chinese blessing wasn't a curse after all. The times she lived in had just become a helluva lot more interesting.

Mattie donned her green silk robe but left it open as she walked to the sideboard and began to mix a pitcher of martinis. It was a warm and sunny late spring day. She would stay naked. She held up her left hand and admired her new engagement ring. Well…mostly.

*** THE END ***

Historical Note

The Gemini Agenda is a work of fiction but there are certain historical elements which provide a foundation and framework for the story.

Winston Churchill. Churchill is portrayed as accurately as we know how, given that it occurs within a wholly fictitious adventure. Churchill traveled to Germany in 1932 to research his biography of his great ancestor the first Duke of Marlborough as depicted in the novel. While in Munich, Hitler backed out of a dinner with Churchill arranged by Putzi Hanfstaengl and, as Churchill later wrote, "Thus Hitler lost his only chance of meeting me." Even at age 57 in the novel, he was the crack shot we make him out to be as well as a man who was so thrilled at the possibility of being in danger that his Scotland Yard bodyguard rarely advised him of it when this was so. We have doubts about the accuracy of all his claims concerning his African hunting prowess in Chapter 89 but there is a photo of him with a white rhino. Churchill's somewhat benign comments about Hitler in Chapter 90 are taken from a 1935 article he wrote and later included in his book *Great Contemporaries*. He was an ardent Zionist, however, and his advice to Hitler through Hanfstaengl on anti-Semitism at the dinner where Hitler was a no-show is accurately portrayed.

Those with only a casual knowledge of Winston Churchill may question his being cast as a key character in an historical thriller. They shouldn't. Saving the world tends to overshadow lesser accomplishments but Churchill was a first-class athlete in his youth, an all-public schools fencing champion, and a championship polo player, a sport he played into his 50s. His detractors — of which there were many before 1940 — dismissed him as an "adventurer" and a "half-breed American." He was both of those things and more. He fought Islamic warriors on the Afghan border and in the Sudan in the late 1890s, bloody no-quarter battles where he killed many men at close range. He escaped from a prison in South Africa during the Boer war in 1899 and made his way over hundreds of miles of enemy territory to freedom. He bagged a rare white rhino in Africa in 1908, drawing the admiration and envy of Theodore Roosevelt who tried to do the same but was not so fortunate. He became a seaplane pilot in the early 1910s after becoming, at age 38, the First Lord of the

British Admiralty. In the First World War and temporarily out of office, he commanded a battalion in the trenches in the bloody Ypres salient where Corporal Adolf Hitler also served and where both men drew sketches in their spare time of the same bombed-out Belgian church. Contrary to some views, Hitler was a talented artist but Churchill was better, a gifted Impressionist whose works pseudonymously won awards in juried shows.

Bourke Cockran *(1854-1923)*. Winston Churchill's real life mentor and oratorical role model was the prominent turn-of-the century New York lawyer, statesman and Congressman William Bourke Cockran whose fictional son's exploits (Cockran was childless) are depicted in *The DeValera Deception, The Parsifal Plot and The Gemini Agenda.*. Churchill's feelings and comments about his mentor in Chapter 1 are accurately portrayed. A Democrat, a close adviser to President Grover Cleveland in his second term, and a contemporary of William Jennings Bryan, Cockran was acclaimed by members of both parties, including his friend and Long Island neighbor Theodore Roosevelt, as America's greatest orator. He was Roosevelt's chief economic adviser in the 1912 presidential campaign and subsequently reviewed galley proofs of the ex-President's autobiography.

Churchill was only 20 years old when he first met Cockran, the two men being brought together in 1895 by Churchill's mother, the American-born heiress Jennie Jerome, with whom Cockran had an affair in Paris in the spring of that year following the death of their respective spouses. Sixty years later, Churchill could still recite from memory the speeches of Bourke Cockran he had learned as a young man. "I owe the best things in my career to him" he once wrote to his first cousin (and Cockran's brother-in-law) Sir Shane Leslie. Those wishing to know more about the Churchill-Cockran relationship are referred to *Becoming Winston Churchill: The Untold Story of Young Winston and His American Mentor,* by Michael McMenamin and Curt Zoller, originally published in hardcover in the U.K. and the U.S. in 2007 by Greenwood World Publishing and in trade paperback in 2009 by Enigma Books.

Adolf Hitler. Hitler's views on German politics in 1932 are accurately portrayed in the dialogue of Randolph Churchill and Kurt von Sturm as well as Hitler himself in Chapter 31.

Hitler's anti-Semitism is well-documented in his own words, both written (in *Mein Kampf*) and spoken. In fact, a monologue on "the Jew as

Parasite" by a fictional SS character in our last novel, *The Parsifal Pursuit,* was taken almost verbatim from Hitler's private conversations in 1931 as recounted by a close confidant, Otto Wagener. But anti-Semitism was not a popular political position in Germany and Hitler was a skilled politician during the years 1930 to 1932 when he was on the cusp of power, tailoring his public and private comments to fit his audience. The fact that he did not utter anti-Semitic comments in private to people like Kurt von Sturm who did not share his racial views is accurately portrayed in the novel as is the absence of overt anti-Semitism in his public speeches during this period. He left that up to the likes of Goebbels and Himmler but there is no doubt that he was as anti-Semitic as any of the other Nazis.

Eugenics. The pseudo-science of eugenics flourished in America during the first forty years of the twentieth century as nowhere else, frequently supported by prominent religious leaders, Protestant, Catholic and Jew alike, as well as politicians of both parties. Even Winston Churchill in the years 1910-1912 once supported sterilization of mental defectives as a method of securing their release from state institutions. While Great Britain never did so, 26 US states passed laws for the compulsory sterilization of mental defectives and through the 1930s, 35,878 men and women were sterilized or castrated. By contrast, Germany had no such laws prior to 1933. The Nazi eugenics laws passed early in 1933 after their ascension to power provided, among other things, for the involuntary sterilization of mental defectives. The Nazis based these laws almost exclusively on model state legislation drafted by American eugenics supporters. All the quotes about eugenics in the novel are accurate, those which begin Parts I through IV of the novel as well as the speech by Lothrop Stoddard in Chapter 2 and the articles Mattie and Cockran read to each other in Ch. 45. The support given to eugenics by the Carnegie Institution and the Rockefeller Foundation actually happened and there really was a Eugenics Record Office and a Station for Experimental Evolution at Cold Spring Harbor on Long Island, all backed by government financial support. The best and most comprehensive account of the eugenics movement can be found in Edwin Black's *War Against the Weak, Eugenics and America's Campaign To Create A Master Race.*

Otmar Freiherr von Verschuer and Josef Mengele. Most people will recognize Josef Mengele as one of the sadistic Nazi doctors at Auschwitz, which he was. But he was also the protégé of Otmar von

Verschuer whose background, articles and official positions are accurately portrayed in the novel. So is the high regard in which he was held by American eugenicists. Verschuer was a racist, an anti-Semite and a dedicated Nazi whose work both inspired and guided Mengele's own. In essence, the experiments on American twins in the novel reflect exactly what Mengele did in 1942 with 3,000 twins at Auschwitz, only 160 of whom survived. Mengele routinely sent blood samples and eyeballs from murdered twins to Verschuer in Berlin. Neither man was ever tried at Nuremberg and, while Mengele was hunted as a war criminal the rest of his life, his mentor Verschuer saw his reputation rehabilitated and he lived in Germany until his death in an automobile accident in 1969. His death in the novel is the only time in our Churchill thrillers we have portrayed the death of an actual historical character before his time. We thought briefly of using another name for the Verschuer character but we really thought he should pay for his crimes against humanity if only in a novel. The most chilling account of Verschuer's and Mengele's work is *Children of the Flames, Dr. Josef Mengele and the Untold Story of the Twins of Auschwitz* by Lucette Matalon Lagnado and Sheila Cohn Dekel.

The Army War College and Military Intelligence Division (MID). From 1919 to 1933, scientific racism was taught as part of the regular curriculum at the US Army War College and books by Charles Davenport, Lothrop Stoddard and Madison Grant were prominently featured in the courses taught and Davenport and Stoddard were often lecturers. General Ralph Van Deman, the founder of the Army's Military Intelligence Division in 1917, did run a private intelligence network in America during the 1930s which worked closely with MID, the FBI, the Office of Naval Intelligence and local police departments.

The Graf Zeppelin. The famed German airship made an historic around-the-world voyage in 1929 sponsored by the media empire of William Randolph Hearst. From 1930 through the crash of the *Hindenburg* in 1937, it conducted regular passenger service between Germany and Brazil, safely flying well over a million miles. The *Graf Zeppelin*, however, was never used for regular service between Germany and America as depicted in the novel. We just like airships.

Autogiros. The Juan de la Cierva-designed autogiro was the next big thing in aviation when it was commercially introduced in the early 1930s. *Fortune* magazine devoted two articles to it in its March, 1931 edition, describing it as "a complex if not revolutionary addition to the science of aerodynamics." It flew and handled like an airplane but could take off and land in short spaces at safe, slow speeds. Lift was provided solely by the blades of its huge hinged rotor, a common feature on today's helicopters.

Michael McMenamin
Patrick McMenamin
November, 2011

Acknowledgments

We owe a debt of gratitude to many people who helped bring this book, our third Winston Churchill Thriller, to light. **Katie McMenamin Sabo**, our daughter and sister and the first writing teacher either of us ever had. With an MFA in Creative Writing from NYU, she really is, as she often reminds us, Rose Wilder Lane to our Laura Ingalls. **Kelly McMenamin Wang**, our other daughter and sister who, with her MBA from Dartmouth, is a really good writer and editor herself and the engine behind the sisters' website www.pixiesdidit.com which offers home and life organization advice based on Myers-Briggs personality types. Patrick's wife **Rebecca Perkins**, the head make-up artist on *Law and Order SVU* and Michael's wife and Patrick's mom, **Carol Breckenridge**, an artist and art therapist, both of whom read and offered critical advice on numerous iterations of the book. Mystery writer **Les Roberts**, our close friend and ever-patient writer mentor, from whom Patrick took a college screenwriting course when he was a junior in high school and who, like any good mentor, validated our dream while continuing to give us candid and insightful advice. **Robert Miller**, the editor and publisher of **Enigma Books**, who published the first paperback edition of Michael's book *Becoming Winston Churchill* and who agreed with us that the world really needed a series of historical thrillers set in the 1930s featuring Winston Churchill. **Richard Langworth**, the author of *Churchill by Himself* and a pre-eminent expert on everything Churchill. **Josh Beatman** and the other creative folks at **Brainchild Studios/NYC** who came up with another killer cover design. **Alexis Dragony**, Michael's former assistant who typed many iterations of the book; her successor **Bonnie Daanish** who did the same as did **Jo Ann Chapman**, none of whom were shy on offering helpful advice. And, finally, to all our good friends and relatives who read our drafts and offered their comments.